I0593806

UNWORTHY HEART

THE DONNELLYS
BOOK ONE

DOROTHY F. SHAW

Red Queen
Publications

PRAISE FOR DOROTHY F. SHAW

"*Unworthy Heart* reminded me of what I love about the romance genre."—The Book Tart

"*Unworthy Heart* by Dorothy F. Shaw made me think, made my heart happy, made me tear up and made me sigh in happiness. Shaw combines heat with heart almost flawlessly. I cannot wait for the follow-up books in this series."—Romance Novel News

"I fell in love with the series from book one…Grab your copy and buckle up for the ride. Dorothy Shaw doesn't do anything halfway."—Beyond the Valley of the Books on *Defensive Heart*

"Holy smokes, can Dorothy Shaw write a freaking awesome sex scene…"—Wicked Good Reads on *Defensive Heart*

"*Defensive Heart* by Dorothy F. Shaw is a good read which gives credence to the statement that opposites do attract."—Harlequin Junkie

"Even though there is plenty of sex in *Shattered Heart*, the author does not neglect the storyline at all – packing it full of romance, danger, trauma, healing, laughs, and the Donnelly family."—Crystal's Many Reviewers

"*Shattered Heart* is an emotional tear-jerker of a romance that had me reaching for the tissues on more than one occasion."—Romance Novel News

"Wow! What a sexy, steamy story that kept me reading from the first page."—Crystal's Many Reviewers on *Stripped Bounty*

"If you are into vanilla, forget this book! Characters larger than life and sex to die for. Dorothy F. Shaw painted a canvas that is both intriguing and close to hardcore."—Amazon Reviewer on *Stripped Bounty*

"Epic story! Rosie and Badger are amazing characters that pull you into the story. The sex is HOT and the ending is perfect!"—Book Addicts PR on *Stripped Bounty*

"I was blown away by how easily the story was told by Dorothy F. Shaw"—CeeriJays Smexy HotReads on *A Few More Rules*

"*A Few More Rules* (a femdom novella) is a super-hot romance that sets the foundation well for a probable HEA between Rig and Beth. This story is a winner."—Romance Novel News

"WOW!!! This erotic, sensual short story will have you panting for more! These two beauties are more than fang bangers. The dark world of lust and sex will feed any appetite you desire."—Bookaholic and More Blog on *Playtime*

"I like books that grab my attention so much that I read a line and end up gasping or commenting out loud... and this one did just that - a few times! I'll definitely be reading it again."—Goodreads Reviewer on *Playtime*

"True to Dorothy Shaw's form, *Avoiding the Badge* is full of everything I love about her writing."—Amanda at Wicked Good Reads

"I liked the way the author brought about the truths that they had been keeping from each other, and I really enjoyed the steps that the two characters took in order to overcome the troubles in their path."—Amazon reviewer on *Avoiding the Badge*

"*Redeeming the Badge* is a second chance romance that is hot as Hades and with a backstory that will twist your heartstrings."—Amazon Reviewer

"This is a tale of love and heartache, dealing with some tough issues such as infertility, endometriosis, and miscarriage. It will tear at your heartstrings and make you believe in true love."—Amazon Reviewer on *Redeeming the Badge*

"Jeff and Tish are a good couple with incredible chemistry that makes you jealous. I can't recommend this series enough." —Amazon Reviewer on *Trusting the Badge*

"*Trusting the Badge* is a quick read for readers who enjoy a focus on relationship building, characters with tragic backstories, and some steamy moments." —Amazon Reviewer

"It was written in a way that I got very emotional reading it, most books don't make me cry. This one did."—Amazon reviewer on *Jaded Heart*

"As usual, Shaw creates characters that can be hard to like. Garrett is not easy to connect to. He treats Angie like crap, but Angie keeps fighting for them. Their flameout moment is painful to read about but very necessary. Garrett has to deal with his past, which he has been avoiding for years and years. With all of this, I still couldn't put the book down."— Romance Novel News on *Jaded Heart*

Unworthy Heart

The Donnellys Book 1
© 2019 Dorothy F. Shaw

Opposites not only attract, sometimes they spontaneously combust.

Ryan Donnelly's past relationship may have failed, but he's determined to make single fatherhood and his career a resounding success. He's got his eye on the top of the ladder at an L.A. marketing firm when his gaze snags on co-worker Maiya Rossini.

She's a feisty, witty, tattooed redhead who's nowhere near his type, but she pushes every one of his hot buttons.

Maiya clawed her way out of her dysfunctional, trailer-park childhood to earn a college degree and establish a promising career. Her future dreams are big, bright and packed with full-throttle fun, but when it comes to matters of the heart and men—especially stuffy corporate types like Ryan—her past slams on the emotional brakes.

In the office and in the bedroom, Maiya and Ryan rub each other in all the *right* ways. Though Maiya is everything Ryan didn't know he wanted, he's got his work cut out for him convincing her she's worthy of love—or the bright light she's brought to his life could slip through his fingers.

DEDICATION

This one's for you, Daddy.
I wish you were here to read it.
But I know you're looking down from above and that you're proud of me.
I love you, and I miss you every single day.

ACKNOWLEDGMENTS

To my dear friend, author Shawna Thomas for being one of the first people to ever edit my writing. You've always encouraged and believed in me when I barely believed in myself. And for tirelessly editing this book from top to bottom and back again in order to help me beat it into an acceptable story that people might actually want to read. You are appreciated more than I could ever express, and I love you dearly.

To my friend, Jen Sylvia, for her awesome editing skills—thank you for taking a ride on the Unworthy Heart train… your help was invaluable.

To my friend, author Nikki Duncan. Thank you for the swift kick in the behind, coupled with an order to "Finish the damn book!" You were exactly what I needed.

To author Melissa Ecker for the endless days and nights of writing sprints when I finally decided to finish a novella that accidentally turned into a full novel and then a series.

Thank you! I could never put a price on the value of the time spent and the fun and laughs that were had. #TUWANDA! To my friends, Jennifer and Amy—two outstanding registered nurses for your help with the medical scenes.

Your expertise was invaluable.

To my dear friend, author Saranna DeWylde for your very helpful critique. Lady, not only are you filled with talent, you're an inspiration and a cherished friend. Thank you.

To my dearest and cherished friend, author Megan Hart.

Thank you for the daily laughs. For being an example of what it takes to do this deal every day, and for reminding me several hundred times that I DO NOT, in fact, suck! For this, I will be forever grateful. And for reading this book, not only once, but twice!

To my friend, author, Christa Desir... You are the bomb. com! And I will always seek your guidance...because you know me too well. Much love and thanks.

To my friend, Jodi G., You breathed life into Jodi's character. When I read her, I still hear your voice. Thank you for letting me give you life in a book.

To my friend Bill J., Our work banter and friendship was truly a muse for this story. Thank you for graciously allowing me to base Ryan's character and style on you.

To author Carrie Clevenger. There are no words except, I love you and thank you.

To my many beta readers: Holly T., Lu E., April (Stitch), Alissa J., Marchelle L., Leslie J., Trenda L., my cousin, Sherri

Z. (Sherri, you read this three times! I love you!), Dawn

V. and Tere H. Thank you! Your feedback was extremely helpful and appreciated. You all rock!

There's an endless list of people I'm probably forgetting

to thank for their help and encouragement since I started this crazy journey into writing six years ago. I want you all to know your help was and is appreciated.

And finally, to my ex-husband, author T.D. Hoffman for his patience, support, plotting help, and, did I say patience? Thank you for always cheering me on and helping me to chase my dream.

**Added with 3rd version re-release: Special thanks to Sunnie Andrews (badass aspiring author and friend) for being an awesome PA and proofreader/beta reader. And fetching coffee and getting my ass to signings ALMOST on time. <3

A NOTE TO READERS

This book contains a lot of graphic, yummy sex. To those prone to lock their bedroom doors, fair warning. In this book, there are no doors, only windows. With no curtains. For those who aren't afraid to keep their eyes wide open: Enjoy the show!

PLAYLIST

Norah Jones - *Come Away with Me*
Shinedown - *I'm Not Alright*
Type O Negative - *Cinnamon Girl*
Drowning Pool - *Bodies*
Saliva - *Click Click Boom*
Rage Against the Machine - *Killing in the Name*
Rammstein - *Du Hast*
Shaggy - *Boombastic*
Ginuwine - *Pony*

My inspirational song for Maiya: Bonnie Raitt - *Nobody's Girl*

CHAPTER ONE

"Cutting it a little close, aren't you, Maiya?"

Dammit, she was. Her hair always took forever when she was in Los Angeles. And the last thing she wanted was to look like crap the first time she met Ryan Donnelly face to face.

"Of course, boss. There's no excitement in actually making it on time." Maiya stepped out of the elevator and pulled off her sunglasses. "Besides, I'm not in the office all that much these days. It takes time to change out of my work-from-home uniform of hair scrunchies, tank tops and boxer briefs to appropriate business attire."

"Very true." Tony tilted his head down, peering at her over the top of his frameless glasses perched on the end of his nose. "Three months is too long for you to not pay a visit."

She brushed her hair away from her face. Relocating from Las Vegas to Los Angeles eight years ago to start her job with Amaryllis Marketing Firm had been a leap of faith for her, but it'd paid off tenfold. And the man in front of her was a huge part of the reason why. Plus, when she had needed to move back to Vegas to care for her mother, Tony had allowed her to stay on, working remotely from home. He'd earned her respect and loyalty in spades, and she couldn't imagine

1

working for anyone else. "Blame the finance group and their travel budgets. You know I'd rather be out here at least once a month."

His handsome smile crinkled the corners of his eyes, and he ushered her into the conference room. "Also true. Regardless, glad to have you here now."

Maiya entered, and excitement raced through her. "Thanks." They grabbed a seat along the back row against the windows, and she nodded to the familiar faces in attendance around the conference room table. She loved connecting with the people she worked with on a daily basis but rarely saw face-to-face. A sense of comfort spilled through her, like she'd come home again.

The senior marketing executive, Mr. Mawbry, spoke to the room, and the conference phone in the center of the table. "Good morning, everyone. Thank you for joining the monthly project status meeting."

Notebook and pencil in hand, Maiya scanned her surroundings. Taking a deep breath, her excitement settled, and pride took its place. Maiya had done hella good for herself sticking with this company. She'd worked her way up the corporate ladder, rung by rung, and found success.

There were a few new faces in attendance, and curiosity pranced through her mind. Did any of them belong to Ryan? They'd only recently started collaborating on a project together. Their conversations, which had started out professional, had begun to slip into the land of flirtation. Dangerous territory, yes, but regardless, Maiya would kill to know what he looked like. She'd checked his Facebook account—in a purely non-stalkerish way—but had come up empty-handed. His page was locked down like Fort Knox.

Sad thing was, she had a feeling Ryan resembled a corporate Ken Doll. Annnd surprise, surprise, Maiya was *nothing* like Barbie.

At least meeting him face to face would be the dose of

reality necessary to evaporate her physical reaction to him and focus on work again. She hoped, anyway.

One of the project managers in attendance kicked the group off and reported on their campaign. Maiya checked her notes for any details she might need to report on for her particular project. At the sound of an additional male voice, her head snapped up. *He sounds familiar.*

The guy turned and looked at her.

Their eyes locked, and a bolt of electricity arced between them. The jolt shot straight to Maiya's toes. *Hello, Gorgeous and totally not my type.* She drew in a deep breath and let her gaze roam over his short, sandy, light-brown hair, high cheekbones and crystal blue-gray eyes. And his lips.

He flashed her a quick smile.

My God, that can't be Ryan. *Jesus, if that's him, I'm in a fuckton of trouble.* Maiya broke their stare and returned her focus to her notepad, tapping it with her pencil—a pale attempt to convince herself the guy *was not* Ryan.

A few minutes later, Mr. Mawbry spoke again. "Ryan, could you please report the status of your campaign?"

Maiya searched the unknown faces, desperate to find him among the team, when Mr. Gorgeous started talking.

"Oh. Shit," she muttered.

Ryan glanced at her, a devilish grin adorning his lips.

Double shit. She couldn't stop herself from staring while he spoke. Especially at his lips. She really liked his lips. This was *so* not good. This wasn't in the plan. It was bad enough his voice got her aching and wet, but…his face. That mouth. Those lips—she could *not* be attracted to him. Absolutely out of the question.

She had to work with him, for fuck's sake!

As the Senior Project Manager assigned, Ryan gave his report. Maiya answered the few questions some of the other executives in attendance had. She had to pry her tongue off the roof of her mouth in order to speak, but she'd managed.

Maybe the corporate ladder hadn't paid off as well as she thought.

The group moved on to the next project on the agenda. Still warm and tingling from the intense eye lock with Ryan, Maiya blew out a harsh breath, trying to cool down. After a few more projects were discussed, the meeting adjourned. She bent to retrieve her things from the floor by her seat. If she didn't get some air and fast, she might spontaneously combust.

A set of long legs entered her line of sight.

Her gaze traveled up his casual khaki pants, over his chest, clad in a pale blue Polo shirt—the color emphasizing the blue in his eyes—and then settled on his lips. *Dammit.* With burning cheeks, she stood and raised her eyes to meet his.

"Maiya Rossini, I assume." Ryan extended his hand to shake hers. "Nice to finally meet you."

She placed her palm in his and drank him in. In hopes of playing it cool, she cleared her throat before speaking. "Ryan Donnelly. Yes, it's nice to meet you, too."

His long fingers curled around her hand, and he smiled. Tingles danced up her arm. Being right in front of him now and touching him, queued up every hormone in her body. *This is crazy!* She was caught between wanting to run in the other direction or throw herself at him and beg him to drag her somewhere private.

They assessed each other for a moment, saying nothing before she mentally kicked herself in the ass and broke the silence. "My team is having a gathering tonight. You joining us?" With regret, she extricated her hand from his very warm one.

"I'll have to see if I can make it. What time again?"

"Thinking of blowing off fun team-building time?" She raised her brows. "Six, I believe. Check your calendar. I'm sure you were sent an invite."

He tilted his head to the side. "I wouldn't dream of

blowing off 'fun team time'. As if you'd let me get away with doing that anyway."

"Good to know." Unable to help herself, she glanced at his lips again. With mammoth effort, she forced her gaze away, took her seat and finished gathering her things.

She was having a hell of a time looking him in the eye, and making small talk wasn't any easier. Her skin was tight all over, and her cheeks were flaming hot. Struck stupid was a damn understatement.

Her reaction bothered her.

And he bothered her.

Ryan stepped a couple feet away to talk to another team member.

Maiya took the opportunity to escape. She needed air. And a cigarette. Maybe a cold drink of water, too. "See you later, Ryan. I gotta run."

"Bye, Maiya. Guess I'll see you la—"

Ducking her head, Maiya rushed from the room.

CHAPTER TWO

RYAN ENTERED THE BANQUET ROOM OF THE RESTAURANT AND glanced around. There were plenty of work faces, but he was interested in finding only one. Zeroing in on the bar, he spotted her, and so did his dick, which jumped to attention in his pants. *Down boy.* After seeing her in person, there was no way in hell he would've blown this little shindig off.

The woman was damn alluring. Pure temptation. Her long, flaming-red hair with streaks of blonde and black in it—not natural, of course—suited her. The thick locks called to him, made him want to run his fingers through them and then grip them tight in his fist. Full lips lined to perfection with a touch of gloss to enhance them—another Siren's call. What flavor did she use? Maybe strawberry? His favorite.

But damn, she was trouble. Trouble with a capital T, wrapped up in a hot body and a pretty face, with a smart mouth. The electricity shooting between them when he caught her gaze earlier today was intense as hell, but also a massive orange neon sign flashing, *Danger! Danger!* Ryan needed to avoid her. Sleeping with anyone from work was off limits in his book. He needed to collaborate with her on his campaign, not wonder what her lips tasted like. Ryan was determined, no matter what the other brain located south of his belt thought, to maintain a professional relationship with her.

No problem.

Easy. Yes. Easy.

He moved through the crowd to get a better view. She still wore her work clothes. A royal blue blouse, tailored to fit her torso, hugged her full breasts, revealing enough cleavage to make his mouth water for more. She probably looked amazing naked. *Damn!* The woman was hotter than hell in four-inch heels and more tempting than the devil himself.

Maiya sat on a stool with her back resting against the bar, glass of wine in hand, talking to her manager. With her long legs crossed, she bounced one high-heeled foot, her damn skirt clinging to her full hips.

The sight was enough to make any man go insane with lust.

Hanging back, Ryan exchanged hellos with some of their colleagues, but every few seconds, he glanced over at her. He was stalling. Nervous even. He rubbed his palms on his thighs. *It's just Maiya.* He needed to get a grip on whatever emotion or fantasy she stirred in him. No biggie, right? They'd talked daily on the phone, and they were professionals.

Ryan drew in a deep breath and did his damnedest to put a lid on his thoughts…and desires. Stepping to the bar, he was careful to stay a few feet away from her. He could do this. With his back turned, he ordered a Jameson on the rocks.

———

MAIYA SPOTTED RYAN WHEN HE ENTERED THE BANQUET ROOM. The air around her had shifted and popped with electricity, dancing along every inch of her skin the minute he walked through the door. She'd been stealing little glances of him while he talked with colleagues, and she chatted with her boss.

He was still in his cut-out-of-a-magazine work attire. So *not* her type. Except for his lips, those were her type. And his eyes, and his… *Gah!*

As she watched him make his way around the room, Maiya decided Ryan was edible. And that little admission annoyed the crap out of her. Regardless, call it denial or self-preservation, she was sticking to her first assessment. Ryan wasn't even in the same room, let alone the same building, as her type. Yet, here she was, salivating over Mr. Corporate Ken Doll.

None of her physical reactions made sense. Maiya dated bad boys—tattooed bikers or musicians. Pretty boys weren't attracted to her. Most times, she intimidated the hell out of them. Even in her teen years. And although she cleaned up nice, she'd never be the type the pretty boys brought home to Momma.

So, what in the hell was with this attraction to Ryan? He made her laugh, yes, and he challenged her daily. But that couldn't be it, right? Annoyed and done with her mental tug of war, Maiya swirled her wine in the glass, took hold of the liquid courage pulsing through her system, and spoke up. "Well, well. Decided to show, huh?"

Ryan glanced over his shoulder, a smoldering fire burning in his eyes. Maiya licked her lips as he turned and faced her. "You were waiting for me, weren't you?"

"Nah, not really. More like curious if you'd actually grace us with your presence. I have it on good authority you never make it to these things." She sipped her wine and met his gaze in flirtatious challenge, hoping he'd take the bait.

A look flashed in his eyes, but was gone faster than she could decipher it. "It's true, I can't always make these events, but I wouldn't have missed this one for the world, Maiya."

Raising her glass, she saluted him. "Hmm. Good to know." Maiya hopped off the stool and sauntered toward the table where Rahul and Jodi were sitting. What did he mean by that? Because *she* was there? No, that couldn't be why... could it? *Damn.* Maiya glanced over her shoulder. He stood there and watched her, a smirk adorning his lips. *Those fucking lips. Kill me.*

Jodi looked up, her blue eyes shining. "Hey, girl."

Maiya tousled Jodi's long blonde curls when she passed behind her and then took a seat. "What's up, chica?"

Rahul's pretty brown eyes, framed by long, dark lashes, smiled right along with his lips. "Hey, Maiya."

Maiya blew a kiss to Rahul across the table. She took in the sight of her two friends, and the deep sense of comfort returned, flowing through her veins. She missed them, Jodi, especially, and having this time with them meant the world to Maiya.

She lived for her business trips to L.A. "Work vacations", she called them. They brought her off-kilter world back to center, giving her what she lacked in Vegas: Freedom and normalcy. Not that she knew what normal was, but what she had here in L.A., with her friends, was the closest she'd ever gotten to it.

The waitress deposited a huge plate of nachos in the center of the table. Maiya leaned back in her seat and sighed. Jodi dug in first, scooping up a chip heaped with meat and cheese, and shoved it in her mouth. "So what's up with you and Ryan?" she said around her mouthful.

"Nice. Your lack of home training's showing." Maiya grabbed her own handful and took a bite. "Nothing. Why do you ask?" She crunched the chip in her mouth.

Rahul chuckled.

Both Maiya and Jodi turned to him. "What?" they said in unison.

"Never mind." Rahul raised both brows and took a swig of his beer.

"Yeah," Jodi continued, "I'm soooo not buying the 'nothing' answer. There's something simmering between you two. It's as plain as the nose on my face."

"I have no idea what you're talking about." Maiya swallowed the last of her wine.

"Mmhm. Right." Jodi shoveled in another helping.

Rahul set down his beer and then ran his palm over his dark, close-cropped hair. "Incoming."

Maiya glanced to her left, and her eyes went wide. Ryan approached their table, two drinks in hand: a glass of wine and a glass two fingers full of amber liquid with ice. *Guess he took the bait.* Her stomach tightened into a knot, and her mouth went dry.

He set the wine next to her empty glass and then took the seat next to her. "Mind if I join you all?"

"Of course not, and thanks for the refill." Maiya took a sip of the fresh wine, trying to drown the nerves break-dancing in her stomach. "I definitely appreciate a man who brings me alcohol."

Ryan exhaled an exaggerated gasp. "Maiya Rossini, that was almost a compliment."

Maiya raised both brows and set her glass down. "I give compliments. Ask Jodi. I tell her how wonderful she is all the time."

"Yes, she does." Jodi sipped her beer.

"Maiya's really quite sweet." Rahul shrugged one shoulder. "You know…when she isn't bossing everyone around and being a bitch." He snickered and motioned like he was about to hide under the table.

Jodi choked on her beer and coughed.

Ryan laughed.

"Haaayy, I am *not* a bitch." Maiya's mouth dropped open, and she looked among the three of them. "Jerks." She laughed.

Ryan cleared his throat, stifling his laughter and raised his hands in defense. "Whoa there. I know better than to say something like that."

Weenie. Maiya shrugged. "Okay, fine. I'm a bitch." She picked up her glass and turned to Jodi. "If getting the job done makes me a bitch, then call me the queen. Am I right, chica?"

Jodi tapped the tip of her beer bottle to Maiya's wineglass. "Got that right, girl."

"I couldn't agree more." Ryan took a swig of his whiskey.

"Oh, great. Thanks for the back-up." Rahul grabbed a chip off the plate.

"Hey, I'm no fool. I've got to work with her." Ryan shook his finger at Rahul.

Maiya brushed her hair off her shoulder and glanced at Ryan. He was being such a suck-up. After all the times he debated, argued and challenged her over work issues during their many phone calls, this new side of him was quite out of character. It made her wonder what his motive was behind it. "Damn straight you do."

Ryan gave her a nod and raised his drink to his lips. Their eyes caught for a moment, but she couldn't help but let hers travel over his face and then zero in on his mouth. He sipped his drink. Maiya licked her lips. *God help me.* Heat radiated through her body, and her nipples hardened. She caught herself before she drooled down her chin and jerked her gaze back to his eyes.

A lazy smile spread across Ryan's mouth.

Maiya's cheeks burned hot.

"You okay there, Maiya?" Ryan asked in a low voice.

She cleared her throat. *Way to go.* He'd caught her staring —and damn, she hated that. Where in the hell had her liquid courage gone? "Yes."

Maiya tried to focus on the conversation in progress with Rahul and Jodi in hopes of distracting herself from the man sitting oh-so-close to her. *What the hell are we talking about?* The waitress had brought another round of drinks and two more plates of snacks to the table, though when that'd happened, she couldn't recall. Everything fell into a slow blur, yet her sensitivity to all things around her popped into hyper-over-drive—or at least, to Ryan being next to her.

Halfway through her third glass of wine, Maiya's head buzzed a little too loud, and she tugged at Jodi's sweater. "Hey, come outside with me. I want to smoke."

"Okie dokie."

With Jodi in tow, Maiya glanced over her shoulder to Rahul and Ryan. "Be back soon." She exited the building, turned to Jodi and fanned herself. "Jeez, I needed some air."

"No kidding. It got a bit steamy in there. I'll ask again, what in the Lord's name is up with you and Ryan?"

"Wha—" Maiya's answer came out in a tipsy squeak. Clearing her throat, she tried again. "What the hell are you talking about?"

"Oh, you know just what I'm talking about."

"There is absolutely nothing going on with me and Ryan."

Jodi rolled her eyes and leaned against the railing enclosing the outdoor patio. "Mmhmm. Okay, Maiya. What-ever you say."

"Well, for fuck's sake. Is it that obvious?" Maiya lit her cigarette and sucked in a long drag, exhaling the gray smoke in a stream above them.

"Hell yeah, it is. There's some serious sexual tension between you two."

"Shit." She took another drag. "This cannot happen, Jodi. You know it as well as I do. What the hell am I going to do?"

A wide grin spread across Jodi's lips. "Fuck him, and then tell me all about it. You know, so I can live vicariously through you."

"Oh my God, Jodi! I can't believe you just dropped an F-bomb!"

"Lighten up, huh?"

Maiya rolled her eyes. "Do you think he'd keep it on the down low?"

"Oh hell, who knows, girl? Who cares? You're both single." She grabbed Maiya's cigarette and took a drag.

"Yeah, but…it's work, you know?" Maiya furrowed her brow, scrunching up her nose. "I don't know. It's a risk." She snatched the cigarette back from Jodi, took a final drag and then put it out in the ashtray.

"You worry too much. Besides, when have you ever been afraid of a little risk?" Jodi ran her fingers through her long hair. "Get in there and work it, like I know you know how to do. You eat guys like Ryan Donnelly for breakfast." She nodded, indicating that was the final say on the matter.

Maiya squinted. "What has gotten into you?"

"What? I'm fine. Come on, let's get back in there." Jodi walked toward the door.

Maiya shook her head in disbelief and followed her friend. "You have *got* to get out more."

When they got back to the table, Ryan was missing. Relief spread through her like a cool drink of water. As Maiya chatted with her friends, she couldn't help but keep an eye on the door in case he showed again. When she finished her wine, Maiya's relief morphed into hot agitation, pulsing hard beneath her skin. He'd left and hadn't said goodbye to her. *Shithead.*

The crowd thinned, and Rahul left for home. Maiya, not ready for the night to end, convinced Jodi to head to Flanagan's. She went into the bathroom first to freshen up. Feeling brave from her wine, she sent a text to Ryan asking him where he'd gone.

A few minutes later, her phone buzzed, the label she'd assigned his number popping up. It made her laugh every time he texted her.

Ryan Painintheass: Oh hey! Sorry, had to
meet a few buddies. What are you up to?

Maiya: Not much. Heading to Flanagan's. You
should come hang out.

Screw it. Maiya wanted another shot at hanging with him.
She also wanted to see if the sparks between them would
continue. If not, fine. At least she'd know for sure, and all
parties involved would be safe. Why not, right?

Ryan Painintheass: Who's going and when are
you heading there?

Maiya: Me and Jodi. Rahul had to get home.
Leaving in about 5 mins.

Ryan Painintheass: I may stop by. My buddies
were just taking off.

Maiya: Cool. See you soon.

Pleased with herself, she applied a new coat of lipstick and
fluffed her hair. Let the games begin. Maiya met Jodi in front
of the restaurant. "I'm ready. Let's go."

Jodi gave her a slanted glance. "Girl, you're up to no
good."

Maiya smirked. "Don't know what you're talking about."

CHAPTER THREE

Ryan had high-tailed it out of the restaurant for a damn good reason. The short amount of time he'd spent next to Maiya at the table had been intense and far too arousing. It was either leave and clear his head or drag her into a corner somewhere and show her just how much her bitchiness turned him on.

The whole situation was crazy. Maiya was the type of woman he steered clear of. A rather hot stove he had no desire to touch again, yet his body didn't seem to care about any of that. It took all of his willpower not to adjust the erection in his pants when they were sitting next to each other. Damn uncomfortable too.

Now, he was heading back into the redheaded-hot burning building again because he just couldn't stay away. He'd have to figure out a way to hang with her tonight *and* keep his distance from her at the same time.

Yeah, right. How the hell was that supposed to happen? She was like a damn sex magnet, all five-foot-eight of her, and his buddy in his pants was all for it. His head—the one on top of his shoulders—kept intervening to remind him she was supposed to be off limits. Not that it mattered, though.

He had no issue with casual sex, but sex with Maiya would be anything but casual. The mere idea of her red hair tangled in his fist and her body bared just for him made his limbs tighten in anticipation.

Ryan ran his palm over his mouth, and a muffled groan slipped past his lips. With one last command to his dick to behave, he got in his car and headed downtown to...to what?

Play with fire?

Test his control?

Yeah, that was it. *Riiighhhtt.*

No. He could do this. Under no circumstances would he have sex with Maiya. He would not kiss her lips. He would not paddle her ass for being such a pain in his. Moreover, he absolutely would *not* enjoy seeing her long legs in the air while he—

"Ah, Jesus. Knock it off." Ryan clenched his teeth and started the car.

When he neared the main strip in front of their office, he spotted the two of them walking on the sidewalk. *Well, well, well. There she is.* Slowing, he rolled down his passenger window and then stopped alongside them. "Hey, there's trouble with a capital M."

Maiya's steps slowed, and she looked over. "You have *got* to be kidding me." She laughed. "That's your car?"

"What? Yes. Why? You don't like it?"

Maiya snorted and rolled her eyes. "Typical."

Jodi laughed, and Maiya resumed her swift stride.

Ryan threw the Porsche in gear and rolled forward a bit, keeping up with her. "What do you mean typical?"

She brushed a lock of hair away from her face. "Just what I said. Typical."

Ryan shook his head. The comment, joking or not, pricked at his nerves. He was *not* typical. He was anything *but* typical. *Damn this woman!* Was it her life mission to agitate him?

He sped past them and then pulled into the lot behind the pub and parked.

When Ryan stepped into the darkness of Flanagan's, he glanced around in search of the pair. Maiya's familiar laugh echoed above the low music and small crowd in the pub. The hair on the back of his neck stood on end, and a bolt of heat shot down his spine.

Following the sound, he moved in her direction. Ryan paused before coming into their line of sight. They were in the back at a table. The mammoth stone fireplace bordering the back wall danced with flames behind them.

Maiya had one leg tucked beneath her. The other crossed over her knee, with her shoe dangling off her foot. Leaning back in her seat, her elbow rested on the back of the chair, and she absently twirled her hair around one finger. She stirred her drink on the table with the fingertip of her other hand. The blaze from the fireplace illuminated her profile, and she glowed in the dim light.

Keeping his eyes trained on her, Ryan took a single step forward, and she turned her head in his direction.

Their gazes locked.

Maiya arched one perfect eyebrow, pulled her finger from her drink, and sucked the liquid dripping from the tip. *Holy hell.* All the blood rushed from Ryan's brain right to his dick.

Control tested, and he'd been served, failing right out of the gate. *So much for that.* Ryan drew in a deep breath and somehow managed to get his feet moving. The seat next to her was empty. Of course, it was empty. *So much for keeping my distance, too.*

Fine plan this turned out to be.

Maiya grinned at Ryan while he pulled the empty chair next to her away from the table and sat. The expression on his face was priceless after the little stunt with her finger. He might've gone a shade or two paler.

He scooted closer to the table. "Typical, huh?"

"Yep."

Ryan waved the waitress over. "Jameson on the rocks, please and uh…and a large glass of water too." He turned to Maiya, leaned close to her ear and whispered, "I am *far* from typical."

She tilted her head to the side, glancing at him from the corner of her eye. "We'll see."

"You will." He pulled away and looked at her friend. "Nice to see you again, Jodi."

"Likewise." She smiled and then sipped her beer.

"Anyone else here?" Ryan shifted his chair closer to the table, bumping Maiya's leg with one of his. Electric tingles ran up her thigh.

"Just saw Joe from the finance team with his girlfriend, Tiffany." Jodi jerked her chin in the direction of where the couple was seated by the bathrooms.

Maiya looked over her shoulder, grateful for the distraction from Ryan's leg against hers. "Didn't even notice. He's a nice guy."

"His girl is a play actress, I guess. She just landed the lead in the play *Gypsy*." Jodi brushed her hair over her shoulder.

"No shit? As in playing the infamous Gypsy Rose Lee?" Maiya shifted in her seat, and her leg rubbed against Ryan's again. *Damn*. "I would love to see that."

"Joe was offering tickets the other day. You can bring a friend. Like me or someone else." Jodi's lips tilted into a grin, and she glanced at Ryan.

"Yeah. Maybe." Maiya pursed her lips and glanced at him, too. He was staring at her, a far-off look in his eyes. Another zing of electricity shot up her leg from where hers still touched his. She waved her hand in front of his face. "Hello?"

He sipped his drink. "Hmm? What'd I miss?"

"Are we boring you?" Maiya raised both brows. "Jodi was telling us about the big show Joe's girlfriend is starring in. Did you hear any of that?"

"Yes, of course I heard it." Leaning back, he cleared his throat. "No, you're not boring me." He turned his attention to Jodi. "It sounds very exciting."

"Oh, Lord." Jodi laughed and took a swig of beer.

Maiya snorted. "Typical."

Ryan's head snapped back in her direction. "You keep saying that, and I'm going to be forced to show you different." He took a long swig of his whiskey.

Maiya watched his lips close over the edge of the glass. *I dare you to show me different.* She stifled a groan. "I doubt that."

Jodi slapped her hand on the table, breaking the moment. "On that note, you two kids have fun. I gotta get home."

Maiya rose and gave Jodi a hug. "Thanks for walking me down here. I'll see you tomorrow."

"Get home safe. Or to the hotel rather." Jodi winked at her. "Have a good night, Ryan."

"You too, Jodi." Ryan nodded.

Maiya shook her head. "I'll be right back." Stepping away from the table, she walked Jodi to the front door and then made a beeline for the bathroom.

Equal parts arousal and frustration thrummed through her veins, and her pulse beat hard in her ears. What was it about him? He was vanilla…too damn vanilla for her. Yet her body didn't seem to care how strait-laced he was. Maiya had intended to annoy him with the *typical* comment. It'd worked; she'd gotten to him for sure. Seeing him all agitated and in a lather amped her libido up ten more notches. Ryan Donnelly did not see himself as typical. My God, anything but.

What the hell had she been thinking, inviting him tonight? A feeble attempt to convince herself she wasn't attracted to him? She didn't even understand the attraction. What she *did* understand was now that she was next to him again, she wanted to lick every inch of his body. The man got her blood boiling at least once a day, sometimes more, and managed to get her body humming with arousal at the same time. With only their phone calls.

Maiya washed and dried her hands. It was probably wise to stop fighting the magnetism. Fuck him out of her system. It was biology—simple, pent-up frustration. And it *had* been a while since she'd had sex. This was a no-brainer. She could have meaningless and sweaty—hopefully satisfying—sex with a colleague and have no issue working with him the next day. Yes, she absolutely could.

Decision made, she walked back to the table.

Ryan was standing with his wallet open in his hand. "You about ready to go?"

"I suppose." She glanced at her watch. "You going to give me a ride to my hotel, or am I calling a cab?"

He crossed his arms. "You want a ride in my typical car?"

"Sure." She shrugged. "I guess if you'd rather the car instead of the bed in my hotel room, I'm game."

"You're bad, Maiya." He shook his head.

She laughed. "Tell me something I don't know."

"I have a BMW too. Still think I'm typical?"

She flipped her hair off her shoulder and headed for the door. *Two cars? Seriously?* "Absofuckinglutely."

"Don't get excited, they're both ten years old. For a second, I worried you might be shocked, however, I have a feeling nothing shocks you, does it?" He followed her outside and then walked beside her, his arm brushing against hers while they made their way to his car.

The small contact was a brand on her skin, right through her jacket and satin blouse. "Not really. But I have a feeling I do a top-notch job of shocking you." It was a lie, she was shocked…a little.

The corner of his mouth tipped into a crooked grin. "I'll deny it till the bitter end. Nope. Not shocked at all."

"What's this? I don't get to drive?" Maiya teased with wide eyes when he opened the passenger door for her.

"Now I know you're in shock because you must've lost your damn mind." He laughed, and the sound rippled over her skin and centered between her thighs.

When she sank into the deep leather seat, Maiya crossed her legs, trying to relieve some of the tension. "I know I teased you, but I do like your car. For being ten years old, it's in perfect condition."

"Stop, please." He placed his hand on his chest in a dramatic display. "I don't think my heart can take the shock."

She turned toward him when he slid behind the wheel. "Ha! See? I do shock you. Oh, come on. I'm being serious. I *do* like your car." She widened her eyes, trying to look as sincere as she could. "Porsches are badass, even if it is a Boxster. And I still think you should let me drive it."

"You're not driving my car."

"Why not?"

"You're nuts."

"I am not. I'm serious."

Ryan shot her a sideways glance. "Yup, totally nuts."

"Fine, we'll see." She crossed her arms and stared out the windshield. "It's a Boxster, for fuck's sake. May as well be a Miata," she mumbled.

"What?"

"Nothing."

Ryan grumbled something back she didn't make out, and she suppressed a giggle. She was having a blast jerking his chain. He had a thing for cars, but she did too. It made her curious what else they had in common.

Ryan made the left into the hotel parking lot, and for a split second, she thought he might pull into the parking garage. Instead, he looped in front of the entrance and stopped. *Damn.* A twinge of disappointment curled in her gut. Taking a deep breath, she pushed the feeling away and turned in her seat to face him. "Thanks for the ride."

He rested his elbow on the windowsill of his door and met her gaze. "Not a problem."

Maiya ran a hand through the length of her hair. "Thanks for coming tonight, too. I had a good time."

"Me too."

They stared at each other for a moment, and then he leaned toward her. She braced for the kiss. Instead, he bypassed her lips and came cheek-to-cheek with her.

With his chest pressed against hers, his heart beat against her own—which was slamming like a bass drum in a marching band. Every inch of her insides quivered from the feel of his stubbled cheek against her face and the pressure of his body against hers. Each sensation ran over and through her. Maiya closed her eyes and placed a trembling hand on his neck.

"Sweet dreams, Maiya." The breath from his whispered words tickled her ear...and then he opened the car door behind her.

The loss of body heat was profound when he pulled away. Shivering, Maiya sighed and opened her eyes. The bastard was grinning. Grinning!

She cleared her throat and schooled her expression in an effort to hide her embarrassment. Obviously, this was all one-sided. "You too, Ryan." Stepping out of the car and closing the door, she started what she considered the "walk of shame" toward the hotel entrance.

"Hey, Maiya."

She froze at the sound of her name and then turned around.

He'd lowered the window farther. "C'mere."

She walked the few steps and bent forward, peering into the car. "You forget something?"

"Yeah. Come here."

She leaned inside the car. Ryan stretched across the console, cupped her face in his hand and gave her a soft, chaste kiss on her lips. When he pulled away, he stroked the tip of his tongue over her top lip. Then he shifted back into his seat as if nothing had happened.

Half hanging in his car, shock and arousal zipped through Maiya's body like a bottle rocket. She swallowed and licked her lips, tasting him. "Mm, thanks." She backed out of the window and straightened next to the car. Her legs had turned to jelly. Such a soft little kiss, and yet it resonated through her entire body, setting it on fire. And she wanted more.

"Good night, Maiya."

"Night, Ryan." She watched while he pulled away and then plopped her ass on the bench outside the hotel entrance and lit a cigarette.

The man was toying with her, and it was working.

CHAPTER FOUR

Ryan released the breath he'd been holding and drove away from the temptation he'd left standing in front of the hotel. God help him. Did she want him the way he wanted her? He shifted in the driver's seat, and the hard bulge in his pants pressed against his zipper.

Between how she poked the bear with her smart-ass comments and then flipped like a light switch, flirting with him by sucking a drop of drink off her fingertip, he hoped she did. Her mixed messages were maddening. Either way, the result was the same: he had a hard-on the size of the Eiffel Tower the entire time they were sitting at the table. Again.

What her smart mouth would feel like around his dick consumed his thoughts while he drove. He bet she gave head like it was an art form. When she'd gone off to the bathroom, Ryan considered following her, with the intention of pinning her against the wall and kissing those sarcastic lips until neither of them could breathe. Thanks to the little fantasy, he needed to taste her and gave in. The brief kiss in the car had been enough to transform his prick into a Maiya-seeking missile. The drive was short, thank God, and he'd definitely be taking care of the problem when he got home.

With the house to himself this week, he sent up a holler of thanks for a hard-earned night of privacy. Ryan stripped his clothes off on the way to the bedroom. Her scent still lingered, and so did her sweet taste. He licked his lips—for probably the thirtieth time since he'd kissed her.

Lying back on the bed, he closed his eyes and palmed his hard length. In an instant, he was back at the pub, in the hallway by the bathrooms with her. Ryan's cock twitched in his fist, and he gritted his teeth. He could've pushed her into the bathroom, locked the door and bent her over one of the sinks. Her sweet ass taunted him, made him want to slide between her full cheeks and then sink inside her wet channel. Arching his back on the bed, he cupped his tight sac in his other hand, massaging, and stroked his shaft with the other. "Goddamn!"

What kind of noises would she make when he filled her with his thickness? How tight would she be wrapped around him as he slid in and out of her cunt? *Fuck!* Ryan sucked a harsh breath through his teeth, and his cock pulsed in his grip. When she came, she'd probably squeeze his dick— something he'd give anything to feel.

Ryan's orgasm hit like a freight train, and his body went rigid. The first hot lash of semen hit his belly, and he arched off the sheets, calling out her name. He stroked again, from base to tip, spurting more creamy fluid down his hand and onto his abs, shivering as his hand passed over the sensitive head.

Blowing out a harsh breath, Ryan stroked his now softening length. He reached for a towel and wiped up the mess he'd shot all over himself. He'd come hard—the fantasy all too real. Rolling off the bed, he stumbled, on tingling legs, to the shower.

Her hot and wet mouth, her sweet lips wrapped around his length. Ryan bit back a moan, and his cock twitched, eager to come back to life. Ignoring his rising desire, he stepped under the spray and tried to push the thoughts of what it might be like to press her against the wall in his shower, wrap her long legs around his hips and fuck them both into a state of exhaustion.

Jesus, it had to happen now. Jacking off wasn't going to be enough.

Ryan would have her.

CHAPTER FIVE

R<small>YAN SAT AT HIS DESK AFTER ATTENDING HIS WEEKLY STAFF</small> meeting, and an instant message popped on his screen.

Maiya Rossini: Hey!

Ryan Donnelly: Well, hello there. How are you today?

Maiya Rossini: I'm fine. You?

Ryan Donnelly: Pretty good. Did you have a good night last night? Sleep well?

Maiya Rossini: Now, Ryan, is that an appropriate work question? Kidding. Yes, I did. You?

Ryan Donnelly: LOL Fair enough. Yes, I did. 😊 So, what's up?

Maiya Rossini: Project issue. Can you meet me in the conf. room at 3pm?

Ryan Donnelly: Uh oh, that doesn't sound good. You want to tell me what's going on?

> Maiya Rossini: A gap's been uncovered. We need to put our heads together and figure out a solution…and fast, too.
>
> Ryan Donnelly: How is it that you know about this before me?
>
> Maiya Rossini: Because I was on an executive call with the client and Tony, and they were doing some testing on their side. Relax, I'm not jumping over your head.
>
> Ryan Donnelly: Sorry, just shocked to find out I've got an issue. I'll see you at 3.
>
> Maiya Rossini: See you then.

It rankled learning there was an issue on his project. The last thing he wanted was to screw up the shot at a promotion. He needed to show his manager he was more than ready to handle his own team. However, it bothered him more knowing Maiya had been the one to find the issue instead of him. Definitely a healthy case of his ego talking, maybe a little bit of male pride, too—which even he had to admit was stupid.

She was senior to him in title and tenure. He didn't have a problem with it, but she wasn't his manager, and he wanted to be able to handle any business or issues on *his* project without her jumping in or getting to them first.

Maiya was a tiger lady, handling her team and any obstacles with a special kind of finesse rarely seen in management. Most people lost their heads when issues arose. Not Maiya. She kept her cool, got people to do whatever it was she needed, and they usually walked away smiling. It was impressive, to say the least. She'd earned her spot at the company and, with it, the respect of all her peers.

With fresh cup of coffee in hand, along with his laptop tucked under his arm, Ryan strolled into the empty conference room at three. Empty except for one person sitting at the table, typing away on her laptop. At the sight of her, all rankled pride and ego smoothed right out. But then his steps faltered, and his breath caught in his throat. Last night's fantasy parked itself front and center in his mind. With his mouth as dry as the desert, he swallowed and unglued his tongue from the roof of his mouth. "Hey, Maiya."

"Hey, Ryan. Pull up a chair. We've got a lot of documents to go through."

"Where's everyone else?"

"Oh, yeah, everyone else. Hmm." She tapped her bottom lip with her fingernail, a contemplative expression on her face and then looked around the room. "Well, looks like it's just us, big guy. Everyone else had somewhere they needed to run off to. You know how it is, families and such. Fun times, right?"

Ryan took the seat next to her and opened his laptop. "My kind of fun."

She'd pulled her hair up into some sort of knot and somehow made it stay with a pencil stuck through it. Amazing. She had a whole sexy, hot-librarian look going, and his dick was more than pleased to send up a salute in approval. Stifling his dirty thoughts, he signed in to his computer. "So, what's going on?"

"It appears we've missed a technical element in the marketing layout." She studied her screen. "We need to go back through our documentation and find where the gap is in the design solution."

"We submitted our mockup to them, and they approved it. I can't imagine what happened." Ryan leaned close to her, causing their shoulders to touch, to peer at the document she was reading on her laptop. The heat of her body penetrated through their layers of clothes, warming his skin, and damn, she smelled good. Too good. He liked it. A slight lingering scent of cigarette smoke was there, but it didn't seem to bother him like he figured it would.

Maiya scrolled through the document. "This is the section

where we should see the design and layout for the particular feature in question. For the life of me, I can't find the miss."

"Let me pull it up on my laptop and search for it, too. I swear we had everything covered." He pulled away and focused on his screen. Though he still sat close to her, their shoulders no longer touched. The immediate loss of her warmth against him sent a shiver rippling through his body.

"Cold?"

Damn, she noticed. "Um, no, not really."

"Okay then. I'm gonna grab some of the crap break room coffee. You need anything?"

He glanced at her. "I'm good. Thanks."

Being stuck at work wasn't such a hardship after all. There may be a mess to clean up for his project, but he couldn't have picked a better person to be stuck with.

Unable to catch her breath, Maiya drew on every ounce of self-control she possessed to keep from running from the conference room. With Ryan close to her while looking at her laptop screen, his scent—clean soap with a hint of cologne— hit her senses like a Mack truck and sent her head spinning.

Every inch of her skin smoldered, lighting up like a Roman candle on the Fourth of July. Only their shoulders touched, and she had to force back the urge to turn her head and press her lips to his neck. They were in the office, for crying out loud! She needed to get her hormones under control and damn fast. There was a lot of work to do— throwing him onto the conference room table and screwing his brains out was *not* on the agenda.

After grabbing her coffee, she did her best to compose herself. She entered the conference room in time to see Ryan scrub his hands over his face and then run his fingers through his hair. She paused, taking in his appearance. With his hair mussed, he still looked hot, but with a shot of cute added in. *Damn.* "Find it yet?"

"Not yet."

She gave his shoulder a quick squeeze when she passed behind him and then took her seat. "Don't worry, we will."

"Maybe it's in one of the many change requests we received via email from them." He leaned back in his chair and stretched.

Giving in to the urge, she glanced at his stomach, where his shirt was pulled tight, and then her gaze traveled to his groin. Jesus, he had a nice body. She cleared her throat. "Good point. I'll start searching my email files."

After an hour or more of searching, they located what they were looking for.

He sighed. "Damn, that's a big miss. Not good."

"Yep. Now comes the analysis and figuring out how we fucked up." Maiya pulled the pencil from her hair and shook out the long length with both hands. "I hate this part. It always makes my brain hurt, you know?"

"Sure as hell do. You want more coffee?"

"Yeah, that'd be great." She ran her fingers under her eyes and then covered her mouth with the back of her hand as a yawn escaped.

"Tired?"

She batted her lashes at him. "Yes, of course. I was up a little late last night."

He gave her a crooked grin and stood. "Me too."

When he left the room, Maiya leaned forward, rested her elbow on the table, chin in her palm, and focused on the data. She wasn't reading anything on the screen, though. Instead, she was absorbed in the memory of the small kiss he'd given her before he left last night. What would a real kiss be like? Better yet, what would he be like in bed?

Lots of men were a disappointment on the mattress: all talk and no action. Ryan might be no different. It would suck, though, risking her job to have a night between the sheets with him only to have him bomb in bed. Maiya glanced at the clock on the wall and then forced her focus back to the computer. If she didn't get this done soon, she might not be able to keep it together.

Ryan placed a fresh cup of coffee next to her on the table. "Any luck?"

Maiya reached for the cup, and their fingers touched.

Snap!

She yanked her hand away, curling her fingers into her other palm. "Ouch!"

He grabbed her hand. "Shit. Are you okay?"

"Yeah. That freaking hurt, though."

"I'm sorry. Damn static electricity. Happens to me all the time here." Pulling her hand to his lips, he kissed the tip of her fingers.

She froze, and their eyes met. *Oh, shit.*

He brushed his lips over her fingertips again. Maiya sucked in a hissing breath, and a whole different jolt of electricity shot up her arm and through her body. Ryan sucked her finger between his tempting lips.

The warm, wet haven of his mouth caused a ravenous hunger to form in her belly, and her nipples tightened beneath her bra to hard points sharp enough to cut glass. "Wow." She exhaled.

He guided her up from her seat to stand in front of him. Removing her fingers from his mouth, he opened her hand and pressed his lips to her palm.

Someone moaned. And she realized it was her.

His blue-gray eyes widened for a moment in response before he closed them and moved to the skin of her wrist, kissing and nipping a spot which had suddenly become an erogenous zone.

Tidal waves of arousal pumped through her veins, and Maiya panted, dragging in breath after breath. Unable to think straight, she didn't know what to do. Should she grab him and press her body close, or push him away and try to regain some sort of professionalism? They weren't exactly alone in the building.

Ryan snaked his arm around her waist, pulling her close to his body. With one action, he'd made the decision for her. And there was no way in hell she would stop him now. Grabbing his shoulder with her free hand, Maiya arched into him. Soft curves met and molded against his hard chest.

Gripping her hips, he kneaded them and pressed her tighter against him. A whirlwind of desperate desire to feel his mouth on her skin blew through her.

"You are so beautiful." His voice was a low rumble, and he placed his lips against her neck.

Maiya's head fell back, giving him full access. He licked and sucked at her pulse point, biting the tender area and then stroking it with his tongue to relieve the sting.

Yes, this is what she craved. Hoping to make her intent clear, she tangled her fingers in his hair and tugged. She didn't want him to stop. "Ryan," she whispered.

He moved his lips up to her ear and nipped the lobe with his teeth. "Yes, Maiya?"

She gasped and gripped his hair tighter.

Ryan growled, kissing down her jawline and then pulled away enough to stare into her eyes. Both of them were breathing heavy. He rested his forehead against hers and then brushed his lips, once, twice over hers.

"Holy shit." She drew in a breath. "Kiss me, dammit."

Ryan chuckled and caught her bottom lip between his teeth, nibbled and then sucked the soft flesh. Maiya moaned, grinding her pelvis against his.

Smoothing his hands lower, he gripped her ass and hitched her closer. His prick was hard against her belly. Rock hard. Excitement ricocheted through her because she'd been the one to inspire every solid inch of his erection.

Ryan wrapped his hand around her thigh, curled her leg around his hip and pressed against her center. A little whimper escaped her, and she rubbed against him. Fuck, this was hot. So hot. Too hot.

Shifting, he lifted her to sit on the conference room table. She spread her legs, and he moved between them and then covered her mouth with his.

Oh, God, finally! Finally! Lightning hit, striking deep in her core at the first contact of their tongues. She tasted the lingering flavor of coffee, but the rest was all Ryan—sweet, like pure honey.

And she wanted more.

Maiya matched his pace. He stroked his tongue over hers and then nipped and suckled at her lips. When he broke the kiss, she let out a gasp.

Ryan ran his tongue down her throat. "You taste so good. I could kiss you forever, everywhere." He licked the juncture of her breasts and tugged at her blouse. "I want to kiss you everywhere."

"Jesus Christ, Ryan. I'm on fire. Don't stop."

"Don't move." Stepping away, Ryan closed and locked the conference room door.

CHAPTER SIX

MAIYA DRAGGED IN AIR, TRYING FOR ALL IT WAS WORTH TO catch her breath. Good Lord, the man kissed like a dream. Ryan was proving better than any fantasy she'd ever had. And still, her mind reeled, a futile attempt to force herself back from the ledge of fuck-up-your-career canyon.

But then he turned to her, hair mussed from her fingers tangling in it, with an I'm-going-to-fuck-your-brains-out gleam in his eyes…

Aaaaand she was a goner.

Maiya leaped off the ledge to career suicide. Nope. There was no going back now. Ryan stalked toward her, a cool and determined expression on his face. Any minuscule lingering doubts she had took a hike. "You look like a man on a mission."

"You could say that." He stepped between her legs.

"You do realize this is a bad idea, right?"

He unbuttoned her shirt. "A very bad idea."

She ran her hands over his arms to his broad shoulders. "We *cannot* have sex in the conference room."

"Why not?" He nipped at the curve of flesh peeking over the top of her bra.

Maiya let her head fall back, drowning in the feel of his hot mouth on her skin. Heat traveled from where his mouth touched and settled between the juncture of her spread legs. "Because you know wh— Oh sweet Jesus."

Ryan clasped his teeth onto her nipple through the lace of her bra.

All rational thought flew out the window, and Maiya fell silent, holding her breath. Threading her fingers through his hair, she gripped the back of his head in one hand and ran her nails down his spine with the other.

Ryan sucked her areola, dampening it through the thin material. His mouth was a raging inferno; the feel of it set her blood to boil. *Sweet Jesus!* He gripped the other breast and squeezed, massaging it.

"I need... Fuck! I need your mouth on my skin. Now." Maiya dug her nails into his back.

With her nipple still in his mouth, he paused and then growled before pulling away. Straightening, he met her stare. His gaze shifted over her face, to her lips and neck, then lower, to her breasts. Dragging the cup of her bra down with one finger, his mouth tipped into a grin, and then he met her eyes again. He looked like a kid in a candy store about to gorge himself on sweet treats.

A wild thrill bounced through Maiya from head to toe, and her body screamed its need for him to be inside it. Her clit throbbed, and her cunt ached. Her nipples hardened to almost painful points. Oh, yes. She wanted this. She wanted him.

With a fingertip, he traced a line from her collarbone to just above the areola on one breast and then circled it. "Pretty light caramel nipples. My very favorite."

He was vocal, and she couldn't deny she liked that. A lot. "I'm glad you like them."

"I'm going to give you exactly what you need." His eyes

were dark and serious, and the dominance in his tone feathered over her body, making her shiver.

"Is this how it's going to be?"

He continued to circle the caramel flesh of her areola with the tip of his finger, causing her nipple to darken and tighten further. "It's how you need it to be."

Maiya gasped. She was dying, fucking dying right there under his masterful touch. "Why is that?"

Ryan stopped the slow, torturous circles, and his brow furrowed in mock consternation. "Because, sweet Maiya, I say it is. Because it won't be any other way between us." He leaned in and bit her stiff nipple…hard.

"Fuck!" She bucked against him. The delicious sting of pleasure—bordering on pain—shot through her breast. Her channel clamped down on itself, and her clit throbbed harder.

Ryan gripped her hip with one hand, stilling her, and released the tender peak. "I'm going to suck and bite your nipples until you beg me to let you come." He took her puckered areola into his mouth again. Pulling the rest of her bra down, he moved to the other, biting and sucking as he'd done to its mate.

Maiya strained against his hold, wanting to rub against the hard length still hidden behind his pants. She was losing control. Ryan taking charge like this annoyed her beyond reason, yet her sex flooded with arousal. Nothing like being turned on and appalled at the same time.

He straightened and gazed at both wet, stiff nipples. "So gorgeous. Look how hard and red your nipples are for me now. You love it, don't you?"

"Fucking hell, Ryan."

His gaze jumped to hers, his eyes stone hard, and he pinched both nipples between his fingers. Maiya hissed through her teeth and then cried out. Her pussy clenched again, and she thought, for the first time in her life, she might end up begging for an orgasm.

"I asked you a question. Now, answer me." The tone in his voice clear; there was no room for her to defy him.

She wasn't sure she could, even if she wanted to. "Yes! Yes, I love it." Any other answer would've been a lie.

Continuing to pinch and tug on her sensitive nipples, he leaned in and licked her upper lip. "Open for me, baby. Let me taste you again."

With her mind a befuddled mess of lust and frustration, she complied, letting him explore her mouth further.

"Good girl." Returning to her mouth, he sucked and lapped at her tongue.

Maiya was swept up in a tornado of stimulation, and the room spun around her. The need to climax rode her like the devil himself was chasing her to hell. Gasping for air between kisses, the pressure inside her body grew. She wanted him inside her, to stretch and fill her, take her as hard as he wanted to. She wrapped her legs around his hips and rocked against him, rubbing her swollen clit against the hard ridge behind his zipper. It wasn't enough, but she'd be damned if she would beg him for release. "Dammit, Ryan."

"All you have to do is ask."

"You're killing me." She rubbed against him again, trying for all it was worth to gain more contact. *Sonofabitch.* "I'm so close... Don't make me... Oh God, please?"

He cupped one breast, rolling her nipple between his fingertips. "Please, what?"

I can't believe I'm doing this, but I don't care anymore. "Please let me come? Please?"

He growled, jerked her off the table and sat in the chair behind them with her astride his lap. "Ride me, Maiya. I want you to come so hard you soak right through those fuck-me pants of yours."

"Oh God. Yes." Aligning her clit with his hard length, she rolled her hips.

Ryan palmed both of her breasts and pressed them

together, and then licked, sucked and bit each nipple. The sting of each bite and the soothing brush of his tongue over the tight peaks made her clit pulse and her channel clench down on itself.

Maiya flew apart. Her orgasm hit with the force of an earthquake, and she bit down on the palm of her hand to keep from screaming his name. Waves of powerful aftershocks traveled through her body, and goose pimples broke out along her heated, sweat-slick skin. Breathless, she slumped against him.

He stroked her hair and back, and they stayed in silence for a few minutes, each trying to catch their breath.

As the crash from the high hit hard, shock at what they'd done parked front and center in her mind. "That was crazy. And I can't believe I begged you."

"You'll beg me the next time, too. Then, when I *let* you come, you'll scream my name." Ryan twined his fingers in her long hair, pulled her head up from his shoulder and kissed her.

Maiya took in his words. They jabbed at her independent side, but she chose to ignore them and focus on the kiss. When she broke from his lips, breathless once again, she rubbed against him one last time. He was still hard. "You didn't come, did you?"

"It's fine."

"The hell it is." She climbed down his lap and knelt in front of him.

"Maiya, what are you doing?"

It was quite clear to her what she was doing: taking back some of the control she'd given over to him. He didn't climax, and she wasn't having it. Plus, the desire to feel him slide between her lips trumped the thoughts of why they should get the hell out of the office before someone caught them in the act. The idea of being caught sent bolts of fear shooting through her, but it also had her pulse pounding with excitement. The risk of it all made everything much more titillating.

"Answer me, Maiya."

She glanced at him and licked her lips but said nothing. "Woman. I'm gonn—"

Maiya ran her palm up his length through his pants, and he gasped. She reached for his belt an—

A knock sounded at the door.

Oh my God! Maiya jumped to her feet and tugged her shirt closed.

"Get under the table." Ryan smoothed his hair and arranged the bulge in his pants, and then walked to the door.

"What? Under the fucking table? Are you nuts?"

"Do as I say, Maiya. Now," he whispered.

She stared at him for a heartbeat and then crawled under the table to the far end, hiding herself in the shadows of the chairs. *Dammit, dammit!*

Ryan opened the door. "Oh, hey, Randy. You need something?"

She fumbled with her buttons but managed to get them all closed and in proper order. Taking deep, even breaths to calm her racing pulse, she sat still, listening to the conversation.

"Yeah, I'm looking for David and Joe. They were supposed to be up here working on some financials," Randy said.

Maiya buried her face in her hands, praying he wouldn't want to come into the room.

"Ah, yeah, you know, I think they were meeting down on three." Ryan stepped from the room and closed the door behind him.

Maiya exhaled the breath she'd been holding, and relief washed through her. She heard their muffled voices beyond the door, and when they faded, she presumed Ryan walked away from the room with Randy. Waiting another minute or two, she climbed from beneath the table. She smoothed her shirt back in place and ran her fingers through her hair.

What the hell had she been thinking? No way... No

goddamn way was she doing this. How the hell did she let this happen? She sat in front of her laptop and began shutting it down, intent on getting out of there before Ryan came back.

RYAN WALKED RANDY TO THE ELEVATORS, MAKING SMALL TALK along the way. "Catch you later, Randy." Ryan gave him a mock salute.

"Later." The man stepped into the elevator, and Ryan watched until the doors closed. Closing his eyes, he pinched the bridge of his nose. *Christ, that was close.* The memory of Maiya on his lap rushed back, full force. Man, she was heaven and hell mixed into one. So responsive to him and his demands, it blew his mind.

He never would've thought she'd yield control to him. It intrigued him and made him leery at the same time. He'd been down a road similar to this in the past and wasn't too keen on traveling it again.

A definite path to hell, fraught with broken hearts and broken people.

Maiya acted different in many ways, though. But what if she wasn't? The same in too many ways, and yet, not. Call him a cynical bastard, but women like Maiya didn't settle down. Ever.

When he got back to the conference room, she was packing up her laptop. "Damn close."

She snorted but said nothing and continued her task.

Closing the door, he leaned against it and crossed his arms. "Why are you leaving?"

"You know as well as I do this is a bad idea."

"Yeah, it is." He shrugged. "Still felt good, though."

She didn't respond, just stood there, lips pursed, head tilted to the side, her red hair pooling around her shoulders. She was even hotter when annoyed. He knew she was wild, but he hadn't pegged her for a runner. Shit, he didn't want her to go. "What? So, you're running?"

She glared at him. "Whatever, Ryan. I'm going back to my hotel." She grabbed her bag and walked toward him. "I'll finish the analysis there."

"I'll come with you."

"No. You go home." She stopped in front of him. "Text me if you have a question about the project. I'm sure I'll be up late."

He watched a figurative mask slide into place over her face. Amazing. In the blink of an eye, she shut him out. "Back to business, huh?"

"Let's just forget this happened." She reached around him for the door handle. "Excuse me."

"Yeah, I figured. Typical." He stepped to the side and opened the door for her.

She stared into his eyes. Her expression changed for a split second, but the emotion was gone before he deciphered it. Looking away, she walked out.

Had the comment hurt her feelings? Doubtful. Based on her behavior, it was more than obvious she didn't care. Why would she? He shut his laptop down. Screw it, if she didn't care, then neither did he. She was right. This was a very bad idea.

When Ryan got home, he set up his laptop and then tossed a frozen dinner in the microwave. His cell rang from the coffee table in the living room. *Maiya.* He ran and snatched it up, not bothering to check the screen. "Hello?"

"Hi, Daddy," the little voice said on the other end of the line.

Ryan sat on the couch. "Hey, little man, how's it going at Nana's house?"

"Good! We made cookies. Nana makes the bestest cookies."

"Yeah, she sure does, Jacob." Ryan leaned back and let his

little boy's sweet voice wrap around him. His son was spending the week of school vacation with Ryan's parents. A pang of sadness rang through him. He missed Jacob more than he'd expected. "So, you're having a fun time, then?"

"Uh-huh, tomorrow we're going to Knott's Berry Farm. Can you come too?"

"No, buddy, I can't. Wish I could, but I have to work." Ryan's mother said something in the background. "Nana says to tell you she'll have me home at seven on Friday. I miss you, Daddy."

"Tell her that'll be fine. I miss you, too, little man." Ryan rubbed the back of his neck. "You better head to bed now. It's getting late. Nana spoils you."

"Nanas are apposst to spoil kids."

"Supposed to." Ryan chuckled. "Yes, I guess they are. I love you, little man. You can call me tomorrow night if you want."

"Love you too."

"Sweet dreams." Ryan listened, and Jacob relayed his message to his grandmother before the phone cut off.

Jacob. Exactly the reminder he needed. Ryan *had* to keep his head on straight for his kid. His little boy was his world, and he'd be damned if he would allow his son to be hurt because he had an attack of horny…or lonely. If he wanted to date, he needed to be dating the right kind of woman. Someone not so wild, maybe a little softer around the edges.

Maiya wasn't that woman.

CHAPTER SEVEN

Maiya rushed from the building as fast as she could. She didn't know if she was more disgusted with herself or Ryan. It wasn't fair to be mad at him, but who the hell cared about fair anyway? She should have pushed him away, should have denied him. And the way she did what he told her to do... Maiya covered her mouth with her hand. The thought made her stomach fold in on itself, and bile burned the back of her throat.

No matter what, she always stayed in control. Her cheeks burned from embarrassment. Giving in like she had freaked her out. Whether she enjoyed it at the time didn't matter either. Who the fuck did he think he was anyway? Some sort of dominant-pounding-his-chest-alpha-male type she'd read about in romance books? *Like hell.* Mr. Ryan Donnelly was nothing but a Porsche-driving pretty boy. Freaking typical snob!

For damn sure, nothing she wanted.

Growing up like she did, in a decrepit old trailer on the outskirts of Vegas, had hardened Maiya. Her mother was always absent. Her father? What father. Maiya was self-made. She took orders from no one. Not bikers, not musicians, and sure as shit, not some stiff shirt from work. The fact she'd graduated high school and earned a bachelor's degree from community college had been a miracle.

Now, at twenty-nine, she had a career, a nice home and badass car. A life—a hella good one at that—and no intention of throwing it down the drain for some too-high- and-mighty guy from work.

Not. Happening.

Pushing open the door to her hotel room, Maiya set her things down and ordered room service, then set up her laptop to finish the analysis on the project. She'd be up past midnight getting all this crap done. Not wanting to talk to anyone, she signed into the work instant messaging system in "invisible" status. She settled at the small oak desk in the hotel with her room service dinner and glass of wine, and worked.

About thirty minutes and an emptied glass of wine later, she noticed Ryan online. She focused on his green status light and visions flashed before her eyes: him kissing her fingers, her lips. Her body on fire for him. She shivered, but then agitation rolled through her.

Tossing down her napkin, Maiya got up and paced behind the desk chair. She should message him, but had no idea what to say. They hadn't had sex, not real sex anyway. It was fake, clothes-on sex, resulting in one amazing orgasm for her. And now, she couldn't even bring herself to talk to him in IM. How the hell would she face him in the office tomorrow? What a fucking mess.

Resuming her seat, she changed her IM status to red. Now he'd know she was online but busy. He'd be working on the project too. At least, she hoped so. If he needed her, he could at least ping her.

An hour and a half and another glass of Chardonnay later, she'd located the info she needed to cover the miss on the project and then prepared a report to email Ryan. The wine settled warmly in her veins, reducing her agitation, and she decided to IM him before sending the note. Pulling up the chat window, Maiya stared at it. *Dammit.* Her internal warning bell clanged as loud as Big Ben's citywide tolling. She should stay away from him. Nothing good would come from pursuing this further.

Guys like Ryan weren't interested in women like her: a chick from the wrong side of the tracks. It was safer with the guys she was used to. Ryan would fuck her until he had his fill and then cast her aside. And who needed that? *Typical.* Yeah, she was the typical one, like he said.

Maiya set her fingers on the keyboard to type out a message…and Ryan signed off—his green status light changing to gray. Relief blanketed her mind. Leaning back, she moved the computer onto her lap and went back to the email she'd started. It contained only the bare facts, and once the report was attached, she hit Send.

Maiya wandered into the bathroom and peeled off her work clothes. She turned on the water for a bath, and her cell phone dinged.

Ryan.

Spinning to bolt from the room, Maiya's feet tangled in the bathmat on the marble floor. With her body in full motion, momentum propelled her forward, and she almost faceplanted into the wall opposite the doorway. Feeling pretty damn stupid at her schoolgirl-with-a-crush reaction, she sucked in a strangled breath and *walked*, in an adult fashion, the rest of the way to her phone. "Fucking. Hell."

FRUSTRATION SWARMED IN RYAN'S MIND WHEN HE READ THE email from Maiya. He retrieved his cell from the kitchen counter. Once back in the family room, Ryan planted his butt on the couch and typed out a text message thanking her. Staring at the unsent message, he didn't know if he was pleased with her for taking the time to finish the research or agitated because she obviously was able to focus...and he wasn't. *Damn her.*

It was a testament to her work ethic, though. She hadn't gotten so far up the corporate ladder without being able to get the job done. At the last minute, he added to the message, inquiring if she was okay. He hit Send and waited. After a few tense minutes, his phone beeped.

Maiya: You're welcome. And... I'm not sure.

Ryan: I'm sorry. You want to talk?

Maiya: Again, not sure.

Ryan: What would it take to convince you? *wags brows*

Lying down, he stretched out on the couch. Unsure of what he was doing, yet knowing full well he, again, wouldn't stop himself.

Maiya: Knock it off. LOL

Ryan: Ah, an "LOL." Are you smiling now?

Maiya: You're a pain in my ass.

Ryan: Speaking of ass, yours is damn fine.

This was like a runaway train. Tragedy was the only destination on the schedule, but he was determined to stay on the ride anyway.

Maiya: LOL. Um, thanks?

Ryan: Haha, I'm serious. So, what are you wearing?

Maiya: Nothing. You?

He stared at her answer for a moment, his mouth dry. Then he typed the next message.

Ryan: Woman, that's hot. I'm still dressed.
Send me a pic. I need to confirm if the rumors
about your many tattoos are true.

Maiya: No fucking way! LOL And we are NOT
talking about my many tattoos. 😜

He chuckled. She wouldn't send him a picture, but he wanted to see what she'd come back with. Her answer wasn't a surprise—though he *did* want to know about her tattoos. She rarely talked about them. Some of the guys in the office had plenty of ideas about what they could be or how many she actually had.

Screw it, Ryan hit "call contact" on the screen and waited for her to answer.

———

MAIYA STARED AT THE PHONE RINGING IN HER HAND, AND HER heart leaped into her throat. She covered her forehead with her palm, sucked in a breath and answered. "Hey."

"I wasn't sure you'd answer."

Pulling the blankets back on the bed, she climbed in. "Why wouldn't I?"

"I don't know. Just wasn't sure."

She listened to him breathing on the other end of the line for what felt like forever. Pulling up her big-girl panties, she broke the awkward silence between them. "I'm sorry about before."

"I'm not."

"Ryan—"

"Listen, Maiya, forget about it, okay? I mean…it's all good. We still have to work together."

There was some rustling in the background. "What are you doing?"

He cleared his throat. "Hmm? Oh, I'm getting naked."

Visions of what his hard, naked body might look like flashed before her eyes, and she bolted upright in the bed. "Fuck. Really?"

"Yes."

She coughed and pulled the mental e-brake, forcing the thoughts of his body to pass right by. "I think… I think I have to go." *Don't think about what his chest might look like or his ass. Or…shit.*

"Do you?"

"Um." She got to her feet. *This is* such *a bad idea.* "Yes, I do. I need to go."

"Well, if you're sure."

"I don't— I can't do this, Ryan. We shouldn't…" She paced next to the bed. "I can't. My job."

"I know," he whispered. "My job, too, Maiya."

A chill zipped down her spine, and not because she was naked. She walked into the bathroom and turned off the running water. "I like you, Ryan. Under other circumstances, maybe." She grabbed a towel, set it on the floor beside the tub and stepped into the hot water.

"I like you too, Maiya. Wait…is that water I just heard?"

"No. Yes. Shit." *Hang up. Hang up the phone!*

"Are you in the bath?" Amazement dripped from his tone. She bit her bottom lip and didn't answer.

"You're in the bathtub right now, aren't you? Answer me." He exhaled. Loud and sounding quite frustrated.

"Yes. Did you just…growl?" Maiya let out a resigned sigh. Once again, she'd given in to his demands. Regardless of whether or not she wanted to. Why did she keep doing that?

And why did it feel so good to know it flustered and pleased him in ways she couldn't even begin to fathom?

"You are going to be the death of me. Is your hair up?"

She touched the scrunchie holding her hair at the top of her head. "What? Why do you— Oh hell." She needed to end this right now. "Good night, Ryan. I'll talk to you tomorrow."

"Mmm. Good night, Maiya."

The call disconnected, and she stared at the screen for a second before tossing it onto the towel next to the tub. There were two more days left of the trip. *Friday. Just have to make it to Friday.* Then she'd go home, and everything would go back to normal.

She'd have to avoid him, though. Maiya slumped in the hot water, contemplating the impossibility of the idea. How to work with him and avoid him at the same time was not going to be easy. She should just sleep with him. A little bump between the sheets. Or in the car. Or in the shower. Or on the — *Stop!*

Truth was, she couldn't *just* sleep with him because…*shit.* Because she liked him. She liked him a little too much. Worse, their sexual chemistry was four-alarm fire hot. She'd end up getting attached and then hurt.

Maiya rubbed her forehead, the effects of the two glasses of wine making their appearance. Her head throbbed, but she had a feeling the ache had more to do with Ryan than the wine.

Casual sex had never been a problem for her, ever. However, sex with Ryan would never be casual. Maiya faced an emotional fork in the road. Sinking lower in the tub, she let the warmth swirl around her. Without a doubt, if she made the wrong choice, it would take her life from simple and smooth to difficult and bumpy.

Just make it to Friday. Maiya closed her eyes. Friday was an eternity away.

CHAPTER EIGHT

THE NEXT MORNING, RYAN STOOD AT HIS KITCHEN WINDOW, coffee mug in hand, peering out at the wooden play gym he'd built for his son.

Jacob would be home on Friday.

Fatigue weighed heavy in his body as if he'd been up all night on baby patrol. Suspended somewhere between semi-sleep and complete consciousness, he dreamed of Maiya. At one point, he rolled over in bed and swore her scent was on his sheets.

Maiya would go home on Friday.

Heaviness settled in his chest, and he rubbed the spot. One day wasn't much time. A befuddled mess of confusion filled his mind. What did he think? He'd get her in bed for a one-night stand and then move on? There was way too much on the line to be playing around like that.

He'd see her today, or maybe he wouldn't. Of course, he could avoid her altogether and work from home. *Coward.* He coughed and then downed the last of his coffee. He needed to be a man about the situation. No sex with Maiya—no nothing with Maiya. The heaviness in his chest increased, and he cringed. Did he really want nothing with Maiya?

He rolled the question around in his mind on his drive to work, tasted it with his tongue. It was bitter. If he was honest, he wanted *something* with her. But what with a woman like her, though? The idea terrified him.

So much to lose. So much to gain. But…what if?

The office buzzed with loud voices and random phones ringing. Ryan walked to his cube, glancing into his neighbors' cubicles along the way. Family pictures, plants, or little cartoon jokes pinned to the gray cloth walls decorated nearly all of them.

Ryan had no personal pictures displayed. No one at work even knew he had a child. Landing this job and all the opportunity it offered, including the salary, had been exactly what he needed for a fresh start. Call him old-fashioned, but he didn't want his being a single parent to limit his chances of rising in the ranks. Companies were far more understanding where women were concerned in regard to single parenting. It was less of an oddity these days for men; still, he didn't want to risk it.

He stared at his bland cubicle walls while his PC started up. A few business certifications and awards were pinned up, and a calendar displaying various racing Porsches—the calendar being the one thing showing even a hint of his personality.

Ryan Donnelly: all business, strait-laced, reliable and, most of all, in control.

"Hey."

He swiveled in his chair and met Maiya's gaze. "Good morning."

"Morning. We have a meeting in conference room six-sixty-four." She leaned forward into his cube, both arms spread out and braced on the portable walls of the entrance.

His skin went tight, tingling all over. *Were her eyes this light yesterday?* He stood and stepped up to her. "When?" He studied her irises. Today, they looked pale hazel with flecks of green and gold surrounding the pupil. "God, your eyes are beautiful."

"Thanks." Her lips quirked into a meek smile. "In ten minutes." Raising her hand, she adjusted his tie.

Snatching her hand, he cupped it between both of his and kissed her knuckles. "Have dinner with me tonight?"

"Ryan, stop." She looked down the hall, stretching to the left and right behind her. "Someone's gonna see."

She tried to pull her hand away, but he held fast to it. "Say yes." He kissed her fingers again. "Please?"

"Ryan, come on." Maiya pinned him with a stare and lowered her voice. "Nothing good can come from this."

"Maybe. Maybe not." He tilted his head to the side. "Come to dinner with me. We'll talk."

"I'll think about it." She tugged her hand free. This time, he let her. "I'll see you at the meeting. Don't be late."

———

MAIYA HURRIED AWAY FROM RYAN'S CUBE, PRAYING NO ONE had noticed them together. What the hell did he think he was doing? "Dinner? Pfft," she mumbled and rushed to the office she used while in town. *No way. Not going.*

Her fingers still tingled from where his soft lips had kissed them. Why in God's name had she reached and adjusted his tie? Her heart thudded in her ears, and she stepped into her temporary office, closing the door behind her.

The man was relentless.

The aroma of clean soap with a slight hint of cologne had funneled through her airway and deep into her lungs when he'd stepped close. Without giving her body permission, she breathed in, taking in his scent, and then held it tight in her lungs as she stared into his sparkling eyes. He looked at her with complete longing, like he wanted her. Really wanted her.

Decisions, decisions. She glanced at the motivational print

hanging on the opposite wall. A man stood, rock-climbing gear loaded on his body, staring at a huge mountain in the distance. The quote read, "Don't let fear keep you from accomplishing your dreams."

She pressed her hand to her pounding chest. The universe was turning against her. "Jesus, I need a cigarette." Work. It was time for work, not time to smoke. Grabbing her notepad and pencil, she exited her office and headed for the conference room. She had a whole hour to stare at him across the table and contemplate her next move.

On her way down the corridor, Jodi fell in beside her. "Hey, girl."

"Hey, Jodi. Ready?"

"Yes, ma'am, let— Whoa, are you okay?" Jodi put her hand on Maiya's arm, halting their forward motion.

Maiya blinked. "Fine. Why?"

"Uh, uh. You are so *not* fine. Your cheeks are flushed, and you look a little frazzled."

"Come on. We're going to be late." Maiya walked forward.

Jodi kept pace while still holding Maiya's arm. "Did something happen with Ryan?"

"I don't want to talk about it."

"Something happened. I knew it." Jodi let out a squeal. "When were you going to tell me?"

"I *do not* want to talk about it." Maiya clamped her mouth closed, gritting her teeth.

"Oh my God. Did you have sex with him?"

They approached the conference room door, and Maiya stopped short, shooting her friend a glare. "Jodi!"

"What? Come on, Maiya. Promise me you'll tell me after the meeting. We'll go downstairs, get a coffee and smoke." Jodi's face beamed with excitement, and she bounced into the conference room, pulling Maiya with her.

"Maybe," Maiya muttered, and they took their seats.

And there he was. Ryan sat opposite from her and met her gaze the second her butt landed in the chair. Maiya swallowed past the bowling ball-sized lump in her throat and tried to focus. Nervous energy thrummed through her body.

She spent the first thirty minutes doodling on her notepad. Every time she dared to glance his way, her heart raced, and she couldn't keep her feet still. The high heel of her shoe started a tap, tap, tap on the carpet, ignoring her mind's orders to quit. Shifting in her seat, crossing and uncrossing her legs, she was desperate to keep one foot planted on the ground.

Jodi rested her hand on Maiya's leg, stilling its bounce. Maiya knocked her hand away, and Jodi smothered a giggle behind her palm.

Ryan spoke, relaying the causes of how the campaign suffered a flaw in the designs and what solutions were being put in place to execute a fix. His words were a muffled blur in her ears because his mouth was the only thing she focused on. She knew how his lips felt on her skin and breasts. Her nipples hardened, and she shifted again in her seat, uncrossing and re-crossing her legs. The fire she'd prayed had died ignited again. *Dammit.* Who was she kidding? It was hopeless. *She* was hopeless and may as well give in.

"Care to add anything, Maiya?" Ryan asked.

"Hmm? Oh! Um, yes." For God's sake, she was too distracted. "Thanks, Ryan." She straightened in her seat and added a few comments to the mix. The meeting adjourned not long after, thank God.

Jodi tugged on Maiya's shirt. "Come on, we have a date."

"Fine, but you're buying."

"No problem." Jodi walked to the door. "Light a fire under it."

Maiya gathered her things. Jodi had no clue how big the fire already burned. "You're lucky I love you."

Maiya leaned back in her seat outside the coffee shop downstairs. The early afternoon sun warmed her skin, and the breeze from the passing cars and buses whipped around her.

Jodi listened while Maiya spilled the goods about what happened two nights ago when he dropped her off from Flanagan's and then what happened yesterday evening in the conference room. "And now he wants to take me to dinner." Maiya took a breath and sipped her coffee.

"Are you going to go? I think you should go."

"I don't know. I'm all in my head about it. I can't afford to get strung out on a guy. Especially one from work."

"It's just dinner." Jodi shrugged. "Use it as an opportunity to…I dunno, get to know him better."

"Maybe." Maiya looked at her watch. Almost noon. Plenty of time to decide still. "I'll think about it and decide later."

"Good plan." Jodi ran her fingers through her blonde hair. "Ready to go back?"

"Sure." Maiya tossed her coffee cup in the nearby trash can. Her anxiety had eased, at least a little, getting the mess off her chest. "I think you smoked yourself into oblivion."

Jodi looped her arm with Maiya's. "Hey, if you're gonna do it, might as well do it right. Right?"

"Thanks, Jodi. I needed this."

"Anytime, girl. You know I love ya."

Maiya nudged Jodi's hip with her own. "I love you, too, sweetie."

When Maiya got to her office, she shut her door and set to get work done. She was determined to salvage some part of this workday, even if she had to stay hidden in her office for the rest of it.

CHAPTER NINE

At the end of the day, Ryan approached Maiya's office. He lingered outside the closed door for a moment and listened for voices. Nothing but silence. Good, she was alone. He inhaled and rolled his head on his shoulders. When he heard and felt the loud pop of bones in his neck, he let out his breath.

Leaning toward the door a little closer, he listened again. This time, he heard her voice. After a soft knock on the door, he opened it. She was facing the window. A quick glance around showed there was no one else in the office with her. He stepped inside, closing the door behind him.

"No, Mom." She ran her hand through her hair. "No, I'm not doing that. Please, stop asking."

He cleared his throat, and she whipped around in the chair. He mouthed a "hello" and shrugged one shoulder. He hadn't meant to intrude.

She rolled her eyes. "I have to go. No. Yes. I'll call you tomorrow." She hung up the receiver and stared at the phone. "You ever notice how many buttons we have on these things? What're they all for?" She shook her head and then looked up at him.

"You okay, Maiya?"

"Yep, fine." She nodded and smiled, but it didn't quite reach her eyes. The same mask she'd shown him yesterday in the conference room slid into place.

He sat in one of the two chairs positioned in front of the desk. "Okay."

"Please, have a seat." She snorted, folded her arms on the desk and leaned forward.

He smirked and leaned forward, too. "Thanks, very kind of you to offer."

Palpable tension bounced between them. He watched her face. The little quirk of her lips. The angle she held her head. Maiya fascinated him. They sized each other up, for how long he wasn't sure. In truth, it didn't matter. He was too caught up with the wonder of what she might be thinking right then.

Without another thought, Ryan reached across the desk, grabbed her by the wrist and pulled her toward him. He kissed her, open-mouthed, stroking over her lips with his tongue, granting her no mercy and no time to pull away.

She resisted but then moaned and opened for him. His kiss swallowed the deep sound. Was that resignation he heard? He cupped Maiya's cheek in his palm, stroked her satin skin with his thumb, and then moved his hand to bury his fingers in her thick, red hair. A zing of arousal shot down his spine, and he caressed the soft strands between his fingers, massaging the back of her head.

She moaned again, this time sounding much like a plea for more. He took the cue and deepened the kiss. She tasted like coffee and...strawberries? *Yes!* Ryan nibbled at her bottom lip and then sought her tongue again.

When he pulled away, they were both breathless. He brushed his lips over hers once more, lingering for a bit, enjoying her sweetness, and realized he could kiss her forever. "Sorry, I just...needed that."

She licked her lips. "Mmm."

"So, dinner?"

"Mmhmm. Yes."

He gave her a final quick kiss. "Good. Let's go." He stood.

"I have to shut down my computer." Still in her seat, she looked up at him. "And I need to drop my car off at the hotel."

Ryan gazed at her, and his stomach knotted at the sight. Lips, swollen from his kisses, cheeks a little flushed. "You're beautiful."

She tilted her head to the side, and her gaze softened, and so did his heart.

They were both quiet while they made their way down the elevator. When they got away from prying eyes, Ryan held her hand and walked her to her car in the parking garage. "See you at the hotel."

"Okay." She smiled and closed the door.

As he followed her rental car, anticipation of what the night would bring pumped through him. She parked in the hotel garage and then emerged and slid into his front seat.

"No, you're not driving." He made a stern face, baiting her.

"I wasn't even going to ask, stud." She stuck out her tongue.

"Oh, ho, ho, ho…you so were. You know you want to drive my car."

She gave him a sideways glance, lips pursed, one perfect brow raised. "Awfully full of yourself. Might need to take you down a peg or ten." Maiya crossed her arms as if deciding she'd be the perfect woman for the job.

He'd make a deal with the devil for the chance to see that. The woman was remarkable. She made him feel calm one minute and then pricked his temper in the next—sometimes, she left him with both emotions at the same time. Hot and cold. Push and pull. Ever the constant challenge. Running his hand over his mouth, he shook his head. The conflicting feelings confused him, and yet, made perfect sense. "Would love to see you try."

MAIYA WATCHED THE PASSING SCENERY OUT OF THE SIDE window while they drove onto the freeway. "So, where you taking me?"

"It's a surprise."

She shifted to face him and frowned. "I hate surprises."

"Seriously?"

"No." She laughed. Maiya *had* to mess with him. Just a little. Why on earth should this be easy for him?

He was taking her somewhere, Lord only knew where, and she was excited. Beyond excited. However, she still needed to take off the edge of seriousness starting between them with a little bit of their familiar banter. Maybe she was addicted to the chaos. Could be why she'd always chased the bad boys.

They were a predictable kind of chaos, though. With the familiar, she knew what to expect. They'd stay around for a short time, and she'd have some fun. And then they'd go. Sometimes it stung, most times not. Ryan was a whole different bag of beans. Her attraction to him was so very unusual compared to the others, and she didn't know how to navigate the unfamiliar terrain.

About thirty minutes later, they pulled into a parking lot and up to the valet attendants. The spotlighted sign above the building glowed with the word "Elise."

He opened his door and handed the keys to the attendant. "Have you been here before?"

"No." She startled a bit when her door was opened, but then took the offered hand of another attendant.

Ryan came around the front of the car, placed his hand on

the small of her back and led them to the door. "Good. A first for both of us, then."

The front door was solid dark wood, adorned with intricate carvings. Ryan held the door open, and she stepped inside. She looked around in awe. The dark paneled walls of the hall were elegant, hosting black-and-white headshots of historical movie stars such as Grace Kelly, John Wayne and several others. "This is beautiful."

"I agree." He paused when she did to study a group photo of actors she didn't recognize. "It's supposed to have the best filet in town."

"Oh, no, really? I'm a vegetarian." She raised her brows. He stopped and turned to her. "Are you kidding me?"

"Maybe." She walked on ahead. He was damn fun to tease and too adorable.

He grunted, and he caught her under the arm. "Woman."

"You're just too easy, Ryan." She smirked, doing nothing to hide her pleasure at teasing him.

He swatted her ass, not hard, but enough to make her jump and squeal. "Quiet, woman. This is a classy joint. There'll be no squealing."

She rolled her eyes and snorted. Ryan circled her wrist in his palm and then wrapped her arm behind her back. Holding it tight with one hand, he kissed her. With her breasts pressed flush against his chest, Maiya melted. And her legs turned to jelly…right about the time the maître d' cleared his throat. *Busted.* She couldn't contain her giggles, and her cheeks flushed hot. Such a strange reaction for her. She never got embarrassed. To this day, the only person who *could* embarrass Maiya was her mother.

His arm slid down around her waist, pinning her to his side. "Ah, yes. Excuse us. We have a reservation for two under Donnelly."

A thousand tingles shot over her skin at the possessiveness of his touch, and she smiled. She couldn't help it.

The restaurant housed a series of different rooms, all lined with elaborate décor and the sounds of classical piano echoed throughout the restaurant. She held Ryan's hand, and they followed the man in the penguin suit to their table. Her eyes widened when they entered their room. Dark, navy-blue carpet blanketed the floor, and several small tables, covered in white linens, were set about in the sizeable space. The back wall housed an enormous mahogany wine rack filled with assorted bottles. The whole room gave off a refined and warm vibe. Gorgeous.

The maître d' pulled out her chair for her. She sat, and then he slid her seat in. "Thank you."

"Your server will be Evelyn this evening. Enjoy your meal." He placed a menu in front of each of them and disappeared from the table with an annoyed look.

"I don't think he likes us." She wrinkled her nose and draped the cloth napkin on her lap.

"Did you see his scowl?"

"Yep. It's a rule in L.A. to have one of those, right?"

"You may be right. I forgot." He slapped his forehead and sighed, and then mimicked the maître d's expression.

Maiya laughed and opened the menu. Holy shit, this place was pricey! Forty bucks for the New York strip and fifty for the bacon-wrapped filet. Oh boy. *How much did he earn at the firm, anyway?* Probably more than her since he'd only been hired last year. If she changed companies, she'd earn more money, but staying with Amaryllis was a better option for her. Also, a sad but true fact of industry and life, women still weren't paid equal to men. "What looks good to you?" She sipped from the cool water glass.

"Aside from the filet, I heard the New York strip is phenomenal, too." He continued eyeing his menu.

"Does it include a salad?"

"I doubt it. These places are always à la carte."

"Hmm. All righty, then. They have garlic five-cheese

mashed potatoes. Those look good. Ooh, and asparagus." She continued to peruse the menu. When she looked up, he was staring at her. "What?"

"Just watching you." He sipped his water. "I like the faces you make when you talk. It's cute."

Maiya cringed and shoved another wave of embarrassment away. What kind of faces did she make?

The waitress appeared in front of their table. Ryan ordered a bottle of Merlot. A few minutes later, she returned with the bottle, opened it and poured a sample for Ryan to taste. He approved, and she poured them each a glass.

Maiya stayed silent and watched the whole scene. It was obvious Ryan was no stranger to finer things. He may not have been to this specific restaurant before, but he'd been to plenty just like it. A feeling of being out of place, inadequate even, settled like a hard knot in her stomach. Looking down, she smoothed the napkin on her lap.

"Have you decided on what you would like?" the waitress asked.

"Yes." Ryan glanced at the menu. "We'll both have the New York strip, medium, mashed potatoes and asparagus, as well." He looked at Maiya, and she nodded.

The waitress left with their menus tucked under her arm. Maiya tried to swallow the nerves rising up her throat. Her heel started its tap, tap, tapping again, and she pressed her free hand on her leg to stop its annoying twitch.

"You okay, Maiya?"

Gah! He asked her that a lot. What *was* her problem? She looked up at him and took a sip of her wine, trying to clear away the gum gluing her tongue to the roof of her mouth. "Mmhmm" was all she managed to get out.

He reached across the table for her hand, and she placed the one from her lap in his. He squeezed her fingers. "Your hands are shaking."

Maiya cleared her throat. "I'm fine, honest." She looked around. "I'm going to find the ladies room."

"All right."

She walked away in search of the bathroom. In this case, a safe place to call *last call* on the little insecurity party she was having.

CHAPTER TEN

RYAN SIPPED HIS WINE WHILE HE WAITED FOR MAIYA TO return. She'd looked like she might be sick before she excused herself from the table. Her face had even gone pale, and the mask he'd gotten used to seeing looked more like a frightened child than the confident woman she'd shown him before.

Was he ever going to get it right with her? Christ, he hoped so. She was still in her work clothes, and he was too, yet she looked perfect to him. Her dark gray, fitted skirt flared around her knees, and her red blouse molded to her body in perfection. Ryan was damn sure the woman could make burlap look good.

He kept his eyes trained on the doorway, awaiting her appearance.

Then, she was there.

As she strutted toward him in her tall black pumps, his stomach launched into a series of somersaults, and he had to swallow a couple of times. Everything slowed to a crawl around them, and all the background noise from the other customers, the staff and the piano playing blended into a hum of white noise.

All he *wanted* to see and hear was her.

"Now it's my turn to ask." She took her seat. "Are you okay? You're looking at me like I'm a present, and you're trying to figure out the best way to unwrap me."

Ryan threw his head back and guffawed. Her comment was perfect, and enough to break the tension and lead the way to idle conversation. She mentioned how nice the restaurant was, how good the wine tasted. He watched her mouth as she spoke, studied the shapes her lips made forming each syllable. He wanted to kiss her again.

Their meal appeared. The waitress poured each of them more wine before excusing herself.

"This looks delicious." She cut into her steak, tasted a piece and closed her eyes.

Again, he watched her, mesmerized. "Is it good?" He raised his glass to his lips.

Still chewing, she opened her eyes slowly. "Mmhmm."

The look in her eyes shot a hammer of lust straight between his legs. His prick swelled in his pants. Clenching his teeth, Ryan swallowed and stared at his dinner.

"Aren't you going to eat?"

His head snapped up to meet her gaze. "Yes. I—" He swallowed. "I just...I was waiting."

"For what?" She scooped up a forkful of mashed potatoes and devoured them.

Christ, she made something as mundane as eating sexy. He shook himself, but his pants got tighter. He cut into his steak. "Nothing."

"Good, huh?"

"Mmhmm." He pressed his lips together and chewed. Much better. If he kept his mouth full, he didn't have to talk. What he wanted to do instead was get them the hell out of there so he could taste every inch of her skin.

They ate in silence for a little while. It gave him the time he needed to calm his raging hard-on. But her eyes widened each time she took another taste of her meal, savoring each morsel. She looked sexy and happy, and that made him happy. "So, tell me about your family."

Maiya looked up and swallowed. "Um, what do you want to know?" She took a drink of her wine.

"Whatever you want to tell me." He took a drink, too. "Siblings?"

"I had an older brother." She wiped her mouth with her napkin and shifted in her seat.

"Had?"

"Yes. He died when I was ten."

"I'm sorry." He studied her eyes. Her pupils were larger than he'd seen them before.

"It was a long time ago." She blinked a couple of times and then studied her plate, spreading her fork through the remains of mashed potatoes.

"You want to tell me about it?" He didn't want to push her, but the words were out before he had a chance to stop them.

"Not really." She shrugged and put her fork down. "Maybe some other time."

"I'd like that."

"What about you?"

"I come from one of those good Irish-Catholic families." He glanced at his drink and then back to her. "Lots of siblings, lots of cousins, and everyone drinks too much."

"Wow. I bet you got into a lot of trouble as a kid." She traced the rim of her wine glass.

"Hell yeah. Gave our parents daily heart attacks. I'm surprised they survived raising all ten of us."

"Holy shit. Ten?"

He raised his glass. "Aye. Six girls 'n four boys, lass."

"Not bad, sir. Not bad a'tall." She laughed. "I guess you were never bored."

"Nope. Never a dull moment in my house growing up." He sat back and smoothed his tie. "Never any privacy, either."

She pouted and batted her long lashes. "Poor baby."

"Teasing me?"

"It's our deal." She licked her lips. "A requirement, I think."

"Well, in that case—" he leaned forward, "—bring it on."

"You love it." She swallowed the last of her wine.

"I'd never admit that." He chuckled. "You want some dessert?"

She gazed at him over the top of her wine glass. "Yep, but not here."

Looking over his shoulder, he signaled the waitress, "Check, please?"

Maiya sat back and giggled.

His mother didn't raise no fool. Maiya decided what she wanted for dessert, and he planned to make sure she got it.

———

MAIYA NIBBLED HER THUMBNAIL AS RYAN PAID. HE'D GROWN up with nine siblings. Amazing. She bet they had family dinner each night at a dining room table inside a nice house. A real house, not one with wheels.

It made her think back to the *typical* label she'd given him. The comment, meant as a teasing joke, probably stung. She'd heard about how kids growing up in large families struggled to be individuals.

Hell, she'd grown up alone and struggled to find her own individuality. Half the time, she had no idea who she was or where she belonged. Mostly, she'd tried to be invisible, especially to her mother.

As she'd grown into a young woman, she was done being invisible, making a point to stand out—in fact, she'd made a hobby of it. At times, Maiya still didn't know who she was deep inside.

She'd be hard-pressed to admit it, but how Ryan grew up

sent little barbs of envy scraping through her veins. As a child, she'd spent many nights longing for his brand of *normal*. As an adult, she'd learned normal didn't fit anyway.

Maiya was fine with being different. Or at least she had been until now. Now, all she could think about was that she didn't fit, and for the first time since she was a kid, she wanted to. More importantly, she wanted to fit with Ryan.

Frustrated with herself, she pushed the thoughts away.

"You ready?" Ryan held out his hand to her.

Was she? Ready or not, this was happening. Time to step up to the plate or get off the field. Standing, she steadied herself, took a deep breath and placed her hand in his. "Yes."

Such a small answer to his small question. Both so much bigger than they appeared.

When they got outside, the cool night air wrapped around her. He let go of her hand and motioned for the valet attendant. Maiya walked off to the side and lit a cigarette. The cool menthol smoke slid into her lungs, and she held it in for a second longer than normal. Her head buzzed, and she exhaled, watching Ryan talk to the attendant. He wasn't a prince coming to rescue her from some fire-breathing, snaggle-toothed dragon, and this wasn't a fairytale. It was just dinner.

Two adults having dinner.

Two adults about to have consensual sex. Nothing more, nothing less.

It didn't matter he'd taken her to one of the nicest places in L.A. It didn't.

Maiya needed to keep her heart locked up and emotions turned off. Safe. She needed to stay safe. But she had a feeling he'd already extricated her heart from its nest of safety. She may as well top off the night with some sweaty sex. Fuck it. An orgasm—or five—ought to send her spinning into oblivion.

When the attendant pulled up with the car, Maiya put out

her cigarette, popped a mint into her mouth and walked over to Ryan.

His gaze was pinned to her. Her breath caught in her throat at the steadfast expression in his gaze. The breeze picked up and blew his tie to the side, and he smoothed it down his chest in what seemed a practiced gesture.

The wine made her movements slow and languid. The nicotine she'd inhaled raced through her blood in fierce competition with the alcohol, making her feel hyper-in-tune to all movement around her. All she focused on was him, though. His sculpted face, his sparkling blue-gray eyes, his edible lips and his broad shoulders.

"Your chariot awaits." Ryan took her hand and helped her into the car. He leaned in when she was seated and placed a light kiss on her cheek. Coming around the car, he slid behind the wheel.

She touched where his lips had been. "That was sweet."

"I can be…on occasion."

They made the drive in relative silence. Norah Jones's "Come Away with Me" played soft and low from the radio, and she hummed along. He traced her fingers, drawing little circles on the back of her hand and then her palm.

The lights of the city glittered in the not-too-far-away distance. Maiya kept her eyes on the passing scenery, and her pulse beat a steady drum beneath his fingertips. The music wove its way in and around her, and she let herself melt into the soft leather of the seat.

Closing her eyes, she took it all in and let herself…feel.

CHAPTER ELEVEN

Ryan glanced at Maiya and then made the turn into the parking garage of her hotel. She was humming, but she looked like she was sleeping. Her expression was soft, relaxed —sweet. He parked in a spot closest to the elevator, turned off the car and looked at her again.

She opened her eyes and blinked a couple of times, and then met his gaze with a modest smile, arching her lips.

"You ready?"

She nodded but said nothing more.

Ryan kissed her fingers and then stepped from the car. He couldn't shake the idea that this was far more than just sex. He wasn't sure how to feel. Thinking about it scared him too much, though, so he pushed the fear aside and opened her car door.

He did things for Maiya he shouldn't, yet he couldn't stop himself. A deep motivation to take care of her, in a way he was sure no one else had, kept rising to the top and propelling him. Opening her car door, helping her in or out of the car, taking her to dinner and ordering her meal for her—but he didn't want it to have to mean anything more than simple, polite gestures. Nevertheless, it did mean more, didn't it? It meant more to him than he was ready to admit to himself, least of all her.

He helped Maiya from the car and curled an arm around her waist. Pressing his body against hers, Ryan kissed her. Slow and easy at first, and then deeper. She breathed a sigh and wrapped her arms around his neck.

A spark caught at the base of his spine, and fire spread, licking slow and easy up his back. Pulling away, Ryan grabbed her hand and tugged her toward the elevator. He needed to get her upstairs now.

When they got in the elevator, she was on him before he even had a chance to blink. He turned them and pressed her against the back wall, shielding her from the elevator camera, enjoying the feel of her soft curves against his body. Running his hands up her sides, he passed his palms over her breasts, thumbed her nipples and kissed her.

Maiya arched and speared her hands into his hair, gripped the strands, and pulled. Ryan growled into her mouth and rubbed his erection against her abdomen. He nipped at her bottom lip, and she clutched his hair tighter. Delving deeper into her mouth, he found her tongue. Heaven. He couldn't stop kissing her, drowning in the taste of her strawberry gloss and the wine from dinner.

Ryan's heart raced, thudding in his ears. The things he planned to do to her once they made it to her room spun through his mind, riding the waves of arousal pulsing through him. She broke the kiss with a gasp for air. Ryan moved to her neck, sucked and grazed his teeth over the soft skin—

The elevator dinged, and the door opened. "Please tell me this is your floor."

She let out a little groan and pushed at his shoulders. "Yes, come on."

He stepped back, and she took his hand and led the way down the hall.

MAIYA TILTED HER HEAD, STUDYING RYAN WHILE HE LEANED against the wall outside her hotel room. The light in his eyes and the expression on his face was all devilish-James-Dean style, and she suspected the bad boy he'd shown her in the conference room was laying in wait under all the polish.

"After you." He gestured with his hand for her to enter.

"Thank you, sir." Stepping inside, she set her purse on the dresser. When she heard the hotel room door close, she turned to face him.

He'd taken two steps into the room and stopped, and then, with a raised brow, spread his arms out at his sides. "Well, you've got me here. What will you do with me?"

"I was going to ask you the same thing."

Ryan walked farther into the room and sat on the bed. Maiya stayed where she was, frozen between the bed and dresser, watching him out of the corner of her eye. Then she felt the heat of his hand on the back of her thigh through her skirt.

"Turn toward me, please."

Annnnd here we go. The bad boy just made his appearance. Front and fucking center. She pivoted and faced him. This was it. From here on out, the rest of the night, he'd dictate how things would go between them. Just like in the conference room.

Ryan removed his tie and unbuttoned the two top buttons of his shirt. His expression was dark, unreadable. Unaffected. "Take off your clothes."

Her stomach jumped like a child on a trampoline. Part fear, part excitement at his commands and change in demeanor. Could she do this? Could she submit to his commands? Giving up control was so foreign to her, but in order to do it, she needed to trust him. And also trust he'd understand how hard it was for her to give him this power over her. It scared her. Mostly because she liked it.

Her throat gone dry, Maiya swallowed. With a deep breath, she took a small step back, pulled her blouse from the confines of her skirt and then raised shaking fingers to the buttons. With care, she unbuttoned them. One, two, three… *Breathe, Maiya…*until she reached the end. She parted the halves of her top and slid it down her arms, revealing her red push-up bra, but also the tattoos covering both arms. Catching the loose fabric, she folded it and placed it on the dresser behind her. Then turned back to him.

He scrubbed his hand over his mouth, but his eyes remained hard, intent on her. "Keep going."

A flush of heat spread up her neck and face, and her heart pounded in her ears. For the first time in her life, Maiya felt self-conscious of her tattoos. Ryan was the only person from work, aside from Jodi, she let see her art. Funny, that's what stood out in her mind. Not the fact she was half-naked in front of him, but that she was covered in ink. What if he didn't like them?

As if knowing her trepidation, he spoke. His expression soft, along with his words. "They're beautiful, baby… You're beautiful." Then, in a blink, his face returned to its former intense focus on her. "Now, keep going."

Hello, whiplash? He went from being the softhearted man she'd come to know in the last week to the bad boy now sitting in front of her and then back again. Two sides of the same coin. Like her. But the speed in which he made the change set her on edge. His actions kept her in a state of doubt, never knowing what to expect, yet knowing without question what she could count on.

Maiya took a deep breath, willing the waves of fear away, and moved her hands to the back of her skirt. Peeling down the zipper, she hooked her thumbs in the waistband and pushed the fabric over her hips. She stood before him, almost, but not quite, naked. Wearing only her red bra and cotton, red lace thong.

"Fucking hell, woman."

She couldn't suppress the nervous giggle that bubbled up. His expression changed. Now, he looked at her like she was a meal and he was a starving man.

The awareness made her belly tighten. Her skin tingled at the promise in his eyes, and her clit answered as well, swelling and throbbing. He couldn't know the effect he was having on her.

"Step closer."

When she did, he traced a line with his fingertip down her stomach to the waistband of her panties. She gasped, and her stomach muscles clenched in response to the feather-light touch.

"Take off your bra."

With no hesitation, Maiya reached behind her, unhooking the clasp. The motion forced her chest to thrust forward, and his gaze fixed on her breasts. She moved her hands around to the front and slid the straps down her arms.

There was no talking aside from his short commands. The low whir of the ventilation system muffled any outside noise in the hotel, and the only other sound was her breathing. She was beyond aroused, and her body hummed in an over-sensitized state. Never before had she been this aware of a man. With her mind a tangled web of emotions, Ryan's eyes were her focal point—a beacon to guide her through the storm raging inside her body and mind. And she locked on to them, desperate to keep herself afloat.

"Touch your nipples for me."

Doing as he asked, she took her nipples between her fingertips and pinched them. They hardened in response, and she gasped at the small sting.

"Nice. I like that." Reaching between her legs, he stroked over her panty-covered mound. "You're hot here, Maiya."

She rocked her hips forward into his fingers. "Yes," she whispered, unable to find her voice. She pinched her nipples again and exhaled a sharp breath.

He watched her and continued his motion, swiping his fingers from her ass to clit. Gentle strokes, back and forth, back and forth…building her climax, but not enough to send her over.

Her insides were molten lava, and each nerve under her skin tingled and sparked. With every sensation, her breath hitched in her chest. Cupping her breasts, she massaged and squeezed them together.

This was the hottest fucking thing she'd ever experienced.

The quiet of the room, his fingers dancing along her covered slit, and the sensations from touching her own breasts. Every action mingled together, creating an atmosphere of pure, unadulterated sexual tension. The air was thick with it.

When Maiya finally came, she wasn't sure she'd survive it.

RYAN'S MOUTH WATERED. MAIYA'S MOISTURE SOAKED through her panties onto his fingers—he had to taste her.

He'd taken all choice away from her, and she liked it. He liked it, too. The hard-on the size of the Empire State Building he was sporting was proof of that. Ryan was intent on ignoring it because each time he passed the pads of his fingers over Maiya's clit her body jerked, and damn him to hell, he wasn't going to stop. Delicious. However, he wanted the last remaining barrier gone. "Take these off."

She let go of her breasts and slid her panties down her thighs. When she bent forward, her breasts swayed close to his mouth. Snaking his tongue out, he licked one peaked nipple.

She grabbed his shoulders and arched into him. "Fuck, Ryan."

He chuckled and sucked the point into his mouth. She

moved to straddle his lap, and he jerked his mouth away. "Stay standing." She protested, and he slapped her ass, one quick, sharp swat. "Be a good girl, Maiya."

"Ryan!" She stayed standing but tightened her grip on his shoulders.

Rewarding her, he dragged his tongue over the flushed tip again and pinched the other. "So sweet. Your nipples taste like candy."

She jerked against him. He smiled around her delicious flesh and trailed his other hand down her torso, following the path to her flat stomach and then between her legs. She had very little pubic hair, and he stroked the fine curls, careful to only graze the top of her clit.

She whimpered, and he ventured lower with his fingers. Running his index finger through her bare and smooth slit, Ryan found the hot wetness he sought. A bolt of lust shot from his spine to his dick, tightening his balls. She was dripping for him.

Ryan groaned and released her nipple from his mouth. He wanted to watch her face when he touched her pussy. Sliding his fingers through her folds again, he held her gaze. "Play with your tits again for me, baby."

Maiya's eyes widened, and then her head fell back on her shoulders. He loved this. Circling her opening with two fingers, he dipped them inside, pulling more slickness out and over her clit. As he rubbed the tight bundle of nerves in little circles, she rolled her hips forward. Fuck, she was killing him. "Oh yeah, that's it, baby. Look at me. I want to see your eyes."

Maiya gazed down at him and panted, little whimpers escaping on each quick breath. She swiped her tongue across her bottom lip and played with her breasts. Cupping them, she massaged and then pinched her nipples between her fingers.

The way he needed her to do.

Back and forth, he moved his fingers, bringing more of

her wetness with him to lubricate her folds. She cried out and tensed. She was close; he could feel it. Her little clit swelling further each time he rubbed it. "Don't come until I tell you, Maiya."

"What? Are you nuts?" Her eyes were wild with shock.

Ryan stopped his movement and pressed his palm against her mound. "You said you'd be good." With his free hand, he slapped her ass. A little harder than the last time.

"Fuck. Fuck. Fuck!" She sucked in a breath and exhaled, closing her eyes. "Yes. Okay. Yes."

"Good girl." He pressed his palm tight to her clit again and drove two fingers inside her. Her pussy clamped down around his fingers, and he almost came in his pants. Dear God, she was tight. Keeping his fingers buried deep, Ryan gripped her mound and lay back on the bed, pulling her with him. "On my face, now."

Maiya climbed over his body and settled her knees on either side of his head, perching herself above his face. She gave him everything he wanted. Deep pleasure and satisfaction from her submission pulsed through his body, and his dick grew harder than he thought possible. With a growl, Ryan latched on to her clit with his mouth.

"Oh— Mmm. Oh, fuck yes!"

Her flavor coated his tongue, and he gripped her thighs. Sweet and tangy honey. She tasted better than he fantasized. Reaching behind her, he stroked two fingers over her opening again, drawing her moisture back over her ass.

She moaned low and long and rolled her hips, grinding herself against his mouth. Dragging his tongue up to her clit, he circled it before sucking it again.

She tensed in his grip. "Ryan! Let me come, please?"

"Come for me." He pressed one finger into her tight asshole and sucked her clit, hard.

Her body jerked, once, twice, and she cried out his name.

Snaking his tongue down to her opening, Ryan tasted her

sweet orgasm, and his cock jerked in his pants. Maiya buried her hands in his hair, holding him tight between her thighs and rode out her climax on his face.

Fine with him; he had no intention of taking his mouth away until she was ready.

Panting, she fell forward on the mattress. Ryan rolled over and sat on the edge of the bed, stroking her back and hair. The long locks were a tangled mass of red heaven. After a few minutes, she glanced over at him. Eyes glossy, cheeks flushed, and a sated expression on her face. She was fucking magnificent.

Ryan licked the remnants of her from his lips and adjusted his dick in his pants.

Maiya blinked a couple of times before the stars peppering her vision cleared. Holy hell, could she even breathe? Yes, she was breathing. Well, what do you know? The man had skills. Not so typical after all—considering that was the most powerful orgasm she'd ever had. He could carry a feather in his cap for the rest of his life, for all she cared. He'd earned it. Maiya rolled over. "My turn."

"You think so, huh?"

She rose from the bed and knelt on the floor in front of him, gazing up into his eyes. "I know so."

He leaned back on his hands. "Since you insist." His tone was casual, yet the bulge in his pants said anything but.

Like unwrapping a present, she unbuckled his belt and pulled down his zipper. She loved presents. She tugged on his pants, sliding them down his hips a bit and then sat back on her heels, gazing at the swollen head peeking from the top of his boxer briefs. She touched the drop of arousal on the tip and raised her finger to her lips, licking it clean. "Mmm. I want that."

Ryan tried to suppress a groan but failed. "Tell me, what specifically do you want, Maiya?"

Her gaze darted to his. "I want to suck your cock, Ryan."

"It's all yours."

Chills raced through her. She dipped her head and licked the length of his shaft through the thin material covering him. His breath came out in a rush, and he raised his hips off the bed.

She stopped when she reached the top of his boxers and then swiped her tongue over the slit of the head, licking another drop of arousal. She hooked one finger over the lip of his boxers and, taking her time, pulled them down.

His shaft, flushed and swollen, bobbed against his abdomen. How long would he last? She wanted to know and reveled in the power she had in that moment. He was hers. This man—this pretty boy. He would be hers...forever.

The thought came out of nowhere and shocked her. No, this was just sex. Right? *Yeah, yes. Just sex.* She circled his shaft with her hand, and the warmth of him sank into her palm. "You've got a gorgeous prick."

He flexed his hips, and she stroked the solid flesh. He wasn't overly long, but he was nice and thick. Anticipation thrummed through her. Maiya couldn't wait to feel him inside her, stretching her inner walls. She clenched her thighs together, and her clit throbbed in time with her heartbeat.

"Suck me, Maiya. Now."

A shiver ran down her spine at the growl lacing his command. She never would've thought it possible, but she couldn't help but love how he sent her body into a tornado of erotic responses by only telling her what to do. She leaned forward and circled the rim with her tongue, once, twice, and then sucked the head between her lips.

"Ah, fuck. Yes." He jerked his pelvis forward. "That's it, baby, let me feel your hot tongue."

Maiya moaned and sucked him deeper until the head bumped the back of her throat.

"Fuck me with your mouth."

Oh, hell yes! Humming, she drew her mouth back up the length to the tip. Maiya wrapped her palm around the base, swirled her tongue around the rim again, and then took him back in. With her other hand, she massaged his sac.

With each pass of her tongue and mouth, Ryan panted and thrust his hips forward. He gripped the back of her head, controlling her movements. A shudder ran through her body from top to toe. Yes! This is what she wanted from him. The sting in her scalp from the hold he had on her hair only made her wilder, hotter, wetter for him. She whimpered and sucked harder.

"Yeah, baby. Oh yeah. Suck my cock. Swallow it," he ground out between clenched teeth.

Maiya gazed up at him. His face was a hard mask of sexual tension—lips pulled tight into a thin line, nostrils flaring with each hard breath he drew in. Seeing him affected in this way, affected by her, was hot as hell. Maiya kept her movements slow, deliberate—taking him into her mouth—stroking her tongue along each inch. With the image of him burned into her mind, she closed her eyes and let out a deep-throated moan around his cock.

He gripped her hair tighter and thrust to her throat. "Fuck, yes!"

Eyes closed, sure of how she must look to him, she sucked harder.

Ryan exploded. His climax hit, and his body seized beneath her. His semen spurted into her mouth, coating her throat. She swallowed and swallowed again. More and more, he came, and she took every ounce.

As his cock finished its pulsing between her lips, he let go of her hair and fell back on the bed. Maiya drew her mouth off him but continued to lick at the head and shaft, cleaning any drops she missed.

He caressed the back of her head. "That was unbelievable."

"Liked that, did you?" She giggled.

"Yes. I like it when you giggle, too."

She pressed her fingers to her tingling lips. "I seem to have developed a habit of it around you."

"That's the kind of habit a man could get used to." He reached for her. "Come here, baby. You missed a drop."

She climbed onto the bed and lay on top of him. "Where?"

He licked her chin and then covered her mouth with his. Spreading his hands out on her lower back, he pulled her tighter against him.

Breaking from his lips, she propped herself up on her elbows and kissed his jaw. "You're overdressed."

"I believe you're right."

"Of course, I'm right. I'm always right." With a giggle, she pressed her lips to his throat.

"You always giggle when you're right?"

She nipped his earlobe. "Maybe."

He rolled them and then moved between her legs. "Bet you think you can get away with anything using your little giggle now, hmm?" He kissed her again.

She moaned, stroked her tongue over his, and tilted her pelvis under him. Maiya was more than ready to have him inside her.

CHAPTER TWELVE

Ryan rested atop her soft body, his head still spinning from the blowjob she'd given him. He pulled away from her lips and shifted from between her legs to lie beside her. They faced each other in the darkness, and he stroked her hair and back.

She nuzzled and kissed his neck and tugged at the buttons of his shirt. When she got them all undone, she parted the two halves, revealing his chest. Sitting up, Ryan rolled the shirt off his shoulders and then lay back down, facing her.

Maiya trailed her tongue from his neck down to his chest. With warm hands, she stroked his skin, following the path her tongue took. She pushed him onto his back, and he let her.

At that point, he'd let her do anything she wanted.

Maiya's long hair tickled his chest and raised his flesh into goosebumps. He ran his fingers through it and raised his face to the top of her head, breathing her in. Coconut and lavender.

She continued her exploration of his chest with her tongue and stopped to lick and suck at one nipple. He gasped when she bit it and tightened his fingers in her hair. Maiya moaned.

She liked it. She liked everything he did to her. In the

conference room, Maiya's body had answered his commands. She'd melted under his touch and orgasmed when he told her to. Tonight, he spanked her a couple of times, and she didn't protest. On the contrary, she'd shown her appreciation by her hot pussy getting wetter for him.

She moved to the other nipple, and he groaned. To him, this woman was such a complex mystery. He traced the designs tattooed on her right arm. A Day of the Dead girl, with a floral background. A mask, much like the one she hid behind, was painted on the girl's face. Maiya had so many sides to her; he could spend years discovering them all. But, she'd eat him up and spit him out before he even got past the first one. Ryan was certain of it.

The thought sobered him.

He smoothed his hand down the back of her head. "Maiya, babe. Hang on. I need a minute."

She stopped and looked up at him, her lips swollen and wet. "Oh, okay." She pulled away and knelt next to him. "Everything all right?"

"Yeah, yeah." Ryan sat up. "Everything's fine." He kissed her cheek and stood. "I'll be right back." He buttoned his pants and headed for the bathroom.

After shutting the door, Ryan leaned on the counter. Panic sped through his veins like a virus, and he ran his fingers through his hair. Fuck, he couldn't do this. She'd never want a man like him. As for his son, what would she want with a child? Wild like she was, Maiya wasn't the kind of woman who stayed home and did the family gig, and he was beginning to think he might want that from her.

Ryan stared at his reflection in the mirror and licked his lips. *Damn.* He could still taste her. Turning away from his reflection, he opened the door and walked into the room. He needed to get out of there. Now.

Maiya had pulled the blankets down and lay beneath the sheets. Her red hair was spread out on the pillow, a sharp contrast to the white case beneath it. He stepped to the foot of the bed and caught her gaze. "Maiya?"

"Yes?"

"I need to go." He reached for his shirt.

She sat up, clutching the sheet to her bare chest. "What? Why?"

"I forgot I had something I need to take care of." He put on his shirt and turned to find his tie.

"You have *got* to be fucking kidding me, right?"

"No." He sighed. "I'm sorry, I just…" He found his tie and shoved it in his pocket. "I have to go."

"I knew it. I fucking knew it." She slapped a hand down on the bed and turned her face away from him.

He stopped and stared at her, though he couldn't see her face. "Knew what?"

"Just go, Ryan."

"Look, I had a good time tonight." He ran his fingers through his hair, feeling like the biggest asshole on the planet. "Come on, Maiya. Don't be this way."

"Go, Ryan." She swiped her fingers across one cheek. "Thanks for dinner."

Was she crying? Why was she crying? "Maiya, I thought…" He took a breath. "I don't know what I thought. I'm sorry."

He left her room, closing the door behind him. Why did it feel like he shut the door in her face? *Because I just did. Shit.* He'd talk to her tomorrow and try to explain. She'd understand. He hoped. But who was he kidding? Ryan wasn't sure he understood. He just knew there was too much to risk. His heart on the line was only a small part of this; he had to consider Jacob, too. It was better this way. At least, that's what he kept telling himself as he got into his car and pulled away from her hotel.

MAIYA COVERED HER FACE WITH HER HANDS. WHAT THE HELL just happened? Everything was fine from her perspective. Son-of-a-bitch. How dare he do this to her? Anger vibrated through her limbs, but if she was honest, it was disappointment that made her skin feel tight. And a boatload of hurt. This was the ultimate rejection. Maiya got up from the bed and tossed on some sweats and a T-shirt. She needed a damn cigarette. When she got downstairs and lit up, she sent a text to Jodi.

> Maiya: Dinner was awesome. Came back to my room. We fooled around. A LOT and then he stopped and just left! WTF??? I'll talk to you tomorrow. I'm too upset to talk now. Luv u.

Why in the hell had he taken her to a nice dinner? Why come up to her room? She leaned back on the bench and listened to the occasional passing car. Confusion raced through her mind. Making sense of this was impossible.

Everything had been perfect, hadn't it? They hadn't had sex, not real sex anyway. She got off, and he did too, but didn't he want to close the deal? Maybe he didn't think she was good enough for actual sex.

The way Ryan knew her body scared her. The way her body responded to him scared her more, but she hadn't wanted it to end. Even now, her body still tingled. Maiya wasn't the kind of woman who took orders from anyone, the bedroom was no exception, but she found she *wanted* to please him. The more she acquiesced to what he wanted, the more he wanted her. It was a dance. A choreographed masterpiece. And though she'd never done this routine before, she fell right in step with him. With ease and without thought, she gave him what he wanted, and then he turned all his pleasure on her.

It was power. And it was wonderful.

Didn't he understand, or did he simply not care? He

couldn't realize the gift she'd given him. Maiya shuddered and rubbed her arms. She'd given him her heart before they even got to the hotel room. With willingness, she laid herself bare and leaped off the ledge.

Instead of catching her, he let her fall.

Maiya brushed away the wetness dripping down her cheeks and took a drag of her cigarette. Damn, this stung. She'd get over it, though. Come hell or high water, she'd do it. No matter how much it hurt right now. Maiya would head home tomorrow and wouldn't have to see him in person for a while. Sure, she'd have to deal with him on the project, but outside of that, she wouldn't speak to him.

This wasn't supposed to be some sort of happy-ever-after. People like her didn't have happy endings. They just did what they had to in order to survive. This was no different.

Ryan Donnelly was about to become a mistake she put behind her. Not the first, but God willing, the last. She put out her cigarette and headed inside. "Pick myself up, dust myself off…" She sang, getting on the elevator. A bath and a good night's sleep were in order. Tomorrow was her last day in town. She'd work, meet with her team, have lunch with Jodi and be on her way back home. Home was safe.

She ran the bath, and her phone buzzed with a reply from Jodi. Glancing at the screen, Maiya tied up her hair and then slipped into the warm water without responding. She closed her eyes, and tears ran down her cheeks.

Tomorrow was another day, but it was still today. And right now, today sucked.

Maiya soaked until the water cooled, and then made her way to the bed. Her chest ached, and her head throbbed from crying. She turned on her side and curled herself around a pillow, willing the visions of Ryan to leave her mind. But she had a feeling it would be a while before they were gone.

Damn him.

GUILT BURNED HOT IN HIS GUT, AND RYAN CURSED HIMSELF A thousand different ways on the drive home. He knew he hurt her. She'd be fine, though. Her pride might be a little bruised, but that was all. Yeah, and maybe if he kept telling himself that story, he might believe it. The burn crept up to his throat, bringing with it a vile taste of regret.

Ryan stepped into the dark kitchen and set his keys down harder than normal. He'd fucked up his chance with her. He knew it. Hell, she'd started crying. He could still see the subtle trembles in her shoulders. She hadn't wanted him to know, though. Maybe she was just frustrated.

His ex had used tears to get what she wanted. But that was Tammy. Maiya, in spite of being like his ex in many ways, *was* different. He knew on an instinctive level she'd never do something so low. His regret intensified, and Ryan cringed. In contrast, she'd tried to hide her tears.

He opened the fridge and stared at the contents—staring but not seeing them. He blinked and pulled out a beer. Dinner had been amazing. Good food and easy conversation, all with an amazing woman—an amazing woman who he'd left naked and crying in her hotel room. Christ, he was an asshole.

The cold brew flowed down his throat, and he mulled over the drive from the restaurant to her hotel. The moment had been surreal. He'd held her hand the whole time and soaked up the soft music she harmonized with. Pure splendor, and he hadn't wanted it to end. With the lights from the freeway and the dashboard reflecting her profile, Maiya had looked like an angel. With a deep sigh, Ryan tossed the empty beer bottle in the recycle bin and headed for the shower.

The water was as hot as he could stand it, and he stood under the spray, arms braced on the wall. The steady stream beat on his head and shoulders. Damn, he'd blown it. Maybe he should call her. No. She'd never want to speak to him again, he was sure. He'd deserve her silence after what he'd done.

Curling his hands into fists, he pressed them against the tile. *Stupid, stupid, stupid.* He shook his head and reached for the soap. After he'd finished cleaning up, he stood a few more minutes under the spray. No amount of soap and water was going to make him feel like less of a dirtbag, though.

Ryan climbed into bed. Tomorrow was Friday, and her last day in town. It was for the best she was leaving. He rolled on his side in the empty bed. She was leaving, but he didn't want her to go.

His last thoughts before he fell asleep were of her and how she'd looked in the hotel bed under the sheets: A red-headed, tattooed angel... With heaven in her eyes and hell between her legs.

No, he didn't want her to go...but his son. He needed to remember what was best for Jacob.

CHAPTER THIRTEEN

MAIYA GOT AN EARLY START ON THE DAY, AND CONSIDERING she wasn't a morning person, was an indication of exactly how much sleep she *didn't* get last night. When the alarm clock went off at six, she'd been lying there wide awake. After packing up and taking a shower, she finished her makeup and hair and then wandered around the room for a few more minutes.

She was stalling.

Sitting on the bed, she did the unthinkable. She called her mother. Mom wasn't the best person to talk to about her love life, so Maiya had no intention of telling her what was going on. She just needed to hear her voice for a minute and pretend she was still a little girl. "Hi, Mommy."

"Emmie? Are you home yet?"

"I'm still in Los Angeles. I fly home today. How are you feeling? Have you been eating?"

"Sure, sure."

Maiya winced as the distinct sound of ice in a glass tinkled in the background. "I'll be by tomorrow to bring you some groceries."

"If you want, not sure I'll be around, though." Her mother coughed.

Apparently, the cold she had was hanging on tight. Damn. And, of course, her mother would be there tomorrow. "All right, I'll see you tomorrow, Mom."

"Bye, Emmie." Her rough smoker's rattle, peppered by the cold, was prevalent through her words.

Maiya sighed. "Bye, Mom."

Thirty minutes after making it to work, Jodi appeared with two coffees in hand. She handed Maiya one of the cups. "Mornin', girl."

"Morning, *chica*. Thanks." Maiya sipped the warm brew.

"Let's go downstairs and smoke. You can tell me what happened."

"All right. Although I can't stay down there long. Too much to get done before I jet out." Maiya stood and grabbed her pack of cigarettes.

They found an open bench in the courtyard and sat. Maiya lit a smoke and then handed the pack to Jodi.

"So, what happened?" Jodi lit a cigarette.

"Well, he took me to Elise for dinner."

"Ooh, nice. Pricey there."

"Yeah, no shit. Have you been? Good lord, the steak is amazing."

Jodi twirled one of her long curls around a finger. "Kevin took me for our one-year anniversary. It's nice."

"Nice is an understatement. I stuck out like a sore thumb." Maiya drew on her smoke. "Anyway, it was great. I mean." She shrugged. "We talked and laughed a lot."

"A unique thumb, but never a sore one." Jodi bumped Maiya's shoulder. "It sounds like you had a good time."

"We did. God, he kissed me in my office before I agreed to go." Maiya traced the edge of her coffee lid. "And then he kissed me at the restaurant too." She took a sip. "He's a fucking fantastic kisser."

"Wow." Jodi blew a low whistle. "So, what happened at the hotel?"

Maiya took a last drag of her smoke and stubbed it out. "The hotel was awesome. Let me tell you, the man has moves I've never encountered before." She ran her fingers through the length of her ponytail. "I can't let myself think about it too much. Good grief."

"Damn, girl. Really?"

"Oh yeah, really." Maiya fanned herself. "He got me off with no problem, and then I got him off. I was naked in the bed, waiting for him to join me after he finished in the bathroom. And instead, he fucking left."

"I couldn't believe it when I read your text."

"He gave me some BS about having something he forgot he had to do... I dunno. It's a mess."

"Damn straight it is!"

"Yeah, well." Maiya rolled her eyes. "I'm completely mortified."

Jodi rubbed Maiya's shoulder. "Don't be. This isn't your fault. He's the asshole, not you."

"I knew better." Maiya looked down at her feet. "I never should have put myself out there. He's not the guy for me."

"You're too good for him, Maiya."

"Oh, come on, Jodi. He's way out of my league."

"Bullshit. That's all I'm gonna say about it." Jodi nodded and stood. "Come on, girl. Back to work."

"Another day, another dollar, right?" Maiya glanced to her left. Ryan was walking toward them and waved to her. "Speak of the devil, and the devil will call." Maiya didn't wave back.

He waved again.

Jodi placed a hand on her hip. "Oh, hell. Don't even."

"Let's go." Maiya stepped away from the bench, pulling her friend with her.

Ryan stopped and watched her walk away from him. Damn, she barely even looked at him.

Dressed in more casual attire, she wore khaki pants, a white long-sleeved blouse and a pair of high-heeled sandals. A tie held all her hair up and away from her face. It surprised him how he noticed minute details about her; he'd never been this way before with a woman. She always managed to hide her tattoos, too. It amazed him. Pretty much everything about her amazed him.

God, he was a moron.

He wasn't sure how to fix this with her—wasn't sure where to begin. Maybe it was best to give her space. There had to be a way, though. Maybe she'd cool off and want to talk to him again.

Might be better if she didn't, though, considering nothing about his situation was going to change. His concerns regarding his son were valid, but he didn't want to leave things like this with her. His care was genuine; he just wasn't sure he wanted to explore that too deeply. However, the thought of not touching her again was maddening.

There was one saving grace: she'd be forced to talk to him about the project. He'd work it from that angle and wear her down. *Christ, what sort of tactic is that, anyway? Wear her down? Dumbass.* He shook his head and entered the building.

On the way to his cube, his cell rang. He checked the number and ducked into a conference room for privacy. "Hey, little man."

"Hi, Daddy!" Jacob's sweet voice came over the line. "I had lots of fun on all the rides. Wait till you see the stuffed monkey Papa got me. I got to see Snoopy, too."

"That's awesome, Jacob." He sat in one of the chairs. "Are you ready to come home tonight?"

"Yup. You miss me, Daddy?"

"I sure do, little man. I'm ready for some guy time. We can watch a movie. Good?"

"Yes." Ryan could hear his son's smile through the phone. "Can we have ice cream sodas, too?"

"You got it. I'll hit the store on the way home." Jacob's excitement helped soothe some of his regret. "See you soon, okay?"

"Love you, Daddy."

"I love you, too, Jacob. Bye."

Ryan disconnected the call and headed to his desk. There was a project with his name on it he needed to manage. All this business with Maiya would have to wait. Four conference calls later and a final run of reports, he leaned back in his seat and stretched. He'd missed lunch, and his head was killing him, too.

Palming up a couple of ibuprofen from his desk drawer, Ryan got up to refill his coffee with the break room sludge. Maybe he'd get lucky, and there'd be something edible in the vending machine.

He chuckled to himself. Lucky? Yeah, there was a thought. He'd graduated high school with honors and a full football scholarship to the University of Washington State. He'd been lucky damn near his whole life until he'd met Tammy the beginning of his senior year of college. She tended bar at a local pub. They were exclusive until he graduated, and when he moved back to California, she'd followed.

He hadn't minded. They got along okay, and she got a job right away. Why not, right? She was fun. Tammy was a bright light in the center of the room people couldn't help but notice. Hell, they *wanted* to notice. A wild spirit and hotter than hell, to boot. A lot like Maiya.

Ryan looked up when he approached the office Maiya was using for the week. It was empty. *Where is she?* He spied her laptop still on the desk. At least she was still in the office. He lingered in the break room for a bit at a table he'd maneuvered so he could see the hall in front of her door.

He had one shot at apologizing to her face-to-face, and he wasn't going to miss it.

Maiya sat in her boss's office reviewing the documents for the next project in the queue. In another month, Ryan's project would be finished, and her team would move on to the next one, which he wouldn't be managing.

Not wanting to see him again, she'd successfully avoided Ryan the remainder of the day, with the exception of the two conference calls she'd been required to attend. She'd stayed at her desk during the calls, with the phone on mute, listening to his voice on the line. Even though he was a mere few feet down the hall from her, she could almost pretend she was home…almost.

A few times, she contemplated sending him a chat message but stopped herself. She was *not* going to give in. It was screwed up what he did last night, and she wasn't about to give him a chance to defend his actions with some lame ass excuse.

She checked her watch—four p.m. She had enough time to grab a coffee and a smoke with Jodi before heading to the airport.

"What time do you head out?" her boss asked.

"In about thirty minutes." She closed her notebook and gathered the paperwork in front of her. "I need to get packed up and say my goodbyes."

Tony leaned forward on his desk. "When do you think you want to come back?"

She cringed but managed to school her features. "I don't know. When do you want me back?"

"The budgets are looking good right now. I'd like you back in a couple of weeks." He stood. "It's always good to have you in the office."

"Thanks, Tony." She gathered her things. "I think I can make that work." *Dammit.*

"Given any thought to relocating back here?"

"I…I can't. My mother's getting worse."

"I'm sorry to hear she isn't doing well." He put his hands in his pockets and rocked on his heels. "I'd be willing to accommodate you having to rush back there if necessary."

"Thanks. You've been very generous to me. It's appreciated." She nodded and pursed her lips. "I'll see you in a couple of weeks."

"Take care, Maiya. Safe flight."

"I'll be sure to tell the pilots." She laughed.

He smiled. "You do that."

Maiya exited his office and walked the long hallway to her own. Before she passed through the door, she spotted Ryan in the break room. With a resigned sigh, she stepped into her office. She sat at the desk and waited.

Five, four, three—

"Hey, can I talk to you for a minute?"

She placed her palms on top of her desk and kept her gaze down. "No."

"Come on, ba—Maiya. For just a minute, then I promise I'll go. I want to—"

"No, Ryan. No. No. *Hell*, no!" Maiya pressed the keys to shut down her computer. "There is nothing you have to say that I want to hear. Save it." She refused to look at him.

His gaze on her was palpable, but she ignored it and stowed her laptop in its bag. She sent a text off to Jodi telling her to meet her downstairs in five. Ryan sighed, and Maiya glanced up, doing her best to appear uncaring. A well-practiced skill she'd used for many years on her mother.

"I'm sorry, Maiya." His voice was low but sure.

She shook her head and looked away.

And then he was gone.

There went the best mistake she *almost* made. Good

riddance. Maiya released a breath she hadn't realized she'd been holding, grabbed her things and left the office.

After a coffee and smoke with Jodi, she headed back to LAX in her rental. The sky was littered with gray clouds, and traffic was murder. By the time she got the rental dropped off and hopped the shuttle to the terminal, it was pouring. One hell of a storm had rolled in, and thanks to traffic and the downpour, she was running late.

The line was eighty miles long for check-in. *Fucking fabulous.* Maiya had no choice but to wait her turn. When she reached the self check-in machine, she'd missed the cut-off time for bags. Nothing to do now but wait for the attendant to come over and give her the drill. As luck would have it, the airline already canceled her flight due to the inclement weather. The next two were overbooked, and the last one of the night wasn't much better.

"How's tomorrow looking?" she asked the desk agent.

"I have a seven, nine and ten-thirty a.m. Which would you prefer?"

She pulled the hair tie from her hair. "I'll take the ten-thirty, I guess." *So much for getting the hell out of Dodge.* Maiya headed out front and grabbed a cab. Maybe she could stay with Jodi for the night, easier than trying to book a room.

After giving the driver the address, she texted Jodi. With the traffic as bad as it was, her friend would be home by the time Maiya got there. She put her headphones in her ears and turned on her iPod. Shinedown's "I'm Not Alright" flowed loud and perfect in her ears, and she laid her head back against the seat.

Maiya always believed everything happened for a reason. She'd ignored Ryan's apology. And now she was stuck here. It didn't have to mean anything if she didn't want it to. It didn't mean she should hear him out.

Or did it? *Crap. Yes, it does.* Grabbing her phone, she pulled up the browser and did a quick search on his first and last name. Ding, ding, ding…jackpot, baby! She was doing this. After relaying the new address to the driver, she sent Jodi another text letting her know her change in plans.

Was she nuts?

Yep, for sure.

She was being spontaneous, following her gut—the least she could do was hear him out. And it bothered her that she'd been such a bitch to him in the office. If his explanation was lame, then fine, at least she'd know for sure. All good. If it sounded legit, then maybe they could start over. At the very least, it wouldn't be so awkward working together.

Nervous tension wove its way from her stomach to her hands. She flexed them a couple of times and shifted in the seat, trying to get comfortable. Ryan lived about thirty minutes past the office. She had at least an hour or more before she got there, plenty of time to calm her nerves. She hoped.

CHAPTER FOURTEEN

THE SOUND OF A CAR PULLING UP IN HIS CUL-DE-SAC GOT Ryan's attention. It wasn't even seven yet, and all of Los Angeles was in gridlock, but his mother managed to get where she was going on time. The woman had skills.

He opened the front door, and his mouth dropped open.

"Hi."

"Maiya?" He blinked. "What are you doing here?" He looked to her right and eyed her suitcase and computer bag.

"My flight got canceled." She gripped the end of her ponytail and squeezed the excess water from it. "Can I come in?"

"Uh... Um, yeah... sure." He glanced past her to the street. "I'm sorry, yes, please come in." Shifting to the side, he motioned for her to enter. Her hair was wet from the storm. Not like he would turn her away under these circumstances. He wasn't that much of an asshole.

She motioned to her bags. "Can I leave these here by the door?"

"Yeah, that's fine. Can I get you something to drink? Coffee? A towel, maybe?"

"Coffee'd be great, thanks." She looked around. "Don't worry about the towel. I'm fine. Nice house."

"Thanks. Coffee's this way." He turned and walked through the hall to the kitchen. Nervous energy bounced around his insides. Jacob would be home any minute. Maybe they'd be late, and Maiya would be gone before they got there. *Yeah, right, not my mother.*

"I love these types of homes. It's a California bungalow, right? A big one, though."

"Yeah. I've been fixing it up for a while. Done most of the work myself." He pulled two mugs from the cabinet and poured them each coffee. "I finished the kitchen a few months ago." He opened the fridge. "You want cream, right?"

She turned in a circle, taking in the space. "It's beautiful. Ah, yeah, cream and sugar." The look on her face told him she was both shocked and impressed.

"Thanks. I'm pretty happy with it." He set the cream and sugar on the table. "Have a seat." He watched her while she sat at the table. *What the hell is she doing here?* The nervous tension in his arms migrated to his shoulders, and he tilted his head and cracked his neck. Pushing the cream and sugar her way, Ryan took a seat at the opposite end of the table. "Help yourself."

"Thanks."

Any minute now, his son would be walking through the door. Had she even noticed the drawings on the refrigerator or the ever-present toy cars and trucks scattered in the hall? Ryan swallowed the lump in his throat and waited for her to take a sip of her coffee before he spoke.

She beat him to it.

"So, I'm sorry to barge in on you, but I thought we should talk." She cupped her mug in both hands.

"How'd you find me?"

"Spokeo. It's a site online you should probably opt out of." She sipped her coffee.

"You make a habit of looking up people and just showing up at their house?" He didn't mean it to sound so harsh, but he was a little peeved she'd shown up uninvited.

Maiya choked on her coffee.

He handed her a napkin. "Sorry."

Pressing it to her lips, she cleared her throat. "No, of course not. I figured since I was such a bitch earlier, it was maybe best to do this in person."

Where were his parents and son? "Did the great Maiya Rossini just admit to being a bitch?" He sipped his coffee. "I'm skeptical."

"You're teasing me, right?"

"Yeah." He watched her. "I'm teasing you, Maiya." He looked away and shifted in his seat. This was *so not* how he imagined this conversation would go.

"Why'd you leave, Ryan?" Her voice sounded timid. As if she wasn't sure she was ready to hear the reason.

He paused, contemplating how best to explain. He got his answer when he heard the front door open. "The reason just got home. Excuse me a moment." Not waiting for a response, he left the room and headed for the front door.

Nothing like ripping the bandage off, right? He neared the entrance, and Jacob jumped into his arms, squealing.

"Hi, Daddy!"

"Hey, little man. So glad you're home." He squeezed his son and then kissed his mother on the cheek. "Hey, Mom."

"Sorry we're late, honey. Traffic was horrible." She set Jacob's bag inside the door. "I have to go, Dad's waiting. Looks like the rain's going to be here for the night."

Thank God she wasn't staying. He wouldn't have to introduce her to Maiya, too. One person at a time.

"Run upstairs and get your jammies on." He put Jacob down. "Thanks, Mom."

"Wait a minute there." His mother tugged at Jacob's T-shirt. "Give Nana a kiss and hug, tiger."

Jacob wrapped his little arms around her neck and kissed her cheek. "Thank you, Nana. Love you."

"Love you too!" She faced Ryan, and Jacob ran up the stairs. "All right, honey. Enjoy your weekend." She kissed Ryan on his cheek and turned to leave. "Call me."

"Sure thing." He shut the front door and then hollered up the stairs. "Come down to the kitchen when you're done, little man."

———

MAIYA WAITED IN SILENCE AT THE TABLE, LISTENING TO THE voices in the other room. She swore she heard a child's voice, and a woman too, but figured it must be one of Ryan's nieces or nephews.

"Hey," she said when Ryan came back into the kitchen. "Did you need me to get out of your hair?"

"No—well, I'll leave that up to you to decide." He opened the freezer and took out a carton of ice cream. "Do you like ice cream sodas?"

"Yes. Wait. Back up. What do you mean, let me decide?"

"You'll see." He pulled three mugs from the cupboard.

"Are you babysitting tonight or something?"

"Not exactly."

A little boy with sandy, light-brown hair came walking in the room dressed in a set of Sponge Bob pajamas. The child glanced at her before focusing on Ryan. "Are we still having ice cream sodas, Daddy?"

Daddy? Whoa… What. The. Fuck.

Maiya stood.

"Sure are, little man. C'mere, there's a friend I'd like you to meet."

The little boy turned and faced her, his eyes wide as though he hadn't noticed her a moment ago. He tilted his head to the side. Was he sizing her up? Then he smiled.

"Jacob, this is Miss Maiya. She's a friend from work. Go shake her hand."

She looked from Jacob's sweet face to Ryan's handsome one. Shock settled heavy in her mind like a brick. *Holy fucking shit.* Maiya blinked, and shook her head, and then focused on Jacob's face again.

Ryan Donnelly had a son.

The little boy blushed and tugged on Ryan's shirtsleeve.

Ryan knelt on one knee. "What is it, little man?"

Jacob leaned toward Ryan's ear and whispered something she couldn't hear.

Ryan squeezed the child's shoulder. "Yup, you're right." He stood. "Don't be rude. Go say hello."

Maiya stayed still while the scene played out. She didn't want to move—afraid she might alter the moment in some way. It was all too damn surreal. Ryan had a son. *Does anyone else know?*

"I'm not rude, Daddy." The little boy frowned and moved forward and stretched out his small hand. "I'm Jacob."

Oh my God, how adorable was this kid? He had the brightest set of green eyes she'd ever seen. Bending forward, she took Jacob's warm palm in hers. "Nice to meet you, Jacob. I'm Maiya."

He blushed. "Are you going to stay for ice cream? Daddy makes the bestest ice cream sodas."

She looked up at Ryan, who was back at the counter loading each mug with ice cream. "Looks that way." She smiled at Jacob. "It's okay? I don't want to intrude."

Jacob shrugged and shifted his little hips. "I guess."

She straightened, and the little boy ran off into what must be a family room. A moment later, the distant sound of the TV flowed into the room.

Ryan grabbed a bottle of soda from the refrigerator. "Like I said, up to you if you want to stay or not."

"Does anyone at work know?"

"No."

"Why not?"

He poured soda into each mug. "It's complicated."

She stepped closer and leaned against the counter next to him. What the hell was complicated about telling people he had a child? "Are you divorced?"

He shook his head. "No."

"Jesus Christ, you're married?"

"God no…" His grimaced. "We were never married."

A wave of relief spread through her, and she blew out a breath and ran a hand over the top of her head. *Thank God for that, at least.*

"Do you still see her? Does Jacob see her?" She couldn't stop the questions from tumbling out. "Do you love her?" She slapped a hand over her mouth. *Jeez, Maiya, shut up!*

He clasped her hand and pulled it away from her mouth. Pressing her fingers to his lips, he shook his head. "No. No. And, no."

Maiya glanced at his lips and then back to his eyes. God, she loved his lips. Remembering what they felt like against her own made her knees go weak. They stood there a moment, caught in each other's gaze. A small space separated them, and if he took one single step forward, their bodies would meet. A desperate need to feel those lips again rose inside her. Maiya wanted him to move closer.

The spell was broken, however, when the TV sounds got louder. An effective reminder they weren't alone. Ryan stepped away from her and then pulled some whipped cream and a jar of cherries from the fridge.

"Were you going to tell me? I mean, is that why you ran out of my hotel room?"

"I don't know. I hadn't gotten that far." He started putting the ingredients away. "We can talk more later, if you want. Right now, let's have some ice cream sodas and watch a movie." He handed her a mug. "If you don't want to stay, I understand." He grabbed the other two mugs and walked toward the sounds of the television.

RYAN STEPPED INTO THE FAMILY ROOM AND SET ONE MUG ON the coffee table for his son. "You ready to start the movie, little man?"

"Is that pretty lady staying?" Jacob knelt in front of the table.

"Her name is Maiya, and yes, she's pretty, and yes, I think she's staying. Is it okay?"

Maiya walked in the room.

Had she heard what he said to Jacob? For whatever reason, embarrassment tingled in his chest, which was crazy because he told her how beautiful she was every opportunity he had.

"Yup, it's okay." Jacob turned to Maiya. "My daddy thinks you're pretty."

Maiya looked from Ryan to his son and back again, a smile on her face. "Yeah? Well, thanks. I think your dad's pretty, too."

"Hey, now. Ratting your dad out isn't cool." Ryan pulled a DVD from its case. "Besides, you said she was pretty first." He stuck out his tongue at Jacob.

Jacob fell to his side in a fit of giggles. "Boys aren't pretty. That's silly."

"Sure they are." Maiya sat on the couch. "You're pretty, too."

Jacob sobered, righting himself. "I'm not pretty. I'm handsome. That's what Nana says."

Ryan chuckled and turned on the movie. "Go easy on her, little man."

"Oh, my." Maiya feigned a shocked look. "Yes, you're

right. Handsome is a much better word." She winked at his little boy.

Jacob smiled and took a sip of his soda. "Mmm, yummy."

"Holy cow, did the great Maiya Rossini just admit to being wrong?" Ryan teased and sat beside her.

"No, I said he was right." She rolled her eyes and sipped her soda. "Mmm, this *is* yummy." She licked her lips.

Ryan tracked the movement of her tongue. What the hell? Hello, bad timing. His son was right there, on the floor in front of him, yet his brain filled with images of how hot that mouth truly was. *Damn. Button it up, dude.* Now was not the time.

The movie started one of those Disney ones with more adult comedy in it than any kid was aware of. They sat in relative silence, aside from the giggles bubbling up from Jacob. Ryan kept his hands to himself, not wanting to be inappropriate or give Jacob any idea this woman was more than a friend. She wasn't really more than a friend, anyway.

He sure as hell didn't think Jacob was ready for him to have some fling hanging around the house. His son might get attached, and then when she was gone, he'd be hurt. Jacob had been hurt enough. Ryan wasn't about to add to it.

About halfway through the movie, Jacob climbed up on the couch and laid his head on Ryan's lap. He stroked his son's hair and noticed Maiya looked over a few times. What did she think about his son? What did she think about him now? He glanced at her. She caught his gaze, but he couldn't tell from the look in her eyes what she was thinking.

As expected, Jacob fell asleep before the movie ended. Ryan stood and then picked up his son. "I'll be right back," he whispered and carried Jacob out of the room.

After tucking Jacob into bed, Ryan sat on the edge, staring at him in the dim light. He was so grateful to have his son in his life. Hell, for the first three years, he didn't even know if Tammy terminated the pregnancy or if she had their baby. Once he knew, his only concern had been to find his little boy.

The memory played through his thoughts, and anxiety curled in his gut. He struggled not to scoop Jacob into his arms and hold him tight. Instead, Ryan leaned forward and pressed a kiss to his precious son's forehead. "I love you."

Ryan tucked the blankets a little tighter around Jacob and then left the room.

CHAPTER FIFTEEN

Maiya rinsed their mugs in the sink and then loaded them in the dishwasher. Ryan seemed to be taking a while, so she wandered around the lower level of his home. Now, she noticed the things she hadn't seen when she'd first gotten there. A pair of kid's sneakers by the front door. A random toy or three lingered in each room, and crayon-colored pictures hung on the fridge door.

There was only one baby picture in the formal living room —a young, red-haired woman holding a child. She was smiling. Was this Jacob's mother? Maiya took it into her hands and stared at the image. It didn't escape her notice that she resembled the woman in the picture. She'd give that more thought later.

Maybe it wasn't the mother, but Maiya could see from the picture she had the same green eyes Jacob had. It had to be her. Damn, she was pretty too. A pang of jealousy rose in Maiya's gut. Before she could give the nasty emotion any thought, Ryan entered the living room behind her. She set the picture back in its place and turned to face him.

He glanced at the picture. "Her name was Tammy."

"Was?"

"She died about a year ago."

"Oh, wow." She covered her mouth with her hand. "I'm sorry, Ryan."

"Some days, I am, too." He shrugged. "Some days, I'm just glad Jacob is safe."

The comment caught her off guard. She was afraid to even ask what he meant—wasn't sure she wanted to know.

They faced each other in the dim room, and silence settled around them until finally, he spoke. "I'm sorry I left last night." He stepped forward, closing the distance between them.

She placed one hand on his chest. "Why did you?"

"Many reasons, but the biggest is asleep upstairs." He looked away and took a breath. "I need to make sure his life is stable. You understand, right?" He rubbed her arms.

"Of course I do."

"I don't really date, and if I do, I don't bring anyone home to meet him."

"I see. I didn't know we were dating, Ryan."

"We're not." He leaned in and brushed his lips over hers. "We're just…having fun, I guess."

Her tummy quivered, and a bolt of excitement shot through her at the light touch of his lips, but it was diffused when a pool of disappointment welled up, too. Guys like Ryan didn't date girls like her. She swallowed the hard lump in her throat and forced a smile. "Fun…sure. Exactly what I was thinking, too."

Maiya wound her arms around his neck and pressed her lips to his, hoping to hide the unexpected feelings that no doubt were plastered all over her face. He grabbed her waist, pulled her closer and deepened the kiss.

She let him, knowing full well it couldn't go beyond this, not with his son asleep upstairs. Regardless, heat spread through her, loosening her limbs. At the same time, the juncture between her legs tightened, and she flexed her thighs in response. Breathless, she broke the kiss. "I should probably go."

"Probably." He kissed her again. "But I don't think I want you to go."

She looked toward the stairs. "Yeah, but…"

"Hang out a little longer. Watch a movie or something." For someone who was adamant about not dating, he sure did want to spend a lot of time with her. Part of her wanted to take him up on his offer, and her body warmed further at the idea of cuddling with him on the couch. But the prospect of having this time alone with him made her want more than he was willing to give. She'd be wise not to think about it so much because she was already too invested in him. The little case of the feels she tripped and fell on last night still lingered. If she gave them light, she might not be able to keep her heart in check. "You think that's a good idea?"

"It's a great idea. Besides, it's still raining out, and a perfect night for a movie." He grabbed her hand and tugged her toward the family room.

She let him lead her into the other room, though his actions pricked at her independent side. "Okay then. I guess I'm staying a bit longer."

He hadn't waited for an answer, just made the decision for her. Why did she give him this kind of control over her? It was as if she didn't know how to say no to the man.

"You want something else to drink?" He paused in the kitchen. "It's amazing how chilly it gets when it rains."

"Coffee?" She rubbed her arms. "It is a little chilly." She *did* feel a chill, but she was certain it was more from the loss of his body heat and how he elevated her internal temperature to a thousand degrees when he was close to her.

"You got it." He kissed her cheek and moved to the counter. "Why don't you pick a movie from the pay channel?"

"In the mood for anything specific?" She rubbed her

cheek with her fingertips. "It may not be a good idea to trust me to the movie picking."

"I trust you." He filled the coffee machine with grounds. "Besides, if it sucks, it'll be your fault and not mine." He chuckled.

"Fabulous." She rolled her eyes and left the room. Damn, what kind of movie would he want to watch? He probably figured she'd pick some chick flick. Boy, wouldn't he be surprised.

RYAN STARTED THE COFFEE BREWING AND SORTED THROUGH A couple of pieces of mail. Maiya was in his house. She'd met his son and didn't freak out. She acted as if she liked him, too. It'd shocked him. He didn't figure her for a kid person. Many people were nice to kids, but that didn't make them kid people. *Jacob likes her, too.* He chuckled, remembering how Jacob had whispered to him that Maiya was pretty. Yeah, she was pretty. Also, funny and smart and…

He shook his head. Maiya was many things.

He fixed her coffee the way he'd seen her do it and walked into the family room, both mugs in his hands. He stopped short when he caught sight of her.

Maiya sat on one end of the couch, legs curled under her, with the Afghan from the back of the couch over her lap. She'd taken her hair down from its ponytail, and the sandals she'd worn were on the floor. The lights were off, yet the glare from the TV highlighted her.

His chest tightened at the sight. She fit perfectly among his things.

Maiya was a puzzle piece he never imagined fitting into his world. With her wild red hair, her tattoos and her bright-as-the-sun smile, she managed to fit anywhere she went. From a rough biker bar to a fine restaurant, she was comfortable in her own skin. It made him envious. Could he ever dare be like that?

He liked it, liked her. Damn, he wasn't supposed to like her this much.

She looked over at him then and tilted her head to the side.

Their gazes locked, and he walked the rest of the way into the room. "Any luck?"

"Yep, all ready to go." She took the offered coffee and sipped from it. "Perfect." A satisfied look graced her face.

"I'm good like that." He sat on the couch and kicked off his shoes. "Feet cold?"

Maiya set her mug on the table. "A little."

"Let me rub them." He slid over and patted his lap.

She crinkled her nose. "Really?"

"Yes, really. I *am* a nice guy, you know." He palmed one of her feet. "Jesus, they're like little ice cubes."

She scooped up the remote. "I know you're a nice guy, Ryan. That's part of the problem."

"Oh, yeah? What problem is that?"

She eyed him and arched her brow but didn't answer. He tickled her toes.

"Hey!" Maiya yanked her foot away. "None of that now."

He grabbed it again. "Tell me?"

"No." She laughed when he raised his hand, threatening another tickle. "Let's watch the movie. And no more tickling, or you might get kicked in the face."

He rolled his eyes and squeezed her foot. "Fine. What chick flick did you pick?"

"I didn't, smart ass. It's *Fast Five.*"

"Oh, damn. Really?"

She snorted and turned back to the television.

"You're amazing."

"Why, because I picked a movie you'd like too?" Maiya

gathered up her hair in a loose bun and wrapped a tie around it.

"Exactly."

"Wait till you see how I drive your car."

He squeezed her foot again. "You are *not* driving my car."

"Bet I am."

"Bet you're not." He tugged her pinkie toe. "Shh, watch the movie. You talk too much."

"I do not!" She stuck her tongue out. "You do."

"You're still talking."

"Be quiet. Pain in my ass."

"Now that's gonna earn you a spanking."

"Let's hope so." She wiggled her toes. "Just no tickling. Now hush, it's starting."

He mumbled a curse under his breath. She *wanted* him to spank her. Damn, that was hot. His cock twitched in his pants. Ryan rubbed her feet and ankles and watched the movie. A bit later, he moved her legs off his lap and motioned for her to shift. He slid in behind her and then covered them both with the blanket.

Maiya glanced over her shoulder at him, her expression blank, but her eyes…her eyes held something in them he was unable to decipher. He kissed her shoulder and wrapped an arm around her waist. She settled her bottom against his groin and rested her arm over his, cradling his hand in hers.

Ryan pressed his nose to her hair, breathing her in. Maiya fit against him as if she was made to be there. Each soft curve melted into his hard angles. The scent of her shampoo teased his senses, and the softness of the loose strands from the bun caressed his cheeks.

He sighed, pulled his hand from beneath hers and ran it along her hip to her thigh, studying the curve of her body. She felt so good. Ryan didn't want to stop touching her. Continuing his exploration, he ran his hand up the front of her leg to her stomach and along her ribs. She flowed like a perfect landscape, and he wanted to explore each hill and valley. Ryan touched his lips to her shoulder again and then her neck.

She let out a soft breath and shifted her hips against him. Fuck, she was like heaven in his hands, and his cock definitely woke up and took notice. If she kept pressing against him like this, he was going to be hard enough to pound nails. How the hell did he get so lucky to have her here in his arms again? Ryan tugged at her shirt and pulled it from the confines of her pants.

He needed to feel her soft skin. She moaned when his hand made contact. Trailing his fingers up her stomach to her breasts, he stroked through the center of her cleavage. So warm. He cupped one full mound in his palm and squeezed. She arched against him, and he rocked his hips forward, pressing his hard length against her ass. He sucked at the tender skin of her neck and then dragged his tongue to her ear lobe and nipped it. "I want you," he whispered.

"We can't." She grabbed his thigh. "Can we?"

Tugging one cup of her bra aside, he found her nipple and rolled it between his finger and thumb. Maiya's breath hitched, and she shifted to her back.

Propping himself on one elbow, he gazed at her. "How quiet can you be?"

She giggled. "I don't know. You want to gag me?"

He raised both brows. "You'd like that, wouldn't you?" He tugged her nipple, and she groaned, biting her bottom lip.

"I don't know." She rolled to her side, facing him. "I've never been gagged before. Then again, I've never been spanked before either." Raising a leg over his hip, she pressed her center against his groin.

"You liked that too, didn't you?" He gripped her ass and ground against her.

She leaned in and sucked at his neck. "What do you think?"

"I think you liked it...a lot." He ran his hand up her back

and unhooked her bra. "I think you liked it so much you want me to spank you again."

His mind raced. Could he have sex with her with his son home? Married couples did, of course, but Maiya wasn't his wife. Hell, she wasn't even his girlfriend.

"Maybe." She ran her nails down his side.

He growled, and she rubbed against him.

My God, he wanted to be inside her heat. "You're a naughty girl, aren't you?" He tugged at the buttons on her shirt, opening each one.

She reached between them and stroked his cock through his jeans. "Does it turn you on?"

Ryan pulled her shirt apart and pushed her bra up, revealing her breasts. With a thrust of his hips, he pressed himself into her hand and then flicked one of her tight nipples with his thumb. "Yes."

She jerked against him, so he did it again.

CHAPTER SIXTEEN

Maiya whimpered, clawing at his jeans while he played with her nipples. It was the most intense kind of torture, and it drove her nuts that he had this much control over her body. She responded to him even when she was angry. Had her body consulted her mind, they would've been in all-out war, but she was sure her body would win.

Maiya's nipples peaked in impossible tightness, tingling each time he passed his fingers over them. She'd never been into pain during sex before, but she wanted him to bite them and suck them and give her that delicious bit of sting.

She wasn't certain she could give herself over to him in some sort of submissive role, but her body sure as hell was on board because of how he responded when she did what he asked. It made her want to see how far he would go with this kind of game. Maiya unbuttoned his pants and tugged down the zipper. "Ryan, do you want me to be your naughty girl?"

He dipped his head and flicked his tongue over her nipple. "I'd have to punish you if you were naughty." He circled the tip with his tongue and then sucked it into his hot mouth.

She hissed, arching her back. "Fuck, but...but do you want that?" She managed to get her hand down his boxers and gripped his length in her fist. His skin was like satin in her palm.

"Hell, woman. Yes, I want that."

He wants *to punish me for being naughty.* Maiya had to see what would come next.

Ryan shifted his hips forward, driving his length through her palm, and then snaked his arm up Maiya's back and into her loose bun. Tugging her head back, he bit her neck.

"What else?" She writhed against him, still stroking his prick. "You want me to be your slut, hmm?"

Ryan pulled his mouth from her throat and gripped her hair tighter. "You are fucking killing me." He kissed her hard, driving his tongue into her mouth.

Maiya stroked it with her own, tasting and drinking him in. When he pulled away, he bit her bottom lip. The sting of pain drew a whimper from her throat, and she gripped his prick tighter in her hand. "Tell me I'm your slut, Ryan."

Ryan grabbed her hand, stilling her motion. "Be careful, Maiya."

"Make me your slut, Ryan." She licked at his bottom lip. "Please?"

She couldn't believe the words flying from her mouth. She never talked like this—never wanted to be anyone's slut, either. But as the words slipped past her lips, he grew harder in her palm, and a thrill sprinted through her. She loved it.

The power filling her when he responded to the dirty words she used aroused her body and mind more than she could've ever imagined.

Ryan rolled over her and then settled between Maiya's thighs. Using one hand, he pinned her hands above her head. "I'm about to fuck you good and proper." He trailed the fingers of his free hand down her cheek and then cupped her chin. "Tell me you want it, Maiya."

Circling her legs around his hips, Maiya met his eyes.

"Which part? That I want you inside me?" She rolled her pelvis. "Or that I want to be your slut?"

Ryan moved his hand to her throat and gripped it lightly. "Yes." He kissed her but then paused and looked up at her. "Is this okay?" He flexed his fingers on her throat.

Maiya thought she might explode into a million pieces beneath him. Her mind twirled in confusion while anticipation thrummed through her at a steady pace—her clit pulsing in time with it. The man had his damn hand around her throat, and she knew for sure this was *not* something she liked or ever wanted anyone to do to her. He wasn't choking her, just making his presence known, but with him, it turned her on. "I can't believe I'm going to say this, but, yeah. It's okay."

She arched against him again. Her nipples scraping across his shirt sent a bolt of electricity through her. She needed her hands free; she wanted to rip his shirt off and drag her nails down his back.

EVERY MUSCLE IN RYAN'S BODY WAS STRUNG TIGHTER THAN A suspension bridge wire. Maiya was driving him into a lust-filled madness. Even through their clothing, the heat of her core scalded him. The things she'd been saying to him were enough to make him go alpha male on her fine ass and slide his dick in her every hole until she begged him to stop, then begged him to start again.

He'd always liked things rougher in bed, but he never had a partner who was as into it as he was. Tammy wasn't interested in this sort of play. There had been a few women he'd screwed around with in the years before and after Tammy, but he never had a woman want him to call her his slut. Or respond to him the way Maiya did.

For Christ's sake, she practically begged him. That had to

be a big deal to her. When he circled her neck with his hand, he did it more to see what she'd do. When would she call a foul on the play, so to speak? He was beginning to think she wouldn't because when he tightened his grip with gentle but firm pressure, she got hotter and writhed against him more. Even still, he needed to be sure and was rewarded with the answer he hoped for. Adding to everything, she *wanted* to be spanked, *she wanted* him to call her his slut, and she *wanted* him to take control. Ryan was all too willing to give her what she wanted and more.

Rising to his knees, he released her wrists and ran his palms over her breasts. "Leave your hands above your head."

"But I can't touch you if I do." She pouted.

He pinched and tugged her nipples. "I know." She mumbled a curse but obeyed his command. "Good girl."

He wanted to push her to see how far she'd let him go, but he had to remember tonight was not the night for testing limits. Even so, he intended on making her come so hard she'd never forget his name. The need to feel her writhe beneath him and scrape her nails down his back while she came all over his cock trumped everything else. He'd happily kiss her lips to keep her little moans and whimpers quiet. He groaned —the thoughts alone were enough to bring him to the edge.

Ryan leaned forward and sucked each pretty, caramel-tipped nipple, circling each peak one at a time with his tongue. God, he was glad Jacob was a sound sleeper. With his mouth on her soft skin, Maiya panted and whimpered, arching beneath him. Moving his hands to her pants, he made quick work of the button and zipper, then pushed them over her hips. He ran his tongue down the center of her stomach to her belly button, and she arched again. Ryan placed one hand on her hip, stilling her. "Don't move, baby."

"I can't help it. You're making me crazy, Ryan."

"Impatient little slut, aren't you?"

"Oh!" She gripped his hair in her hands. "Oh fuck. Say it again."

He stopped and looked up at her. "Where are your hands supposed to be?"

She stared at him, her breath heaving in and out of her lungs. Her eyes were heavy-lidded, her cheeks flushed with arousal. She didn't say a word, just raised her hands back above her head and then licked her lips.

She was a fantasy come to life, and he blinked a couple of times to make sure he wasn't dreaming. "Maiya, I want you. My God, I want you now."

She nodded, drawing in a breath.

He pulled her pants the rest of the way off her legs and then stood and shed his own clothes. "Take your shirt and bra off." Ryan grabbed his wallet out of his pants and removed a condom.

She did as he asked and tossed them on his pile of clothes. "Ryan, are you sure about this?"

He knelt between her legs on the couch and pulled the Afghan around them. "No, but it's happening because I can't wait another goddamn minute to make you mine."

"Let me do this." She took the condom from him and tore the package open.

Mine… Ryan gazed at her through heavy lids. Maybe she hadn't noticed his slip about making her his. The statement had shot from him before he'd had a chance to stop it. His head fell back, and he had to take a couple of deep breaths while she teased the head with her fingertips before sheathing his length in the thin barrier.

He smoothed his hands down her inner thighs. Gripping behind her knees, he raised her legs, spreading them farther. Ryan glanced at her core, and his head spun with desire. The delicate skin of her sex was flushed and swollen with arousal. Her clit was hard beneath its hood of skin and protruded just enough to taunt him. He licked his lips. "You've got the prettiest pussy I've ever seen."

Running his finger through her folds, he gathered moisture to spread around the taut bundle of nerves.

She gasped, and her hips rose off the cushion. "Jesus, Ryan. The things you say to me. I think you could make me come with words alone."

"Yeah?" He chuckled. "That'd be fun to try. You taste like heaven, Maiya. Do you know that?" He ran his fingers through her folds again and dipped two inside her opening. "Have you ever tasted yourself?" He raised his hand, her moisture glistening on his fingertips. She sucked in a breath, and then her throat bobbed as she swallowed. "Lick my fingers, baby. Taste how sweet your honey is."

She parted her lips, and he pressed his fingers inside the warmth of her mouth. Maiya's eyes fluttered closed, and she sucked them, curling her tongue around the sides of each finger.

"The things you'll do for me." He shook his head. "It's amazing." Ryan pulled his fingers from her mouth and then sucked them between his own lips. Leaning forward, he settled between her welcoming thighs and kissed her, long and deep, and with all the passion welling up inside him. Ryan was starving for her, and he might never get his fill. He pressed his hardened length into her mound and shifted his pelvis forward, dragging the shaft over her clit.

Maiya rocked her hips in time with his and moaned into his mouth. Back and forth, they moved while he kissed her until they both gasped for breath. "Ryan, please?"

He thrust forward again. "Ask me to fuck you, Maiya. I need you to say it." He gritted his teeth, trying to maintain some control of himself—once he was inside her, he'd be lost.

She gripped the back of his hair. "Fuck your slut, Ryan." She bit his lip and then released it. "Please?"

"Jesus, where have you been all my life?" He raised his hips, positioned the head at her slick opening and slid in until his hips met hers.

She cried out and then bit his shoulder. He held himself still for a moment, allowing her time to adjust. Pausing gave him a chance to breathe, too. She was tight and hot and wet. Her internal muscles flexed around him, squeezing his prick, and his need for her skyrocketed to the moon. Ryan shifted his hips, pulled out, and then slid back inside her. Her walls flexed again, and he growled, grabbed her hips and moved inside her. "Woman, you feel like heaven."

———

Maiya couldn't stop her body's reaction to him when he slid inside her. Her inner walls spasmed, gripping his prick over and over again. Mini orgasms spread through her, and her whole body shook in response.

She couldn't stop them—why should she stop them? She'd never felt this kind of pleasure with anyone. Even the orgasms she'd given herself weren't this good. It was like her body had been waiting for his cock to be inside of her for her entire life —in complete awareness of what it would do for her.

She was filled with his thickness, and her body kept sucking him in deeper. Each time her channel rippled, Ryan growled and pressed into her again. She whimpered and sucked at his neck and shoulder, struggling to keep herself quiet. Maiya grabbed his ass, digging her nails in. "Ryan. Oh, God."

She panted and raised her legs higher, changing the angle of her hips. The shift of her pelvis caused him to graze over her G-spot, drawing a cry from her throat. He kissed her, swallowing her cries. Pulling from her lips, Ryan raised himself up on his fists. Sweat dripped from his body onto her chest.

Maiya gripped his biceps. "Harder. Fuck your slut harder."

His jaw tightened, and then his gaze traveled down the

length of their bodies to where they were joined. She looked, too.

Ryan slid out to the edge of the head. "Look at me. You want it harder, slut?"

Meeting his eyes, a nod was all she managed. He slammed into her with such force the lamp on the end table jiggled. *Holy God.* Maiya bit down on her bottom lip to keep from screaming, the pleasure rolling through her. The pressure was like nothing she'd ever experienced in her life. Her insides tightened with each push, sending waves of heat through her body until every nerve tingled.

He shuttled, slow but with power, into her. Maiya held on to his arms, panting in time with his movement as the orgasm built from deep inside her core. Her cunt spasmed again...

Ryan groaned, and his eyes rolled back in his head. "Maiya, baby, you keep doing that, and I'm not going to last."

"I can't..." She tried to catch her breath. "I can't help it. Oh God, Ryan!"

Shifting his weight to one arm, he smoothed his palm down her chest to one breast and pinched her nipple. She hissed and bit his arm, and her core tightened around his length again.

"Maiya, you're killing me." He dragged his hand away and circled her neck again.

She released a ragged breath and gripped his ass with one hand. Ryan growled when she dug her nails into his skin and then increased his momentum, fucking her with hard, concentrated thrusts. The head of his dick dragged over her g-spot, and his pelvis rubbed her clit with each roll of his hips. Maiya's orgasm rushed fast and hard at her with the equal stimulation of her clit and g-spot. "Don't stop. I'm gonna come."

He squeezed his hand a little tighter, not enough to cut off her breath, but enough to feel the pressure. "Not until I say you can. Your pussy, all wet and tight, feels like it was made for me. So damn good." He kissed her, catching and biting her tongue.

Whimpering, she held on to his ass while he continued the incredible repetitive motion. Over and over and over, he moved within her, and over and over, she met each thrust. Higher and higher, she climbed until she gripped her legs around him as tight as she could. "Ryan!"

"Come, Maiya. Come for me." He released her neck and grabbed both of her hips, tilting her pelvis off the couch.

She exploded and buried her face in his neck to stifle her scream. The spasms were endless. Little tremors spread from deep inside her channel and clit through her body to her limbs. She closed her eyes, unable to breathe.

"Yes!" He gripped her tighter, drilling into her. "That's it, baby, your cunt is—"

Still trying to catch her breath, she looked at him. His face was tight, his lips pulled back from his gritted teeth. A magnificent expression she'd never forget.

Ryan reared up on his knees, pulling her by the hips with him. Sweat glistened on his chest and abs. He had a death grip on her waist with her ass raised clear off the couch, and he ground her against his pelvis, sliding her up and down his cock. Throwing his head back, he came with a deep moan. His cock jerked with his climax in her core. Every muscle from his neck to his chest and abs was tight.

He was fucking beautiful.

Gazing at him through a lust-filled haze, Maiya was overcome. Another burst of small orgasms lit off deep inside. The room spun around her, and she closed her eyes. She might actually be dying. If she did, at least she'd been fucked good and proper like he'd said.

Ryan collapsed over her, and they lay pressed together while their breathing calmed. The smell of their sweat and sex permeated her senses. She stroked her hands up his back, enjoying the slickness of his cooling skin and then ran her fingers through his hair.

With his face buried in the crook of her neck, he pressed a soft kiss behind her ear, and then shifted and rolled to his side to lie beside her.

"Brrr." She shivered. "Where's the blanket?"

"Over there." He raised his arm and pointed without looking.

"Where?" She raised her head in search.

"Here." Ryan sat up and grabbed the blanket from the opposite end of the couch and then covered them both. He kissed her cheek and settled next to her. "Better?"

"Yes." She sighed and curled against him. "You wore me out."

"Me?" He chuckled. "Hell, woman, you about killed me."

She traced the contours of his chest and then kissed his collarbone. "It would be a good death, though, right?"

"The best," he whispered.

CHAPTER SEVENTEEN

MAIYA SETTLED CLOSE TO HIM WITH HER HAND PRESSED TO HIS heart. The beat was steady and sure against her palm. Had sex ever been this amazing before? Considering the various lovers and boyfriends she'd had in her past—the answer was an easy one.

No.

Already, the tension low in her tummy was building. She wanted him again. Nope, sex had *never* been like this before. Ever. Maiya kissed his neck and licked the salt from his sweat from her lips. Breathing him in, she basked in a post-orgasm bliss she'd never experienced before. *I could get used to this.* She smoothed her hand over his shoulder and then down his arm. What if it *was* always like this with him? But, oh God, what if it hadn't been as good for him as it was for her? Doubt crept in, and Maiya's mind raced. Fuck.

Maiya closed her eyes and worked on getting her emotions under control. So what if it wasn't the same for him as it was her? She never cared before, and she shouldn't care now. This was just sex. Casual sex. Mind-blowing, unbelievable, never-in-her-life-been-like-this-before sex, but still, just sex. And now, it was time to go. Staying the night wasn't an option. Not that he offered. But if he did, she'd decline. Shifting, she made to roll away and met with the resistance of his arm around her waist.

"Where you going?" His words came out in a sleepy voice.

"I...uhh. I should probably go. You know, time to get out of your hair. Jodi's waiting for me."

RYAN ROSE ON ONE ELBOW AND LOOKED AT HER. "YOU DON'T have to go yet."

She bit her bottom lip.

God, he loved when she did that. Her hair had pulled free of its knot and fell in messy, layered strands around her face. Her cheeks were flushed, and her lips were still swollen from his kisses. He'd never seen anyone so beautiful in all his life.

"Sure I do." She leaned over the side of the couch and returned with her cell phone. "It's better if I go."

"I wish you wouldn't."

She sat up, placing the phone to her ear. A moment passed, and then she relayed his address to the person on the other end of the line, most likely the cab company. Damn, she was leaving in a cab. Didn't that just make him feel like a piece of crap.

Disconnecting the call, she turned back to him. "I had a really great time."

"Me, too." He shrugged, trying to hide his disappointment. She needed to go, but he didn't want her to. He hadn't expected to want her to stay, though. Maybe he should see if she wanted to spend the night in the guest room or something. But then he'd have to explain to Jacob why she was still there in the morning.

Nope. She was right. It was better she leave.

Maiya scooped up her clothes and made quick work of

putting herself back together. "Bathroom?" She ran her fingers through her hair.

"There's a small one off the hall past the kitchen."

"Thanks." Appearing apathetic, she got up and padded from the room.

At some point between the mind-blowing sex and a few minutes ago, she slid her mask into place. He hated it, but there wasn't much to say at this point. He had no idea if it was an act or if she was, in fact, that shut off.

After disposing of the condom, Ryan put on his boxers and pants. Sitting again, he rested his head in his hands. There was an undeniable chemistry between them. He'd never been this sexually in tune with another person in his life. They moved together with precision. She knew just how to touch him, and her body responded to each stroke and caress he gave it. It was magic.

"My hair tie over there anywhere?"

Yanked from his thoughts, he looked up as she stepped into the room. "Um, I don't know. Let's see." He ran his hand along the cushions and then in between them. "Bingo." He held the tie out to her.

She took the tie from him, scooped her hair up in her hands and secured it. "Thanks."

"You're gorgeous, you know?"

She dipped her chin and avoided his gaze. "You're tired."

"Yeah, but—" he stood, "—it's still true." Circling her waist, he pulled her close. She stiffened, but he gave her no opportunity to pull away. He kissed her instead. Little sips from her lips, her tongue.

She rose on tiptoe and wrapped her arms around his neck. Ryan pulled her tighter against him and deepened the kiss. She tasted as sweet as always, and he cringed inside at how much he craved it.

Ryan was in trouble.

He wanted her, and it scared him because he'd been positive up until now; he didn't want anything serious. Not anything full-time anyway. Plus, Jacob didn't need the complication in his life or the risk of getting attached to someone only to lose them again. Maybe they could just see each other when she was in town. That'd be okay, right? It wasn't full-time, so it might work.

The faint sounds of a horn outside drew his attention, and Ryan pulled away from her lips.

She stepped back and pressed her fingers to her lips. "Looks like my ride's here."

"Let me walk you to the door." He scooped up his shirt and pulled it on.

She grabbed her sandals. "You don't have to."

"Of course, I have to. I'm not that much of an asshole, Maiya." He grabbed their coffee mugs and walked past her toward the kitchen.

No. She couldn't be his girlfriend, and for the most part, he'd keep her away from Jacob. Maiya would break his heart. He'd survive. But Ryan couldn't let her break his son's heart, too.

MAIYA WATCHED RYAN DISAPPEAR INTO THE KITCHEN. HAD SHE offended him? Damn, she didn't mean to. She put on her sandals and followed after him. Coming up behind him, she touched his back. "Hey, I'm sorry. I didn't mean to hurt your feelings."

He shrugged, rinsing their mugs in the sink. "No big deal." He turned and dried his hands on his pants. "Come on, you better hurry before the taxi leaves." He grabbed her hand and led her to the front entryway.

"I really did have an amazing time tonight."

He opened the door. "Me too."

"Jacob is a great kid. I enjoyed meeting him."

"Thanks. He's my miracle." His expression softened, and he smiled.

"I fly out tomorrow."

With a sigh, he pulled her close. "When are you coming back?"

"A couple weeks, I think. You want me to come back?" Maiya tilted her head to the side and searched his face for any hint of his feelings.

He paused and then kissed her lips. "Yeah, I want you to come back."

She kissed him again and then pulled from his embrace. "Bye, Ryan."

"See ya, Maiya."

It was still drizzling and quite cool outside. Maiya shivered and scurried to the cab and got inside. She peered out the window at Ryan. He stood in the doorway, his features obscured by the shadows the porch light cast over his face. Maiya rubbed her chilled arms. Leaving might be a mistake. But, no, his son was home. Jacob didn't need to wake up to her being there in the morning. That'd be awkward, to say the least. Plus, spending the night would complicate things further. Neither of them needed that.

Pulling out her cell phone, she shot a text to Jodi, letting her know she was on her way. Damn, it was already after midnight. Knowing Jodi, she'd be up waiting for her anyway. She'd for sure want the deets on the happenings between her and Ryan.

Explaining the gravity of how she'd had the best sex of her life and how it had forever altered her was *not* going to be easy.

CHAPTER EIGHTEEN

"WHAT'S UP, CHICKADEE?" JODI SMILED, WRAPPED IN A PINK fuzzy bathrobe and pink bunny slippers. Her blonde hair was piled high on her head in a messy knot, coffee mug in hand. "Come onnnn in."

Maiya laughed and stepped into her friend's house. "Hubby sleeping?"

"Oh girl, hell yeah, he is. That man goes to bed when the kids do. You'd think we were old or something." Jodi shut the door behind them. "Where are your bags?"

Maiya whipped around. "Oh shit! I left them at Ryan's." Right then, her phone buzzed in her hand. A text from Ryan.

> Ryan Painintheass: Babe, you left your
> suitcase and bag here.

She showed Jodi the screen.

"He called you babe? Aw, that's too sweet." Jodi grabbed her hand and tugged it toward her again. "Wait. What do you have him labeled in your phone?"

"Stop." Maiya laughed and pulled her arm away. "I need

to text him back." She shot a quick message back, letting him know she'd call in the morning.

"Oh, girl. You have a look on your face I've never seen before." She tugged Maiya toward the kitchen. "We're not going to bed till you tell me every last dirty detail."

Maiya trailed behind her. "I figured."

After about an hour of questioning, Jodi let Maiya go to sleep. Maiya was exhausted. Staring at the small digital clock on the nightstand, Maiya watched the numbers change at a snail's pace. She'd poured it all out to her friend—her excitement, how incredible the sex had been and her fears. Per usual, Jodi listened, but then gave her opinion. "You only live once, girl," Jodi had said.

Her friend was right, of course, but it didn't make the situation any easier.

Maiya couldn't shake Ryan from her thoughts. He was weaving his way into her heart, and that just plain pissed her off. She absolutely, under no circumstances, could allow herself to fall for Ryan Donnelly. And there was no way on God's green and blue earth he was going to fall for her. No matter how soft and intense his kisses were. No matter that he knew every divine way to touch her. No matter what she thought, she might see in his eyes. Maiya needed to get her walls in place around her heart, and she needed to do it fast.

Rubbing her temples, she tried to relax, but it was no use. Her mind wandered for the better part of the night from the sex to his kisses, to his son and the way Ryan was with him. He was a good dad, and it warmed her heart.

A son. *Ryan has a son.* She didn't even know if she wanted kids of her own, and now there was this adorable little boy who said she was pretty. Dammit, she couldn't fall for him, either.

Morpheus was not going to bless her with any sleep. Rolling over, she stared at the windows and watched while the sun rose and glittered in the window. At six-thirty, Maiya got up and took a shower.

Tugging on a borrowed pair of sweats and a T-shirt, she wandered to the kitchen and was treated to a messy-faced blonde two-year-old in her high chair. Maiya blew raspberries on the toddler's neck and then kissed Jodi on the cheek.

"Coffee's hot in the pot," Jodi said. "You look like hell. Did you sleep at all?"

Maiya grunted an unintelligible response and poured herself a cup.

"I'll take that as a no." Jodi sipped her coffee.

"I need to call Ryan and ask him to bring my bags." She grabbed a bagel and tossed it in the toaster. "You think he's up yet? Maybe I should text him instead."

"I guess text him. He might be up. How old is his son again?"

Maiya pulled the hot bagel from the toaster and spread jelly on it. "I didn't ask. I dunno, five or so?"

"You didn't ask?" Jodi shook her head. "Finish your waffle, Megan."

"No. Why?" Maiya asked with a mouthful of bagel.

"Piggy." She rolled her eyes. "Because this shi—stuff is important." Jodi eyed her daughter.

"Whatever." Maiya took a seat at the table. "It doesn't matter how old he is. I'm sure I won't be seeing much of the kid anyway." She made a face at Megan, tickled her belly and then grabbed her phone and sent a text to Ryan.

"He's nuts if he doesn't let you see his kid. You're great with my kids."

Maiya glanced at Jodi and shrugged one shoulder. Her phone buzzed with his reply. She sent him Jodi's address and set down her phone. "Where's Jared?"

"He's playing golf. Been gone an hour already."

"Golf?" Maiya scoffed. "You guys are like 'real' yuppies, I swear."

Jodi pinched her arm. "Bite your tongue!"

"Ow! Shit, woman."

Jodi pinched her again. "Watch your mouth."

Maiya rubbed her arm and laughed. "Sooorryyy."

Megan started laughing. "Funny, Myma." She scooped another piece of waffle into her mouth.

"Yes, Auntie Myma is funny, silly girl," Maiya crooned to Megan, still rubbing her arm. "Hey, let me borrow some makeup, please?"

"Of course. Can't have lover boy seeing you *au naturel* now, can we?" Jodi snorted.

Maiya rolled her eyes and left the room in pursuit of a more suitable face.

SLEEP WAS A NO-GO LAST NIGHT SINCE RYAN WAS WEATHERING a horrible case of Maiya on the brain. The woman had wormed her way into his head from the moment he'd laid eyes on her. Damn if he knew what to do with her, either. Part of him wanted to keep her. Make her his, like he'd let slip the night before. Another part of him wanted to run as fast as he could in the other direction.

He finished tying Jacob's shoes. She kept changing temperatures on him. One minute, she was hot and all over him, and the next, she was cold and distant. He wasn't much different, though. He *had* left her naked and willing in her hotel room, but he'd done his best to make it up to her, too.

"Are we going to see that pretty lady, Daddy?"

"Sure are." He mussed his son's hair and stood. "She forgot her suitcase here last night when she left. We need to take it to her."

"Why does she have a suitcase?" Jacob shifted his little body side to side. "Is she going on a trip?"

"She's going home. She doesn't live here by us." He grabbed his keys.

"Where does she live?"

He chuckled. "You ask a lot of questions, you know that?"

"Uh-huh. Can I bring my truck?"

"Yes, little man. You can bring your truck." He walked toward the back door. "Quick, grab it. We need to go."

Thirty minutes and a hundred more questions from Jacob later, Ryan pulled into Jodi's driveway. Jacob hopped out of the car and went running toward the front door before Ryan had even turned off the vehicle.

"Hey, Jacob!" Ryan jogged up to his son. "You need to wait for Daddy."

"Sorry. I forgot," his little boy said, looking at least a little guilty.

He eyed Jacob and rang the bell. The door swung open, and Ryan looked down. A little blond-haired boy about Jacob's age stood there.

"Anthony! Mommy said *do not* open the door." Jodi appeared at the door. "Come on in, you two."

"Nice to see I'm not the only one." He stepped inside, ushering Jacob with him.

Jodi laughed. "No kidding." She knelt down. "Hey there, I'm Miss Jodi." She held her hand out to Jacob.

"Hi," Jacob said, but didn't raise his hand. "Jacob, can you shake Miss Jodi's hand?"

Jacob looked up at him, holding his truck tight in his hands, and then around Jodi to see where Anthony had gone.

"You want to go play, Jacob? It's okay. You can go." She stood and focused on Ryan. "You want some coffee?"

"That'd be great." He followed behind her. "They look about the same age. I hadn't realized."

She glanced over her shoulder at him and snorted. "Neither did I."

"Touché."

Jodi grinned. "Have a seat. The Gorgeous Redhead will be done in a minute, I'm sure." She sat a cup of coffee in front of Ryan and excused herself for a moment. A minute later, a little girl, cradling a sippy cup in the crook of her arm, wandered his way with Jodi behind her. "Sorry, it was way too quiet. Had to make sure this one wasn't ripping my walls down."

"How many kids do you have?"

"Two, and that's plenty," Jodi said.

Maiya leaned inside the kitchen doorway. "Jodi, do you have— Oh, hey, Ryan. I hadn't heard you come in."

He stood and walked to her. "Morning." She turned her head, and his kiss landed on the corner of her lips. *Hmm.* She wasn't as happy to see him as he was her. *Great.*

"Morning. Thanks for bringing me my stuff."

"No problem. Do you need a ride to the airport?"

"I was going to take a cab. Jodi's kind of got her hands full."

Jodi rested a hand on her hip. "You didn't even ask me. I can take you. I *do know* how to function on a daily basis, you know?"

"Well, I just figured…" Maiya wrinkled her nose. "I didn't want to bother you."

Bingo. Giving her a ride was, at least, a chance for Ryan to spend a little more time with her. "I can take you. It's not a problem. I'm heading in that direction anyway."

Maiya looked at him and bit her top lip. "All right. I guess that'll work." She shrugged a shoulder. "My bags? I need to change."

"I'll go get it." Ryan ran outside, and grabbed the suitcase from the back of the car, and then brought it inside. Maiya thanked him and disappeared somewhere in the house.

He resumed his seat at the kitchen table, and his nerves tap-danced in his stomach. Why the hell was he nervous? Also, why was she acting so distant? *Ugh, this woman.* He didn't think he'd ever get it right with her. The images from last night were embedded in his mind, but he couldn't recall anything he'd done to piss her off. Damn, he wasn't up for this kind of dramatic roller coaster ride.

She needed to figure out what she wanted. Ryan's head fell forward, and he chuckled. Maybe *he* needed to figure out what the hell *he* wanted first.

"Something funny, Ryan?" Jodi looked over from the sink.

"Nah, just lost in thought." The sounds of the boys playing off in another room filled his ears, and every few minutes, they'd race by the entryway.

Jodi dismantled a series of sippy cups and rinsed them. "Boys are playing nice."

"Yeah, they are. How old is Anthony?"

"He'll be six in September." Jodi loaded the cups in the dishwasher.

"Nice. Jacob'll be six in December."

"We should get them together again."

"Yeah, that'd be cool. Thanks." He brought her his coffee cup. "Hey, Jodi, do me a favor, will you?"

"Sure." She looked at him.

"Don't say anything in the office about Jacob. It's not something I let people know about." He leaned against the counter. "I just…I don't want them thinking I can't do my job, you know, since I'm a single father."

"Is that why you haven't told anyone? Jeez, Ryan. They won't care."

"I don't want to risk it. I'd appreciate the favor."

"All right." Jodi closed the dishwasher and started it. "My lips are sealed."

"Thanks." He blew out a relieved breath and glanced over to the kitchen doorway right as Maiya returned.

"Okay, I'm ready. Better go now, or I'll miss my flight." She walked over to Jodi and kissed her cheek. "I'll call you later. Thanks for letting me crash here."

"Sure thing. I gots da setup, yo. Perfect fo' crashin'." Jodi snapped her fingers in a zigzag pattern.

"Did—" Maiya dipped her chin and raised her brows. "Did you just try to go all gangsta? Cuz… Oh my God, please don't."

Ryan laughed. It was spectacular to see how well the two got along. They seemed total opposites, too.

She hugged Maiya. "I'll do it again if you don't get gone this instant."

"Let me get Jacob and your bags. I'll meet you at the car." He walked in the general direction of the noise.

After finding Jacob, he poked his head back in the kitchen. Jodi was hugging Maiya again. He swore he heard Jodi say something about "hanging on to him," but he wasn't sure. "Hey, sorry to interrupt… Nice seeing you, Jodi. We'll have to talk about getting the kids together again." He left the room and headed to the car, Jacob and luggage in tow.

THE FIRST THING MAIYA NOTICED WHEN SHE GOT OUTSIDE WAS Ryan wasn't driving the Porsche. It was the BMW he'd mentioned before. An X5 SUV or, wait, they called them SAVs, didn't they? She chuckled, opened the door and slid into yet another plush leather seat. "So, I guess you were serious when you said you had a Beemer." She smoothed her fingers across the wood grain strip in the door. "I like these, they're nice."

"Thanks. And, the proper term is Bimmer."

"What? Oh, please. Like that matters."

He snorted a laugh and shook his head.

She squinted her eyes at him and furrowed her brow. "What's so funny?"

"I figured I'd get another 'typical' comment from you, is all."

"Ohh, that. Yeah, well, the word coming to mind this time is spoiled yuppie."

He frowned. "I am not a…a yuppie."

"What's a yuppie, Daddy?" Jacob asked from the back seat.

Damn. She'd forgotten Jacob was there. Whoops.

"I'll tell you when you're older." Ryan eyed Maiya. "Okay, fine. It might appear that I am a bit…yuppie-ish."

She burst into a fit of laughter.

The ride went by pretty fast, even with the little bit of traffic on the freeway. Jacob asked her a ton of questions. The kid was adorable and smart. So smart. Ryan answered any questions directed at him with ease and a tone of patience laced through his words.

Having never met the man who impregnated her mother, it intrigued Maiya to see how Ryan interacted with his son. He was a single father. Therefore, he had to play both roles for this kid. Coach Little League and wipe sick noses. Was it hard on him, or did it come easy? One thing was for sure: Ryan loved his son. It meant a lot to her, though it shouldn't. It wasn't like they were dating. She didn't need to concern herself with whether or not Ryan was a good father.

They pulled up to the departures area at the airport. Maiya hopped out and then opened Jacob's door. "It was really nice meeting you, Jacob." She smiled. "Be good for your daddy."

He flashed a big grin and waved. "Bye, Miss Maiya."

She shut the door and walked to the back of the car.

Ryan had already pulled out her suitcase and computer bag and set them on the curb. "You sure you don't want me to park and help you inside?"

"Nah, I'm good. Thanks."

He pulled her into an embrace. "Yeah, you are."

She stiffened but relaxed when he stroked his hand up and

down her back. Unable to stop herself, Maiya wrapped her arms around him.

He nuzzled her hair. "Will you call me?"

"Do you want me to call you?"

"Yes." He pulled back from her. "I want to see you again."

"Of course, you'll see me again. I'll be back in two weeks." She tilted her head to the side. "We still have a project to finish."

He rubbed her arms. "That's not what I meant. I want to spend time with you again, outside of work."

"We'll see."

His brows drew together in a look of confusion, but then he brushed a soft kiss over her lips. Warmth spread through her, and when he pulled away, she licked her lips.

"Call me when you're on the ground, okay?"

She blinked, her mind caught in a haze. "Sure."

He stepped away from her and rounded the back of the car.

Maiya stood, lips still tingling and watched him drive off.

How did this man do this to her? It was just a kiss and a pretty damn chaste one at that. But now she'd be thinking about him the whole damn flight home.

CHAPTER NINETEEN

Ryan couldn't keep his eyes off the damn clock—or his watch, his phone, the clock on the stove or the microwave. Take your pick, didn't matter which one. Maiya would be landing soon. Would she call? Maybe he should call her? Ryan stifled a growl. A little distraction was needed. "Little man, want to go to the park?"

Jacob looked up from his Legos. "Yes!"

Grabbing a couple of water bottles, he walked while Jacob rode his bicycle to the park. His phone buzzed in his pocket. Pulling it out, he read the screen.

> Maiya: Hey, I'm home. Don't have time to call right now. Maybe later.

> Ryan: Okay, thanks for letting me know.

Disappointment settled over him like a storm cloud. He probably wouldn't hear from her tonight. Maybe he'd try and call her tomorrow though. Ryan sighed and shoved his phone back in his pocket. No. He wouldn't call her.

Boyfriends did those things, and he wasn't her boyfriend. He had no intention of being her boyfriend, either. A lump rose in his throat, and Ryan swallowed it down. Why did the idea of not being her boyfriend upset him? Unless... Did he *want* Maiya to be his girlfriend?

He shook his head, helped Jacob park his bike and took a seat on a nearby bench. His son ran off toward a couple kids playing on the enormous wooden structure made to look like a castle in the middle of the playground.

The sun shined bright, warming his face while he watched his son play and tried to unravel the elastic ball of thoughts bouncing around his brain. After about an hour on the Maiya merry-go-round, his phone rang. He swiped the screen. "Hey, Mom. What's up?"

"I'm making a pot roast. Care to come for dinner?"

He glanced over at Jacob. "That sounds great. Time?"

"Six-ish should work. Your brother is here."

"Which one?"

"Your favorite one."

"No shit? When did Jimmy get into town? The bastard didn't even call me."

"Language, please." She sighed. "Last night sometime. I woke up, and he was in the kitchen."

"Sorry, Mom." He cringed, amazed at how she managed to still make him feel ten. "Can I bring anything?"

"Just yourself and my sweet grandson, of course."

"That can be arranged." He scanned the play area, finding Jacob again. "See you in a couple hours."

Cool, Jimmy was in town. Why hadn't the ass let him know? Damn, he'd missed his brother. Maybe he'd come stay at Ryan's place instead of their parents. Jimmy was fourteen months older than Ryan. Damn near Irish twins and flanked on either side by their two sisters, Cyn and Angie.

When they were kids, they'd fought incessantly, but as teens, they were inseparable even though they were total opposites in all things, including women. Ryan played sports in high school. Jimmy was in drama and art classes. They rarely hung out during school hours and didn't share the same group of friends. But they always ended up together by the end of the night. Plain and simple, they were best friends.

Now, Jimmy lived in New York City and was a big, hotshot artist. Saying Ryan was proud of his brother was an understatement. Jimmy had had several showings of his work and sold a lot of it.

Ryan called over to Jacob and let him know they were leaving in five minutes. Jacob waved and ran back up the maze to the slide. Ryan leaned back and crossed his arms, watching his son while he swooped down the plastic yellow spiral for maybe the twentieth time since they'd gotten there.

———

MAIYA TUGGED HER SUITCASE BEHIND HER ON THE WAY TO THE long-term parking garage. Mötley Crüe's "Girls Girls Girls" spilled from her phone in her bag, the ringtone telling her exactly who it was. "Home sweet home." Stopping, she grabbed the phone and swiped the screen. "Hello, Heather."

"Hey! You busy?"

"Who me? No. Why would I be busy?" Maiya rolled her eyes. The sarcasm in her tone was totally lost on Heather.

"Good. I need a ride."

Wedging the phone between her ear and shoulder, Maiya continued the trek. "Why? Where's your car?"

"It got towed."

"Jesus, again, Heather?" Maiya stopped and repositioned the phone. Her damn neck was starting to cramp.

"Don't lecture me. It wasn't my fault."

Maiya sighed. "Yeah, yeah. It's never your fault."

"Emmmmmm, pleeeease?"

Maiya cringed at the sing-songy whine smothering Heather's words. "Ugh. I'm leaving the airport now. It's going to be a little while before I can get you. I have to stop home first and then hit the grocery for Mom. You're going to have to wait until I do that."

"I thought you said you weren't busy."

"Just that whole flying home from a business trip thing, right? Plus, my mother. I mean, what could be busy about that?" She let out an exasperated sigh. "I'll grab you *and then* drop you off on the way to Mom's. Be ready, please, because I'm leaving you if you're not."

"Thanks! I owe ya, Em."

"I'll add it to your tab. See you in a bit." She hung up before her friend commented further.

Heather Walsh was Maiya's oldest friend and allergic to anything relating to responsibility. Growing up, they lived in the same trailer park, went to the same schools and got into trouble together—lots of trouble. But while Maiya worked her way through college, Heather partied her way right out the door.

Arriving home, Maiya ran upstairs and dropped her bags. After changing her clothes, she pulled a brush through her hair and then made her way back out the door. It was a little past two-thirty by the time she pulled up to Heather's apartment complex in her black Infiniti.

Retrieving her cell from her purse, she sent Heather a text letting her know she was there. And waited. And waited. And wai—impatience won out, and she dialed Heather's number, listening while it rang and rang and then hit voicemail.

"Dammit, Heather! I am so kicking your ass if you flaked." Maiya hit End and rested her forehead on her steering wheel, her left eye twitching. This additional agitation wasn't on the to-do list, not when she still had to deal with her mother today.

She glanced up through her windshield at the cement stairs leading to Heather's apartment. Maiya didn't feel much like hiking up the three flights and banging on the door. Though she'd burn off a little restless energy and calories climbing them. *Screw this.* She dialed Heather's number again and was greeted with a sleepy "Hello."

"Get your ass down here. I told you to be ready, or I was leaving you."

A yawn. Then, a cough. "Em?"

"No. It's your Great Aunt Sally. Of course, it's Em! Light a fire under it." Maiya disconnected the call, got out of the car and lit a cigarette. It'd be at least seven minutes before her friend dragged her butt downstairs.

True to her prediction, seven minutes later, Heather puttered down the steps. Her petite frame wrapped in a pair of faded and torn blue jeans, a white tank and no bra. Maiya rolled her eyes and got back behind the wheel. When Heather was in and buckled up, she pulled away.

"You love me." Heather pulled down the visor, applied her lipstick and then ran her fingers through her dark brown hair.

"You're lucky I do. Where's the car this time? And please tell me you have money to spring it from the tow yard."

"Actually, yes, I do. I didn't pay rent yet, so…all good." Heather shrugged with an added grin and closed the visor.

"Then how will you pay rent? Heather, I swear to Christ, you really need to get your shit together."

"Don't lecture, Em." Heather looked down at her hands. "Dunno, I'll figure it out."

"Chica, you always say that, but one of these days, you *really* do need to figure it out." Maiya reached over and squeezed her friend's arm. She loved Heather, but the girl hadn't ever grown up. She was still hitting the bars, weekend or weeknight, didn't matter. And getting into any number of risky situations with crazy guys. Or not paying her rent. Or having her car towed. The list was never-ending. They just weren't the same people anymore.

Correction: Maiya wasn't the same person anymore.

Heather was still the same and failed to notice that Maiya had changed. She still considered Maiya her best friend and bore no shame calling her to bail her out of the various dramas she landed herself in. Maiya put up with it because that's what a person did for their oldest friend, but she was getting real sick of it. Heather represented everything about the past that Maiya wanted to forget, yet couldn't manage to escape.

When they got to the tow yard, Heather gave her a peck on the cheek and got out. "I'll call you later. Love ya, Em."

"Love you too." At least Heather hadn't asked for money. This time.

As luck would have it, the tow yard was right around the corner from where her mother lived. Maiya pulled up in front of her childhood home and parked. She paused, taking in the rusted aluminum sides of the single-wide trailer. She hated going there, but she did it every weekend and sometimes a few days during the week.

Her mother was getting sicker, though the woman wouldn't admit it. She still smoked close to two packs of cigarettes a day and drank like a damn fish, with no quitting in sight. The doctor wanted Joanie on an oxygen tank for her emphysema—no deal there, either. They didn't discuss the drinking with her doctor, but he knew of her habit. Maiya made sure he did. It was only a matter of time before her mother got too sick and needed to be hospitalized.

For now, the woman planted her ass in her thirty-year-old orange-striped recliner inside her forty-year-old single wide trailer and swallowed her booze and inhaled nicotine. It wasn't pretty, but it was reality.

Taking in a deep breath to steel her anxiety, she got out of the car and then hefted the four bags of groceries from the trunk toward the trailer. As per usual, the door was unlocked, and Maiya glanced over at the recliner nestled in the corner and made her way from the small living room to the kitchen. Her mother was stretched out in the chair, napping, with the TV tuned to some soap opera. Her age-imprinted face at ease, and her dark hair, tied in a loose braid with plenty of gray threading through it, lay over her shoulder.

Maiya bit her bottom lip, swallowing past the knot in her throat, and emptied one of the grocery bags. She'd never get used to this. Hated having to do it. "That's what good daughters do, even when their mothers don't appreciate it." A friend she'd had in Los Angeles drilled the statement into her mind a few years ago. The girl had been a member of a twelve-step recovery group for families and tried to convince Maiya to go with her. Some of the things she told Maiya had stuck, but Maiya didn't need that stuff. She was doing fine all on her own—at least as far as she was concerned.

Careful to keep her steps light, Maiya made her way to her mother's bedroom. After making the bed, she stopped by the bathroom, deposited a new supply of shampoo and toothpaste, and then did a quick cleanup of the sink. She needed to hire a maid, but her mother wasn't agreeable to having strangers in the house. Funny, having strangers in the house when Maiya was a kid was commonplace.

In a constant battle to air the metal box out, she opened windows along the way. The trailer smelled of stale cigarette smoke, booze and mildew. The place still had the same mustard-yellow shag carpeting and brown plaid furniture Maiya had grown up with. Her and Jeremy's old bedroom was now a dumping ground for out-of-date newspapers and old magazines. All the white vinyl wallboards were yellowed by the years of cigarette smoke. It was gross and made Maiya's skin crawl.

Maiya might smoke, but never in her house or car. And nowhere near the amount her mother did. The smell lingered, attaching itself to everything. Maiya hated that, but her mother was perfectly content with all of it.

Back in the kitchen, she leaned over the sink and cranked the window open. When she turned, her mother was behind her. Maiya jumped, pressing her hand to her chest to calm her racing heart.

"Why do you do that? You're gonna make it all dusty in here, Emmie." Empty glass in hand, she stepped past Maiya, retrieved a handful of ice from the freezer and then poured herself a fresh gin and tonic.

Maiya winced at the use of the childhood nickname her older brother Jeremy had given her. She looked over her mother's weathered and worn features. The years hadn't been kind, but mostly, it was the booze that'd stolen her mother's beauty. Leaning her hip against the counter, Maiya crossed her arms. "I do it because it reeks in here, Mom."

"It does not." Her mother raised the glass to her lips and took a healthy gulp.

Not exactly healthy, in Maiya's opinion. She looked away, unable to bear the sight.

Setting the drink down, her mother pulled a cigarette from her soft pack, popped it between her lips and lit it. She coughed on the exhale, and Maiya winced again. "I didn't think you were comin' today."

"Don't I always come?"

"I suppose you do." Her mother sneezed and reached for a tissue.

"Bless you. Are you hungry?"

"I could eat, I guess." Her mother blew her nose. "I don't even know what's in there. Make what you want." She picked up her glass and shuffled back to the living room.

Maiya stared at the floor, and her eyes burned with unshed tears. How the hell had she ended up back here, in this trailer —hell, in the state of Nevada again? She'd escaped her mother's drinking a long time ago, and the demons haunting her when she lived in this trailer had gone elsewhere. Except now she had to visit regularly, so she hadn't really escaped after all.

She *had* done it, though, hadn't she? She'd made it out of this hellhole, made it out of Vegas, too. Some days, taking the job with her company so long ago felt like it'd all been a wonderful dream. Or maybe it wasn't. Maybe she was actually in Los Angeles, living in her little apartment and working in the office with everyone else, and what she faced now was merely a nightmare. Any minute now, she'd wake up.

Any minute now.

Wake up, Maiya!

She closed her eyes and drew in a deep breath. Opening them, she glanced around the kitchen. *Damn, still here.* Dragging herself away from the rabbit hole of self-pity, Maiya put the rest of the groceries away. Asleep or not, this *was* a nightmare. The kind a person lived day in and day out. The kind a person didn't wake up from…ever.

Because they weren't sleeping.

From the living room, another cough echoed into the kitchen—not unusual, considering her mother's emphysema —then another sneeze, followed by more coughing. Which sounded a little too moist for Maiya's liking. The woman struggled to breathe as it was because the COPD had gotten so bad, plus her liver wasn't functioning very well. The last thing her mother needed was bronchitis, or worse, pneumonia. Maiya glanced over her shoulder from the counter. "Mommy, that cough isn't sounding good."

"It's just a cold. I'm fine."

"I'll dig out the nebulizer before I go. Can't have it getting any worse." Maiya wandered to the living room. Glancing at the side table next to her mother's chair, she saw the many crumpled tissues.

"I hate that thing. It makes me all shaky."

"Got news for ya, Mom. It's not the breathing machine making you all shaky."

"All right, Miss Bigwig-Corporate-Girl, what's it from?"

Maiya bit her tongue, shaking her head. "Never mind." There was no point going there. It was like trying to explain to a fish what water was. Instead, she gathered up the empty glasses and snotty tissues on the end table. She didn't miss the yellowed hue in the whites of her mother's eyes. "You want a turkey sandwich?"

"That's fine." Joanie coughed a few more times before finally catching her breath.

Maiya grabbed a glass of water and brought it to her. "Here, Mom."

"What's that?"

"It's water. Please drink it."

"I don't need that, I have my drink right here."

"Take it anyway." Maiya set the glass on the end table and then walked back to the kitchen. Her mother grumbled something about her always being a pain in the ass, but Maiya ignored it and made her mother lunch.

Loading the plate on a tray, she brought it into the living room and then set it on her mother's lap. "There you go. I got some of those chocolate-striped cookies you like so much. You can have those later after dinner."

Maiya walked away to open the remaining windows. Her mother's wet cough echoed through the trailer. That damn minor cold was probably full-blown bronchitis already. She went back into the living room and sat on the couch. "Mom, I really think you should do a breathing treatment when you finish your sandwich and try to lay off the smokes today, too."

Joanie looked up from her plate, mouth full of food. "I'm fine."

"You need to get this cold under control now, or you're going to end up in the damn hospital," she chastised. "And we know how much you love that. You can't drink there."

"Watch your tone, and don't talk to me like I'm stupid. I said I was fine!" Joanie coughed again and then swallowed the remains of her drink. "Last I checked, I was still your mother, and you were still my kid."

"Have it your way, Mom." Maiya sighed. "I'm only trying to help you."

"If you want to help me, get your fat ass off that couch and refill my gin and tonic."

Maiya stared at the television, red coating her vision, and bit her tongue again. She needed to shut up and allow the nasty insult to fall flat in the middle of the room. What she wanted to do instead was tell her mother to kiss her "fat ass" and then hand her the whole bottle of booze.

Be a good daughter. Be a good daughter. Be a good daughter. Be a good daughter.

When her temper cooled, she was able to speak again. "You have an appointment next week with your doctor." Maiya glanced at her. "They want to do blood work for your liver."

Her mother put the sandwich down, moved the tray and stood. "I'll get my own damn drink."

"Oh my God, look at your stomach!" Maiya jumped up. "You're all bloated." She touched her mother's abdomen with her fingertips. "It's hard, too."

Joanie swatted her hand away and pulled her royal blue threadbare sweater closed. "I'm fine. I'm old, my belly's chubby. It happens."

Still shocked at her mother's appearance, Maiya's feet were rooted to the shag carpet in the living room. How had she missed this? Though, to be fair, she rarely saw her up and mobile when she was there. Her mom stayed in that damn orange-striped chair while Maiya moved around her, fixing her a meal and tidying up the trailer. "You should see the doctor sooner. I'm calling."

Joanie glared over her shoulder. "Don't you dare. I'm fine, and I'll be the same in two weeks time." She returned, drink in hand, and sat in her chair. "Don't get yourself all in a lather."

"But—" Maiya shut her mouth, pressing her lips together. Turning, she sat on the couch again. "Fine."

"So, who's the new flavor of the month?" Joanie sipped her drink.

"Wha…" Maiya frowned. "What makes you think there's a flavor of the month?"

"Because you're *my* daughter." Joanie snorted. "You got a look about you like you been laid recently. I can always tell when you have."

"God, Mom. Do you have to be so damn crass?"

"Crass? Do you have to be so damn sensitive? I know what I see is all." Joanie shrugged and bit into the remaining piece of her turkey sandwich. "So, who is he?"

"I'm not talking to you about this."

"You think you would've learned something by now." She shook her head. "He another biker?"

"No, he's not another biker. And he isn't a flavor of the month, either." Maiya scowled, ran her fingers through her hair and blew out a breath. Was it getting hot in there? She was sweating. And dammit, her mother always set her on edge. Jesus, she needed to get out of there; her anxiety level was on maximum overdrive.

"Something more?" Her mother raised her brows. "You think he might be more, Emmie?"

"No— Yes… I don't know!" Maiya shook her head, agitated. "Why do you care?"

"What? A mother can't ask about her daughter's love life?"

"Not *my* mother." Maiya crossed her arms. "You're more interested in telling me how I'll be alone forever."

"Only because you push everyone away who comes near you." Joanie set the drink on the side table. "You been pushing me away for years." She started coughing and grabbed a tissue, pressing it to her lips.

"I push you away? Oh, that's rich." Her mother coughed and coughed—the rattle erupting from her lungs sounded horrid, but Maiya pressed on. "You've been pushing me away since Je—"

"Don't!" Joanie sputtered between coughs. "Don't say his name." She coughed a few more times, fanning herself with the tissue.

"You sound horrible, Mom. You're doing a treatment right now." Maiya retrieved the nebulizer and medicine for it. When she returned, she loaded it with the steroid and then fixed the mask over her mother's mouth and nose.

Joanie sat back, eyes closed and breathed in the vaporized medicine. While the machine did its job, Maiya busied herself preparing a meal for her mother to have for dinner. When the treatment was done, she cleaned and put the machine away.

Joanie had settled in her chair and appeared to be napping. Maiya covered her with a blanket and then smoothed her mother's hair from her forehead. Her coloring looked a little off, too. It worried Maiya more than she wanted it to. She kissed her mother's cheek. "Get some rest, Mom. I'll call you in a couple of days."

Joanie nodded but didn't open her eyes.

When Maiya got in her car, she waited there for a few minutes, trying to quell the fear tightening her chest. She pressed her forehead against the steering wheel, and her tears fell. She loved her mother, she did. But she didn't like her. And sometimes she hated her, though she'd never say it out loud. At least not anymore. Years ago, she had no qualms about telling people how she hated her mother. And it didn't matter to her that they looked at her with horror and pity in their eyes.

People didn't hate their mothers; it was considered unnatural.

Wiping her wet cheeks with the back of her hand, Maiya pulled away from the trailer. She'd go back in a couple of days. Her mother managed okay without her there every day, still, but soon enough, Maiya would have to go daily. Then she'd insist on bringing in a care person for a couple of hours a day. Maiya was smart enough to know she wouldn't be a good caretaker. It wouldn't be healthy for her or her mother.

Ryan occupied her thoughts while she drove the rest of the way home. Was he going to be another flavor of the month? She wasn't sure. She had the sneaking suspicion she wanted more than a month, but she wouldn't admit it. Even to herself. And then there was his little boy.

Ryan didn't want to confuse his son. She couldn't blame him. It scared her, the prospect of being in his life. In both their lives.

Fairytales didn't come true in real life, not the happily-ever-after kind anyway. People made their own happiness, rescued themselves like she'd done. Ryan was not her Prince Charming. He was a single dad with a darling child.

A normal. Nice. Guy.

And Maiya had no idea what the hell he wanted with her.

CHAPTER TWENTY

RYAN MADE HIS WAY UP THE FRONT WALKWAY TO HIS PARENTS' house with Jacob half asleep in his arms. The door opened before he reached it, and his brother stood behind the metal security door.

"What up, my brotha?" Jimmy's mouth spread into a goofy smile. His jet-black hair was a spiky mess and in desperate need of a trim. Their dad always gave him shit for it when Jimmy was in town.

Ryan laughed. "Same old, same old. Now open the damn door, would you?"

"Yes, sir. Right away, sir." Jimmy opened the door and stepped to the side.

Jacob raised his head and let out a loud yawn. "Hi, Uncle Jimmy."

"What's up, little man? C'mere, let me get a look at you." Jimmy took Jacob into his arms for a hug.

Ryan squeezed his brother's shoulder and walked to the kitchen. "Hey, Mom." He kissed her cheek. "Where's Dad?"

"Out back." Roseanne tossed a salad for dinner. "Jimmy have Jacob?"

"Yup. You look pretty today." He leaned against the

counter next to her, admiring how young she still looked, her short blonde hair done to perfection.

Her hazel eyes sparkled, and she smiled. "Thank you. Dinner will be ready in about ten minutes. Now, get out of my kitchen."

"Yes, ma'am." He snagged a slice of cucumber off the cutting board on his way past. Laughing, she swatted his hand away.

Ryan found Jacob in the bedroom his parents kept for their grandkids, showing Jimmy his new set of Matchbox cars and track. Ryan took a seat on the bed and observed while Jacob giggled with excitement each time a car made a successful lap and didn't fall off.

Jimmy didn't appear to be someone great with kids. The man was over six feet tall, slender, with their father's darker features. Plus, tattoos and piercings galore. He looked more like someone to steer clear of in a dark alley than a potential babysitter.

"I've never seen a track this cool before. You're pretty lucky, little man." Jimmy pulled Jacob into his lap and let out a mock groan. "My gosh, you're getting too big. I can hardly believe it. Let me see your muscles."

Jacob flexed his little arm when his uncle circled it with his hand. "Daddy says I gots manly man arms." A proud smile stretched from ear to ear. "I'm strong."

"Whoa. You *are* strong. Promise you won't beat me up?" Jimmy asked with wide eyes.

Jacob hugged him. "You're silly, Uncle Jimmy."

Jimmy looked at Ryan and flashed him a wide grin. "All right, little man, let me up. I need to give a proper hello to your daddy."

"I'm gonna go find Papa." Jacob ran out of the room.

Jimmy got to his feet and clasped fists with Ryan. "How ya been, man?"

They pulled each other into an embrace. Slaps on the

back included. "Great. Things are great." Ryan stepped back from him. "Why the hell didn't you tell me you were coming into town?"

"You sound like a chickie."

"Whatever, dude." Ryan laughed. "I didn't think we'd see you until the holidays."

"I had to settle some business. I'm working a deal for some of my stuff to be used in this new swank hotel in Hollywood."

"No kidding? That's awesome." Ryan clapped him on the shoulder. "You're kicking ass. Congratulations, bro."

"Thanks. Sometimes, I can't believe these crazy people want to display my funky industrial art on their walls." He shrugged. "Fuck it. It's their money, right? I'll take it."

"Don't ask me, I have no eye for artsy stuff. You know that." He turned toward the door. "Let's get a beer and find Dad."

"Reading my mind, Ry."

They settled on the back patio, a beer in hand, and watched their father help Jacob knock around a plastic golf ball. Jimmy leaned back in his seat, crossed his long legs at the ankle and looked at Ryan. His hazel eyes flashed with something akin to mischief in them.

"Uh oh. You look like the cat who ate the canary." Ryan tipped back his beer.

Jimmy wagged his brows. "Wanna go to Vegas tonight?"

"Dude, you're nuts."

"I don't like the sounds coming from both of you," their father called over to them.

"Wha—" Ryan leaned forward. "It's him, Dad. You know he's the troublemaker."

"I know you're both the troublemakers," Joseph Sr. said, then focused back on Jacob.

"Come on, Mom and Dad will watch Jacob. We can fly in tonight and back out tomorrow morning," Jimmy whispered.

Ryan shook his head. "I dunno, man. I can't just do that kind of thing, you know that." He took a swig of beer.

"Yeah, yeah, I know. But hey, when was the last time we got to hang out? I'm asking Mom."

"Why do I feel like I'm sixteen again?" Ryan chuckled. "Fine, go ask her."

Jimmy stood. "Shit, sixteen? I think twenty-one is better."

"Right, so we can both drink legally *and* be prosecuted as adults in a court of law?"

"You got it." Jimmy gave him a thumbs-up and walked in the house. "Hey, Mom?"

Vegas? He could handle some Vegas right now. Blowing off some steam with his brother might be just what he needed. Ryan leaned back in the chair and mulled it over. Realization barreled through his mind. *Maiya.* Maiya lived in Vegas. Ryan rushed into the kitchen to help butter Mom up. When he got inside, Jimmy had already charmed (bribed) her to take Jacob for tonight and tomorrow.

His brother had a smile that got him whatever he wanted, and if it didn't, he found a way to get what he wanted anyway. Out of all the boys, Jimmy was the silver-tongued devil of the Donnelly family; considering his tongue was now pierced, the label was never truer. Ryan searched his mother's face, wanting to be sure she was really on board with this. "Are you sure, Mom?"

"It's fine." She kissed his cheek. "Go have some fun with your brother."

"Told you she'd do it," Jimmy gloated. "Ooh, Mom. This looks delicious."

"Thank you, James. You two are on clean up." She winked and moved the platter of pot roast and vegetables to the table. "Someone call your father and Jacob to the table, please."

Neither one was a request, even if she did say "please". When Roseanne Donnelly told her kids to do something, they did it. The woman had raised ten of them, and not one dared to defy her, even now. Excitement bounced through Ryan, and he exchanged a grin with Jimmy.

Talk about feeling like kids again.

———

It'd been a long day, and all Maiya wanted to do was curl up on the couch with a movie. She stared at her phone several times, even picked it up once or twice to text Ryan. But in the end, she decided to leave it alone. If he really wanted to talk, he'd contact her.

Her phone buzzed, and she grabbed it up so fast she almost flung it across the room. "Shit." She checked the text.

Heather: You home?

Maiya: Watching TV. You?

Heather: Get off the couch. Let's go shake our asses at the club.

Maiya: I'm too tired.

Maiya curled her feet under her, and the phone buzzed again.

Heather: Maiya, come on. You're only 29. Live a little. Get your lazy ass up and meet me at the club. It's freak night.

Maiya: Fuck's sake, Heather. Leave my ass out of this! What time?

Heather: YAY! Ten. I'll meet you at the back bar.

Maiya: Fine. See ya there.

Tossing her phone on the couch, Maiya blew out a breath.

So much for a quiet night at home. At least she'd work out some stress on the dance floor. A few drinks would be nice too. Plus, Heather and any drama following her would make for a great distraction.

She dragged her worn-out ass off the couch and made her way to the bathroom. Time to do her hair, and since it'd dried all pulled up in a scrunchie, she needed to wet it and dry it and curl it and... Oh hell. What was she thinking? Baseball cap. Jeans. Done.

An hour later, Maiya pulled into the parking lot behind the club, finding a spot in the far back. She checked her lips in the mirror and then gathered all the essentials. Walking around to the front of the large, two-story building, she glanced at the club's twenty-foot pink neon sign. It flickered in spots but was pretty against the star-filled Vegas sky.

Tangled was located about five miles off The Strip. Each night was a different theme, and tonight was Freak Night—one of her favorite nights to go dancing there. Freak night meant any local goth, metalhead, patchouli-wearing, hookah-smoking, Harley-riding, tattooed or pierced freak within a twenty-mile radius showed up—a melting pot of anyone who ever rebelled against societal norms, and even those who didn't. College boys and girls—pretty boys and girls, as she liked to call them—mixed in the fray with the dropouts, blue-collar workers and day laborers. And the DJ played anything from Nine Inch Nails to Yaz.

It was cool, and what made it even cooler was her choice of dress on these nights: Jeans, tank top, work boots or Chucks, and always her cap. Tonight, she wore a low-cut, white cotton ribbed tank with a black bra, faded blue jeans and her black work boots. Simple and comfy.

Maiya bypassed the long line in her usual fashion and headed for the door of the club. When she stepped in front of the head bouncer, he pulled her into a hug. She gave him a squeeze. "Hiya, Jay. Good to see you, hon."

Jay was a six-foot-five, two-hundred-and-fifty-pound, muscle-bound black man. But to her, he was a teddy bear who gave awesome hugs. The man had a smile genuine enough to light up every heart on The Strip, coupled with gorgeous deep-brown eyes. He'd make some lucky girl a happy woman one day if he ever managed to stop playing with the clientele.

"Always a pleasure, sweetness. Go on in, the door's always open for you, gorgeous."

"Aw, thanks, honey. You're too good to me." She kissed his cheek and walked inside.

The first thing to hit Maiya was the sweet smell of vapor from the fog machine. They had multiple smoke eaters and a vaulted ceiling, so there was only a slight lingering of cigarette smoke. She smoked, but she didn't want to bathe in it. Most times, she took her smoke breaks on the outdoor terrace running along the side of the building on the second floor.

Tangled had a Victorian goth meets industrial steel feel to it—dark and easy for her to lose herself deep within the beat of the music, drinks and the movement of the bodies around her. Perfect.

Maiya walked around the edge of the large oval dance floor toward the back bar with a smile. She was glad she'd come. Being in the club was better than sitting home waiting for her phone to ring. A few friends nodded their greetings. Among them, a former bedmate or two. Maybe she'd take one home tonight. Maiya groaned. The idea soured before she could fully consider it. And Ryan was the reason.

Ryan wasn't her man, and he sure as hell hadn't made any claim on her. Glancing around the crowd, she sighed. Maiya was free to do as she pleased. So why did the thought of letting another man touch her make her want to hurk up her dinner? Brushing off the feeling, Maiya tossed Eric, the head bartender, her credit card.

Eric propped his elbows on the bar top. "How ya doin', sexy?"

"I'm fucking fabulous. Vodka cranberry?" Stretching over the bar top, she gave him a peck on the cheek.

"Coming right up. Heather's here. She said tell you she'd be right back."

Maiya smiled. "Fucking fabulous."

He laughed and slid the drink her way. "Here you go. This one's on me."

"Triple fucking fabulous." She sipped the cocktail through the straw. "Everything will be fucking fabulous tonight because I deem it so."

"Anything you say, Maiya." He shook his head. "Crazy girl. Lookin' hot tonight."

She tipped her hat. "Fabulous, I'm looking fucking fabulous, Eric."

"That too, sexy. That too."

She faced the dance floor and waited for Heather to come back from wherever she'd gone off to. Type O Negative's cover of "Cinnamon Girl" came on, and Maiya set her drink on the bar. "Eric, I'm dancing. Tell Heather, yeah?"

He gave her a nod, and she walked to the dance floor. A minute later, Heather was next to her. Maiya pulled the brim of her hat low and got down to business. Moving in time with Peter Steele's deep voice, she let her stress fly free. The tension in her shoulders eased a bit. She loved to dance, and she needed to lose herself for a little while. The fog blasted from overhead and the corners of the floor. White mist rolled between the crowds, creating the illusion of separation.

And then she was lost to the music.

CHAPTER TWENTY-ONE

Ryan walked up the jetway with his duffel bag in hand and navigated around a group, taking pictures when they reached the terminal. "Where are we going to stay?"

"Dunno yet, we can figure it out later. Maybe we can pick up a couple of chickies like back in the day and crash with them?" Jimmy ran his fingers through his mop of hair.

Ryan raised his brows. "Wow. Classy."

"Relax, Momma's Boy. I'll get us a room somewhere close to the club."

"Fuck off. You're one to talk."

Jimmy blew a breath on his knuckles and shined them on his chest. "I don't deny it."

"Anywayyyy. Where's this club we're going to?"

"It's not on The Strip. Which makes it badass." Jimmy flashed him his Cheshire cat grin.

"That smirk is what has me worried." Ryan stopped before they got on the escalator. "Should I be worried?"

"Nah, it's all good, bro. You'll love this place. All kinds of people hang there." Jimmy clapped him on the shoulder and walked past him onto the escalator.

Ryan paused, knowing full well he *should* be worried. Guaranteed, tonight would be wild and crazy and full of Jimmy-induced fun. Should he even call Maiya and let her know he was in town? He wasn't sure if he wanted Jimmy near her, though. The two would probably hit it off big time. *Hey, Maiya, this is my brother. I know he's your type, but could you please not want him?* Jealousy poked his insides like a pin.

"Come on," Jimmy yelled from halfway down the escalator, snapping Ryan from his thoughts.

Damn, he'd never been jealous of his brother. They'd never had the same taste in women, still didn't. Ryan cringed. But Maiya was every bit Jimmy's type. Shoving the thoughts aside, he stepped onto the escalator. Pulling his phone from his pocket, he checked it for missed calls. A razor of disappointment sliced through him. She wasn't going to call him, and man, that just sucked.

After a quick check-in at a hotel, they headed to the club. Ryan got out of the taxi and took in the mammoth white-brick building. "You sure I'm dressed okay for this place?"

"Yeah. Stop worrying, will you?" Jimmy paid the cabby. "When did you become this much of a pansy ass?"

Ryan crossed his arms. "Oh, now, that was harsh. Take that shit back, or I'll tell the first girl that talks to you that you used to wet the bed."

"You wouldn't."

"The hell I won't." Ryan laughed.

Jimmy threw his arm over Ryan's shoulder. "I am totally getting your uptight ass drunk tonight."

Ryan looked at the towering neon sign. "Tangled, huh?"

"The one and only. This place speaks my language."

"James Donnelly." The bouncer smiled when they reached the entrance. "To what do we owe the pleasure this fine Vegas night?"

Jimmy shook the bouncer's hand. "Jay, my man, nice to see you. Just flew in from L.A. Brought my brother along to party for the night. Ryan, this is Jay. Good man. Makes sure this club stays clean."

Ryan looked up to meet Jay's gaze when he shook the big man's hand. He was colossal in size. "Nice to meet you."

"Go on in. I'll let Gino know to get you a table upstairs in the corner."

"Right on. Thanks, Jay." Jimmy walked past the bouncer, and Ryan followed, thanking the bouncer too.

They made it halfway through the entrance corridor before Ryan stopped and realized he was staring at his brother's artwork. "You sold work to them?" He turned in a circle, taking in the walls. "That's awesome."

"Yeah, no biggie, though. It was a couple years ago when they opened. I told you about it at the time, but you were a little busy then."

"Shit. I guess so. Sorry, man." Ryan shook his head. Jimmy would never get used to the fact his art had gotten so popular. His brother was humble and immensely talented, and Ryan was so damn proud of him it made his chest ache.

His brother squeezed his shoulder. "It's cool. I know you love me. Come on, you can make it up to me by buying me a drink."

"Absofuckinglutely." Ryan laughed, remembering Maiya using the same word on him.

Another bouncer, probably Gino, met them when they entered the main area. He bent and said something to Jimmy Ryan couldn't hear, and then they were traveling up a curving wrought iron staircase to a loft that circled the perimeter of the club. They moved to a stout table nestled between two plush chairs in the back corner and took a seat. A moment later, a waitress came over and took their drink order. Ryan handed her his credit card. "This place is off the hook."

"No shit, right? I love it. Check out the crowd on the dance floor."

Ryan walked to the railing. A blast of fog shot from the

ceiling into the center of the floor, and the crowd went nuts. The DJ queued up Drowning Pool's "Bodies" and a mosh pit formed in the center of the floor. Ryan threw his head back and laughed.

Joining him at the railing, Jimmy handed him his Jameson on the rocks. Ryan bent to his ear. "Makes you want to go down there and get in it, huh?"

"Hell yeah!" Jimmy took a gulp of Guinness.

Next on deck was Saliva's "Click Click Boom". The mosh pit continued, arms flying while guys—and girls—moved in and out, and around the center—the outer fence of people doing their job, keeping everyone in the pit. The song changed, and Rage Against the Machine's "Killing in the Name" blared through the speakers. Ryan was in awe, listening to the boiling cauldron of metal and rap power echoing through the club.

The crowd shifted, and the outer circle widened. His eye caught a tattooed girl on the edge, pushing guys twice her size back into the fray. In between shoves, she danced... and was magnificent. Kind of reminded him of Maiya.

The girl tilted her head back and laughed at something the chick next to her said, and at the same time, a bit of the fog cleared. Ryan tightened his grip on the railing. Holy shit, it *was* Maiya.

Rammstein's "Du Hast" blared from the speakers, and Ryan watched her—he watched every move she made. Pulling the brim of her hat lower, Maiya danced. Her body moving in time with the hard industrial metal beat.

Like a badass, she shoved with her hands and elbows, keeping the rowdy ones who broke the circle within the pit. Her display was downright sexy and made his dick so hard he wanted to scream.

The mosh pit broke up, and Maiya walked off the floor toward the back of the bar.

He watched until he couldn't see her anymore. "Be right back, bro." Ryan left his drink and made his way down the stairs, heading in the direction she'd gone. He spotted her talking to the same dark-haired chick she'd been next to on the floor. Not wanting her to see him yet, Ryan stayed behind one of the large pillars, ensuring he had a clear view of her, and then sent her a text.

> Ryan: Hey, bummed I haven't heard from you. You still up?

Then he waited.

Maiya pulled her phone from her back pocket and read the text, but then lowered her hand. She wasn't going to respond? *You* have got *to be kidding me.* Disappointment settled hard in his chest. Thirty seconds later, she stepped away from her friend and started typing on the screen. Relief washed through him, and he exhaled a harsh breath.

> Maiya: Hey, sorry. One of my friends dragged me out. Why aren't you sleeping?

> Ryan: My brother came into town and he dragged me out too.

> Maiya: That's cool. Where'd you two go?

Typing the next message, he walked up behind her and hit Send.

> Ryan: We're at a club called Tangled in Vegas...

Ryan waited a bare second, then wrapped his arms around her waist from behind and bent to her ear. "Where are you?"

She jumped and turned her head with a glare harsh enough to scare a mercenary. "Holy fucking shit, Ryan. You scared me." She blew out a breath and then spun inside his embrace to face him, wearing a far different expression now. "You coulda got punched, you know?" She laughed.

"Believe me, I braced for it." He tugged on the brim of her hat. "Not to sound creepy, but I was watching you on the dance floor. I think you might have one hell of a right hook in you."

"You were watching me?" She raised her brows. "And you didn't go running in the other direction?"

"Why on earth would I run from you?" He snugged her tighter against him. "I think I'd much rather be up close and personal." He kissed her then, a soft stroke of his lips over hers.

Yes, Jimmy was a genius. Vegas had been exactly what he needed.

HOLY MOTHER OF GOD AND ALL THE SAINTS, RYAN, WAS there. And not only was he there, he was standing in front of her. She was in his arms. And he'd just kissed her.

In spite of what he'd said, Maiya couldn't imagine what he must've been thinking when he saw her on the dance floor. She'd been going all out, venting her tension, but Maiya never expected to run into anyone from work… especially Ryan. She stared into his crystal eyes. "How long were you watching me?"

"Since they played Drowning Pool." He caressed her back with one hand, and she shivered.

"That's a really long time, like four songs long time." Circling her arms around his neck, she pulled him down for another kiss.

"I know. Couldn't keep my eyes off you." He nipped her bottom lip. "Made me hard."

Maiya gasped and gripped his hair between her fingers. "Are you still hard?"

He pulled her closer, pressing his groin to hers. "You tell me."

The solid ridge of his erection sent a thrill zipping through her from head to toe. "Damn. I guess so, huh? I want!"

Yeah, she'd definitely had a few too many drinks because in an instant, all the fears about whether Ryan did or did not want her, or if letting him touch her again was the right thing to do, went "see ya later, bye-bye". Maiya was buzzing hard, and the only man who'd ever made her come like lightning struck her body had his arms around her.

With a hard-on.

Just for her.

Mmm!

"You want?" His lips slanted into a devilish grin. "Have you been a good girl, Maiya?"

She loved when he went all dominant male on her. She couldn't help it. The man reduced her to an enormous puddle of boiling hormones. She wanted to rub herself up and down his body like a cat in heat. Hell, *her* cat wasn't just in heat, the damn thing was on fire for him. "That depends."

"Oh? On what?" He nuzzled her neck.

She tilted her head to the side and rolled her hips forward. "On the reward or the punishment."

Ryan muttered a curse and bit her neck. "I guess you'll have to take your chances."

"Then I've been both." She giggled.

He gripped her ass. "I fucking love the sound of your laugh." He pulled away and gazed at her, his eyes alive with delight.

For a moment, she imagined herself as the woman he

perceived. She was sure he saw her much different than she saw herself. With shaking fingers, she traced his lips.

Ryan bit her fingertip and then brushed the tip of his nose over hers. "Come dance with me."

Shaggy's "Boombastic" played through the sound system, and Ryan led her to the center of the floor. The dance floor thumped like a heartbeat, the whole crowd moving in time with the music. As the heavy bass of the music vibrated in her chest, Maiya discovered another talent Ryan had— the man could dance.

He snugged up behind her, one hand on her hip, pulling her ass tight to his groin and rocked his hips in time with the song. Bending at the waist, she kept her ass against his pelvis and moved in unison with him. Wanting to see his face, Maiya stepped away and spun around to face him. Fog drifted around them, and he jerked his chin at her, urging her closer.

The expression in his eyes—part predator, part prey— gave her a new definition for the word sexy, and lust zipped through her. Maiya raised her hands over her head and moved closer, pressing her body against his, then slid one leg between his thighs. Ryan framed her sides with his arms, and they shifted from side to side.

They were matched, in perfect time with each other. She shouldn't have been surprised; the man rocked her world in bed, why wouldn't he be able to rock the dance floor? So many sides to Ryan Donnelly. What else would she find if given enough time with him?

She'd had her doubts and suspicions before meeting him in person, but after this past week, she knew for sure—he wasn't the vanilla preppy boy she'd mistaken him for. He was a bright businessman and a soft, loving father. He was romantic, and he was a smartass. As if that wasn't enough, adding to the prize, he was dominant as hell in bed. The man was turning out to be a match for her in more ways than she ever dared to imagine.

Ginuwine's "Pony" came on, and she popped her shoulders. "I love this song."

"Me too." He spun her and pulled her back against his chest again.

She glanced at him over her shoulder and ground her ass against him. His warm breath brushed her ear, and he slapped her thigh. The sting through the denim made her shiver all over. Leaning forward, she rolled her hips, sliding her ass over the bulge in his jeans.

He yanked her back up. "Don't think you won't get punished later for teasing me like this."

She turned to face him. "You love it."

"That—" he bent his head and ran his tongue up the side of her neck, "—is beside the point."

Another blast of vapor blew around them, making the dance floor a haze of blurry bodies. But she could still see Ryan. All she wanted to see was him. Ryan pressed his thigh between her legs and urged her hips forward. She rocked her pelvis, rubbing her clit against his leg. With each sway of their bodies, she ground against his thigh, and her clit pulsed.

The whole scene felt like something out of a wet dream. The music, the smell of sweat and booze, and the way she rode his leg to the beat. Ryan was building her up, and she let him. There had been a few times she swore the managers of the club were drugging the crowd with a liquid form of ecstasy via the fog machines, but it'd always been a joke. She felt drugged now, though. So much so she wanted to find a dark corner and beg him to fuck her against the wall.

Ryan ran the flat of his hand up her arm and then cupped her face. "That's it, baby. Getting hot for me?"

She gazed into his eyes. He slid his palm down to her throat, circling his fingers around her neck and rubbed the front of her throat with his thumb. Her eyes widened, chills racing through her body. Forward and back, forward and back, she rode his leg. It was delicious.

A muscle twitched in his clenched jaw, and he squeezed her throat ever so slightly. Then he kissed her. Wet, hot and wild. His tongue moved into her mouth, and she chased it, sucking and tangling hers with it. And her heart cracked open. It was too much... He was larger than life, everything she needed and never knew she wanted. Maiya couldn't stop her feelings now if she tried.

This was going to hurt like hell.

CHAPTER TWENTY-TWO

RYAN DROWNED IN HER. HER BODY, HER TASTE, HER SMELL. He wanted to sink into the depths of Maiya and stay there for as many hours as he could sta—

Abruptly, she pulled away from his kiss and then stepped from his embrace, her gaze darting away.

"You okay, baby?"

"Yeah, I just need some air." She fanned herself. "There's a patio upstairs."

"Done." He grabbed her hand, leading her off the dance floor toward the stairs. He had her go in front of him, in part so she could lead the way to the patio, but mostly to keep an eye on her. She looked a little pale.

When they reached the second floor, she turned in the opposite direction from where he'd been with Jimmy and led him to an exit he hadn't noticed before. She pushed through a set of glass-and-wrought-iron doors and stepped onto a huge, covered veranda running along the side of the building. The cool air hit him like a blast, but he shook it off and followed her to a small plastic table and chairs in the farthest corner.

The patio had about twenty or so patrons milling about and a small bar in the middle to keep the spirits flowing.

Similar to balconies in New Orleans, decorative wrought-iron railings spanned the edge of the patio and rose from each support post to join the roofline, forming arches between each one. "I'll get us a couple of waters." His phone buzzed in his pocket as he paid the attendant. Ignoring it for the moment, he returned to the table and handed Maiya a water bottle.

"Thanks." She cracked the lid and took a long drink.

"Any time, baby."

He palmed his phone and checked the message. It was Jimmy, wondering where he was. He'd been gone longer than he thought; it only seemed like one or two songs, but must've been more. Sending off a reply, he let his brother know they were on the patio upstairs.

Ryan got a single word back from him: *We're?*

Maiya was about to meet his brother. No way to avoid it now. He ran his hand through his hair. She was going to dig his brother. A lot. "My brother's on his way up."

Maiya lit a cigarette. "Oh yeah? Cool. Wonder where Heather is."

"Heather?"

"Yeah, my friend that dragged me out tonight. She's most likely shaking her ass on the dance floor." She blew out a breath. "Sorry, I think the heat got to me."

He reached for her hand. "It's all good. Feeling better?"

"Yes." She leaned in for a kiss, and he met her lips across the table.

"Hey, Ry."

Ryan straightened in his seat. "Hey, bro. Sorry, I ran into a friend."

Jimmy smiled at Maiya. "I see that."

Damn his brother and his panty-dropping grin. Ryan cleared his throat. "Maiya Rossini, this is my brother, Jimmy."

"James," Jimmy corrected.

"Nice to meet you." Maiya accepted Jimmy's hand. Jimmy kissed her knuckles. "Pleasure's all mine."

Maiya giggled. Ryan rolled his eyes and cleared his throat. His brother was always a killer with the ladies.

"You okay, Ry?" Jimmy asked.

Ryan took a swig off his water bottle. "I'm good."

"There you are," a woman said from behind Jimmy.

Jimmy turned and stepped to the side.

"Thank God you found me. I had no idea where I was." Maiya made a face of mock relief and then smiled.

"Bitch. One minute you were there, the next you were gone-baby-gone." The girl laughed. "Hey, what's up? I'm Heather," she said to both him and Jimmy.

"Oh, sorry. Ryan and James Donnelly, this is Heather Walsh."

They did the all-around handshake exchange and head nod.

"I'm starving." Heather stretched her arms over her head. "You want to get something to eat?" She was looking at Maiya.

"I guess." Maiya motioned to Ryan. "You two want to come with?"

Ryan shrugged and looked at his brother. "You ready to get out of here?"

Jimmy hesitated a second. "Yeah, I'm game. There's an all-night diner a couple miles from here."

"We'd love to. Let's go." Ryan stood and grabbed Maiya's hand.

When they got downstairs, Jimmy stopped and stared at the dance floor, then turned in the direction of the front bar. "Gimme a sec," Jimmy said and stepped away from them.

"What're we doing?" Maiya asked.

"Don't know." He turned to her. "Jimmy said he needed a second. Maybe he's tabbing us out."

"Shit. I almost forgot that myself." She tugged his hand and walked in the direction of the back bar.

Ryan glanced over and saw Jimmy talking to a woman.

"Hey, wait, I think mine's at the front bar. You go do yours and meet me back here." He kissed Maiya's cheek and sent her off with a pat on her ass. She smiled back at him as she walked away, tugging her friend with her. Heather glanced over her shoulder at him.

She was a petite and pretty brunette with a shapely body, a pierced nose and tattoo work on both arms. Maybe she'd be a good distraction for Jimmy. At least he hoped so. Ryan turned and scanned the area in front of the bar, looking for his brother again.

He was still talking to that woman. Ryan walked over in their direction. As he neared them, he was awestruck by her stunning features: tiny, pert nose, bright blue eyes and pouty, full lips. Her blonde hair was up in one of those twists women somehow managed to get to stay in place on the back of their heads. He tapped Jimmy's shoulder. "Hey."

His brother turned. "Hey, Ryan, what's up?"

"Did you tab us out?"

"Ah shit, no. You mind grabbing it?"

"No problem." He eyed the woman behind his brother.

Jimmy cleared his throat and stepped to the side. "Ryan, this is Sonja Martin. She's in town for business."

"Nice to meet you." She smiled and shook his hand.

No wonder his brother was talking to her. There was definitely something intriguing about the woman. It took Ryan a second, but he managed to get his mouth moving. "Nice to meet you, too." Letting go of her hand, he excused himself to take care of the bill.

She was gorgeous and not Jimmy's type. At all. Not that his brother didn't date beautiful women, he did, but this woman was a straight-up high-class businesswoman. Jimmy dated women like, well, like Heather and his Maiya— Wait, when the hell did he start referring to Maiya as his? Ryan shook his head and let the question hang in his peripherals while he took care of their bar tab.

A set of arms wrapped around his waist from behind. *Maiya.* His pulse quickened, and he covered her arms with his, glancing over his shoulder at her. "All set?"

"Mmhmm." She kissed his cheek. "I'm glad you're here."

"Me too." He turned, circled his arms around her waist and then kissed her soft lips.

Heather made an inelegant scoffing noise. "Okay, love-birds. Let's go, I'm starving. Where's your brother?"

Ryan looked over to where Jimmy had been. "He's talking to some gorgeous woman who's completely not his type."

"Gorgeous, huh?" Maiya stepped from his embrace.

He motioned with his head. "Check her out. The blonde at the table."

"Ah. Yeah, she's very pretty. Now that you mention it, she seems more your type."

"Yeah, I guess." He shrugged and turned to look at Maiya, but she was gone. She'd started walking away toward the door.

"Way to go, asshole." Heather walked past him, shooting him a nasty glare, and followed Maiya.

Way to go is right.

MAIYA WALKED TO THE CAR AS FAST AS HER LEGS COULD carry her.

Time. To. Go.

Heather called her name, but she didn't stop to wait for her. Nope. It was time to go.

She was well aware she wasn't Ryan's type. There was no need for him to rub it in. Asshole. Out of all the clubs in Vegas, and he shows up in the same one she's at? He should be on The Strip, like the rest of the yuppies.

By the time she reached the car, her face was wet. *Dammit, don't cry.* She swiped her hands over her cheeks and then bent to fish the key fob from her boot.

A hand rested on her back. "I'm fine, Heather." She straightened.

"I didn't mean it how it sounded."

Maiya froze at the sound of Ryan's voice and then turned to face him. "It doesn't matter." *It matters.* A lot.

"It sure looks to me like it matters."

Maiya dropped her head and bit her lip. "No. It's fine. It's true, though. I'm not your type." She glanced up and noticed Heather off in the distance. He must have asked her to give them some privacy, and Heather looked pissed about it.

Ryan grabbed her by the loops of her jeans and pulled her close. She went reluctantly, but did go.

"I'm not yours, either."

The overhead lights in the lot cast shadows over his face and made his eyes appear much darker than the clear blue-gray she was used to. "I know." She lowered her voice. "Doesn't mean I want to be reminded of it. No one likes to hear they don't measure up, you know?" Her voice hitched, and she dropped her head again.

"Is that what you think, Maiya?" He placed his finger under her chin, raising her head, and she closed her eyes. "Tell me."

"What is this?" She glanced around at the sea of parked cars and then back to him. "What are we doing, Ryan?"

He paused, opened his mouth and then shut it again. She had no idea what they were doing, and it was obvious he didn't either. *Fucking fabulous.*

Ryan frowned, a look of confusion on his face. "What do you want it to be?"

She stepped back and put her hands on her hips. "Oh no. Nope. You're not going to set me up. I'm not going to go all vulnerable and lay myself bare for you. Whatever this is—"

she motioned her hand between them, "—if *it's* even anything at all, will be defined by both of us."

He flashed his "I'm going to eat you up" smile. The one he used to let her know she was about to be dinner. *Fat chance, buddy!* She crossed her arms. "What are you smiling at?"

"You."

"You're a pain in my ass, you know that?" She pulled her hat off, ran her fingers through her hair and then rushed to put it back on. She was feeling exposed enough; she didn't need her hat-head on display, too.

He pulled her close again, but this time wrapped his arms around her. "I love the way you fight with me." He dipped his head to kiss her.

She dodged it. "You think you can just kiss me now? You better earn these lips, buddy." Okay, maybe his fat chance had graduated to a slim one.

"Earn them? Now wait a minu—"

"Hey, can we go eat? I'm still starving, you know!" Heather yelled.

Maiya craned her neck to the side and looked at her friend. "How could I forget? Are you meeting us there or riding with me?"

"I'll meet you there. Don't want to get towed. Again." Heather laughed and walked toward her car.

"No shit!"

"I want to ride with you." Ryan nuzzled her neck. "Can I ride with you?"

She cursed and slapped his shoulder. He nibbled her ear. "You forgive me?"

"The jury's still out. I'll tell you after breakfast." Those little caresses of his had her blood pumping.

"Sweet, you're letting me spend the night?" He pulled away, his eyes wide and a freaking adorable smile on his face. He looked like a kid who just got his favorite toy on his birthday.

"No. I meant after we get done eating breakfast *at* the diner."

"Too late." He backed away from her. "Get the car and meet me out front. I'll go drag my brother away from some blonde."

"Fine. You're still a pain in my ass, though."

Pulling onto the street, Maiya waited in front by the curb for Ryan and James to come out. It took a few minutes, plus one explicit text message where she threatened to torture specific body parts before they exited the club.

James climbed in her tiny back seat, and Ryan took the front. He shut the door. "Nice car, baby."

"I know." She took off into traffic. Pedal to the floor. "And no, you can't drive it."

"Guess she told you, bro." His brother leaned forward and stuck his head between the two front seats. "Did you see that woman? Man, she's beautiful."

"Yeah, who was she?" Ryan fiddled with the buttons on the navigation system.

"Sonja-the-lawyer. I just met her." James sat back in his seat and let out a sigh. "She's a criminal defense attorney. Fucking hot, huh?"

"Which part?" Maiya eyed him in the rearview. "The way she looks or the lawyer part?"

"Both." James leaned forward again. "I think she's the girl of my dreams."

"That's a woman, Jimmy. Not a girl." Ryan looked over his shoulder at his brother. "She's also out of your league."

"Fuck you, bro. I'm gonna marry her, you watch."

"I bet he does." Maiya swatted Ryan's hand away from the dash. "Good luck, James." She caught his gaze in the rearview.

"You can call me Jimmy."

"That's very sweet of you, Jimmy. I will, thanks."

"Are you flirting with my brother?" Ryan poked her thigh.

"What?" She glanced at him and then focused back on the road. "Why would I flirt with your brother?"

He leaned close to her. "Because he is your type, you know?" The low tone of his voice washed through her.

"Maybe I'm in the mood for something different."

Ryan ran his hand up her thigh and slid it between her legs, cupping her sex. Her insides went tight, and she released a slow, measured breath. *Easy, girl, focus on the road.*

He kissed her cheek. "Me too."

Maiya pulled into the diner parking lot. Heather was probably beyond pissed at them, but knowing her, she'd already ordered food. She owed Maiya anyway; she'd just knock this one off Heather's long list. Once inside, they piled into the booth with her friend.

Heather grunted at them and sipped her coffee. Not ten minutes later, Jimmy had her laughing. Maiya was surprised it'd taken that long. After they'd stuffed themselves full of pancakes and eggs, Maiya yawned, and Ryan glided his hand between her crossed legs.

Gripping her thigh, he pressed the edge of his pinky finger against her denim-covered clit. Sweet baby J, this man enjoyed tormenting her. She watched as he traced his tongue along the seam of his lips, and she coughed, stifling the whimper erupting from her mouth.

Ryan moved his hand to her back and rubbed it. "You okay?"

"Fine. Thank you." She cleared her throat. "Had a little tickle in my throat."

Heather was too focused on Ryan's brother to notice.

Jimmy hadn't, either. Ryan smiled, wrapped his arm around her waist and slid her closer and then settled his hand between her thighs again. She squeezed them together and let a grin slant one side of her mouth.

He bent to her ear. "You're getting wet, aren't you?" He nipped the tender skin of her neck.

"Mmhmm." Swallowing hard, Maiya gripped her coffee cup between both hands and turned her head toward the window, trying to focus on something other than the intense pressure against her clit. Her body responded like a dragster off the starting line. The tiny bundle of nerves pulsed, sending little waves of pleasure through her.

"I can feel how hot you are." His warm breath brushed over her ear before he licked the lobe.

She shivered and grabbed his wrist, digging her nails in. He chuckled. Maiya glanced across the table, and Heather was whispering in Jimmy's ear. Laughter erupted from one of the other tables. This was getting interesting. The diner had filled with the late nightclub crowd, and the noise level echoed like white noise in her ears. Waiters and waitresses buzzed from table to table, coffee pots or trays filled with food in hand.

And Maiya sat there with Ryan's hand between her legs, shifting her pelvis ever so slightly while he kept pressure against her clit. She was going to come. Shaking her head, she looked at him, pleading with her eyes to take her home and fuck her. Now.

She gasped and dropped her head when he stroked his hand up and down once, then twice. Maiya was about to lose control. Crossing her legs, she squeezed her thighs together. "Now."

Ryan gave her the barest of nods and then signaled the waitress for the check.

CHAPTER TWENTY-THREE

Ryan chuckled at Maiya's whispered demand. He couldn't figure out what it was in particular about her that had him walking around like an eighteen-year-old boy in heat. All he had to do was think about her, and his prick got stone hard. Pussy whipped. That's what Jimmy would say. He'd probably be right. Maiya had a cunt that gripped him like a fist and a mouth that made his toes curl. Being pussy whipped was fine, as long as it was her doing the whipping. "You 'bout ready to get out of here?" Ryan directed his question to the whole group.

Jimmy and Heather appeared rather comfy, and relief flowed through him. Good. His brother would be leaving Maiya alone, but he was pretty sure Jimmy already figured out she was Ryan's.

Damn. Again, with the *his*. Apparently, his heart had already made up its mind and started sending "you've got feelings for her" messages to Ryan's brain. His brain kept trying to convince his heart this was simple lust and things should stay this way; there was Jacob to consider.

But he liked her. A lot. He liked their conversations. He liked their banter. He even liked her passionate bitch temper.

"I'm gonna catch a ride with Heather back to the hotel. You planning on meeting me there?" Jimmy pulled his wallet from his back pocket.

Ryan looked at Maiya. "I don't know. Maiya, am I meeting him there later?" She smiled at him but said nothing. "Tell you what." He glanced at his brother again. "I'll shoot you a text if I am heading your way, cool?"

"I'll leave my phone on." Jimmy tossed thirty bucks on the table and got up, pulling Heather with him. The chick wore a grin from ear to ear. So much for Sonja-the-lawyer.

"Talk to you later, Heather," Maiya said.

"Count on it," Heather called over her shoulder as she walked, or was being tugged rather, behind his brother. The man made picking up women an art form.

Ryan tossed another twenty on top of the bill and stood. "Ready, baby?"

"I like it when you call me that."

"Yeah?" Helping her to her feet, he pulled her close and kissed her cheek. "Good, because I like calling you that."

They made their way to her black Infiniti G37 coupe. The woman had taste. Maiya was a professional businesswoman by day and a kick-ass tattooed chick who rocked the hell out of a mosh pit by night. Those were just two sides of her; there were so many more. He just knew it. Ryan wanted to get to know all of them. Even the one that made her close herself off to him in a split second.

The car chirped, the locks clicked open, and she tossed him the keys. Surprised, he caught them. "You're seriously going to let me drive your sexy car?"

"I trust you. Even if you do drive a Porsche." She got in the passenger seat.

He stared at the empty spot she'd occupied a second ago and guffawed. Damn, she made him laugh! Another plus on the growing list of reasons why he needed to see more of her.

The drive to her house was both too fast and far too long.

Maiya spent the entire trip leaning over the center console, stroking and touching him. She kissed and nipped at his neck, ran her hand up and down his thigh, teasing and then grazed the bulge in his jeans with her nails.

Ryan kept a tight grip on the steering wheel with one hand. With the other, he held the back of her head and neck when he wasn't shifting gears. He was damn grateful the nav system was already programmed to direct him to her house.

Maiya had a modern two-story Tuscan-style home. It was cookie-cutter track housing, but she'd painted her exterior a deep burgundy compared to the other bland beige colors in the neighborhood.

When he pulled into her garage, and the door was closing, she crawled across the console and straddled his lap.

"Hey, baby." He gazed up at her.

She kissed him and moaned, tangling her tongue with his. Her firm breasts pressed hard against his chest. Damn, the car was tight quarters, and so was the space inside his jeans. Somehow, he managed to get the door open and them out of the car with her still wrapped around him.

Maiya circled his waist with her long legs. He hoisted her higher and walked into the house. Reaching over, she deactivated the alarm system, switched on a light and then kissed him again.

MAIYA HAD GIVEN IN TO WHAT HER BODY SCREAMED FOR. It was ridiculous to fight it. He pissed her off daily but always made her laugh too. And then he made her body hum and crave his touch. She was thoroughly and irrevocably screwed. "Go to the left, then up the stairs."

Ryan set her down at the bottom of the steps. "Trying to kill me, woman?" He swatted her behind and turned her to face the stairs.

"What? You sayin' I'm fat?" She peered over her shoulder at him and raised a brow.

"You know damn good and well you're not fat." Cupping her breasts, he massaged them. "Now, run. The sooner you get your hot ass up the stairs, the sooner you can wrap your legs around me again. This time, naked."

She started up the stairs, navigating each step slowly. "You love telling me what to do, don't you?"

Ryan stayed a step behind her. "Only as much as you love me telling you what to do." He grabbed her ass and then swatted it again.

Maiya squealed and ran up the rest of the stairs. She couldn't get up to her bedroom fast enough, pulling off her tank top before she stepped through the door. The hat went with it. Hat head be damned, she was going to get fucked good and proper. Again. Two days in a row. Hot damn! Moving to the nightstand, Maiya turned on the small lamp.

Ryan entered the room and closed them in. He stood motionless, staring at her, with his back to the door, an impassive expression on his face. But the heat in his gaze penetrated straight to her insides. "Take off your bra."

A shiver tickled her spine. Reaching behind her back, she unhooked it. Anticipation sped through her veins, and she let the bra fall to the floor next to her.

Ryan took off his shirt. "Now the pants."

Nodding, Maiya tugged the button of her jeans open and slid the zipper down. She watched his eyes, then let her gaze roam down his body. He had such a gorgeous chest. A slight bit of hair, a little darker than what was on his head, covered his pecs and then arrowed down the center of his tight abs. He was muscled without being bulky; more sleek swimmer than bodybuilder. Ryan's stomach muscles bunched and flexed when he grabbed his belt and tugged the buckle free. Bending forward with her breasts exposed for him, Maiya kept her gaze locked on his abs and then the fly of his jeans. The bulge of his erection behind the denim made her mouth water, and her cunt clenched in anticipation of him filling her. She removed her boots and then took off her jeans.

"Christ, you have amazing tits." He slid off his shoes and unzipped his pants.

Nervous energy vibrated through her, quickening her breath. "I'm glad you like them."

"You better lose the panties, or I'm going to rip them off you." Ryan walked forward, the top button and zipper open on his pants.

The pale green waistband of his boxer briefs was visible, and the crown of his cock peeked out from the top, tempting her. Maiya licked her lips, and her stomach flip-flopped. He looked like a predator stalking his prey.

Stepping back while he approached, Maiya stopped when the back of her bare legs met the bed. *Oh God.* Her stomach somersaulted again, and she clenched her fists at her sides, unable to meet his gaze now. She focused instead on the steady pulse on the side of his neck and melted under the soft caress of his palm down her arm.

Ryan settled his hand on her waist, stroked her side with his thumb, and then grabbed the thin strap of her thong panties and tugged, snapping it.

Her breath caught. "Hey! I liked those." She gazed at him and tried not to giggle.

"I told you to take them off." He urged her onto the bed. "I'll buy you a new pair." Leaning forward, he sucked one nipple into his mouth and tore the remaining strap of her panties.

Maiya buried her fingers in his hair. "Well, in that case—" She gasped when he tugged on her nipple with his teeth, and little electric stings blasted through it.

He pulled what was left of her panties off and stroked his fingers through her slick folds. "So wet for me."

Her hips shot up off the bed, and she ground her teeth

together. Moving to the other nipple, he took it between his teeth.

"Fuuuuck." She gripped his hair tighter, and he growled against her skin.

Ryan moved his hands to her sides and pulled away from her breast, a tender look in his eyes. And she melted. In one quick motion, he picked her up and tossed her back onto the pillows. A squeal of giggles erupted from her, and she landed in the softness of her comforter.

A self-satisfied grin spread across his lips. He pushed his pants and boxer briefs off and then climbed onto the bed between her legs. "There's that sound I like so much."

Maiya loved the weight of his body on top of her. She looped her arms under his and caressed his back. Raising her head, she placed gentle kisses along his jaw, his chin and then his edible lips. A sudden, frantic need to touch and taste— drink all of him in, as if she were dying of thirst— possessed her entire being.

Ryan rested his upper body weight on his forearms, cradling her within them. He buried his fingers in her hair and pressed his hard length right against her core. His lips parted on a gasp.

Maiya caressed his bottom lip with her tongue and sucked it gently. Releasing it, she flicked her tongue over his top lip and then slanted her mouth over his. Breathing fast and hard, he gripped her hair tighter in his fists while their tongues danced and tumbled together. Pulling his mouth from hers, Ryan tilted her head back and ran his lips down her throat.

She arched and undulated her body, rolling her hips forward. The length of his prick dragged over her clit and through her wetness, and she gasped. Thrusting forward again, he bit her neck.

"Baby." She sucked in a breath. "Condom…drawer. Oh God. Ryan."

"Patience." Ryan pushed back onto his haunches between

her legs and dragged his hands down her shoulders to her breasts and squeezed them together. Bending forward, he licked up the center of her cleavage and pinched her nipples between his fingertips.

A loud curse tore from Maiya, and she tossed her head from side to side on the pillow. She loved the little sting of pain he caused when he pinched or bit her nipples. When his hot tongue touched her sweat-slick skin, goose bumps broke out along her limbs. It was a tidal wave of sensations, crashing into one another, then re-building, causing her body to tense and the lips of her cunt to soften and swell at the same time.

Ryan let go of her breasts and moved one hand to her throat, cuffing it loosely between his fingers and thumb. He ran his other hand down her body, cupped her mound and drove two fingers deep inside her core.

A guttural cry came from the center of Maiya's chest, and she bucked her hips off the mattress. She was on the verge of orgasm. In the space of a heartbeat, he'd driven her there. Body and mind running headlong toward the finish line.

With his fingers buried deep inside her, he gripped her mound hard, compressing her clit beneath his palm. "Mine," he said through clenched teeth and increased the constriction on her throat. "Say it."

"Oh my God." The pressure on her throat was intense, though she could definitely still breathe. The sheer excitement of the damage he could do kicked her heart rate even higher. But she knew he wouldn't hurt her. He hadn't, and he wouldn't.

RYAN WANTED—NO, *NEEDED*—MAIYA TO TELL HIM. HE needed to hear her say her cunt belonged to him and him alone. Hell, if he had any idea why, though. He'd played with and always enjoyed the control thing in bed, leaving it alone if his partner didn't like it.

But with Maiya, God, Maiya made him *crave* that control. More importantly, he wanted her to crave it, too. He wasn't sure where this came from, but he was damn sure, with her, it felt right.

His hard-as-steel prick throbbed while he gazed at her in reverence. With his hand cupping her neck, her head was tilted back, and her red hair was spread out on the pale pillowcase beneath her. She was panting, and her cheeks were flushed—her lips swollen from his kisses. She looked like a fucking goddess. Pulling his fingers free of her tight channel, he sucked them between his lips and then delivered a quick stinging slap to her cunt. "Say. It."

Maiya screamed and gripped his wrist, where he held her neck. "Oh my God!" She bared her teeth. "Fuck. Me. Now. Ryan!"

He delivered another slap, and her hips shot off the bed. "Tell me what I want to hear, Maiya." Caressing and circling the edge of her opening with his fingertips, he spread her slickness up and over her tight clit. She was soaked for him— her juices running down her ass and coating her anus. With trembling legs, she rocked her hips, trying to gain more contact. She was going to come soon, and if he wasn't careful, he was too. Ryan toyed with her, using soft strokes on her tight clit in contrast to the stinging slaps. "You like that, don't you?" He sank his fingers inside her again as deep as he could get them. "You like when I slap your hot cunt?"

"Yes." Maiya thrust her pelvis forward, forcing his fingers in deeper.

"Whose pussy is this, Maiya?' He loosened his grip on her throat.

She grabbed his wrist and held it in place, whimpering in pleasure. Ryan was careful to only apply enough force so she could feel the pressure, but her breathing wasn't constricted.

He'd done it last night at his house and asked her if it was okay. She'd agreed. He loved it, and based on her reaction, she did, too. Need built inside him. He wanted to bury himself deep inside her tight inferno. So sweet, so wet, so... his. "Say it."

She gazed at him through the veil of her lashes and licked her lips. He started to pull his fingers out. A little deprivation would earn her submission.

"Yours!" She gasped. "My pussy is yours."

"Good girl." Ryan leaned forward, tightened his grip on her neck again and kissed her hard on the lips. She sucked his tongue into her mouth. The head of his prick nudged at her opening. Maiya gasped. He pulled away. "Condom, baby?"

"Nightstand." She brushed her hair back from her face. Fishing a condom from the drawer, Ryan tore the package with his teeth and rolled the latex down his shaft. Cupping his heavy balls in his palm, he groaned, then focused on her again. Long legs spread for him, cunt slick and glistening with her juices. The sight was enough to drive a sane man mad.

"I'm going to make you come, then I'm going to put my cock in that hot pussy and make you beg to come again." He slid down the bed and lay between her legs, and then gripped her hip with one hand to keep her still. Ryan spread her labia with his fingers and sucked her clit between his lips. Her flavor hit his tongue, and the head of his cock throbbed.

Raising her legs over his shoulders, she got to her elbows and then went off like a rocket. Her head rolled back, and she moaned deep and long, and her body trembled. At once, he rose from between her legs and pushed her down on the bed. He gripped her thighs and scooted her closer. Tucking the head inside her opening, he paused, ready to drive into her in one thrust.

She was still panting, her walls pulsing around the head of his dick from her orgasm. Ryan gritted his teeth, and his balls tightened. Call him a merciless bastard, but he wanted to be deep inside her snug sheath while it spasmed and clenched in release. And he wanted to see if she'd come again when he drove his thickness inside her.

"*Ppp... Mmm... Please?*" Her voice was thick with need.

Covering her body with his, he slid his hands under her ass. "Hold on to me." He angled her hips off the bed and, with one thrust, drove the rest of the way inside her. Maiya cried out and grabbed his ass, digging her nails in.

He pulled out and plunged deep again and then rolled his hips, grinding against her clit. He let out a curse when her cunt rippled and tightened around his shaft, another orgasm rolling through her. They were both slick with sweat. Ryan's chest slid against her breasts as he drove into her with punishing thrusts.

Soft whimpers escaped Maiya's lips, and she ran her hands up and down his back. Gripping her jaw in his hand, Ryan increased his pace and kissed her hard, swallowing her cries. He rose to his knees, hauled her hips off the bed and slammed into her cunt, grunting with each slap of his pelvis to hers. "I love fucking you." Ryan gritted his teeth, nearing his climax. "I can't get enough of your tight cunt."

"Don't stop. Oh God, don't stop."

He gripped her full hips harder. "Mine."

"Yes!" Arching her back, she came, her channel squeezing his dick like a vice.

Ryan drove into her one final time, and the muscles in his body seized with his climax, his prick jerking over and over inside her as he orgasmed. Gasping for breath, he fell forward with her in his arms, collapsing to the side of her. Maiya's body shook, and she rolled over, curling against him.

Wrapping his arms tighter around her, Ryan smoothed her hair down her back. "Holy shit."

She sat up and pulled the blankets over them.

"Hang on a sec, baby." He got up and headed to the bathroom to take care of the condom. When he returned, she'd shifted onto her side. He climbed in behind her and tucked her close to his body.

"Mmm." Maiya turned her face toward his.

He kissed her cheek and then her lips. "Sleep, babe." He ran his hand along her arm to her side, caressing her soft skin. She lay her head back down on the pillow.

Pressing his face into her hair, he breathed in her now familiar scent of lavender and coconut. Ryan explored her soft curves, stroking down her waist to her hip and back again, listening to her breathing even out. He smiled when her body jerked a little as she fell into a deeper sleep.

CHAPTER TWENTY-FOUR

MAIYA WOKE WITH RYAN'S WARM BODY PRESSED AGAINST HER back. She snuggled a little closer, enjoying the weight of his arm around her waist and his hand cradling one breast.

"Morning, sleepy head." His whispered words wrapped around her, warming her further.

She sighed when his lips landed on her shoulder. He'd woken her a few times during the night for more sex. It'd been incredible. The last time had been slow and gentle. He explored her face, her neck, and damn near every centimeter of her body with his fingertips—like she was some kind of fine china. No one had ever touched her with such tenderness before. It *did* scare her, but she'd been so enraptured by the look in his eyes and the feel of his hands on her body, she couldn't have run away if she tried. Besides, where would she have gone? They were at *her* house, after all. "What time is it?"

"Almost seven. Mind if I use your shower?"

"Good God, seven?" She turned over and pressed her face against his neck. "Don't wanna get up yet."

Chuckling, he stroked his fingers through her hair and caressed her back. Maiya shivered and wrapped an arm and leg around him. He smelled wonderful still, even after all the sex and sweating. Fuck's sake, the man was perfect.

"Come take a shower with me," he whispered.

She kissed his throat. "Start the water, I'll be right there."

"Don't leave me hangin', woman." He pinched her ass and rolled away, getting out of the bed.

She yelped and tried to swat his ass but missed. "I do love to watch you walk away, though."

Turning when he reached the bathroom, he winked at her and then escaped through the door. She heard the water start, and then minutes later, he yelled from the bathroom, "Maiya, come onnnnn in, baby. It's nice and warmmm."

Oy, this man! With a shake of her head, she tossed the covers back. Maiya groaned when her stiff muscles protested. Her body ached in places she didn't know even existed. She took her time getting to the bathroom. Couldn't let him think she was too eager. It was a wonder she hadn't raced after him, though. What would he do to her in there?

When she reached the steam-filled bathroom, she paused in front of the glass shower doors and admired the view. Ryan had his back to the spray, spreading soapsuds over his body with his hands. The water and bubbles sluiced down his lean, muscled chest, and then his taut stomach muscles…and lower, lower… *Sweet Jesus.*

Lust coiled tight like a spring in Maiya's belly. Her gaze followed the path of his hands, and when he stroked his semi-erect penis in his soapy palm, she bit her bottom lip and groaned.

"Like what you see, Maiya?"

Busted. She jerked her gaze to his face.

Ryan opened the shower door, wearing that devilish smile of his. "Coming?"

"God, I hope so." She stepped into the space with him and kissed him.

An hour later, Maiya stood at her kitchen counter, making

coffee. They'd spent at least forty-five minutes in the shower, and the water had run cold by the time he had his way with her. He'd pressed her against the cool, tiled wall and fucked her. And that was *after* he'd gone to his knees and devoured her sex like a man who was starving to death.

Ryan came in and helped himself to some bagels in the breadbox and toasted up two. One for each of them. How sweet. She watched him from the corner of her eye as he made himself at home. "Cream cheese?"

She filled the coffee pot with water and turned it on. "Yep, in the fridge. Get the jelly, too."

"Jelly, too?" He chuckled and retrieved the items. "Living on the edge, huh?"

"You know it." Grabbing some utensils and plates, she set them on the counter. "What time is your flight?"

"Eleven. Still trying to wake Jimmy's ass up. Haven't heard back from him yet."

"I'll call Heather. She never turns off her cell." Heather's phone rang and rang and went to voicemail. Maiya hung up and redialed.

This time, she was greeted by a sleep-laden, grumpy voice. "Do you know what time it is?"

"Yep. But I bet you don't." Maiya laughed. "Could you hand the phone to Jimmy, please?"

"He's not here. Dropped him at the hotel last night."

"Oh. Well, shit. All right. Go back to sleep." Maiya disconnected the call.

Ryan grabbed a coffee mug from her cupboard. "What's up?"

"Heather dropped your brother at the hotel last night." She crossed her arms. "Kinda shocked. I figured they hooked up."

"Still possible. Knowing Jimmy, he took off afterward." Right then, Ryan's phone rang and he pulled it from his pocket. "Speak of the devil."

He answered and then turned and walked to her living room, cell pressed to his ear.

Guess he needs privacy. After pouring herself a cup of coffee, Maiya spread cream cheese and jelly on her halved bagel.

Ryan wandered back in, planted a kiss on her cheek and then poured his own coffee. "Thanks."

"Welcome," she said around a mouthful of bagel. *Oh yeah. Talk with my mouth full. Keep 'em coming back for more.*

He raised both brows, a slight curve on his edible lips, and leaned against the counter next to her. "He's going to meet me at the airport." Grabbing the other half of her bagel, he took a bite.

"Hey, get your own, thief."

He swallowed. "Yours needed sampling."

"You need a ride?" She sipped her coffee.

He bit into his own bagel and tilted his head side to side.

She licked some cream cheese off her finger. "Was that an answer?"

"I don't want to put you out. I can take a cab." He sipped his coffee, but his gaze was focused on her mouth.

She licked her lips.

"Woman."

"Ohhh, come onnnn!" She rolled her eyes. "You cannot tell me you want more sex? Really?"

Looping a finger in a belt loop on her jeans, he tugged her close.

She set her coffee cup on the counter. "Keep doing that, and you're going to rip my pants."

He kissed the corner of her mouth. "I'll buy you new ones."

"I'll have you know I can buy my own jeans, mister." She wrapped her arms around his neck. "But you do owe me a pair of underwear. And they weren't cheap."

He sucked her bottom lip. "I don't think I can ever have too much sex."

With me? Please, say me. "Nympho." She should let him take a cab. "Suit yourself."

He swatted her ass. "Yeah, well. What can I say? Sex with you is... Mmm..." He kissed her again. "Unlike anything else."

Her heart brightened; at least it wasn't only her thinking the sex was nuclear.

He nuzzled her neck. "You really want to take me to the airport?"

"It's the least I can do." Desire sizzled in her veins, and she tried to douse it. "I owe you one for taking me yesterday." There. She'd said it without sounding too breathy or affected by his attention.

Damn, she was screwed. She needed to get some space from him and clear her head. He'd go home today, and then she'd have two weeks to get her head straight before going back to L.A. and facing him again.

"Okay."

Pulling away, she sat at the table. "Good. Now, eat your breakfast."

"Told you I'd be here for breakfast." He chuckled and bit into his bagel.

She laughed. "Whatever."

"Mmm, music to my ears." He took the seat across from her and, with a smile a mile wide, ate his bagel and drank his coffee.

Maiya shook her head and thought—for about the hundredth time—she was going to get her heart broken. *Gotta find a way to get it back out of his reach.*

RYAN KISSED MAIYA GOODBYE IN THE CAR AFTER SHE PARKED at the airport's curb. The night they'd spent together had been incredible. But he sensed she was holding a part of herself back. Not that he blamed her. He was holding back a degree or two also.

He still wasn't sure what they were doing or what had started to develop between them. She'd asked him last night, and he didn't have an answer; he just knew he wanted more time with her. He really wished she lived in L.A.

"How do you know Maiya?" His brother shifted in his seat on the plane.

"Have I told you, you look like hell today?" Ryan flipped through the magazine he'd found in the seat pocket. "I know her from work."

"You're fucking someone from work?" Jimmy cracked the cap of his water bottle. "I'm getting too old for this shit, bro."

"You can say that again. We both are." Ryan glanced out the window at the clouds.

"Looking at her, I wouldn't have suspected you worked together. What does she do there, admin assistant or something?"

"She's the associate director of development and testing. She hides all the tats when she's in the office. Most of them, anyway."

"No shit? Sounds like a big deal. More than meets the eye, huh?"

"Jimmy, you have no idea, man." Ryan looked at his brother. "Every time I think I have her figured out, she knocks me on my ass again."

Jimmy laughed and sipped his water.

"What's so funny?"

"You're falling for her."

"Don't be stupid. Not going to happen. She's way too wild for me." Ryan looked away. "I like her, though."

"Mom meet her yet?"

"Hell no… Jacob did, though." He pinched the bridge of his nose. "You think she's like Tammy? I mean…she's wild like Tammy was."

"Let me get this straight. She outranks you at work, which means she may even make more money than you do." Jimmy took another swig of water.

"Yeah, and?"

"She's got her own car, house, career—"

"She also plays in mosh pits and is covered in tattoos." Ryan closed the magazine. "I don't know what to think. She's a goddamn anomaly."

"Dude, chill." Jimmy fanned Ryan with his napkin until he batted it away. "Nah, I don't think she's like Tammy. Tammy was on a one-way road to nowhere. 'Bout time you let that shit go too."

Ryan focused on his brother's face but said nothing. Jimmy was right. Ryan did need to let it go. His guilt and resentment over what happened still held him hostage. But he knew, deep down inside, Maiya was nothing like Tammy. "You're one to talk. You haven't been serious with anyone since you ended it with—"

"Don't even say her name, Ry." Jimmy cleared his throat. "Besides, we're talking about you, not me, right now. What did Jacob think of her?"

"Go easy, Mr. Sensitive. Jacob likes her, thinks she's pretty." Ryan shrugged. "Kids, right? What do they know?"

"Shit. Dude, sometimes kids know everything."

The flight attendant handed Ryan the coffee he ordered. "So, Heather?"

Jimmy scrubbed his hand over his face. "Let's not go there, either. I was gonna, but wasn't feelin' it. I sent her home." Leaning forward, he pulled a business card from his back pocket. It was the one the blonde woman had given to him in the club.

Ryan motioned to the card in his brother's hand. "That why you weren't feeling it?"

"Maybe." Jimmy studied the card. "Dunno."

"Gonna call her?"

Jimmy flicked the edge of the card with his thumb. "I want to, but then again...dunno."

"She's different for you. As different as Maiya is for me."

"Who knows, maybe there's hope for both of us then, right?"

"We sound like a couple of chickies."

"Like I said, getting too old for this shit." Jimmy ran his fingers over the embossed lettering on the card. "We'll see."

Turning back to the window, Ryan thought about Maiya, and then an idea came to him. When the plane touched down in L.A., he sent an email to Joe from the finance team.

MAIYA LOVED AND HATED THAT RYAN HAD COME AND GONE. She started the week like normal: Worked from her home office, talked to Ryan during work hours—about work things only. But at night, he would call her after he'd gotten Jacob to bed. In between, they exchanged text messages.

In a feeble attempt to keep her heart from seeking his attention, Maiya refused to be the one to initiate contact. Each day, she'd wait for him to text or call first. She'd lounge on the couch, ready to read a book or watch some TV, and sure enough, her phone would ring. Sometimes, she'd let it ring a few times before answering, wanting to make him sweat a little, but she answered. She always answered.

Not a day passed where Ryan didn't communicate with her in some way. What the hell was this exactly? If he didn't want a relationship with anyone, least of all her, then why was he acting this way? Maiya couldn't figure it out. He'd managed to dodge the question last weekend at the bar, and there was no way in hell she'd ask him again. Whatever it was, she wasn't going to let herself get used to it. Eventually, he'd get bored and move on from her.

And then? No more Ryan. A lump rose in Maiya's throat,

thick and tight in her airway. He was worming his way past her defenses because, Lord, the idea of no more Ryan made her insides ache.

Wednesday, she took her mother to her doctor's appointment, where they took four vials of blood. The way Joanie bitched, they may as well have taken thirty. Her mother had taken off the technician's head, poor kid. The doctor expressed his concern—in a calm tone—regarding her mother's now bronchitis, the visible jaundice in her eyes and skin and her distended belly. Which, of course, were the exact things Maiya worried most about. Never mind how her lung function had deteriorated.

The doc wanted her mother to schedule an appointment and get the fluid drained from her abdomen. Of course, Joanie told him she'd rather wait. Things were not looking good in the Mom department. Maiya tried to broach the subject again in the car, but Joanie shrugged it off. When they got home, her mother promptly made herself a drink. The woman must have a death wish—either that or a major case of denial. Maiya was willing to bet the house on the latter. And there was nothing she could do about any of it. Not like the woman could be declared incompetent because she was a stubborn drunk.

The following week, Maiya slipped, mentioning her mother's appointment to Ryan when she talked to him. The accidental comment had opened a can of worms she wasn't prepared to dive into. He wanted to know what happened, how her mother was, was anything treatable, how Maiya was handling the stress. To her horror, she found herself answering all his questions, including the details of how frustrated she felt and even how worried she'd been.

Apparently, she'd contracted a bad case of diarrhea of the mouth. Maiya had been shouldering the burden alone for a long time and wasn't in the habit of talking about her struggles. But Ryan sounded genuinely interested, and she couldn't help but tell him all of it. The relief to share was too great. She stopped herself from telling him her mother's illnesses were a result of her alcoholism, though. She wasn't ready to head down that road.

"So, when do you fly in?" Ryan asked on the other end of the phone.

"Monday. I'll get there around noon."

"Do you think you can come early, maybe on Saturday?"

"I guess I can see about changing my flight. Why?" Maiya tried to keep the sudden butterflies of excitement swirling in her belly to a minimum. "There'll be a change fee."

"Look into it, I'll pay the change fee."

"I don't want you to do that." She walked to her back porch and lit a cigarette. "Tell me why you want me to come early." She exhaled a plume of gray smoke.

"It's a surprise."

She could hear his smile through the phone. "Ryan."

"Maiya."

She frowned. "What are you up to?"

"Come on, baby. Get the flight changed and get here early. Bring something pretty to wear, too."

She took another drag of her smoke. "Define pretty."

"A dress would be nice. Doesn't have to be too fancy. Are you smoking?"

"A dress?" She rolled her eyes and sat in one of the cushioned patio chairs. "Yeah, I'm smoking. Why?"

"Yes, a dress. Just curious. I can hear you exhaling."

She took another draw from the menthol stick and exhaled, keeping her mouth close to the phone.

"Stop. You're getting me all hot and bothered."

"Hot and bothered, huh?" She stubbed out the cigarette and lowered her voice. "That could be fun."

"Playing with fire, woman."

"Maybe I like getting burned." The irony of the statement was probably lost on him.

"My kind of fire doesn't burn." He chuckled. "Let me know tomorrow about the flight?"

Maybe it wasn't lost on him after all. She hesitated a moment but then answered. "Sure, what the hell."

"Sweet dreams, Maiya."

"You too." She tapped her nail on the armrest. "Night." Maiya sighed and lit another smoke.

She had a love-hate relationship with surprises. What if it was someplace she hated? What if it was something wonderful? She groaned and rubbed the spot between her eyes. The man asked her to do something, and she did it. She had a love-hate relationship with that, too. As if she couldn't manage to tell him no.

Ryan was an Alpha male through and through—not that anyone could tell by looking at him. Maiya wasn't sure if it was the tone of voice he used when he went from asking to telling her to do something, or because he was dominant in bed. Either way, the little spell he had her under was working. A little too well.

She finished her cigarette and, once inside, grabbed her laptop to see about changing her flight.

———

THE FIRST THING RYAN DID WHEN HE ARRIVED IN THE OFFICE was send Maiya an IM.

> Ryan Donnelly: So?
>
> Maiya Rossini: What?
>
> Ryan Donnelly: Can you change your flight?
>
> Maiya Rossini: Good morning to you, too! 😜
>
> Ryan Donnelly: LOL. Sorry. Good Morning. Can you change your flight?

Maiya Rossini: Ugh. I cannot believe I am doing this.

Ryan Donnelly: Can you see me smiling from there? What time do you get in?

Maiya Rossini: Practically. It's bigger than the signs on the strip. LOL. I get in around 2pm.

Ryan Donnelly: Sweet! I'll pick you up at your hotel at 6. Dinner then... I'm not gonna tell you. Neener, neener. 😜

Maiya Rossini: Can you see me rolling my eyes from there? Fine. Now, go work on my project. Slacker.

Ryan Donnelly: LOLOL. Anything you say, ma'am. I'll text you later.

Maiya Rossini: ....

Ryan chuckled at her reply. It was definitely an insert-curse-word-here response. He leaned back in his seat, and excitement raced through him. Being away from her the last week and a half had sucked, but talking to her every day had made it bearable.

Maybe he should've called her instead of messaging her. He loved the sound of her voice in the morning. Always raspy and sexy, most likely because she smoked. He didn't care for smoking, yet her smoking didn't seem to bother him. Not much seemed to bother him at all where Maiya was concerned.

Ryan clasped his hands behind his head and contemplated his dilemma. How could a woman so similar to Tammy, so very much not his type, be so appealing? *Was* she similar to his ex, or was it merely his first impressions he refused to let go of? Maybe Jimmy was right; she was nothing like Tammy.

Ryan leaned forward and thumbed through his project files. Best get to work and try to keep his mind off her. He chuckled. *Good luck with that.* Since coming face to face with her, he hadn't stopped thinking about her. It'd only been a short time, and he was acting like a guy in love. Not that he was in love, of course. No, no. Ryan didn't believe in love at first sight, or first weeks. He definitely wasn't in love.

He just liked her. A lot.

A whole lot.

MAIYA CHEWED HER THUMBNAIL AND STARED AT THE IM window for a few minutes before closing it. Cursing herself the whole time, she'd changed her plane ticket, hotel and rental car, and since he was now aware, there was no going back. Beyond nervous and doubting her decision, she did the only thing she could think of. She called Jodi.

"You're coming in early? Where's he taking you? Are you staying at the hotel, or do you want to come here?"

"Damn, girl. Take a breath, would you?" Maiya laughed and walked to the back patio, coffee in hand. "I'm staying at my usual."

"Well, where's he taking you?"

"He won't tell me. All I know is we're doing dinner." Maiya lit a cigarette. "He said I should wear a dress." She inhaled a long drag and then exhaled a plume of gray haze. "Said nothing too fancy."

"Oh my God, girl. Are you excited or crapping your pants?"

"I don't know." Maiya stared at the mountains in the distance. "Maybe a little of both."

"This is way more than sex, obviously. Did you have the talk with him?"

"I asked him, ya know, when he was here, what was going on between us. He didn't have an answer."

"Wait, what? When the hell was he there?"

"Oh, shit." Maiya cringed. "I didn't tell you, did I?"

"Hell no, you didn't tell me!"

"Sorry."

"When did he come there?" Jodi sounded impatient.

"He showed up here last Saturday night. I was with Heather at Tangled, and he was just…there."

"Did he know you were there? What did you do?"

"Jodi, damn. Easy." Maiya snorted and put out her cigarette. "He came into town with his brother for the night. They showed up there." She sipped her coffee. "He didn't know where I was or that I was even out."

"Did he go home with you?"

"Nosy ass."

"That would be a yes. Was it as good as last time?" Jodi asked in a hushed tone.

"Now you're whispering? Why the hell are you whispering?"

"Just answer my question, will you?"

Getting up, Maiya walked back to her office. "It was better."

"Lord, be still my beating heart."

"Yeah, yeah. Don't remind me. My thighs catch fire whenever I think about it." Maiya flopped in her office chair. "The sex is the best I've ever had. The stuff he does to me." Closing her eyes, she drew in a breath. "It's… It's… Shit, I can't even find the right words."

Jodi let out a high-pitched squeal, and Maiya pulled the headset away from her ear. "Ouch!"

"Sorry." Her friend laughed. "You better text me Saturday night when you're back at your hotel… Well, if you make it back to your hotel. Otherwise, you can call me in the morning."

Maiya doodled a heart on her notepad. "I'm glad you're getting such a kick out of this."

"I am! I told you, I'm living vicariously through you. It's better than soap operas."

"And I'm going to get my heart crushed like a character in one of those ridiculous shows, too."

"Oh, stop. You only live once, remember?"

"I know." Maiya sighed. "Just not looking forward to the pain."

Jodi tsk'd her. "Doom and gloom. Knock it off and enjoy it while it lasts."

"All right, fine. You win. But you're buying a gallon of chocolate ice cream when he breaks my heart and spending the weekend here with me."

"Deal," Jodi said. "Love ya, girl. Talk soon."

Maiya disconnected the call and stared at the heart she'd drawn, and then added a crack to the center of it. *What am I, fifteen?* Groaning, she scribbled it out.

CHAPTER TWENTY-FIVE

RYAN LACED HIS FINGERS THROUGH MAIYA'S WHEN THE HOUSE lights came up in the theatre. She looked more than stunning in the black dress she wore. It hugged her body like a glove. He loved staring at her in it, but he couldn't wait to get her out of it.

She'd pinned her gorgeous red hair in a twist on the back of her head, and little curling tendrils hung down here and there, framing her face. Even with all her tattoo work, she looked...classy. In fact, he was sure the woman would make burlap look classy. He shook his head, smiling at the thought and looked at their joined hands.

"What are you smiling about?"

"Have I told you how beautiful you look tonight?"

"Um, let me see." She tilted her head to the side. "I think that makes the tenth time. Wait, maybe the eleventh."

He raised their joined hands and kissed her fingertips. "Just checking."

"Did you like the play?"

"I did. Did you?" He stood, pulling her up with him.

"I thought it was fantastic. Tiffany did a wonderful job."

He cupped his hand behind her neck and pulled her close

to him. "She did." He paused, letting his gaze roam over her face. "I need to kiss you."

He meant it, too. It was a need, one he was powerless to deny. She stroked her warm fingers down his cheek, and the expression in her hazel eyes stole his breath. Emotion swirled within the flecks of gold and green. The most obvious being desire. But fear, maybe even a little hope, was there too. And love. Was it love he recognized or his own wishful thinking? Did he want her to love him?

She licked her lips and swallowed. "I'll let you."

Ryan stroked the side of Maiya's neck with his thumb and then took her lips in a soft, unhurried kiss. She arched and gripped his arm when his tongue stroked over hers. The crowd around them milled up the aisles on their way to the exits, but none of them existed as he tasted her, swallowed her and sought for more.

Cupping both sides of her face in his hands, he deepened the kiss. He wanted this woman more than he'd ever wanted a woman in his life. The thought startled him a little, but the need curling in his gut all night far surpassed any fear his mind held. Ryan pulled away, nipping at her bottom lip.

Maiya pressed her forehead to his, trembling. "That was one hell of a kiss."

"Well, I missed you." He kissed the tip of her nose.

She closed her eyes. "I don't know what I'm supposed to do with you."

"Take me back to your hotel room, and you can do the first thing that comes to mind." Pressing his hips against hers, he let her feel the consequence of their kiss.

"Rawrr. Did I do that?"

Taking her hand, Ryan led her up the aisle toward the exit. "Do you have any idea how many times I jacked off the past two weeks thinking of you?"

She stopped short, halting his forward motion. "Fucking hell, Ryan!" She put her hand over her mouth and looked around at the other patrons, and then began again in a lower tone. "Do you have any idea how hot that is? Jesus, I think I just had a mini orgasm."

He gazed over his shoulder at her. "If you're a good girl, I'll let you watch me after I get you naked." He smiled and then escorted her out of the theatre.

———

AFTER MISSING THE SLOT THREE TIMES, MAIYA HIT HER MARK and inserted the key card into her hotel room door lock.

Ryan kept nipping the tender skin on the back of her neck and running his hands over her breasts and up and down her body. And she was unable to focus on the simple task of unlocking the damn door. The man had hands like the devil and a tongue that should be registered as a lethal torture device—of course, if someone considered getting sucked and licked to death torture.

Maiya motioned toward the tray holding a basket of fresh strawberries and two small bowls, one with whipped cream, the other chocolate syrup. "Where did that come from?"

"I ordered it." He walked farther into the room. "C'mere."

She set her purse and beaded satin shawl on the dresser and moved to him.

Ryan framed her waist with his hands and kissed the side of her neck. "You smell delicious." His breath was warm on her skin, and he trailed open-mouthed kisses down her neck to her collarbone. With a tight grip on his shoulders, her head fell back. The room spun around her, almost as if she were drunk.

He moved his hands from her waist, around to the small of her back and onto her ass. He paused there, massaging her buttocks through her dress, and then tugged up the hem. "Thigh-highs and garter?" He trailed his fingertips along the black lace tops of her hose and then traced up the two attached garter straps.

Maiya gazed into his eyes. With her body pressed against his from chest to thigh, her heart thundered in her ears. "I thought you might appreciate them."

With the fingertips of one hand, he teased the tender skin at the crease where buttock met thigh and then trailed one finger from the other down the small strip of material of her G-string between her buttocks, stroking over her anus. "Very much so."

Moaning, she arched her back, angling her ass up and urging him on.

He slid his fingers over her center through the thin material. "You're wet. Soaked straight through your panties. Always so wet for me, Maiya." He nipped her earlobe. "Whose cunt is this? Tell me."

Heat sped through her veins, and her whole body pulsated with desire. She whimpered and arched again. "Yours." She drew in a shuddering breath. "Fuck. Ryan, please?" Running her fingertips over his upper back, she scraped at his shirt with her nails.

"Please, what?" He tugged the strip of material aside and circled her entrance with two fingertips, drew out her wetness and coated her clit with it. "Is this what you want, baby?"

Her knees went weak. She was going to die. Right then and there. Beneath his fingers and his mouth. He overwhelmed her in every way possible. It was almost too much. He captured her mouth again with a hard and sure kiss and slid two fingers inside the tight entrance of her cunt.

She bucked her hips and whimpered into his mouth. He slid them deeper and then withdrew them before repeating the motion. Over and over, he stroked her, all while continuing his assault of her mouth, lapping and swirling his tongue with hers.

Maiya threaded her fingers through his hair and gripped

the soft strands tight in her fists, trying to anchor herself. She couldn't breathe, needed to, but didn't want to stop kissing him.

He broke the kiss and then nipped her chin. "You're so hot. I can feel you squeezing my fingers in your tight little channel. You're close, aren't you, baby?" He kissed her again, not giving her a chance to answer.

All she managed was a nod as she writhed against him. Her orgasm hovered just out of reach. The room spun faster, and her knees buckled. Catching her around her waist, he rotated them and laid her on the bed. Ryan pushed her dress up over her thighs.

"I need you inside me. Oh God, Ryan, fuck me, please."

"Patience, baby." He knelt between her legs. "For God's sake, look at you."

The sound of his breathy voice made her rise. She wrapped her arms around his neck and kissed him. Ryan broke the kiss and then tugged his tie free. He tossed it aside and then moved his hands behind her back and unzipped her dress.

She unbuttoned his shirt and ran kisses down his jaw to his neck. Ryan groaned and gripped her sides with force when she bit the tender spot below his ear. Excitement raced through her. She loved how she got to him.

Pushing his shirt off his shoulders, Maiya splayed her hands on his chest and kissed and licked her way to each nipple. He nudged her back a bit and pulled her dress down to her waist and off her arms.

She gazed at him. The fleshy mounds of her breasts arched at the top of her bra, and he caressed the tops of each with the backs of his fingers. She tumbled head over feet like a tidal wave from the expression in his eyes while he whispered, almost reverently, again about her beauty. She couldn't hold it back any longer.

And as her heart opened, it broke a little too. Ryan would

hurt her, she was sure, but she gave in to it anyway. "Ryan." His name spilled from her lips in a low tone, unsure if she was asking a question or stating a fact, and a little afraid that if she spoke too loudly, she'd break the spell between them.

Ryan ran one hand up her chest to her neck and cupped her face. Trembling, she leaned into it, letting him hold her.

Raising his other hand, he cradled her face between both and kissed her. Feather-light kisses over her eyes, her nose, her cheeks and then her lips. "Shh. I've got you, baby."

Maiya fell and hoped like hell when she hit bottom, she wouldn't shatter.

CHAPTER TWENTY-SIX

SHE QUIVERED BENEATH RYAN'S TOUCH. WAS SHE AS SCARED as he was? Ryan didn't want to examine it too closely, but Maiya was all he could think about anymore. Instead, he followed his desires and ignored his fears. Maiya fit him.

Breaking the kiss, he urged her back onto the bed and then tugged her dress off. Christ, she was amazing, framed in matching black lace lingerie. Her voluptuous breasts called to him from the confines of her bra, and he ran his hands down the swell of them to her stomach. "Take off your bra."

After running her hand over the top of his head, she arched and unsnapped her bra. Ryan painted a line down the center of her abs with his tongue and then circled her belly button, tickling her soft spots. Her tummy jumped from his attentions. A beat of pride at knowing her body so well rolled through him. Unsnapping each garter strap from her hose, he removed the belt from her waist and then hooked his thumbs under the thin straps of her panties and slid them down her thighs. She lay still, gazing at him while he unwrapped his present.

As he moved over her body, he took little sips of her sweet skin. She was a gift. His gift. Maiya was the best present he'd ever gotten, and he savored every second of the act as if it might be his last chance. "If I could tie you to this bed, I would. We'll do that next time we're at my house." Wasting no time, he leaned over, grabbed the chocolate syrup and then poured a line down her stomach.

"Ryan!" She buried her hands in his hair.

Ryan licked the sticky, warm sweetness from her flesh. "I didn't think you'd taste sweeter. I was wrong. You taste incredible with a side of chocolate."

She giggled. "You're crazy."

"Crazy for you, maybe." Using his fingers, he scooped some whipped cream from the bowl and spread a generous amount over each nipple. "Let's see how you taste with this." He sucked one coated areola between his lips.

"Holy shit." She sucked in a ragged breath.

"Mm. That's good." He moved to the other nipple.

She anchored her legs around his hips. "I want a taste."

"Are you kidding? Pfft. I'm not sharing." He chuckled and bit her nipple and was rewarded with her squeal of pleasure. He loved it. Ryan took a strawberry, dipped it in the chocolate and brought it to her nipple. She watched, eyes wide, her teeth planted on her bottom lip.

Ryan exhaled a harsh breath at the sight of her luscious mouth and circled the hard tip of her nipple with the berry. Dragging it up the swell of her breast, he brought it to her lips and held it just out of reach. "Lick it."

A drop of chocolate dribbled onto her bottom lip. She raised one brow and smiled. The tip of her pink tongue snaked out, and she licked the syrup away. With a quick movement, she reared up and bit the end off the berry.

Ryan almost came in his pants. "Eager, huh?" Taking a bite, he hummed. "Everything tastes better with a little Maiya mixed in."

"Can't argue that. My turn." She unbuttoned his pants.

He let her push them down, along with his boxers, freeing

his shaft. It was hard-as-steel for her, like always. "Yeah, right. You argue about everything, especially when I'm involved."

She scooped some whipped cream from the bowl and spread it over the head of his cock. "Shut up." Maiya swallowed him to the back of her throat, all the white cream disappearing into her mouth.

His moan of approval echoed in the silence of the room. Zings of arousal pumped up and down his spine. Ryan's head fell back, and he took a deep breath, trying to regain some control. At this rate, he'd be climaxing in two seconds, like a teenager. But damn, her mouth was a mix of heaven and hell. Delicious torture.

In an effort to distract himself, he poured chocolate syrup down the middle of her back. She gasped, her mouth still full of his prick. Drawing back up his length, she sucked a little harder on the head.

"Fuck!" Clenching his teeth, he breathed rapidly through his nose. When his head stopped spinning, he smeared the chocolate down her back and ass.

She arched and then pulled him from her mouth. "Don't you get any syrup near my kitty. I might have to take a pound of flesh if you do." She sucked him between her lips again and cupped his scrotum in her hand, squeezing gently.

"I won't…" He panted. "Damn, baby. If you keep that up, I'm not going to last."

She rolled her tongue over the head.

That. Was. It.

Grabbing her arms, Ryan pulled her away, spun her, and bent her forward onto all fours. She glanced over her shoulder at him, a slight grin tilting her lips. "I wasn't done." Her hair was still up in its twist, but much of it had fallen loose, cascading over her shoulders. She looked so damn sexy, his breath caught in his throat. Ryan swallowed a couple times, allowing himself a moment to learn how to breathe again.

Applying a little pressure to her upper back, he pushed her farther down on the bed. "Ass in the air."

Giggling, she wiggled her hips.

He slapped her bottom. Once. Hard enough to sting and make her squeal. "Testing me, Maiya?"

"If I say yes, will you spank me again?"

She was taunting him. Damn woman. He smoothed his palms over her ass cheeks and up her back, smearing more of the chocolate. Scooping a big handful of whipped cream, he added it to the chocolate and then leaned forward and licked a line up her spine. She moaned and pressed her ass against his prick.

"Cock slut." Ryan straightened and slapped her ass again but then smoothed his hand over the red mark he'd made, soothing it. "Don't move." He removed his pants and boxers and then positioned himself behind her on the bed again.

Maiya remained on her knees, her head lowered to the bed, her ass in the air. Open and willing, the way he loved her to be. Running two fingers through her folds, finding how slick she was, he murmured an oath of thanks.

"Oh. God." Maiya rocked back against his fingers. "I need you inside me."

"I'm not done eating cream and chocolate off your delectable skin."

She shifted her hips back again. "Ryan Donnelly, if you don't fuck me right this minute, I'm going to get myself off. You can watch from the corner."

"Is that so?" He slapped one butt cheek. "I will fuck this pussy when I am—" he slapped the other cheek, "—damn—" another, "—good—" one more on each side. She arched her back farther, crying out when each slap landed. "And ready." Grabbing his dick, Ryan positioned himself at her entrance and slid fully inside her with one thrust.

Maiya's ass cheeks burned with a delicious sting from the spanking he'd delivered. Her clit pulsed hard when he landed each hit. She was on the verge of orgasm when his thickness filled her.

Warm.

Satin.

Uh, oh.

"Baby…I got so caught up." Ryan sounded horrified. He was stock still, holding her hips firm in his hands.

He hadn't put on a condom. The muscles inside her channel clenched around him, and she let out a moan. "It's okay, birth control pills."

"Jesus, you feel—"

She gripped the blankets, desperate to feel him move inside her. They were skin-to-skin, no condom to protect them. Pregnancy wasn't a concern. They'd talk about it after. "Ryan. I need you."

He pulled his hips back and slid deep again. Yanked from her thoughts, she sucked in a hard breath. The rub of his bare skin in her channel sent tremors through her limbs.

Ryan leaned forward and licked up her back again. "So tight and warm." He pumped his hips, gliding in and out of her in long, deliberate strokes. "I knew you'd feel this amazing wrapped around me."

Maiya widened her legs farther, opening herself for him. "Fuck, you feel so good."

Gasping, Ryan sped up his strokes. His pelvis slapped into her ass, and she cried out, uncaring how loud she was being. "Mine."

Her walls clenched down on him again, and her orgasm rushed to the surface. Reaching between her legs, Maiya rubbed her clit. "I want to come, babe."

"Not yet."

Reaching farther back, she cupped his sac, massaging it. "Then fuck me harder."

"You're such a bad girl tonight." He leaned over her, blanketing her with his body and rewarded her with what she wanted. Ryan banged into her, and her grip slid from his scrotum.

Maiya rubbed her clit again. "Fuck your cock slut, Ryan."

"Oh my God, Maiya." He groaned and bit down hard on her shoulder.

"Ryan!" The feel of his teeth in her flesh brought her orgasm forward. It slammed into her, wild and fierce. Her channel clamped down, squeezing him with each pulse. "Inside me," she panted. "Finish inside me."

Thrusting two more times, Ryan gripped her hips hard and hollered her name. His cock jerked, spurting deep within her. Resting his forehead on her shoulder, he sucked in ragged breaths.

Maiya froze, barely breathing, while the overwhelming sensations of Ryan's orgasm echoed through her core. After a long moment, she moaned and slid flat on the bed. He remained on top and inside her—his weight a comfort, bringing her back to her body. Ryan rolled to the side but kept one leg draped over the backs of hers. Remaining on her stomach, Maiya turned her head to face him.

Ryan pushed her hair from her face and then drew his fingers down her back. "You're all sticky."

She smiled, sated and ready to fall asleep. "Mmm. I bet."

Ryan got up and then returned a moment later with a wet washcloth. The cloth was warm against her skin as he wiped the stickiness away. Maiya didn't want to think about anything more than how she felt right then. Especially that they hadn't used a condom. He'd always been prepared when they were together before, and she hoped to hell he was clean.

Pushing the thoughts away, she shifted closer to Ryan. His sweet breath was warm on her cheek, his hands gentle and soothing on her back. He murmured something she couldn't decipher.

Sleep took her instead.

———

"I'M KEEPING YOU," RYAN MUMBLED WHEN HER BREATHS became soft and even, knowing she wouldn't hear him.

Setting the washcloth aside, he lay next to her, watching her sleep. He trailed his fingertips up and down her back, tracing her tattoos. Taking her from behind had been unbelievable. Watching the designs flex and move while her body shifted and writhed proved to be the most erotic experience of his life.

She had the tiniest waist that flared into full hips and an incredible heart-shaped ass. Bared before him, it was almost painful to look at her and realize she was his. Smart and funny and bitchy and sexy—damn, she was sexy.

Problem was, he'd been too chicken to make her his. Officially his, anyway. He still worried about Jacob. What she would think of being with a man who already had a kid? If Jacob didn't like her once he got to know her, or if it didn't work between them, Jacob could get hurt.

So many ifs.

Ryan didn't have the answers. Stupid, and he knew it was, he wished someone could tell him what would happen so he could make a decision one way or the other. Pulling her closer, he cradled her warm body. He'd talk to Jimmy about it tomorrow while they were at the zoo with Jacob. His brother would tell him he was being an ass again, but he just needed to be sure.

Ryan had slept about five hours by the time light shone through the hotel room window. He'd roused at some point and made love to her again in the middle of the night. Keeping it soft and slow. Intimate.

Maiya lay curled on her side, her ass tucked against his

groin. Kissing her shoulder, he rose from the bed in search of his clothes. After locating them, he dressed in silence.

She'd burrowed farther under the blankets, still sound asleep. Taking a seat on the edge next to her, he pulled the blanket down, drew a lock of her red hair away from her face and kissed her cheek.

She stirred and opened her eyes. "Are you leaving?"

"I've got a date with my brother and Jacob at the zoo in a couple of hours."

She rolled to her back. "Aw, that's sweet. I love the zoo."

"Do you?"

Maiya sat up and clutched the sheet to her chest. "Yeah, I mean, who doesn't love the zoo?"

"It'll be a good day. The weather should be cool enough." He stroked a finger down her nose to the tip.

"Yeah." Her brow furrowed. "Have fun."

He smoothed the lines on her forehead with his thumb. "I'll call you later, okay?"

"Sure."

Ryan headed for the door but then turned back to her. "Everything okay?"

"Yeah, fine. I'm going to get a little more sleep." She smiled, but he could tell it was forced. "Have fun," she repeated.

"Babe. I...I just—"

"Don't." She held up her hand. "Go have fun with your family." Turning away from him, she fluffed her pillow and then lay back down.

Damn. He'd hurt her again. "Okay. I'll text you later." Not wanting to be any more of an asshole, Ryan left the room.

Ryan pushed the down button for the elevator. Some time was all he needed to settle the emotions and fears continuing to dog him. *Grow some balls.* After today, he'd get past his issues or leave her alone.

He didn't want to hurt her. He didn't want to hurt anyone.

UNABLE TO GET COMFORTABLE, MAIYA TOSSED AND TURNED IN the hotel bed. But how could she, with a mountain of hurt feelings stealing all her comfort? *He doesn't want me around his kid. Fucking fabulous.* It stung. A lot. And dammit, she didn't want it to.

She was plenty good enough to screw. Plenty good enough to dress up and take to dinner and a show. But not good enough for his family. For his son.

Fine. Whatever. Throwing off the covers, Maiya headed for the shower. She wasn't about to let it get to her. She'd wash him off her body and right the hell out of her heart in the process.

Hot water rained over her face and chest, and Maiya gave in, allowing herself to cry for a few minutes. The tears released some tension, and the warm water soothed her aching muscles. As usual, she was deliciously sore in all the right places. The memory of his body and the dirty words he used played through her mind, and instant lust swirled in her belly. Maiya cursed her body and finished scrubbing the last remnants of their night off her skin.

Once she'd gotten herself cleaned up and ready to face the world, she scooped up her phone and called Jodi.

"Meet me at the coffee shop." The sound of Jodi starting her car echoed in the background. "I'm heading there now. No kids. Adult girls day only."

"All right. Maybe we can get toes done, too?"

"Oh, hell yes. See you in a few."

Maiya left her hotel room. She could do this. No problem. Yep. *Lying to yourself isn't a good thing, girl.* For the love of all things holy, she wasn't fooling anyone, least of all herself.

CHAPTER TWENTY-SEVEN

BUBBLES SWIRLED AROUND MAIYA'S FEET IN THE HOT WATER AT the nail salon, and she wiggled her toes. "I'm going to stop seeing him. I think."

"That's the fourth time you've said that since we've been out today."

"I'm serious, Jodi."

"Yeah, I hear you. But, um...who are you trying to convince exactly, me or you?"

Maiya glared at Jodi and then rolled her eyes. "I *am* serious."

"So am I, girl. When did you pick up so many issues?"

The man working on Jodi's feet murmured something to the nail tech next to him that Maiya couldn't hear. "When in the hell did you think I didn't already *have* issues?" Maiya tucked a hair behind her ear. "Shit, girl. I'm all fucked up. Sorry to blow the image to bits."

A woman walked by with her young daughter in tow and shot Maiya a look. *Ah, hell.* Maiya cringed, realizing her colorful language.

"Can't you let things be easy? You worry too much." The nail tech rubbed Jodi's calf, and her friend moaned. "The sex is good. You get along… Well, you get along in a weird way, but still, it works. Stop complicating it."

"I'm not." The smell of the nail chemicals tickled her nose, and she sneezed. "Okay, maybe I am. It's confusing, Jodi." Her friend raised a single perfect brow. "He pulls me close and says all these wonderful things, but then he doesn't want me around his kid. What the fuck am I supposed to think?"

"You don't know that. Not for sure, anyway. And besides, if I were a single parent, I'd be damn sure I was serious about someone before I let them spend any regular time with my kids." Jodi reached over and squeezed Maiya's arm. "He's probably as nervous about this as you are."

"Don't you think it's a sign?"

"A sign of what? That he's a good father? Oh, maybe a sign he likes you and wants to spend more time with you? No, wait. A sign the sex is cartwheel-worthy?"

"Cart-what?" Maiya burst out laughing. "You crack me the hell up. Crazy ass."

"Yeah, you love me. Now, chill and enjoy your pedi."

Maiya let out a breath, sounding a lot like a snore. "Fine."

The nail tech looked at her with wide eyes and then focused back on Maiya's feet.

Bottom line, she needed to have a conversation with Ryan. They were getting too involved, and feelings were blossoming in her heart at a high rate of speed. She'd been trying like hell to get them under control but was failing miserably. Maybe she should break it off or, at the very least, slow things down.

For two people who were only getting to know each other, who also lived in different states, for fuck's sake, they sure saw a lot of each other. And a whirlwind romance all about the "oh my God, the sex is off the charts, and it's just so wonderful to be together" could only end in heartbreak. Falling for someone was fucking fabulous. It was. But the inevitable hitting-the-ground-with-her-ass part was far from fabulous.

"Stop thinking about it. I can see the wrinkle between your brows getting deeper."

"I hate you." Maiya rubbed the spot between her eyes. "Is it really getting deeper?"

Jodi laughed. "I love you, too."

RYAN WAITED WITH JACOB AT THE ENTRANCE OF THE ZOO FOR Jimmy to arrive.

"Can I get a stuffed monkey today?"

Ryan tickled his son's stomach, and Jacob giggled. "You're a stuffed monkey."

"I need a stuffed monkey, Dad."

"Don't you have a stuffed monkey already?"

Jacob's little brow furrowed in a serious expression. "He needs a friend. Monkeys get lonely."

"Hmm. You have a point." He sat Jacob on the bench next to him. "We sure wouldn't want your monkey to be lonely."

"You get lonely, too."

Ryan looked at his son. "What makes you say that?"

"You don't have a wife." Jacob shrugged. "Daddies are supposed to have wives. That's what Toby at after-school care said."

"Some daddies have wives, yes. Sometimes they don't." He pulled Jacob onto his lap. "What do you think?"

"If you had a wife, then I'd have a new mommy, right?"

From the mouths of babes. Ryan had been blessed with such a smart kid. He swallowed, his throat feeling drier than the Mohave Desert. "I suppose so, yes. If I had a wife, then you'd have a mommy." He re-tied one of Jacob's sneaker laces and continued. "You think you want a mommy?"

Tilting his head to the side, Jacob pursed his little bow-shaped lips, looking as if he was giving the idea a great deal of thought. Ryan fought to smother his grin. His son was being so serious he didn't want to appear like he didn't appreciate it.

"Would I getta pick who my new mommy would be?"

God, he loved this kid. "Get to," Ryan corrected. "I'll make you a deal. If Daddy finds someone he likes enough to make her his wife, I'll make sure you agree first, okay?"

Jacob smiled, and his eyes sparkled. "Deal."

Ryan looked over and spotted Jimmy walking toward them. About time his brother showed up.

"Uncle Jimmy!" Jacob hopped off Ryan's lap in hot pursuit of his uncle.

Ryan stood. Damn, that was a heavy conversation. He'd be running all of it by his brother, along with a few other things.

Ryan and Jimmy ambled along the walkway, and Jacob ran up ahead of them.

"So, let me get this straight," Jimmy mumbled around a mouthful of roasted almonds. "You left a naked woman, a woman you have feelings for, in bed this morning to come to the zoo with me and your son?"

Ryan glanced at his brother and rolled his eyes.

"Okay, yeah, I get it. Jacob's your priority. And he should be. But, dude, why didn't you invite her to come with us?"

"Because...I don't know." Ryan ran his fingers through his hair. "Hey, Jacob," he hollered. "You're getting too far away. Wait for us."

"What do you mean you don't know?"

"I'm worried about Jacob."

"How so?"

"I don't want a bunch of women in and out of his life. Keeping things stable for him is important."

Jacob ran up to them. "Daddy, can we feed the goats?"

"A bunch of women?" Jimmy asked.

"Yes." Ryan took Jacob's hand.

"Dude, you have got to be kidding me, right?"

"What?" Ryan looked from his brother to Jacob. "Come on, little man." Walking Jacob toward the goat pen, he looked at his brother and shook his head. "The 'yes' was for Jacob about the goats, idiot."

Jimmy laughed and tossed another handful of nuts in his mouth. "You got a parade of women in and out of your bed all of a sudden?"

He and Jimmy grabbed a bench in the goat area and watched while Jacob fed a couple of the animals. "Hell no. I told you, just her."

"Ry, how many women have you brought home for Jacob to meet? Hell, how many have you even dated in the last couple of years since you got Jacob?"

"None, and a few."

"Exactly."

Agitation pricked at Ryan's gut. He wished Jimmy would get to the damn point. "Exactly, what?"

"This one's different, and Jacob already met her. Why in the hell not invite her along?" Jimmy leaned back and crossed his feet at the ankle. "You like her. I bet you like her a lot more than you're willing to admit. I saw the way you were with her in Vegas."

"I don't have a great track record for picking the right women. Neither do you."

"Not talking about me, so I'm going to ignore that. You made one bad choice. You need to let that shit go. It's old baggage."

His brother was right, even though he had no room to talk, either. Jimmy's heart had been shattered during college, and he'd been single since. Tired of doubting himself, Ryan blew an exasperated breath. "So, you think I should've invited her along?"

"Damn, grow some nuts." Jimmy glanced at him. "On

second thought, here, have some of mine." Jimmy tilted the bag of almonds toward him.

Ryan pushed the paper sack away. "You're an ass."

"Yeah, but I'm right."

"I should call her, invite her to dinner tonight." Ryan grabbed his phone. "Go play with your nephew. Give me a little privacy."

"'Bout time." Jimmy clapped Ryan on the shoulder and headed for Jacob.

As he looked for Maiya's number, Ryan's cell rang in his hand. He cringed when he saw the caller ID—Tammy's parents.

"Hello, Bernice."

"Hello, Ryan. I'm surprised you picked up this time. I seem to only get your voicemail these days."

Getting up, Ryan strode over to the edge of the enclosed area. Not answering was preferable. He dreaded these conversations. "I've been a little busy lately."

Bernice let out a very unladylike snort. "That's always your answer."

"Is there something you needed?"

"It's been a while since we've seen Jacob. I'd like to set up a visit."

"Fine. When were you thinking of coming?"

"Robert and I were thinking Jacob should come here to visit this time."

When Ryan obtained custody of Jacob, he'd had to fight Tammy's parents to hold on to it after Tammy passed. The entire process had been an ordeal from hell. Every bit of his life, past and present, had been dragged out into the open. But he'd fought them tooth and nail and won.

In the end, they were granted visitation. Two weeks a year, but the agreement was they had to come to him. Ryan accepted the arrangement; however, he figured at some point they'd try to change the terms. He just didn't think they'd try so soon. Drawing in a deep breath, he sought for a calm tone. "That's not the visitation agreement, Bernice."

"He's getting bigger, Ryan. He should be able to come and spend time here with us."

"He's five, Bernice. Five."

"I know how old he is. Look, I really don't want to have to take this back to court." Her threatening words came through the receiver in a clipped tone.

"You won't win. And if I remember correctly, the last court venture about broke the bank for you two. You sure you want to go through all that again?"

"We'll do what's necessary. We have the right to see our grandson." Bernice exhaled. "I don't want to fight about this."

"Of course, you have the right to see your grandson." Ryan gripped one of the fence posts. "Two weeks a year. Here. Where he lives. Not out of state."

"We're not the enemy."

Ryan clenched the phone in his hand. "Really? You could've fooled me."

"We love him, you know." Her voice quivered.

"Look. I'm not willing to send him two states away for a week. Not yet."

"When? When will you be willing?" Bernice whined.

"I don't know. However, if I am, I'll let you know. Until then, you're welcome to take me back to court." He disconnected the call.

Ryan stuffed his phone back in his pocket and braced his hands on the fencing. His heart thundered in his ears, and an ache started behind his eyes. If he'd had his way, they never would've been near Jacob again. Tammy's parents kept his son a secret from him, and because of it, Jacob endured a year of neglect, and God only knew what else. It was unforgivable.

"What was that all about?" Jimmy asked when Ryan returned to the bench.

"I'll tell you later."

"You and Maiya have a fight or something?"

"Nah, nothing like that. I'll call her in a little bit."

Jacob looked over from one of the goats. "I'm hungry, Daddy."

"Me too, little man. Let's go grab some lunch." Jimmy stood and tossed the empty bag of almonds in the trash can.

"We need to wash our hands first." Ryan took Jacob's hand and followed his brother from the area, agitation still bubbling in his gut.

Bernice had to be out of her mind to think he'd let his five-year-old child leave the state.

As if he'd ever trust them again.

CHAPTER TWENTY-EIGHT

After stopping at the grocery store to purchase a bottle of wine for her and Ryan and a bottle of chocolate milk for Jacob, Maiya waited on the porch in front of Ryan's door and drew in a deep breath. Sweet lord. *Get. A. Grip.* Nervous energy radiated from her limbs, and she clenched her free hand in a fist.

In the morning, he'd been all tongue-tied about the zoo, and as a result, she'd been convinced he hadn't wanted her around his son. Now, she was joining him and Jacob for dinner. Once again, the man surprised her. Putting the bag down next to her, Maiya shook out her hands to relieve some tension and rang the doorbell. Shifting her weight from foot to foot, she waited.

Jimmy opened the door with a grin the size of a freight train. "Why hellooo, Mzzz Maiya. You're looking especially pretty this evening." He leaned against the doorframe.

She smiled, shaking her head. The man had way too much sexy packed into one body, and yet, it did nothing for her. "Hello, Jimmy. Thank you." She grabbed the bag at her feet. "Very nice to see you again."

"Ooh, you brought goodies? Here, let me take that."

Jimmy pulled the sack from her hand. Stepping aside, he waved her past. "Come on in."

"Thanks. It smells delicious in here. He cooked?"

"Sure did. You know the way to the kitchen, I assume. He's back there chef-ing it up for you."

"You're staying too, right?"

"Actually, I'm not. Was just hanging around until you got here."

She walked into the kitchen and found Ryan in front of the stove, stirring a big pot of something.

Setting the spoon down, he walked straight to her. "Hey, baby." He wrapped his arms around her and kissed her right on the lips.

Maiya stiffened, her eyes going wide, trying to scan the room for where Jacob was.

Ryan chuckled. "Relax, babe."

"Nice choice." Jimmy held up the bottle of merlot she'd picked. "Damn, and chocolate milk too? Hey, Ry, this must be for you." Jimmy lobbed the small container of milk to Ryan.

Turning, Ryan caught the bottle against his chest.

Maiya gasped but then laughed. "You two are like a couple of kids." She sat at the table. "Where's Jacob?"

"Psshaw. Your point?" Ryan grabbed a cup with a lid and straw. Setting the cup down, he filled it with the milk. "He's in the family room. And I happen to take great pride in my juvenile behavior."

Jimmy opened the bottle of wine she'd brought and set it on the counter. "Head's up!" Jimmy shot the cork at Ryan's head.

Ryan ducked, and the cork whizzed by him. "Better pick that up, you delinquent." He faced the family room and hollered for his son. "Jacob, come here."

Maiya's nervous tension eased watching the banter between Ryan and his brother.

Jacob came running in but stopped short when he saw Maiya, his little mouth curving into a huge smile.

She smiled back. "Hi, Jacob."

Jacob giggled and ran to his father; a sweet blush colored his cheeks. *This kid couldn't be any cuter.*

"Hey, little man, don't be rude. Say hello to Maiya."

"It's okay, Ryan. He's just being a little shy."

"I don't hafta call her Miss anymore?"

Ryan chuckled. "I think just Maiya is fine from now on."

"'Kay." Jacob nodded with wide eyes.

Maiya raised her brows. Apparently, something had changed, and Ryan had decided he'd had enough of the formalities. Interesting. Maybe he'd clue her in later.

Jimmy leaned a hip against the counter. "She brought you a present, little dude. You need to let her know you appreciate it."

"You gots me a present?" Jacob's face lit up like it was Christmas morning.

"*Got* me a present," Ryan corrected.

Jacob's little brow furrowed. "Daddy."

"Well? Don't look like that. Here." Ryan handed Jacob the plastic cup. "It's your present."

"I brought you your very own chocolate milk. You like chocolate, right?" Shifting in her seat, Maiya tucked her hands under her legs and sat on them.

Jacob took a long sip from the straw and then came running toward her. "I love chocolate milk." Jacob hugged her. "Thank you, Maiya."

The hug both delighted and shocked her. She raised her hand, offering a high five. "Cool beans. You're welcome."

Jacob slapped her palm and ran off to the family room. "Be careful not to spill," Ryan called after him and then went back to the stove.

"Whelp, looks like it's time for me to go." Jimmy walked

over to her and gave her a peck on the cheek. "Have a nice dinner, Red."

Another surprise. These people sure were affectionate. It stunned her into silence, and she reminded herself to close her mouth in case it was gaping open.

"Hey, now." Ryan crossed his arms with an expression on his face resembling something like a cross between appreciation and...jealousy?

Could he be jealous of his brother? That was, for sure, a warning in his tone. Holy hell. He *was* jealous. She couldn't help but smile, and her face heated with what she knew was a rare, honest-to-God blush.

Jimmy let out a sharp laugh and clapped his brother on the back. "No worries, Ry. I know she's your girl, even if you haven't admitted it to yourself yet."

Ryan gaped at him for a moment before he shook his head and extended his arms to his sides in an are-you-insane gesture before moving back to the stove.

"Yes, sir, I did just say that out loud. Heading to Mom's. I'll shoot you a call tomorrow." With that, Jimmy left the kitchen.

"My brother's an ass." Ryan stirred the contents of the pot. "I hope you like spaghetti."

Getting up from her seat, Maiya walked to him. She placed her hand on his shoulder. "Is it true?"

Ryan tensed and stilled his movement of the spoon. Setting it aside, he turned around and then placed his palm against her cheek. "I don't know. Is it?"

Maiya closed her eyes and leaned into the warmth of his touch. "I don't know what to think."

He slid his hand around the back of her neck and pulled her close. "I know when I'm not with you, I can't stop thinking about you," he whispered, and his lips grazed hers.

"But?" Her heartbeat quickened, becoming a loud throb pulsing in her ears.

Soft and slow, Ryan kissed her, taking little sips from her lips. Placing her hands on his shoulders, she pressed herself against his hard body. Tingles pulsed along Maiya's spine, and her heart skipped a few beats. She was utterly defenseless and laid bare when he was tender like this with her.

He pulled away and pressed his forehead to hers. "There is no *but.*"

"Ryan." She cringed at how whiny she sounded. "We need to talk."

"After dinner and after Jacob goes to sleep." He kissed the tip of her nose. "Taste my sauce. I have to try and impress my Italian girl."

She smiled. "Okay." He spooned up a bit of sauce for her to taste. Blowing on the edge, she closed her lips over the end. Still holding the spoon, he kept his eyes on her mouth when she licked the sauce from her lips. "Mmm. I think it's better than mine."

"I doubt that. Too much Irish flowing in my veins. You'll have to make me yours."

"It's been forever since I made sauce." Maiya moved to the bottle Jimmy had opened for them. "You want some wine?"

"Hell, yes. Glasses are to the right of the fridge. Thanks, baby." Pulling a pot from one of the lower cabinets, he filled it with water. "Hey, how's your mom doing?"

Maiya poured them each some wine. "I declare a subject change immediately. Shall we toast?" She held out his glass.

After setting the pot of water on the burner, he took the wine from her. He gave her an odd look but then raised his glass. "To family."

"Family?" She shook her head, smiling. "All right, family." She tapped her glass to his and then took a sip. "Mmm, it's yum."

He leaned forward and stole a quick peck from her lips. "Quite. Not yummier than you, though."

She raised her fingertips to her tingling lips. "Anything I can do to help?"

"You mind setting the table?"

"Sure." As she moved around the space, gathering the items for the table and setting them in place, she felt Ryan's gaze on her. She turned to look at him. "What? Am I doing it wrong?"

He was leaning against the counter, arms and legs crossed, and a slow, devious smile spread over his lips. "You look good in my kitchen."

"I see that look in your eyes."

"Yeah?" He strode to her. "What look is that?" Circling his arms around her waist, Ryan pulled her close.

Warmth spread over her skin the minute her body met his. No matter how many times she touched him, kissed him or had sex with him, her body leaped into immediate arousal. Often, before she even realized it or had a chance to stop it. Hunger swirled in her belly—not the kind food would satisfy, either. "The one that means you're thinking about what I might look like bent over your kitchen table."

She didn't think she'd ever tire of touching this man. Granted, they hadn't been involved sexually for long, but from the moment she laid eyes on him in the conference room, a fire had erupted between them and had only grown hotter every time they were near each other.

No. That wasn't accurate, was it? In truth, Ryan Donnelly had stirred something inside her even before meeting him face to face. Each phone call, every interaction over work issues, birthed this attraction inside her. Something about this man drew her to him, and Maiya realized, staring into his blue-gray crystalline eyes, she quite possibly was lost forever.

She'd gone head over heels for him.

Ryan chuckled and smoothed one hand down her lower back to her ass, palming one cheek. "Maybe." He nuzzled her neck.

"Daddy, is it almost dinner?"

Ryan and Maiya jumped apart like a bomb had been set off between them.

Jacob giggled. "Were you kissing?"

Ryan coughed. "No. I was just giving Maiya a hug."

Maiya busied herself with gathering items from the fridge for the table.

"Dinner'll be ready in about ten minutes, buddy. Why don't you go wash your hands?"

Jacob frowned. "Janet at school tried to kiss me the other day. I ran."

"Uh oh." Maiya raised both brows. "You don't like kisses, I guess?"

"Yucky. Not from her. Reegan can kiss me if she wants, though." Jacob marched toward the bathroom. "You should kiss my dad. I bet he'd like it."

Ryan stopped and looked at Maiya. "Did he just say that?"

"No comment."

Draining the pasta, Ryan finished getting dinner prepared, and then they all sat at the table. This was what families did. They had dinner together. A brief feeling of being an outsider rose in Maiya's stomach, but she pushed it down. Ryan had invited her to share a meal with him and his son. She intended to enjoy it for the gift it was.

Jacob rattled on about the zoo. He'd placed two stuffed monkeys on the empty chair at the table. What a bright and inquisitive five-year-old he was. And Maiya listened in awe while he explained how his monkey had been lonely, so his daddy had bought him another today at the zoo.

"That's very sweet, Jacob."

"Yup. I told Daddy he gets lonely, too, 'cause he doesn't have a wife."

Ryan looked at Jacob, pausing mid-motion, a mound of spaghetti hanging from his fork. "Um…"

Maiya raised a brow. "Is that so?"

"Yup. He said if he found a wife, then I'd have a new mommy."

Ryan set his fork down, picked up his glass of wine, took a big gulp and then leaned back in his seat.

"A new mommy?"

"Mmhm. I getta help pick her. We made a deal. Right, Daddy?"

Ryan coughed and wiped his mouth with his napkin. "Get to. And we sure did." He winked at Jacob, but Maiya didn't miss that his cheeks had gone flaming red.

The man was blushing! *Ha!* Picking up her glass of wine, she took a swallow and tried to process what she was hearing his little boy tell her. No. He couldn't possibly be considering her. "Anyone you have your eye on?" She took a bite of her food.

"I dunno." Jacob looked at his father, who was now trying to smother a laugh and failing miserably.

Ryan's cheeks burned a brighter crimson if that was even possible. "Finish your dinner, little man."

Jacob nodded and took another bite.

Maiya stared at her plate and twirled her fork in the spaghetti, trying for all it was worth not to read into this entire conversation. But curiosity piqued—regardless if it tended to kill the cat.

RYAN MIGHT UP AND DIE OF EMBARRASSMENT. A DESPERATE need to climb under the table and hide rose up inside him, but he stayed in his seat and continued eating. He should've anticipated Jacob mentioning their conversation at the zoo today. In truth, he'd meant what he said to his son about having a say in such an enormous decision.

He hadn't thought about marriage in years, and now the topic had come up twice in one day. But the idea of being married wasn't uncomfortable like he figured it might be. The notion of Jacob having a mother again, one who would always be there for him, warmed his heart.

He was more concerned with what was going through Maiya's head. Did it freak her out? Did she think he wanted that with her? Ryan took another sip of wine. She'd deflected his question about her mother pretty fast, too, and that puzzled him. He watched and listened while she ate and talked with his son. Jacob liked her. That was good. Really good.

"I'm done, Daddy. Do I getta have dessert?"

"*Get to* have," Ryan corrected. "Put your plate by the sink, please, and then go get your PJs on. When you finish, you can have two Oreo cookies. Sound good?"

"With milk, too?"

"Did you finish all your chocolate milk?" Maiya asked.

"Uh-huh." Jacob got up and placed his plate by the sink.

"I'll get your dessert ready for you. Head on upstairs and find PJs."

"Wanna see my room, Maiya? I have a fort in there."

Maiya looked from Jacob to Ryan, seeking permission. He appreciated it. "If you want, it's fine with me."

"I'd love to." Rising, Maiya held her hand out to Jacob.

"Uncle Jimmy helped me make it." His son took Maiya's palm in his little one and pulled her behind him out of the kitchen.

Ryan cleared the table. He'd gotten the dishwasher loaded by the time Maiya and Jacob came back downstairs. "Cookies and milk are on the table, little man."

"I would have done that," Maiya said.

"Done what?"

"The dishes." She moved to the sink and started washing the saucepan. "You cooked. I clean. That's the way it worked in my house with me and my brother."

"All right then, I'll dry." He rubbed her lower back.

"Thanks, baby." Ryan glanced at his son. "Did Maiya like your fort?"

"Mmhm. She even climbed inside with me," Jacob said around a mouthful of Oreos.

"It's a pretty excellent fort, Jacob. Your uncle is cool for making it for you." Rinsing the pot, she handed it over to Ryan. "My brother used to make forts for me when I was a little girl."

"You have a brother? What's his name?" Jacob took a drink of his milk.

Ryan looked at Maiya. She'd only talked about her brother to him once and had revealed very little.

She started on the pasta pot. "His name was Jeremy."

"Does he live near you?"

"No, honey. He doesn't." She looked at Ryan.

The request was clear in her eyes, and he nodded. "Her brother is in heaven, little man."

"Oh. He prolly knows Mommy." Jacob gobbled the last piece of cookie, swinging his legs back and forth under the chair.

"Maybe." Maiya scrubbed the pot, rinsed it and then handed it to Ryan.

After drying it, he put it away. "Okay, little man. It's time for bed. Let's head upstairs, get your teeth brushed, and you tucked in."

"Already?"

"Yes, already. It's seven o'clock. And you have school tomorrow."

Jacob shuffled over to them with his empty cup of milk. "Can Maiya come up and tuck me in too?"

"If she wants, sure." Ryan picked up his son. "Care to join us, Maiya?"

She reached for the cup from his son. "I wouldn't miss it."

Jacob dived from Ryan's arms into hers. Maiya let out an "oof" when she caught him. It shocked Ryan. It shocked her, too, because her eyes got wide as silver dollars when she looked at him, but then she smiled. His stomach dropped, and his heart launched into his throat. She wrapped her arms around his son's tiny waist and nuzzled his little neck, inspiring a giggle from Jacob.

Other than family, he hadn't seen his son in a woman's arms in forever. It was odd, but in a good sort of way. He swallowed past the lump in his throat and followed them upstairs. This woman had found a place in his heart with ease, and now it appeared she'd found a place in his son's, too. It pleased him more than it scared him. It was a good thing. It felt right.

He held her hand, and they descended the stairs after getting Jacob settled in bed. Maiya read his son three stories before Ryan declared official lights out. His mind had ping-ponged all over the place while he listened to her soft voice lull his son into dreams.

Fear, amazement, pride and complete admiration for Maiya filled him. She'd fallen into rhythm, helping Jacob pick out books, getting him settled under the blankets and lying down beside him to read what he'd chosen.

All of it led him to one conclusion: he wanted her to be his. No. Theirs. He wanted Maiya in his *and* his son's life. Done deal.

When they reached the bottom of the stairs, Ryan pulled her into an embrace. Holding her soft body tight to his, he chastised himself for holding back from her in favor of old wounds long overdue to be healed. He just hoped Maiya wanted him *and* his son as much as Ryan wanted her.

MAIYA PRESSED HER MOUTH AND NOSE AGAINST RYAN'S NECK, breathing him in. His skin carried the scent of fresh air from being outdoors half the day at the zoo.

Loosening his arms, he ran his hands up and down her back. "I'm sorry," he whispered.

She looked up at him. "For what?"

His gaze roamed over her face, a sad expression in his eyes, but then a small smile curved his lips, and he caressed her cheek with his fingertips. "For a few things, and for today."

She covered his hand, cradling her cheek with her own. "I don't understand."

"I know." Ryan stroked his thumb over her bottom lip. "How about I make coffee? We can talk."

"Sounds kind of ominous."

"Not at all." He gave her a soft kiss. "But I understand why you might think so." Taking her hand in his, he pulled her down the hall into the kitchen.

She waited at the kitchen table while he readied the coffee pot. Confusion settled like a thick storm cloud, and her mind wandered in all sorts of directions. She chewed on her lip, contemplating if she'd stepped over some sort of line with his son. Or was he ending their relationship— or whatever it was they were doing? She tapped the tip of one nail on the table and bounced her knee, trying to dispel some of her nervous energy.

Ryan remained silent the entire time the coffee brewed, and he put some Oreo cookies on a plate. When she thought she might burst clean out of her skin, he spoke. "I should have invited you to the zoo today with us."

"Ryan, it's... You don't—"

"Let me finish." He glanced at her, and she clamped her mouth closed. "I was scared. No, that's a lie. I *am* scared." He filled two mugs, adding cream and sugar to hers, fixing it the way she liked. Such a simple thing, yet it made her insides turn to mush.

This amazing, wonderfully surprising man remembered how she liked her coffee. "What are you scared about?"

He handed her the mug and then took a seat opposite her.

He raised his mug to his lips and blew on the hot liquid before sipping it. "A few things, I guess."

"I'm sorry, but I'm in desperate need of a cigarette. Can we go outside?"

"You should quit smoking."

"I should do a lot of things. Indulge me." She got up, grabbed her smokes from her purse and headed toward the back door in the family room.

He followed and opened the slider for her. "It's chilly. You want one of my jackets?"

"No. I'm okay for now." She sipped her coffee. "Mmm, perfect again." Taking a seat on one of his cushioned patio chairs, she lit up. The gray smoke swirled from the end, and she exhaled a stream of it, savoring the first drag.

"Better?" He pulled an ashtray from behind the outdoor bar on his patio, slid it toward her and then sat a few feet away in the matching chair.

"Much. Go on, please."

He ran his fingers through his hair, mussing it, and stared out at the backyard. "I don't know where to start."

With her nerves feeling more settled, thanks to the nicotine running through her system, Maiya waited for him to gather his thoughts. They hadn't turned on the outside light, and the clear sky and glow from the moon bathed the strong features of his face. His eyes were cast in a dark shadow, but his cheeks, lips and chin were highlighted. What a beautiful view he made.

He leaned forward in his seat, bracing his elbows on his knees. "I told you about Jacob's mother, how she died."

She took another puff off her cigarette. "You told me she died, but not how."

"She overdosed. Heroin." He blew out a breath.

"Jesus Christ, Ryan. I'm sorry."

"Thanks. I gained custody of Jacob about a year before the end." He smoothed his palm over his face. "She'd been clean when she got pregnant and… I was happy, you know? Surprised but happy. I asked her to marry me." He shook his head and then sipped his coffee. "When I woke up the next morning, she was gone. It took me almost three years to find her *and* my son. Christ, I didn't even know I had a son."

"Holy shit."

"When I found her, she was so deep in her addiction she readily signed him over to me. It was horrible watching her kill herself with the drugs after that." He looked at her. "But none of that has anything to do with what scares me now."

She needed to give him something of hers—a fair trade for him sharing something so deep and personal with her. She also wanted him to know she knew what it felt like to watch someone destroy themself with an addiction they couldn't control. "My mother's a chronic alcoholic." She drew on her cigarette. "That's why she's sick now."

"I'm sorry. Was she like this when you were a kid?"

"Yeah. It wasn't happy land, that's for damn sure." She put out her cigarette and lit another.

He raised a brow.

She giggled. "What? Don't look at me like that."

He leaned back in his seat again. "I love that sound."

"I love that you make me make it so often." She smiled. "What scares you? Tell me, please?"

"I don't want this to come out wrong."

"Just say it."

"You're a lot like her."

She scoffed. "You can't be serious?" He couldn't mean what he was saying. Considering what he'd shared with her about his ex, the idea hit her like a knife in the chest.

"Hear me out."

"Okay, fine. Finish." Maiya sipped her coffee and tried to keep an open mind.

"You're like her in the good ways. Tammy was the person in a room full of people who stood out. Everyone noticed her.

And if they didn't, she made sure by the end of the night they had. It's why you remind me of her. People see you, Maiya. They can't help but see you. For one thing, you're beautiful."

She laughed, shaking her head in denial of his compliment. But at least this was a line of thinking that was the good kind of stab in the chest.

He smiled. "You are! For another, you have this intoxicating personality. People want to be near you. I want to be near you."

"Thank you, and I want to be near you, too. But you still haven't told me what scares you."

"It's stupid. The more I say it out loud, the more stupid it sounds. I just… Jacob, you know? He lost his mother, and it was hard on him, but he's okay. I mean, he remembers her, just not like I remember her. Tammy wasn't always on drugs. There was a time when she was like you are now, except she really never was." He shook his head and pinched the bridge of his nose between his fingers. "I don't even think I'm making any sense."

"I think I understand."

Shock skittered across his features. "You do?"

"What if, right?" Taking a long drag, she exhaled and watched the smoke waft away on the breeze. "What if I come into your life and then I disappear? What if you get hurt, or worse, Jacob gets hurt? Again."

"Yes." He blew out a breath, grabbed his mug and took a long sip of his coffee.

"What if you decide you want someone better? What if you wake up and realize I'm someone who somehow landed a great job but is really nothing but a tattooed girl from the wrong side of the tracks with an alcoholic mother?" She stared at her feet. "What if you wake up one day and realize I'm not good enough for you?"

"Of course, you're… God, you think I would do that?"

She shrugged a shoulder. "Do you think I would do what you fear?"

Ryan sighed. "What if…"

"Exactly."

"I see you with my son, and it freaks me out, and at the same time, it feels right." He stared into his coffee. "I mean, you've only been around him twice, and already he can't stay away from you. You're like some sort of drug, but a good one."

"I'm not sure that's a flattering reference considering what you told me about Tammy and my experience with my mother, but I'll take it for what it's worth." She laughed.

"So, what do we do now? You realize I'm a package deal here, right?"

"You having a child doesn't bother me. I think Jacob is a bright and sweet little boy. As far as us? I don't know. What do *you* want exactly?"

"I want you." He met her eyes. "I want you in my life. But I don't know what that looks like or how it'll work. I'm fuzzy on anything beyond that."

"Dating?" She peered through the darkness at the backyard. "As in, exclusively, monogamously, dating?" She put out her cigarette. It surprised her how calm her voice sounded because her heart had launched into a rapid beat, and a lump lodged itself in her throat. Was this really happening?

"Yes."

She cleared her throat and reached for some calm. "Wow." She pulled her hair over one shoulder. "I didn't expect this. You're sure?"

"Very."

Fuck, she needed to sort out her thoughts. Yes, she'd fallen for him, but she hadn't meant to. She didn't belong with a guy like Ryan and was convinced even if he thought he wanted her, he'd change his mind. She'd be hurt either way. *God, I need Jodi.* Maiya wanted him. Of course, she wanted him. *I just don't think he really knows what he wants.* He was a risk she wasn't sure she would survive. "Let's see how this week goes." Picking up her coffee, she stood. "Let's just see, okay?"

"I'm sure about this, Maiya." He stepped to her. "But I guess we'll see how the week goes."

Anxiety coursed through her. Damn, she was going to have a heart attack if she didn't get out of there. "It's late. I better get back to my hotel. We have work tomorrow."

"Okay." He sighed and brushed her hair away from her face, and then kissed her cheek. "Let me walk you out."

She kissed him goodbye at the door, and he held her close a lot longer than in the past. Maybe he was afraid she didn't want what he did. Even so, how could he want *her*?

She'd been smart enough to earn an education and make something of herself. But, so what? Getting a college degree and a good job didn't change what existed inside. Her family defined dysfunction. She was still Maiya Rossini, a girl who grew up in a trailer park on the shit-side of town, had a mother who was drunk more often than not, and a brother who died far too young.

She'd never forgive herself for Jeremy's death. Her mother damn sure wouldn't, either. Getting into her rental car, she headed for the hotel. *"You're so selfish. It's your fault he's gone, Emmie!"* Her mother's words echoed in her mind. Maiya did her best to focus on the road and turned up the radio, trying to drown out her mother's voice and the memory of that horrid day.

She didn't need this shit. Didn't need or want the memories that having these feelings for Ryan brought up. The man had no idea what he was asking her for. He was too good for her and deserved someone so much better. And sweet Jacob? Well, that little boy deserved a mother who was respectable.

Maiya knew in her heart she could never live up to what they needed. She would fall short. It didn't matter if she'd fallen for him or his son; she had to find a way to walk away.

None of it mattered. *Fuck!* She slammed the heel of her hand on the steering wheel and then gripped it tight. Maiya was screwed six ways from Sunday because not only had she fallen for Ryan, she didn't think she was strong enough to walk away now. She wanted him, and he wanted her. Didn't she deserve that? Didn't she deserve a happy life?

Maiya blew out an exasperated breath and pulled into the hotel parking garage. No, she didn't. Things were quite clear to her now. She didn't deserve any of it. As far as she was concerned, sticking around made her worse than unworthy. It made her selfish, just like her mother always said she was.

CHAPTER TWENTY-NINE

THE FOLLOWING AFTERNOON, RYAN WALKED INTO THE BREAK room to grab a cup of crap coffee and found the best thing he'd seen all day standing in front of him. His Maiya. He moved to her. "Hey, baby."

Placing her palm on his chest, she halted his movement before he leaned in and gave her a kiss. "Hold it right there, lover boy. We're at work. No kissy kissy here."

He grabbed a cup for his coffee. "True. Okay, how about you meet me in the conference room at three?"

"Very funny. So, when are you going to tell people around here about Jacob?" She turned and leaned against the counter.

"I don't know. I guess I figured after I got this project done." He sipped the hot brew. "Ugh, this stuff is crap."

"Tell me about it." She toyed with the hair draped over her shoulder. "You didn't have to keep him a secret, you know."

"I thought it was best to wait, that's all."

"Can't wait to see how it will go over if news of you and me gets out." She rolled her eyes.

He set his foam cup on the counter and crossed his arms.

"Is there a 'you and me'? I mean, an official you and me? Like officially?"

Her gaze fell to her feet. "Dunno yet. Giving it the week, remember?"

"You're being stubborn."

She glanced at him. "Maybe. Or maybe I'm being smart."

"Bahh! No fun. Come out with me tonight?" He ran a fingertip down her arm.

Maiya sucked in a breath and closed her eyes. Aha! She craved his touch as much as he craved touching her. The urge to grab hold of her and kiss her until she didn't remember her name overwhelmed him. He leaned close to her. "I fucking love how you respond to my touch."

"Pfft. Whatever." She pushed him away. "Knock it off. You're not playing fair."

"Nope, and I won't. Ever."

"Where do you want to go tonight?"

"It's a great place; you'll love it. The atmosphere is out of this world."

"Oh lord. Where?" She sipped her coffee.

He laughed. "Chuck E. Cheese."

She slapped her hand over her mouth and then grabbed a napkin to wipe her chin. "Sounds positively romantic. Damn, I almost spit coffee across the floor."

"I know. That was awesome." Leaning in, he kissed her cheek before she could stop him. "I'll pick you up at six."

"Dammit. Stop that before someone sees." She giggled. "Fine, I'll be ready at six. Jeans will be suitable attire, yes?"

He wagged his brows and smiled. "Yes. Then I can peel them off you later."

"You're incorrigible, you know that?"

"And you love it. See you at six, baby." Turning on his heel, he walked out.

Maiya was waiting for him outside the main entrance of her hotel. Damn, she looked good. Her hair was down and curled around her shoulders. A royal blue fitted T-shirt met the low waist of her faded jeans, which hugged her curves to perfection. The shirt had the word *Angel* in pink glitter across her gorgeous breasts. A little set of red devil horns framed the letter A. Pretty damn accurate from his perspective.

When she got in the SUV, Jacob greeted her. "Hi, Maiya."

She turned. "Hi, sweetheart. Are you excited about playing some games?"

"Yup. Daddy says I can have twenty tokens this time. And Auntie Cyn is coming too. She's bringing her boyfriend."

Maiya looked at Ryan. "Oh?"

"Hey, babe." He leaned in and gave her a chaste kiss on the lips.

She glanced in the back seat at Jacob and then back to him. "I'm meeting your sister?"

Ryan put the vehicle in gear and navigated from the lot. "Yeah, that okay?"

"Of course. Just shocked, is all." She put on her seat belt. "Where in the birth order is she?"

"She's right before Jimmy. Two years older than him." He rubbed her thigh. "You'll like her. Though I think her boyfriend is a knob."

"A knob?" She laughed. "Awesome. If I'd known I was meeting more of your family, I would have dressed a little nicer."

"Why? You look fine. She's going to love you. I'm sure Jimmy already told her all about you."

"Uh, oh. That could be disastrous." She wrung her hands in her lap.

Ryan covered her hands with one of his. "Baby, don't worry. She'll love you."

"I'm not exactly the girl you bring home to mom, Ryan."

"Like hell. Can you trust me?" He glanced at her. "Trust me?"

She blew out a breath. "I do. I really do. I just—okay."

It shocked him to see her unsure of herself. My God, she was Maiya Rossini: Confident, kick-ass businesswoman. Strong, smart and the definition of sexy. That she would worry about being liked was surprising. He supposed meeting someone's family was nerve-racking for anyone the first time, but her reaction seemed like something more.

MAIYA CHECKED HER LIPSTICK AND HAIR IN THE VISOR MIRROR when he parked in front of the building. *Jesus. Fucking. Christ.* She hadn't been prepared to meet more of his family. She would've worn long sleeves, at least. Jimmy had been a surprise, but he was pretty much her kind of people.

She dug in her purse, trying to calm the nerves bouncing through her. Except Jimmy had been raised in the same nice family Ryan had, and he wasn't some loser like the guys she knew who resembled him. Either way, Jimmy had been easy to meet, but a sister? Good Lord. It terrified her.

Glancing at Ryan, she realized he was watching her, a grin the size of California across his sweet lips. Now, she felt even more self-conscious. "What?"

"You look beautiful, baby." He rubbed her thigh. "And, damn, you're pretty cute when you're nervous too."

She cringed. "Is it that obvious?"

"Ahhh…yes. Your face is like an open book. I love it. Much better than the mask you've shown me before."

"Wha…?" She frowned. "What mask? I don't know what you're talking about." She opened her door and got out.

"Your story, tell it like you want to." Chuckling, he stepped out of the truck, then opened the back door and helped Jacob out.

She walked around the back of the vehicle and put her hands on her hips. "Great. I've lost my edge. It's your fault, you know."

Jacob came running up to her and wrapped his arms around her legs.

She looked down and then back at Ryan. He was grinning again. Damn, he was too gorgeous with that crooked smile on his face.

"Hiya, sweetheart." She picked up Jacob. "You're spoiling me with all these hugs."

Jacob kissed her cheek. "I like hugging you."

She gasped. "Kisses for me, too?" She tickled his side.

Squirming in her arms, he giggled. "Daddy gots to give you a kiss. It was my turn."

"Is that so?" Ryan got closer. "So, you think you can steal kisses then?"

"Yes!" Jacob yelled, gripping her shoulders and bouncing.

"Whoa, easy there. I don't want to drop you." She laughed.

Jacob rubbed his little hands down her arms. "You have tattoos like Uncle Jimmy. That's cool."

She smiled. She hadn't given thought to the fact that Jacob hadn't seen her tattoos on display yet. "I do, yes. So, you like them?"

"Yup!" Jacob bounced again.

"You can put him down if you want, baby."

"Nope. I got him. Lead the way." Relief spread through her. Maiya moved forward, Ryan's palm on her lower back, and Jacob in her arms. The child was a fantastic distraction from her nerves.

If someone had told her a month ago, she'd be kinda-sorta...dating?—*did I just think that?*—a man completely not her type, holding his five-year-old son in her arms *and* going to Chuck E. Cheese for dinner with them both, she would've told them they were out of their flipping gourd.

Life was beyond strange and full of amazing sometimes. Maiya nuzzled Jacob's neck, and the nerves that had been screaming her name fell silent. She could do this.

They stepped inside the establishment, and the over-whelming noise from the kids running around playing battered her ears. After getting the obligatory hand stamps, they made their way to the food counter and ordered a couple of pizzas.

Ryan purchased a whole mess of tokens for Jacob, and they found a booth to sit in. Several kids surrounded the many arcade games, filling the large, purple-carpeted space. Others climbed into the plastic maze of green tubes suspended from the ceiling and exited the many yellow slides, only to make their way back up the tunnels again.

Parents wandered around in search of their kids, who had to be in there somewhere. No wonder they stamped the kids' and parents' hands with matching stamps. There was no other way to ensure a kid didn't leave with someone they shouldn't. Maiya had never visited the popular kid's attraction and stared with wide eyes at all the activity surrounding them. "This is complete and utter madness."

"Hell, yeah, it is. Jacob loves it, too. What kid wouldn't, though?"

"Can I go in the maze, Daddy?"

"Sure. Take your shoes off and leave them here. I'll be watching for you to come down the slide."

Jacob took off running and then disappeared into a plastic tube. A few minutes later, he popped out of one of the yellow slides, waved to them and ran right back in the cylinders again.

"Yeah, he'll be in there until I have to drag him out to eat."

Maiya focused on the slide Jacob had come out of the first time, waiting for his little head to appear. She didn't like not being able to see him the whole time.

"Here comes trouble." Ryan's gaze focused over Maiya's shoulder.

"Uh, huh. Look who's talking?"

Maiya turned in her seat, and a woman bearing a slight resemblance to Ryan came up to the table. *Ah, this must be Cyn…I hope.*

The woman kissed Ryan on the cheek. "Good to see you." She looked at Maiya. "Hi, I'm Cyn, Ryan's sister. You are?" She held her hand out for Maiya to shake.

"Cyn, this is my…" He hesitated as if not knowing what label to give her. "This is my good friend, Maiya. Maiya, this is my sister."

Awkwardness settled around Maiya. With a nervous smile, she clasped Cyn's hand in her own and shook it. "Pleasure to meet you."

His sister was on the petite side, with a shapely body. Her short hair was cut into a bob, framing her face, but was darker than Ryan's, more of a chestnut brown.

"Likewise." Cyn slid into the booth next to Ryan.

"Where's Carlos?"

Cyn snorted and rolled her eyes. "Where he always is. 'Busy.' Whatever. Where's the little man?"

"You need to dump that guy."

"Yeah, yeah. Tell me something I don't already know." She looked at Maiya. "Love it when my baby brother gives me relationship advice. As if hearing it from my older siblings *and* my mother isn't enough."

Maiya rolled her eyes. "I hear you there. The minute my mother starts asking me questions about my relationship status, I make a break for it."

Ryan leaned his elbow on the table. "Jacob's in the tubes playing."

"Sweet. I'm gonna go hunt his cute butt down." Cyn kicked off her shoes and headed toward the tubes in search of Jacob.

Maiya pulled her hair over one shoulder. "She's gorgeous."

"Yeah she is. Her boyfriend is a major asshole, though. Wish she'd leave him."

"So you said."

Ryan glanced behind them. "Pizza should be here in a minute."

"Good. I'm starving." As Maiya finished her statement, the pizza arrived.

"I'll go find Jacob and Cyn."

"No, I'll go." She stood.

"I hate to see you go, but I love to watch you walk away." He grinned.

She leaned close to his ear. "You know you're a complete dork, right?" Laughing, she pulled away.

"Yes, but I'm your dork." He tugged her down for a kiss. "Go find my boy and sister before this pie gets cold."

"Yes, sir! You get drinks." *My dork, huh?*

"Yes, ma'am!"

She gave him a salute and then went in search of Jacob and Cyn.

They sat at the booth, eating the pizza and chatting. Jacob bounced in the seat like there were ants in his pants and asked every two minutes if he could go play again. Ryan made him sit and finish one slice before taking off with him to play the Skee-ball machine. Alone with Cyn— *oh, Lord*— Maiya braced herself for a possible onslaught of questions.

"I have to say, your hair is freaking gorgeous. And your tattoos? Wow. Amazing work." Cyn smiled, glancing over Maiya's arms.

Maiya widened her eyes, shocked at the compliments. "Thanks. I guess I'm a bit on the wild side."

"You were expecting me to grill you on your intentions regarding my brother, huh?"

Maiya laughed. "Guilty."

"Eh. Ryan's a big boy. He likes you. That much I can tell."

Maiya leaned forward, resting her elbows on the table. "So, he's mentioned me?"

"Nope. But you wouldn't be here with him and Jacob, or with me for that matter, if he didn't." Cyn picked at the cheese left on her plate. "He doesn't do that. You know, bring women around. So, you must be special."

Maiya eyed a mother trying to calm her child in the midst of a temper tantrum. "We work together."

"That's what Jimmy said. He also said you're senior to Ryan in the company." Cyn's lips tilted into a devious smirk. "I happen to think that's fucking priceless."

"Oh shit." Maiya snorted a laugh. "I guess you're all really close, huh? You talk a lot?"

"Pretty much. There's a ton of us. Thank God our parents stopped when they did. You have any siblings?"

Maiya cringed. She hated having to tell people about her brother. They always wanted to know what happened, and she loathed sharing it. "One brother." She looked at her plate.

"You close with him?"

"I was."

"Was? But not now? Crap, I'm sorry. You must think I'm totally rude. None of my business."

"No. It's okay." Maiya waved her hand, dismissing Cyn's worry. "He died when I was ten."

"Oh God. I'm so sorry." Cyn reached across the table and covered Maiya's hand with hers. "Truly."

"Thanks." Maiya focused on Cyn's hand. It was warm and also comforting. "It was a long time ago. I miss him, but I was young, so it sometimes feels like he was a dream. Does that make sense?"

"Perfect sense." Cyn squeezed her hand and then released it. "What'ya say we go find the boys?"

"Sure." They stood. "Hey, Cyn."

"Yeah?"

"Thanks for not asking me what happened." Maiya

brushed a stray hair out of her eyes. "It may've been a long time ago, but it's still hard to talk about."

Cyn hugged her. Maiya stiffened at the unexpected embrace. Forcing herself to relax, she patted Cyn's back.

"No problem." Cyn pulled away, her expression soft but without pity. "Maybe someday, if you want, you can tell me about it." She smiled, grabbed Maiya's hand, and they set out to find Ryan and Jacob.

Maiya was awestruck. Was his whole family like this, like the families she watched on TV as a kid? Both Jimmy and Cyn made her feel accepted, so maybe they were all this way. If so, she was way out of her league. God help Maiya if he wanted her to meet his parents. She would definitely have to have a few drinks to calm her nerves before that adventure.

Ryan cuffed her wrist in his hand. "Come on."

"Where you taking me? Should I call for help?"

"I'm going to take you into the tunnels and do naughty things to you."

"Ryan!" She tugged on his hold, looked around, and then bent to his ear and lowered her voice. "There are kids here."

He pulled her close and spoke against her ear, his breath feathering over her hair. "Let me tell you something. It's been two days since I've been inside you. You keep whispering in my ear, your breath all warm and beckoning, I *will* find a dark corner and take you from behind." He nuzzled and then bit her neck.

Maiya's skin tingled, and heat pooled low in her tummy from the commanding tone lacing his words. She'd never let him fuck her here, but for crying out loud, the idea of it had her slick and throbbing for that very thing. "Damn, Ryan."

"That's right." He nodded. "I want to race you." He pointed in the direction of two motorcycle games set up side by side.

"You are *totally* on. Be prepared to lose, Mr. Donnelly."

She tossed her hair over her shoulders and sauntered to the game.

Ryan mounted one of the simulated speed bikes. "I'll have you know, at one time, I was the number one winner on this game." He inserted the tokens into the machine.

She snorted and mounted her own bike. "And when was that? Tenth grade?"

"Pfft. Doesn't matter. I got this. Be prepared to be left in the dust."

Maiya gripped the handlebars. "Bring it."

Three games later, she'd won every single round.

"One more." His face was serious, the determination evident in his tone.

Cyn propped a hip against the machine beside them. "You have to learn when to cut your losses, little brother."

Maiya cracked her knuckles. "Stubborn male."

"You mean mule?" Cyn laughed.

"That's one way of putting it." Maiya laughed, too. "Aw, come on. You're not *really* bothered by me kicking your as— butt, right?"

Ryan got off the motorcycle. "Fine. Just don't tell Jimmy. I'll never live it down."

"Sooo gonna tell Jimmy." Maiya grinned and straightened her T-shirt.

Cyn blurted a laugh. "I already texted him."

"Fabulous." He rolled his eyes and cleared his throat. "Excuse me. I have some games to play with my son." He kissed Maiya on the cheek. "Payback is a bitch, isn't it?" He laughed and then wandered over to Jacob, who was playing one of the dance games.

Maiya knew exactly what kind of payback to look forward to. "I'm *sooo* going to milk this one for all it's worth."

"I would. Do me proud." Cyn glanced around. "I need the ladies' room. I'll find you all in a bit."

Maiya smiled and then went and found Ryan and Jacob.

They played games another hour or so, moving from machine to machine. She laughed a lot. Between Jacob and his adorableness and the sibling banter between Ryan and Cyn, she couldn't help the smile that filled her heart. So, this is what it felt like to be part of a family.

They weren't her family, but she sure as hell didn't feel like an outsider, either. It'd be amazing to have happiness like this all of the time.

CHAPTER THIRTY

RYAN HAD WANTED MAIYA TO COME BACK TO HIS HOUSE, BUT she declined, using the morning meeting as the reason. It felt more like she was playing things safe with him, though. If he'd gotten her back at his place, he would have stripped her bare and then tortured her delicious body for hours.

He wanted her begging and breathless, on the brink of orgasm and dripping wet for him, before he gave in and took her. Fire raced through his blood, and he groaned. The thought of how incredible it was to be buried deep inside her wet heat had his dick standing up and taking notice inside his jeans. They'd had such a great time out; he couldn't wait to do it again. But he wanted her there with him, in his bed. Not in some hotel across town. She was right, though; they both had work tomorrow.

After he'd gotten Jacob settled and in bed, he sent her a text.

Ryan: Miss me?

Maiya: Maybe. ☺

Ryan: Who's being stubborn now?

Maiya: Okay fine. I miss you. Happy?

Ryan: Yes. I miss you too. I want you in my bed.

Maiya: Are you in your bed now?

Ryan: No. But I can be. You?

Maiya: Give me 5 minutes then call me.

Ryan: Making demands?

Maiya: I'll make it worth your while.

Ryan: In your bed naked. Now. 5 minutes I'm calling.

Ryan stood, stripped off his clothes and then climbed beneath the covers. She hadn't responded to the last text, but he wasn't worried about it. She'd be ready when he called. Eyeing the clock, he watched the minutes count down. When time was up, he dialed her number.

"Hey, you."

He palmed his stiff cock. "Baby, your voice is so sexy. Have I told you that?"

She giggled, and it rippled over his skin. "I don't know, maybe?"

"Are you wet for me?"

"Mmhmm."

"God damn. Whose pussy is that, baby?"

"Yours." Her voice was breathless.

Sweet music to his ears. "Close your eyes and rub your clit. Tease it for me." He pumped his fist slowly along his shaft. "Is it nice and swollen?"

She let out a little whimper, and his prick throbbed in his hand. "Yes. So good. I wish you were inside me right now."

"Two fingers, deep inside your wet heat. Right now." Jesus,

he couldn't get enough of her. Her voice, her little whimpers of pleasure. His head spun like he was drunk.

"Oh God, baby. I'm clo—" She sucked in a breath and moaned. "I'm so close."

"Ah, baby, not yet. Wait for me. Damn, my prick is rock hard."

"Please?" she begged. "I'm dripping down my ass, I can't —God, please, fuck!"

On the verge of coming himself, he pumped his dick faster, listening to her beg. "What are you, Maiya?" His voice sounded husky to his own ears. "Tell me, and I'll let you come."

She gasped. "I'm your slut."

"Come for me, my dirty girl." He listened to her hard breaths puffing through the phone, and his cock throbbed in his palm.

"Yes! Oh, God, yes. Yours." Her moans grew louder through her release.

"Mine!" He gritted his teeth and stroked twice more, and then gripped the base of his shaft and cupped his balls. His climax struck like an anvil, and his seed ran from the tip, down the length and onto his fist. "Jesus Christ."

She was gasping, trying to catch her breath. When she finally did, she spoke. "God, that was good, but I'd rather have the real thing."

"Tell me about it." He chuckled. "Hang on, baby. I need to wipe up." Setting the phone down, he found a towel and hurried back after he'd cleaned up and got under the blankets. "Okay. I'm back."

"Shit, the bed's all wet."

He tucked his arm behind his head. "Lucky it's a big bed; you can move to the other side."

She yawned. "Very true."

"Ready to sleep?" Ryan rolled to his side.

"Mmhmm. You?"

"Yes." He smothered a yawn with his hand. "Wishing you were here with me, though."

"You're going to become a bad habit if I start sleeping next to you. Besides, Jacob's there."

"I'm absolutely fine with being your habit, but I'd prefer I be a good one and not a bad one." He adjusted his pillow. "Yeah. You're right, I'd worry about freaking Jacob out."

"Besides, early status meeting, remember? I'll see you then."

"Ugh. Hate the early ones. They're before I can get Jacob to school. I'll have to dial in to it from home, but I'll be there right after."

"Okay. Night, Ryan."

"Sweet dreams, baby." Disconnecting the call, he rolled over to his other side and hugged the pillow.

The echoes of Maiya's moans swam in his mind, sending a chill through his body. Maybe if he tried *really* hard, he'd fool his mind into believing it was *her* in his arms instead of the pillow.

CHAPTER THIRTY-ONE

Maiya made it into the office in time for the damn seven a.m. meeting. No matter how early she went to bed, she'd never be a morning person. At least she'd gotten some decent sleep after the incredible call with Ryan.

Sweet baby Jesus, the man made her skin ache to be touched, but by him only. And his voice? Holy hell, he had a sexy voice. His words during the call came rushing to the forefront of her mind and flowed over and through her body like hot lava. Phone sex had never been that good before.

An hour and a half later, Ryan graced the doorway of her office with a fresh coffee from the shop on the corner. He stepped inside in silence and shut the door. Setting her coffee in front of her, Ryan pulled her up from her seat and kissed her. Hard and open-mouthed, he stroked his tongue over hers. He kissed her like he was starved for her.

Maiya was plenty fine with being his meal. She was so amped up from the kiss her whole body quivered in his arms. When he released her, they were both breathing heavy, and it was all she could do not to let him bend her over her desk and fuck her fast and hard right there in her office.

Plopping back down in her seat after he'd left, she

grabbed a few papers and fanned herself, trying to cool the raging heat. After a few minutes, she tried getting back to work but had no luck focusing. An hour later, she gave up and sent an IM to Jodi telling her to meet her downstairs for a smoke.

Maiya leaned against the brick wall of her office building, watching the traffic pass on the busy street. She'd already smoked one cigarette and lit another by the time Jodi got downstairs.

"I was away from my computer when you sent that message. What's up?" Jodi leaned against the wall next to Maiya.

"I needed some air." Maiya exhaled a plume of gray smoke. "I *do not* want to be working today. I can't focus for shit."

"Uh oh." Jodi smiled but then covered her mouth with her hand.

Maiya looked at her. "What?"

"It's happened, hasn't it?" Jodi clasped her hands together. "I knew it!"

"What the hell are you talking about? Nothing's happened."

"You're in love with Ryan Donnelly."

Maiya glared at her. "Fuck you, I am not."

"Oh, yes. You sure are."

"Dammit, Jodi. I *am not.*" She took a long drag of her cigarette. "I just…" She exhaled the smoke and stared at the traffic again. "I like him. A lot."

"Maiya." Jodi placed her hand on her shoulder. "It's okay."

"He wants to date, as in boyfriend-and-girlfriend- exclusively date." She looked at Jodi.

"That's good. Hell, that's great. I'm happy for you."

Maiya stubbed out her cigarette and lit another. "I told him we'd see how the week went."

"Why? I mean, you love him, honey. Even if you can't admit it to yourself yet."

"Will you quit saying that? I am *not* in love with Ryan. For fuck's sake, Jodi!" She shook her head. Frustration burned her gut, hotter than the tip of her cigarette.

"Okay, okay. Fine. You don't love him. But you like him, so why are you hesitating to be in a committed relationship with him?" Jodi grabbed the cigarette from Maiya's fingers and took a drag.

In no mood to share, she lit another cigarette and then stared at her feet. "It's complicated."

"Only if you make it so."

Maiya placed the cigarette between her lips and held her hands out in front of her. They were trembling. "Dammit." She clenched her hands into fists. "We don't even live in the same state."

"Come on, really? Girl, you don't even live six hours from here. It's barely an hour flight, and you've got enough miles from work travel to fly free every weekend for the next year."

"I can't fly here every weekend, Jodi. I've got a life in Vegas, you know? My mom and stuff." What the hell did Jodi think? Maiya couldn't just drop her life, all her responsibilities, because Mister Wonderful, Ryan Donnelly, wanted her to be his girlfriend. *Not gonna happen.*

"You're scared." Jodi poked her in the shoulder. "Look at me, Maiya."

Maiya looked over and exhaled a plume of smoke in Jodi's face. She was not scared.

Jodi fanned it away. "Okay, gross." She placed her hand on Maiya's cheek, and her expression softened. "Don't do this, sweetie. Don't miss this because of fear."

Maiya's eyes welled up with tears, and she blinked, trying to stop them from breaching her lower lids. Jodi pulled her into an embrace. She buried her face in her friend's thick curls and sobbed. "I can't do this, Jodi. I don't think I can do this."

"Of course, you can." Jodi rubbed her back. "You deserve this, sweetie." Pulling away, she fished a tissue from her purse and handed it to Maiya. "I don't know anyone else who deserves it more."

"Thanks." Maiya swiped carefully under each eye with the little white square. "We'll see." She sniffled. "It's complicated."

Jodi pursed her lips. "Yeah, you said that already."

They stayed against the wall until they'd finished smoking and then walked inside together, neither one saying anything more on the subject. She was grateful Jodi knew when to drop it. The conversation ventured way too close to territory Maiya wasn't ready to explore.

And sure, yes, in those moments when they were alone, and she was in his arms, Maiya let herself feel everything and more for him. She put her heart in his hands, but after it was done, and she had some space from him, she always took it right back. She had to. Maiya couldn't let herself be in love with Ryan. It wasn't an option.

Jodi didn't understand. Any day now, Ryan would figure out he deserved better, and he'd drop her like a hot potato. Then where would she be? Flat on her ass, with a shattered heart, is where. It would be more than she could bear.

Maiya walked into her office and shut the door behind her. She had to find a way to tell him no. *Yeah, like I've been able to do so far?* She laughed. *I am well and truly fucked.*

An IM message popped up on her screen.

> Ryan Donnelly: Dinner tonight, my house. 6pm.
>
> Maiya Rossini: I don't know. I'm kinda tired.
>
> Ryan Donnelly: Pshaw, tired schmired. We'll watch a movie with Jacob and I'll rub your feet after he goes to bed.

Dammit. She exhaled a hard breath, trying to figure out

how the hell to tell this man no. It was like the word didn't exist for her where he was concerned. He would *definitely* be rubbing more than her feet. Her clit throbbed, and she squirmed in her seat from the images flying through her mind of the last time he had her on his couch after Jacob had gone to bed. Good God.

> Ryan Donnelly: Hello? You still there?
>
> Maiya Rossini: Yes. Just thinking.
>
> Ryan Donnelly: About?
>
> Maiya Rossini: About why I can't seem to ever tell you NO!
>
> Ryan Donnelly: LOL can't say I'm upset about that. See you at 6, baby.
>
> Maiya Rossini: Ugh. Fine. See you then.
>
> Ryan Donnelly: Ha! That's my girl.

She rolled her eyes.
Yep, I'm fucked.

RYAN GRABBED A SIX-PACK OF BEER ON HIS WAY TO PICK UP Jacob and then ordered a couple dozen wings to be delivered when he got home. While they waited for Maiya and their dinner to arrive, he made Jacob help clean up the little messes made from their morning hustle to get out the door.

His son grumbled the whole time about wanting to play with his Hot Wheels, but Ryan wouldn't let him off the hook until he'd done his age-appropriate share.

The doorbell rang, and Jacob ran for the door, complaints forgotten. "Maiya's here!"

"Wait for me, Jacob." Ryan rushed after him, opening the

door when they reached it. His son's excitement was intoxicating.

Maiya stood on his front porch, a paper bag in her hands with the name Manny's Wings printed on the side. Her beautiful lips curved into a crooked grin. "Delivery."

"Damn, did that arrive the same time you did?" Heaven help him, she looked fine as hell. She was clad in a black tank top and blue jeans with her hair drawn up in a high ponytail. Positively edible.

"Yeah. No big deal. Are you going to let me in, or are we eating on the porch?"

He coughed a laugh and stepped aside to let her pass. The woman never failed to make him chuckle. He kissed her on the cheek, and Jacob wrapped his little arms around her legs, halting her movement. His child was making a habit of doing that. He guessed it was a good thing.

Maiya stopped and looked down at Jacob. "Hey there, sweetie. Did you have a good day?" She smoothed a hand over his son's hair.

"Yes. We had a fire day," Jacob said.

Ryan took the bag from Maiya's hands. "You had a what?"

"A fire day. They made the alarm go off, and we all hadda go outside in a line. No running or talking."

"Ohhh." Ryan breathed a sigh of relief. "You mean you had a fire drill today?"

Jacob looked confused. "That's what I said."

"More or less." Maiya bent down and hugged his son. "I think you scared your daddy and me for a minute there." She mussed his hair.

"Why?"

"Don't worry about it. Go get your cars. Maiya and I are going to set up dinner." Ryan took her hand and led her toward the kitchen.

Jacob ran off toward the family room. A minute or so later, the sound of the television made its way into the kitchen.

Maiya grabbed plates out of the cabinet. "That child is way too smart for his age. He sure has the TV figured out, huh?"

"He *is* male, after all. I think we all come out knowing how to operate electronics." Stepping behind her, he wrapped his arms around her waist and nuzzled her neck. "Mm, you smell good."

She sighed, covered his arms with her own and rested the back of her head on his shoulder. "You feel good."

They stood together for a few precious minutes, swaying back and forth. Satisfaction spread through him. Next to his son, there was nothing better in the world than holding her in his arms. Complete opposites, yet by some miracle, she matched him in more ways than he'd ever imagined. Maiya fit against him in odd, yet perfect precision.

Somehow, in the last few weeks, Maiya had carved a spot in his world, spun it off its axis, and then balanced it again. He was sure she had no idea it'd even happened, but Ryan intended to let her know. He just had to figure out how. Her stomach rumbled, pulling him from his thoughts. "Let's get you fed." Kissing her cheek, Ryan stepped away and arranged the wings on a serving platter. "I got hot and honey ones."

"Sounds great." Maiya set the plates out. "I looove the hot stuff."

"Why does this not surprise me?"

"Oh, shoosh your face. I surprise you all the time." She grabbed a lidded cup and straw for Jacob and opened the fridge. "What do you want him to drink tonight?"

"Milk, if you please. There's beer in there for us."

"Plying me with booze, I see."

"Yes, ma'am. Ain't no shame in my game. Whatever it takes."

"O.M.G. If you start doing the cabbage patch, I might have to beat you with a hot wing."

"Oh yeah, baby. You know I can rock those moves all over this kitchen. Do not eeeven tempt me."

After setting their drinks on the table, Maiya turned, put her hands on her hips and tilted her head to the side, regarding him. Ryan tried like hell to hide his smile because all of a sudden, she looked really damn serious.

"Yes?"

"Are you trying to scare your child? Or the neighbors?" She pointed at her chest. "Or me, for that matter?" Unable to keep it together, she busted up laughing at her own comments.

"Fail!" He pointed his finger at her. "You couldn't hold that one together long enough to get a reaction from me." He started busting a move—cabbage patching it right over to her. "Who's yer daddy? Uh-huh, oh-yeah." Spinning around, he shook his ass in front of her, well aware he was making a total moron of himself. But he didn't care because Maiya was laughing so hard she had to sit down.

"Stop—" She gasped for a breath. "Stop, oh my God, you're killing me." Clutching her stomach, Maiya laughed harder.

Jacob must've heard the commotion because he came running into the kitchen and stopped short. His little mouth split in a wide grin, and he watched his father lose all dignity in their kitchen. "Daddy, you're silly."

Maiya scooped him up onto her lap. "Yes, he sure is. Are you ready to eat, sweetheart?"

Jacob nodded, and she stood and carried him to his seat. Still chuckling, Ryan sat at the table and dished out a couple of wings to Jacob. Maiya took her seat and followed suit, adding wings to her plate. They ate, chatted and joked around, enjoying dinner together.

Man, how life had changed in such a short time.

MAIYA BUSIED HERSELF, CLEARING THE TABLE WHILE RYAN took his son upstairs for a bath. It'd gotten too late for Jacob to stay up for a movie, and the little man, bless his heart, wasn't too happy about it.

She'd promised him, as he pouted, that she'd come up once done in the kitchen and read him three stories again like she had the other night. Poor thing was likely overtired from the activities at Chuck E. Cheese the night before, and then the whole school thing.

After she finished reading with Jacob, she and Ryan made their way back downstairs. She eyed the door across the hall from Jacob's room before they descended the stairs. Must be Ryan's bedroom, the one she'd yet to see.

What did his room look like? She hadn't thought much about it until now. Would he have it decorated much like downstairs? Guys usually didn't care how their sleeping space looked. Hell, most guys rarely changed their sheets, and some were fine with not even sleeping on sheets at all. Gross-out city for sure. But Ryan…he probably had clean, pressed sheets on his bed. She chuckled. Shit, she bet he made his bed every morning right when he got out of it too.

"What's got you giggling?" He grabbed two more beers from the fridge.

"Ohhh nuthin'." She grinned. "Just had a funny thought."

He popped both caps and handed her the cold bottle. "Not gonna share?"

"Nah." Maiya grabbed her smokes from her purse.

"Thanks for cleaning up, babe."

"No need for thanks. You cooked, sort of. I cleaned." She made a beeline for the back porch.

He followed her. "I could get used to this arrangement."

"And now, I need to smoke." She opened the sliding glass door. Settling on the lounger, she stretched her legs out.

Ryan picked up her feet, sat on the end of the lounge and placed them in his lap.

She lit her coffin nail and inhaled deep, watching him

while he slipped off her black Converse and then her socks. She exhaled the smoke away from him. "Do *not* crack my toes."

Smiling, he started rubbing her arches. "How about I just tickle them?"

"So, you *want* to get kicked in the face?"

He raised a hand to his chest and gasped. "You'd do that to me?" He pouted. "Meanie."

"Killing me." She moaned when he rubbed the ball of her foot.

"Ditto." He ran his thumbs down the arch to her heel. "Feel good, baby?"

"Mmhmm." Maiya watched his hands on her foot.

He switched to the other and started the same deep massage at the ball of that foot. He found and rubbed the tight little tendons in her arch. It hurt a little, but it was a good kind of pain. Similar to sex with him. A little bit of pain, meant to bring pleasure, mixed in. A zing of arousal shot through her at the thought, and she shivered.

"Cold, baby?"

She crooked one corner of her lip in a grin. "Not really."

He raised his eyebrows, studying her for a moment, and then returned his focus back to her foot. Taking one last pull on her smoke, she stubbed it out in the ashtray on the little table next to her.

"Ready to go inside?"

"Yes. I'm so tired." She smothered a yawn behind her hand.

Ryan stood and grabbed both their beers. Picking up her socks and sneakers, she followed him into the house. He set the two bottles on the coffee table, careful to put them on coasters.

"You're the only guy I know who does that."

He looked up as he sat on the sofa. "Does what?" He patted the cushion next to him. "Lie down, baby."

She stretched out on the couch. "The coaster thing."

"My mother." Pulling the Afghan off the back of the couch, Ryan crawled behind her and then covered them both with the blanket.

"Let me guess." She snuggled her ass against his hips. "It was like a requirement in your house as a kid, right?"

"Pretty much." He nuzzled her neck. "Wasn't like that at yours?"

Grabbing the remote, she clicked on the TV. "Hell no. Trust me; there was nothing so normal as coasters in my house growing up." She flipped through the channels.

He smoothed his palm down her side to her hip. "Care to share what it *was* like?"

"Ooh, *Wedding Crashers*." She set the remote down. "I love this movie."

"I'll take that as a no, then." He kissed her shoulder.

She turned her head to look at him. "I will. Just not tonight, okay?"

"Whenever you want, baby." He traced the seam of her lips with a fingertip.

Nodding, she kissed his finger before turning back to the TV. A comforting silence settled between them. Ryan wrapped his arm snug around her waist, moving his hand on occasion over her stomach and hip and then returning to her tummy. A sense of ease flowed through her. Maiya felt secure. Safe. Cared for.

Different. So very different.

She sighed, and her body softened against his.

CHAPTER THIRTY-TWO

"Wake up, Daddy. I'm hungry."

Ryan heard his son's request through his sleepy haze. When he opened his eyes, he was treated to the sight of flaming red hair and the feeling of his arm around Maiya's waist. Then Ryan shifted his gaze and met the inquisitive set of young eyes belonging to Jacob—who was standing in front of them.

In the living room.

Them...

They were sleeping on the couch.

Fuck.

"Uhh... Hey, little man." He glanced at the clock on the DVD player: Six a.m. At least they hadn't overslept for work. Ryan squeezed Maiya's side. "Wake up, babe."

With a moan, she arched her back and pushed her ass against his—*oh hell.* Yup, into his morning wood. Dammit.

"Are you hungry, Maiya?"

Maiya shot up like a bomb went off beneath her... and slammed into Ryan, cracking him in the face with her forearm.

"Owww!" Ryan clamped his hand over his jaw and chin.

"Shit!" She looked—panic coating her features— between him and Jacob, and then back to Ryan. She touched his face. "Oh, God. I'm so sorry."

"Why are you sleepin' on the couch?"

Ryan rubbed his palm over his now sore jaw. "Um."

"I'm sorry, sweetie. I guess we fell asleep watching a movie. I better get going." Peeling the Afghan off of them, she rose.

Ryan grabbed the blanket and held it against his groin in order to conceal his morning arousal, and then got himself into a sitting position.

"But it's breakfast time." Jacob fiddled with the waist of his pajamas as if Maiya leaving so soon was nowhere near as important as breakfast. Amazing.

"Uh…oh, um, okay. Let's get some breakfast, but then I have to leave for work." Maiya grabbed his little hand and let Jacob lead her into the kitchen.

Ryan shook his head, got up and headed for the bath-room. When he returned, Maiya was at the table with his son, eating cereal. His chest tightened at the sight. They looked so normal together. Ryan kissed the top of his son's head and proceeded to make a pot of coffee.

Maiya took off after she finished the cereal and a cup of coffee. Getting himself and Jacob ready, Ryan got his son off to school on the bus and then drove into work.

After a long day in the office and only seeing Maiya a couple of times in the morning, Ryan picked up Jacob and made his way home. Damn, he was starved for the sight of her.

"Daddy?"

He looked up from the stove. "Yes, little man?"

"Can Maiya come back for a movie tonight since we dint' getta watch one last night?"

Ryan set the burner to low. "Didn't and get to, little man." He smiled. "I can call her and ask. She was pretty busy today at work, though, so she may not want to." Jacob's brows drew together. Ryan walked over to him at the table. "I'll let you know what she says. You and I can still watch a movie either way, okay?"

"'Kay." Jacob went back to coloring his picture. Ryan stepped away and slid the biscuits in the oven when Jacob spoke up again. "If she comes, I think you should sleep in your bed this time. You're too big for the couch, Daddy."

Ryan froze, but for his mouth dropping open. When he turned around, Jacob's focus was trained on his picture, blue crayon in hand, coloring a balloon. As if he hadn't said anything of importance. Only when Ryan managed to close his mouth and organize his thoughts was he able to speak. "Jacob?"

His son looked up at him.

"What did you think about Maiya sleeping over?"

"Told you. You should sleep in your bed instead." Jacob tilted his head to the side, studying his picture.

"Right. So, it didn't upset you at all?"

"I think Maiya is nice. And pretty."

Ryan walked over and knelt in front of him. "She definitely is both of those things. Hey, you know you can always tell Daddy if something makes you feel sad or upset at all, right?"

"I know." Jacob eyed his box of crayons. "What color should I make the pony?"

Ryan leaned forward, kissed his son's cheek and pulled out the yellow crayon. "This one."

Jacob giggled. "Daddy, ponies aren't yellow."

"They can be. It's your picture. You can make them any color you want. If you don't like yellow, then pick another." Ryan smiled and went back to making dinner.

Wonders never ceased. He'd been torturing himself for no reason because it was obvious Jacob had no issue with Maiya being around. At all. Huh. He supposed most kids would be okay until, of course, the person they'd grown attached to wasn't coming around anymore. Ryan hoped after this week, Maiya would want to stay around.

He checked the biscuits in the oven and then dialed Maiya.

SHOCK STILL VIBRATED THROUGH MAIYA OVER WHAT JACOB said about their chosen sleeping location. It was obvious the child had no issue with her being there that morning. She was also convinced she might've lost her damn mind because she'd packed a bag to spend the night—plus a couple of changes of clothes. Just in case. God help her, she wanted to sleep in Ryan's bed. Wanted to see his personal space and smell his sheets. And, for fuck's sake, she was horny as hell. Crazy or not, she was staying there.

Maiya pulled into his driveway, let go of the wheel and flexed her hands. They ached, and it dawned on her she'd had a death grip on the steering wheel the whole drive there. Nervous energy raced through her limbs. *Why am I nervous?* She closed her eyes and concentrated on her breathing. Not like this was their first time in bed together. Not even their first time sleeping next to each other.

Waking up next to him had made all of this more personal, though. Not that sex wasn't personal, but sleeping next to someone was *really* personal. Way more intimate. When a person slept, they were vulnerable. And then there was cuddling—which was pretty much unavoidable with Ryan. He seemed to love wrapping his arms around her and keeping her close. Maiya didn't have a shot in the world of not becoming more attached to him.

Ryan had vaulted over all of Maiya's walls, and it'd left her raw and exposed. What made it worse was she'd let him. If she was going to be honest with herself, she'd *wanted* him to bust through her barriers and bring her out of the detached, dark place she'd existed in forever.

The front door opened, and Jacob came running out. Damn, she'd been sitting in the car for who knows how long, trying to sort through her mess of thoughts and feelings. Ryan followed and scooped his son up into his arms. Time to jump in with both feet. Maiya got out of the car and pulled her small bag from the backseat.

"Hey, baby." Ryan zigzagged across the lawn toward her. She waved. "Hi."

"Hiiiii, Maiyaaa." Jacob waved and giggled while Ryan held him over his head, moving him in the air like an airplane.

"Hey, sweetie. Not sick of me yet?"

When he reached her, Ryan snorted and kissed her cheek. Then Jacob kissed her cheek, too.

"Oh my gosh! Kisses from both of you?" She smiled, her cheeks tingling. "You boys are gonna make me blush."

"You're awfully pretty when you do." Ryan put his son down. "Jacob thinks you're pretty. Don't you, little man?"

"Daddy!" Jacob buried his face in Ryan's thigh. "You're emmarrissing me."

"Aw." Maiya knelt down. "Don't be embarrassed." She kissed Jacob's forehead, and his color deepened to an adorable shade of pink. "Come on. I'll race you to the house."

With a wide grin, Jacob gazed up at her and then took off running for the door. Maiya laughed and ran after him. When they got inside, Jacob hightailed it to the backyard.

"I hope you like chili. It's not regular chili, though," Ryan said.

"What exactly does 'not regular' mean?" She grabbed three bowls from the cabinet.

"I like when you do that."

"Huh?" She glanced at him. "Do what?"

"That." Crossing his arms, he jerked his chin in her direction.

Maiya set the bowls on the kitchen table at each place and then grabbed napkins from the holder. "What are you talking about?"

Turning, she rested her ass against the table and let her gaze travel over his body. He still wore his work clothes. Gray dress pants hugged his solid thighs and pooled in the perfect length at each ankle. A pale blue dress shirt stretched tight over his equally solid chest. The sleeves rolled up to mid-forearm gave her a nice view of his strong arms. His tie was missing, and the top button of his shirt was open, providing the smallest glimpse of the golden tone of his chest.

Maiya gripped the sides of the table. The sight of him made her go all wobbly-kneed.

"It's sweet chili." Opening the oven, Ryan pulled out a cookie sheet full of biscuits and set them on the stovetop.

She shook her head, dragging her thoughts away from his body, and walked over to retrieve spoons from the silverware drawer. "I'm sure I'll love the chili." With those in hand, she grabbed three small plates for the biscuits. "So, what is it that you like me doing?"

He snagged her by the waist and pulled her close. Maiya gripped the small plates and spoons to avoid dropping them. Ryan buried his face in her hair and pressed soft kisses behind her ear, then her jaw, before traveling to her lips. "That you come in and start getting ready for dinner with me." He kissed her again. "It feels good. Feels right to me."

"I didn't realize setting the table was such a big deal." She kissed his nose. "You're a strange man." She tried to pull away, but he held her still.

"Not strange. Just appreciative is all." He cupped her chin in his hand. "It means a lot to me, babe. So…thanks." He kissed her again and then let her go.

She hadn't expected the praise. And she didn't know how she felt about it. She hadn't meant it as a huge gesture or anything—just doing the right thing and helping out where she could. As she arranged the small plates and spoons on the table, Ryan's cell phone rang. She glanced at him.

"Ryan Donnelly." He turned and faced the stove. "Yes. Are you kidding me? No. Christ, okay fine."

Figuring he might need some privacy, she made her way to the family room. She could still hear him, however.

"Yes, I'll stop by tomorrow on my lunch break. Around twelve-thirty. Are they out of their damn minds?" There was a long pause, and then he continued. "Okay, no problem. See you then." Ryan let out a loud curse. "Baby, where'd you go?"

She stepped back into the kitchen. "I was giving you some privacy."

"Yeah, thanks." He ran his palm over his head and then rubbed the back of his neck.

"Everything okay?"

"Yes. No." He shook his head. "I don't know." His brow furrowed, and his beautiful mouth turned down into a frown.

"Wow. I don't think I've ever seen you so upset." She walked over to him and pulled him into an embrace. "You want to tell me about it?" She rubbed his back.

"Fuck." Sighing, he wrapped his arms around her waist. "It was my attorney. Tammy's parents have filed for additional visitation."

"Oh." She tried to keep the shock from her voice but failed. Damn. She was never good at keeping her emotions from bleeding into her words. "I hadn't realized they saw him now."

"They rarely see him. And it's always here in town. Goddammit!" He shook his head. "We'll talk more about it after Jacob goes to bed."

"All right." She kissed his cheek and moved away. "Dinner almost ready?"

"About five minutes or so." He glanced at the stove and

then back to her. "Let's go see what the little man is up to. He's too quiet." Ryan grabbed her hand and led her to the back door.

CHAPTER THIRTY-THREE

Ryan managed to get through their dinner without losing it. But the movie with Jacob was a little harder to sit through without getting up and working off some of the damn nervous energy racking his system. He couldn't wrap his head around the fact these people were already challenging him on visitation. At least they weren't seeking custody again.

By the time he got Jacob settled into bed, restless nerves had taken over his body, and he was crawling out of every inch of his skin. He took Maiya by the hand, pulled her into his bedroom and then shut the door.

Overcome by the tension devouring his system, he turned and pressed her against the door, kissing her as though he was a drowning man and she was his life raft. "I need you." He gasped for a breath before capturing her mouth again. "I need you now." Not giving her a chance to answer, he pulled up her skirt and hoisted her off her feet.

"Wrap your legs around me." He carried her away from the door to the other wall and ran one hand up her thigh, finding skin. "Goddamn. Thigh highs? I fucking love these on you."

"I know." Something sounding like a growl rose up from

her throat, and she grabbed his shirt and ripped it open, sending buttons flying in all directions. She licked a line from the top of his chest to his throat and then bit his neck.

Ryan let out his own growl, and his need to be inside her went into overdrive, rumbling through him. He tugged her panties to the side and somehow managed to get his pants undone. With his dick free, he stroked through her moist, hot slit with the tip. "Jesus, you're wet."

Pushing his shirt over his shoulders, she gripped the flesh and dug her nails in. "I'm always wet for you."

"Fuck yes, you are." Gripping her full ass in his palms, he positioned himself at her entrance and then slid into her heat in one thrust.

Bliss.

Heaven.

God help him.

Ryan pressed his forehead against hers and held still a moment, allowing her time to adjust and giving himself time to breathe. Maiya pressed her lips to his with a whimper and rocked her hips.

He took it as his cue to get his ass moving. He pulled his length out, leaving the head nestled inside her, and then slid back in again, pressing her harder against the wall. Mindless with the sensations of her channel gripping his cock, he needed to pound into her. Pound her through the wall if he had to. "Eager little slut, aren't you?"

She tilted her pelvis forward. "I'm *your* eager slut."

Ryan came undone. With relentless strokes, he slammed into her. Aside from his torn shirt, they were both still clothed, but he needed to feel her skin beneath his hands and mouth. He grabbed at her top and tore it open, revealing lace-covered breasts.

Taut nipples stood at attention through the thin fabric. He kept a tight grip on her ass with one hand and gripped one full breast in the other. Tugging the fabric down, he ran his thumb over the hard tip.

She bucked against him and dug her nails deeper into his shoulders. "Oh, fuck. Yes! Pinch it, please?" She rocked her hips forward, meeting his relentless thrusts.

Ryan rolled the solid peak between thumb and forefinger and then pinched as she'd so sweetly begged him to do. "I can't stop thinking about how your pussy grips my prick. I need to fuck you every day, Maiya." He dipped his head and sucked the entire areola into his mouth.

She gasped and ran her fingers through his hair. The taste of her swept through him, overwhelming his senses. He loved how she tasted—how she felt. He couldn't get enough of her —wanted all of her and more.

His. She was his.

"I love how you feel inside me." She raked her nails down his back and buried her face in his neck, running her tongue along his skin.

The sounds of their lovemaking—his groans, her whimpers—resonated around them, driving his desire to make her mindless. He slowed his movements and, with shorter thrusts, ground against her clit. "I want to hear you scream my name."

Her channel clenched in little spasms, and he knew she was on the verge of climax.

"Whose pussy is this?" *Thrust.* "Whose?" *Thrust.*

"I'm coming, Ryan. Oh. God."

He thrust harder. "Whose? Tell me!"

"Yours!"

Ryan clamped a hand over her mouth, quieting her, leaving her to breathe and moan through her nose. "That's. Fucking. Right." His voice was low and gravely. Each word said in time with the drive of his hips. "Come for me, my dirty slut. Come all over my dick."

Seizing in his arms, a low guttural cry emerged from

Maiya's chest, vibrating in the palm of his hand still clasped over her mouth. Her orgasm crested, her body trembling in his arms.

"Jesus. Yes, yes!" Ryan pulled his hand from her mouth, gripped her ass tighter and threw his head back. Bucking against her, wild with lust, he gave in to what his body was aching for. The clenching of her tight channel around his throbbing prick sent Ryan flying right over the edge after her. Over and over, he spurted inside her and spots formed behind his closed eyes.

Ryan held her tight to his body, resting his head on her shoulder. Thank God for the wall supporting them, otherwise he'd have fallen with her to the ground. Ryan didn't care. All he wanted was to stay buried deep inside her.

Soft whimpers escaped her with each breath she took, and she trailed featherlike kisses over his shoulder and neck. Raising his head, he sought her lips, sucked her tongue and once again, basked in her taste. When he was finally able to pull them away from the wall, he carried her to the bed and laid her down. He tugged the blankets down beneath her and then removed his shirt and undressed her. "I'm not done with you."

When they were both naked, he climbed back between her welcoming thighs. The heat of skin-on-skin contact seared him to the bone, and Ryan sucked in a breath. She was so warm, so willing; a playground of delight he couldn't wait to explore a thousand times over. When he'd left no part of her untouched by his hands or mouth, he fucked her again.

This time, a little slower.

MAIYA LAY WITH HER HEAD ON RYAN'S CHEST, LISTENING TO the smooth, steady beat of his heart. He stroked his fingers up and down her spine as they basked in the post-coital bliss that came after incredible, mind-altering sex.

The sex had been out of this world. Then again, when hadn't it been that way with him? Fast and furious, biting and scratching, a complete tornado of sexual desire and release. Downright intense is what it was.

What happened after he laid her on his bed was no less intense, but was…different.

His movements had been slow, calculating. He'd made her mindless with each touch, kiss and stroke he delivered to her body. However, his words, falling in whispered tones, had sent her to a place she'd never been before. *You just don't understand. You don't get it. Being apart from you isn't an option anymore. I need you, baby. So badly.*

He'd said these and many other things to her several times while he possessed her body. His words shocked her, and all she could say in response was, *I'm right here, I'm right here with you.* Anything more wasn't possible.

This was so much more than sex. It was making love.

Ryan had been making love to her body, her mind *and* her heart. The emotions his words and movements conjured within her were almost too much to bear, and she was power-less to stop any of it.

She could no more hold back the tidal wave of his feelings than she could her own. And she drowned in all of them.

"Do you need anything?"

"No, I'm fine." She traced the contours of his ribs and snuggled closer.

Kissing the top of her head, he ran his fingers through her hair. "You feel so wonderful."

She raised her head to look at him. It was dark in the room, and she could barely make out the contours of his face. "You want to tell me about the call from the attorney?"

"You sure you want to hear about all that mess?"

She kissed his chest and then laid her head back down. "Only if you want to tell me."

"They already have visitation."

"Okay, so then what more do they want?"

"The deal right now is they get to see him two weeks a year, but they have to come here to do it. It has to be on my turf, not theirs."

"Let me guess, that's not good enough for them anymore?"

"Bingo." He squeezed her closer. "Have I told you how smart you are?"

"I wouldn't go that far. Just coming to the obvious conclusion." Tracing his exposed nipple with her nail, she watched while it tightened to a peak.

"Hey now, I say you're smart, so you are. You're beautiful, too, and if you don't stop toying with my nipple, I'm going to flip you over and show you just how much I appreciate you."

She pinched his nipple. "Is that a threat?"

"One I'll follow through on later." Ryan grabbed her hand. Raising her fingers to his lips, he kissed them.

"In that case, I'll consider it a promise." She smiled. "It's going to be fine, you know that, right?"

He kissed the top of her head. "Yeah. Because there's no other option."

She had no doubt he'd hit the visitation request head-on and win. Closing her eyes, Maiya let out a sigh and snuggled closer, his heart beating a steady drum beneath her ear while he played with her hair.

CHAPTER THIRTY-FOUR

MAIYA WOKE TO THE SOUND OF THE SHOWER RUNNING. SHE rolled to her side, and the usual soreness from spending the night with Ryan made its presence known.

The water shut off, and she sat up and smiled. A few minutes later, he emerged from the bathroom with a blue towel wrapped around his waist. Beads of water clung to his chest, and his hair stuck up in several directions, the obvious result of a run-in with the towel.

"Morning, baby." He stepped into his closet.

Managing a glance around the room, she noted the sparse furnishings. There were two dressers. One, a tall chest of drawers, stood between the entry and bathroom door. The other, its mate, was wide and stout, sat across from the bed. "Morning." She stretched and then flopped back on the pillows. "Do we *have* to go to work today?"

Ryan crawled onto the bed and hovered over her. "You think we can both call in sick?" He nuzzled her neck.

"Doubtful." Yawning, she cupped the back of his wet head. "What time is it?"

"Six-thirty. Jacob'll be up soon. I'm surprised he isn't yet, actually." Ryan got up and walked over to the tall dresser. He dropped the towel to the floor and pulled out a pair of boxer briefs and socks.

Maiya clenched her teeth at the sight of his firm ass and thighs. "Fabulous view in this place." Smiling, she drew the sheets and blankets aside and sat on the edge of the bed.

"You like?" He wiggled a little before he bent to pull his underwear on.

Standing, she gave her own little wiggle. "Very much."

Ryan dropped his socks *and* his jaw.

With hands planted on her hips, Maiya strode past him into the bathroom. She peeked her head back out. "When you're dressed, can you get my bag from downstairs?"

"Damn. Um...what?"

"My bag?" Shaking her head, she laughed. "Close your mouth, Ryan. They're just tits." She turned away and stepped into the shower. With her eyes closed and her hair full of soapy shampoo, Maiya heard the shower door slide open.

"Yes, I will get your bag. And no, they are not 'just tits'. They are *your* tits, and amazing ones at that." He swatted her ass.

She yelped. "Hey!" Cracking one eye open and risking the suds, she looked at him.

The man wore a grin the size of Europe. "Never mind all your ink, too. Hot stuff."

Bending her head back, she let the water wash over her hair, sending the bubbles down her body. He groaned. *Got him.* If he was going to stand there, she may as well give him a show. "Close the door, you're making me cold."

"I know, and your nipples are getting nice and hard. I want to bite them. Like, right now."

"There'll be none of that, Mr. Donnelly. Your sweet little boy will be awake soon, and jeez, don't you think you bit them enough last night?" She covered her sore areolas with her palms.

He ran his fingertip down her arm. "A nipple a day keeps the doctor away."

"Clever. Now shoo. Let me finish." She gave him a quick kiss and then slammed the shower door closed.

"Cold. Real cold, Maiya."

"Yeah, yeah. That's what I was just saying." She couldn't help herself and laughed. "Go get my bag, will you, please?"

"Yes, dear." Ryan exited the bathroom, laughing, too.

Good thing he left when he did. His lust-injected compliments and his light touches had riled her up enough to pull him in the shower with her.

Maiya dried off with the two towels he'd left for her. *Aw, how thoughtful.* Most guys couldn't remember women needed two towels after the shower. He'd also brought her bag, like she'd asked, and left it by the counter. When she poked her head out of the bathroom to thank him, he was nowhere in sight—probably getting Jacob ready.

They were simple things he'd done for her, yet they filled her with a level of joy she'd rarely experienced. Shutting the door, she glanced around his bathroom. It seemed weird, but in a good way, to be in his personal space alone. The temptation to explore filled her mind, but she resisted. The clock was ticking, and they had to go to work.

RYAN HELD HER HAND WHILE THEY DROVE TO WORK. THE morning at home with her had been easy. Jacob had been his normal chipper self at breakfast, eating his cereal and chatting Maiya's ear off. Ryan marveled at how his kid had no issue with her being there with them. As if she'd always been there for breakfast. Maybe the reason Jacob had no issue with Maiya was because she made people want to be around her. His son may not have been this accepting of another woman.

She was the epitome of softness, with hard edges in the

perfect spots. Jacob seemed to see only her softness, which was amazing, while Ryan saw the softness and the hard edges. He wasn't sure which he liked more, but he didn't have to decide. The beauty was, he got to have all of her sides. At least he hoped to have them.

"What are you thinking about?"

He stroked the top of her hand with his thumb, glanced at her and then back to the road. "You."

"Hmm."

"I'm allowed." He squeezed her hand.

"Of course, you're allowed. Is there a porno playing in your mind right now?"

"No, but now that you mentioned it, there probably will be all day."

"Fabulous. Make sure you tell me all the dirty details later." She leaned over the center console and kissed his cheek, and then her soft breath feathered over his ear. "I get to be on top."

Sucking in a breath, Ryan stroked his hand through her hair before gripping the strands between his fingers. "I'm holding you to that tonight."

She ran her hand up his thigh to his groin and cupped him through his dress pants. "Meee-owww."

"Maiya, if you get my dick hard right now, you're going to be sucking it so I can focus at work today."

"Whew! Now, *that* is one hell of a visual."

"I'm so spanking your ass for this tonight. You just wait."

"Yay!" Smiling, she clapped her hands. "Promise?"

"You do realize it's not really a punishment if you enjoy it?" He gripped her thigh. "I'll have to make you beg, then."

She moaned and narrowed her eyes at him. His cock twitched in his pants. Damn, would she ever *not* turn him on? Ryan didn't think it was possible.

He'd successfully managed to get them to work, park and walk inside without taking her in the truck, the garage stairwell, or a wall along the way. Not easy, though. When the elevator doors opened to their floor, they stepped off, hand in hand and damn near smacked into her boss, Tony.

Fuck. They were holding hands, too. Letting go of him, Maiya gave Ryan an "oh shit" look.

He nodded at Tony and walked away. Glancing back before turning the corner, he saw Maiya heading in the other direction, talking with her boss. He hoped she wasn't going to catch hell over them being involved. Some companies didn't allow office romances. He wasn't sure what their company policy was regarding the matter. There'd never been a reason to look something like that up. Turning down the aisle toward his cube, he ran into Jodi. Perfect.

"Good morning, Ryan."

"Good morning, indeed. Just the person I need to see."

Jodi shifted the folders she held in her arms. "Oh yeah? About?"

He looked around to be sure no one was close enough to hear and lowered his voice. "What's the company's policy on office dating?"

Jodi's eyes widened, and then she smiled. A big-ass smile too.

He chuckled. "Okay, you can stop grinning at me like that."

"So, it's official?"

Reluctant to answer the question, Ryan blew out a breath and tilted his head to the side. Maiya hadn't yet agreed to exclusively being his, which pretty much sucked, but beside the point now since her boss clearly saw them.

"Hmm. Follow me to my office." Jodi stepped past him.

He dropped his laptop case in his cube and then made his way to Jodi's office. On his way, he passed Rahul's office and nodded when the guy looked up from his laptop screen. Jodi and Rahul were Maiya's closest friends in L.A.

He should invite them both to dinner or something this

weekend, assuming he could get her to stay for the weekend. He'd have to work on her about it tonight. He stepped into Jodi's office.

"Close the door," she said without looking up from the screen.

"You're bossy." He laughed.

"Hey, I got two kids, a husband and a full-time job. Being bossy comes with the territory. Sit." She motioned to one of the chairs in front of her desk.

"Not going to argue that."

"Believe it or not, I already looked this up a week or so ago. Watching out for my girl, you know."

"Quite nice of you." He took a seat and leaned forward. "So, what does it say?"

"Basically, it's common-sense stuff. Like, if you worked for her or her for you, then it'd be a no-no, but that's not the case, thank the Lord."

Relief washed over him. Letting out a breath, he sat back. "So, we're good?"

"I think so, but it also says something about discretion of management."

"Meaning?"

"I think if your relationship compromises the company in any way, then management reserves the right to either move one of you to a different group or terminate one of you. Not sure which." She frowned at the computer screen.

"That's like two completely different ends of the spectrum." Bending his head forward, he rubbed the back of his neck.

"Yes, but I think you're okay for now. No one knows except us, right? And Rahul. Of course, Rahul knows." She tapped her fingertip to her lips.

"Who told Rahul?"

"I did." She leaned back in her chair, regarding him. "Did something happen?"

"Does Maiya know you told Rahul?"

"Yes. We're friends, Ryan. That's what friends do. Now, did something happen?"

"Tony saw us stepping off the elevator. We were holding hands." Leaning forward again, he rested his elbows on his knees. "He didn't say anything, but Maiya walked off with him."

"Tony is a really great man to work for." Jodi pursed her lips. "I'm betting it's going to be fine." Slapping her hand down on her desk, she stood.

"You think?" He hated the sound of his own voice, a mixture of fear and doubt tainting each word.

"Hell yeah. Don't worry. Come on, you can buy me a cup of coffee downstairs." She smiled and opened the door. "We'll invite Rahul too."

Shaking his head, he followed her out. "Okay, great. Sure."

———

MAIYA SAT IN TONY'S OFFICE FEELING A WHOLE LOT OF nervous. Her palms were sweaty, and the breakfast she ate threatened to make a reappearance. With her luck, if she puked, it'd land all over the top of his desk.

Tony glanced at her over the top of his laptop screen. "You look like you're about to be sick."

She forced a smile. "I'm fine, really." *Please don't fire Ryan. He has a child to care for.*

"Is it serious with him?"

"Define serious?" She crossed her legs.

"Come on, Maiya. I'm a reasonable guy. These things happen." He leaned back in his chair. "Honestly, I'm asking more out of curiosity than anything else, though it's none of my business."

His statement shocked her, and she sat up a little

straighter. "I… I don't know." She fiddled with the cuff on her sleeve. "I don't want him to get into trouble. I mean, I know better, Tony. These things can sometimes get messy. But I won't let that happen." She stood, unable to sit still any longer, and walked to the window in his large office.

"Bah, I'm not concerned about that. I'm sure you'll remain professional, Maiya."

"I appreciate your trust in the matter."

"If he worked for you, or vice versa, we might be having a different discussion. I have to admit, as selfish as I know it might sound, he may be the thing that finally gets you to move back to L.A."

Turning, she paced the area next to his desk. "Can I speak openly?"

He linked his hands over his stomach. "Please do."

"You asked if it was serious. Well, he wants it to be."

"But?"

"But… Ugh, I can't believe I am telling you this." She pivoted and faced him. "Don't take this wrong, but I think I need some fatherly advice." She sank into the chair again, wringing her hands in her lap, quite overwhelmed with the whole situation.

Tony leaned forward, resting his elbows on his desk. "Maiya, look at me." When she did, he continued. "I'm honored, and to tell you the truth, I've always looked upon you like one of my daughters."

"Well, I— Really?" She'd never expected to have him return those feelings. It made sense, though. He'd always taken care of her at work. Encouraged and mentored her even before she worked directly for him. He'd been a stable figure in her career for years now. "That means a lot, Tony. Thanks."

"So, speak freely; you're in good company." He settled back in his seat again.

She took a breath, letting herself relax a little and began

again. "He wants it to be serious, and to be truthful, I'm terrified."

"Of what?"

"Not being good enough." There. She'd said it. Maiya blew out a breath and wiped her forehead with the back of her hand. Damn, she was sweating.

"*Not being*...? Maiya, in all the years I've known you, that has got to be the dumbest thing I have *ever* heard you say."

Shock blasted through her mind so fast she couldn't process. She squared her shoulders, and her jaw dropped.

"Well, it is. Don't look at me like that. You listen carefully to me." He pointed his finger at her. "*You* are an intelligent, beautiful woman. You're full of energy and have more to offer the world than half the people I've met in the last ten years. You are more than good enough, in fact, probably too good for him, and if Ryan Donnelly doesn't treat you as such, then you better dump him right now."

She laughed then. "I don't think I've ever seen you so serious, Tony. Knock it off, you're freaking me out."

"Psshaw." He waved his hand at her. "I mean it."

"I appreciate your kind words. They mean a lot." She relaxed further and crossed her legs. "I think Ryan is a good, kind man. The problem would be me, and yes, maybe my perception is a bit...*off* in regard to this. Either way, I have a lot to think about."

"If there's one thing I've learned over the years, it's not to think too hard on something. Go with your gut and not your head, Maiya. You'd be surprised how right it tends to be."

"So, we have your blessing?"

"Of course." He smiled. "Just don't screw it up. If he's 'the one', then go for it. Jump in with both feet, and don't look back." He chuckled. "Then move your butt to L.A."

Relief washed over her. "Thanks, Tony." She stood. "And thanks for the advice; it's appreciated."

"Any time."

She left his office. On her way to her own, she stopped by Jodi's. "Lunch today?"

Jodi looked up from a pile of paperwork. "Hey, *girrrl*." She grinned. "Yes, please."

"Why do you look like the cat who ate the canary?"

"Do I?" Jodi raised both brows. "What time do you want to eat?"

Maiya checked her schedule on her phone. "How about twelve-thirty?"

"That works. I'll meet you out front."

Maiya placed her hand on her hip. "You didn't answer my question."

"We'll talk at lunch. Now shoo." Jodi waved her hands at Maiya. "I've got a report to get out."

"Suit yourself. I plan on eating. If my mouth is full, I won't be speaking much." Maiya snorted a laugh and walked off before Jodi had a chance to respond.

CHAPTER THIRTY-FIVE

RYAN'S HEAD POUNDED LIKE A JACKHAMMER GOING TO TOWN on a city street. His lunch break had been anything but filling. Instead of picking up a delicious meal, he'd picked up a stack of papers with the word *"visitation"* stamped on every one of them. Ryan rubbed the back of his neck. His attorney intended to handle it with a court-appointed mediator, and if that didn't work, they'd be going to court sometime in the next ninety days.

Bernice and Robert Houston had tap danced all over his last nerve, and he'd about had enough of them. If it weren't for the fact Jacob loved them and the whole court-ordered visitation thing, he would've preferred no contact with them at all. Ryan was beyond ready to pack this whole mess up, with the exception of what special things he'd kept for Jacob in regard to his mother.

On his way back to the office, his father called, inviting him over for a family cookout. Ryan took the opportunity to let him know he'd be bringing a guest. The surprise in his dad's voice was obvious, but of course, he said it was fine. One more mouth around the Donnelly table was never any big deal. Between him and his nine siblings, there was always someone over.

Now, he couldn't wait to tell Maiya what the dinner plans were. Ryan was damn excited for her to meet his family and for them to meet her. Whether they'd like her or not wasn't even a question. *Everyone* loved her.

At first glance, she was almost overwhelming. But in his eyes, and others he'd noticed sneaking glances of her, she was gorgeous. People couldn't help but want to get to know her or hear what opinions she might have on any number of topics. The woman's intelligence was amazing. Plus, she had a wicked sense of humor.

Once settled back at his cube, he waded through the deluge of emails regarding his project and then sent her an IM letting her know dinner would be a cookout at his parents' house.

> Maiya Rossini: You want me to meet your parents? Are you crazy, Ryan?

> Ryan Donnelly: A little, but not in regard to this. Why wouldn't I want you to meet my parents?

> Maiya Rossini: Is it just them, or will anyone else be there?

> Ryan Donnelly: Probably some of my siblings that live close by and their families. Jimmy and Cyn will be there, too. If they're cooking out, Mom's making a feast that could feed the entire neighborhood.

> Maiya Rossini: Oh, Lord. Should we go home...er...I mean, can we stop by your place and change first?

> Ryan Donnelly: Sure. Hey, is this some sort of social anxiety thing you have I'm not aware of?

Maiya Rossini: LOL No. Just when it comes to
your family, I think. I worry I'm too different for
them. I'm not exactly the girl you bring home
to momma if you know what I mean.

He stared at the words in the message window and shook
his head. No way—no fucking way would he tolerate her
thinking she wasn't good enough for him or his family. Ryan
stormed straight to her office. The door was closed when he
got there. Not that he cared. Ryan walked in and closed it
behind him. To hell with knocking.

She looked up from her laptop, eyes wide with shock.
"What are you doing?"

Saying nothing, he stalked around the side of her desk,
gripped her by the arms, pulled her up from her chair and
planted a hard kiss on her mouth. When he broke from her
lips, she was breathing heavy and then reached back, seeking
her chair to sit again.

"What was that for?" She pressed her fingers to her
swollen lips.

Leaning forward, Ryan braced himself on the arms of her
chair. "You are *exactly* the kind of woman I intend to bring
home to 'momma'. And my momma—I don't really call her
that, by the way—is going to love you. So will my father and
my siblings." He pressed another kiss to her lips.

When he pulled back, her hazel eyes had darkened. Lust
or anger, he wasn't sure. Not that it mattered. She needed to
understand this now.

"I just meant I'm not your typical type, Ryan." Maiya
frowned, her brows peaking at the center.

"You *are* my type, Maiya. You're who I want to be with.
Why is it so damn hard for you to accept that?" His tone was
harsher than he'd intended, but it was important she
hear him.

"I'm sorry, okay?" She rubbed her forehead. "I didn't mean to offend you."

Straightening, Ryan ran his fingers through his hair and softened his tone. "You matter to me, baby. I care...deeply about you. I want my family to meet you."

Eyes wide, she blew out a breath. "I don't know what to say. I'm honored, a little shocked, but honored nonetheless." She reached for his hand and held it. "What time are they expecting us?"

"That's my girl." He smiled. "Six-ish. If we can get out of here a little early, we can go home and change first."

"That'd be nice. I don't think high heels and a skirt are the best attire for a cookout." She glanced at her laptop screen. "I'll get wrapped up by four."

"Perfect." He leaned forward and cupped her chin in his hand. "Don't worry. They'll love you." He kissed the tip of her nose and exited as fast as he'd entered.

ONCE AGAIN, MAIYA SAT IN THE FRONT SEAT OF RYAN'S BMW, bubbling over with nervous energy, fidgeting in her purse and then with the radio. It hadn't helped Ryan made her wear a short-sleeve shirt. Her tats would be on display for all of them to see. The drive to his parents' house felt endless, but in reality only took about forty-five minutes with traffic.

They pulled up in front of a sprawling two-story historical colonial set back from the street, and Maiya's mouth dropped open. The house was stunning and confirmed her original assumption. His parents had money—although they may've bought the house years ago when real estate wasn't quite as overpriced as now.

Jacob unbuckled his belt and jumped out of the car, running for the front door before Ryan had turned off the ignition. Cyn greeted her nephew under the portico, scooped him up in her arms and waved to them before disappearing into the house with him.

Ryan grabbed the six-pack of Coronas he'd bought, took her hand and walked toward the door. Every step Maiya took felt like she walked through thick mud.

Just before they entered, Ryan turned and kissed her cheek. "Breathe."

"I swear to God, I am not this much of a freak. I'm fine, honest. Let's go." She gulped her anxiety down and forced a smile.

What *was* her problem? It was just his parents and family; a ton of them, she was sure, but still. She was a damn adult, a corporate professional and a regular badass. She could freaking do this. Game face in place, Maiya stepped through the front door of this gorgeous house and tried like hell not to gawk at the antique décor. It appeared lived in though, warm and welcoming. A place where kids played and adults relaxed. It felt like a home—a real one.

"Mom?" Ryan called out. "In the kitchen!"

"Wow! Your hair is really cool." A young girl with hair hanging in front of one eye walked out from what looked like the formal living room. Did all girls go for that look? Jeez, she was completely out of touch with kids and trends.

"Hey, Julia. Come see," she called over her shoulder.

Another girl, a bit older but with the same hairstyle, came running to them. "Wow! And *ohmygawd* awesome tattoos!"

"Hello there, ladies. This is Maiya. Maiya, these are my two beautiful nieces, Julia and Tori."

Both girls blushed.

"Nice to meet you both." Maiya smiled. "And thanks, I'm glad you like my hair. Yours is pretty cool, too." She wasn't touching the tattoo compliment.

"Our moms won't let us color it yet. You color yours, right? I can kinda tell since it's got, like, three different colors in it. When I grow up, I want to be a hairdresser," Julia said without taking a breath.

Tori looked at Julia. "I'm totally getting tattoos when I'm eighteen. Oh, I didn't tell you. My mom said I can do highlights when I'm thirteen."

"Shut up! She did? I am soooo gonna whine to my mom. That'll be way unfair if you get to and I still can't." Julia pouted and put her hands on her hips.

"We'll see you gorgeous beauty queens in a bit." Ryan shook his head, chuckling and pulled Maiya away.

"It was nice meeting you," Maiya called over her shoulder while he tugged her toward what she assumed was the kitchen. "They're freaking cute."

Ryan squeezed her hand. "My sisters are going to have their hands full when those two hit high school. Serves them right."

Then they entered the greatest kitchen she'd ever seen. With wide eyes, Maiya glanced around the large space. It had one of those stainless steel, professional-chef stoves on one side and a huge island in the center, complete with a prep sink. Dark mocha marble counters topped the antique white cabinets that took up three walls of the space. Beyond the cupboards sat a large rectangular table with enough chairs to seat an army.

At the stove stood a woman about Maiya's height and build with short blonde hair. Not a single gray in sight, either. She turned when they entered and wiped her hands on a towel. "Well, hello there. Your father said you were bringing a guest; I had no idea it was such a pretty one."

Still holding her hand, Ryan walked toward his mother. "Hey, Mom." He kissed her cheek. "This is Maiya Rossini. We work together."

Maiya held out her hand to his mother. *And sleep together.* "Hello, Mrs. Donnelly. It's a pleasure to meet you."

"Please, call me Roseanne." She smiled and took Maiya's offered hand. "It's wonderful to meet you as well, Maiya."

"Everyone else out back?" Ryan asked.

Rosanne moved to the counter. "Naturally."

"Nice to see Mary and Katie both made it out. Cam and Jerry, too?" Ryan pulled two beers from the six-pack and put the remainder in the oversized, to-die-for stainless refrigerator.

Jimmy sauntered into the room. "What? You writing a book?"

"Ahh, here he is, the prodigal son. What up, my brother?" Reaching out, Ryan clasped hands with Jimmy and pulled him into one of those shoulder-to-shoulder manly hugs.

"Same old, same old." Jimmy leaned over and kissed Maiya's cheek. "Hey, darlin'."

"Hey, yourself. Good to see you, Jimmy."

"All right, trouble twins. Out of my kitchen so I can finish prep." Roseanne looked at Maiya. "You get these two together, and it's best to take cover. Oh, and remove any sharp objects." Laughing, Roseanne went over to the island and hacked into a stack of vegetables.

"I've seen them in action, so I have an idea what you're talking about. Can I help at all?"

"Oh no, dear. I've got it. Cooking is what I do for a living, and fortunately, I still love to do it." She looked up from her task. "Go on outside. My kids are all eager to meet the guest Ryan brought to dinner. Jimmy's spent the last half hour teasing them all."

Ryan bumped Jimmy's shoulder with his own. "Dude, what the hell. Seriously?"

Roseanne sliced a cucumber in half. "Language."

"Sorry, Mom," they both said in unison.

With a smile, Ryan held his palm out for Maiya. "Come on, baby. Let's head out back and have a beer."

She took his offered hand, doing her damnedest to stifle a

giggle at how effective Roseanne was at putting them in line. "Guess she told you two."

"Not another word," he mumbled and ushered her into what appeared to be the family room.

Much to her surprise, her anxiety had vanished. She guessed meeting his mother had been the big hurdle she needed to jump. How interesting. Plus, she hadn't so much as glanced at Maiya's tattoos.

On to meet the rest—or part of, at least—his family. They stepped onto the back patio, and...holy shit, there were a lot of people. This wasn't even all of his family. Anxiety slammed back into her tummy like a sledgehammer, and she tightened her grip on Ryan's hand.

Breathe... Breathe...

RYAN PULLED MAIYA FARTHER OUT ONTO THE PATIO. WHEN she squeezed his hand, he leaned over and kissed the side of her head and then let his gaze roam over the patio and back-yard, taking in his family.

His sisters—Katie, Mary and Cyn, along with his sister-in-law, Stephanie—had gathered around one of the outdoor tables on the far end of the patio. His father, Joe Sr., his broth-ers, Joey and Jimmy and his brothers-in-law, Jerry and Camden, were tossing a football around the backyard. His son and his nephews, Steven and Cam Jr., were running around, trying to snatch the ball from the adults.

They made one hell of a motley crew, and not all of his siblings were present. Good thing, too, Maiya might well have had a heart attack. "Come on. It's all good." He led her to the table.

Getting up, Cyn gave her a hug. "Hey, Maiya."

"Hey, Cyn. Nice to see you again."

"Let's do some introductions." Ryan clapped his hands,

rubbing them together. "Don't worry, I don't expect you to remember everyone's name." He nudged Maiya's hip with his own.

"There might be a test later," Katie piped up with a grin.

"Bad form." Ryan chuckled. "I'll go oldest to youngest. How's that?"

Katie tossed a chip at him. "Go for it. Brat."

He went around the table, introducing each sister, stopping to tease each one of them, of course. "Ladies, you know I love every one of you. Now, this is Maiya Rossini. We work together."

"It's nice to meet all of you." Maiya's voice was timid.

"It's nice to meet you, too." Mary stood and shook Maiya's hand, then motioned to her sleeves. "Awesome artwork you have there."

Maiya smiled. "Thanks."

"Join us," Katie said. "Ryan, you go run along and play with the other lesser species."

"Lesser? You just declared war. We're playing Pictionary later, and I am so gonna kick your ass." Ryan rubbed Maiya's lower back.

"Bring it." Cyn grabbed another chair and placed it next to her own. Maiya was nervous, and Cyn must be able to tell. Bless his sister, all of them, actually, because he knew they'd scoop her up. In no more than fifteen minutes, Maiya would be fine.

"Have a seat, babe." He kissed Maiya's cheek. "I'm going to go play with the other cavemen." He grunted, ape-like, at Katie and stepped away from them.

Glancing back, he watched Maiya as she took a seat. When he neared the guys, Jimmy tossed him the ball. Ryan ran toward him, taking him to the ground in a full tackle. *Aw yeah, this is so on!* Jacob jumped on top of both of them, giggling his little head off. A few minutes later, laughter reached his ears from the direction of the ladies. Like he'd thought, Maiya fit right in. Life was definitely good.

Ryan hung with his brothers, and then with Maiya, then back to his brothers. Later, everyone gathered around the patio for dinner. His sisters kept Maiya included in their conversations, and his brothers teased her whenever they had the chance. She laughed and talked with everyone, carving out a space among them like she'd done with him.

After dinner, he carried an empty potato salad bowl into the kitchen and found his mother at the counter. "Thanks, Mom. This was nice."

"It *was* nice." She ran her hands over her hair. "So…?"

"Hmm?" He walked to the sink to rinse out the bowl and put it in the dishwasher. Jimmy was already there, washing pans by hand.

Jimmy set a pot to dry on the rack. "Dude, you know she wants the DL on Maiya."

"You button it up and wash the dishes." Ryan plucked him in the back of the head.

"Oh, you are *so* gonna get payback for that when you least expect it," Jimmy said.

"Not in my kitchen." Their mother sat at the table. "Are you serious about her?"

Ryan approached her and leaned a hip against the island counter. "I'm curious. What do you think, Mom?"

"I think you never bring women around, yet you brought this one. So, yes, I think you're serious about her." Crossing her legs, she propped her elbow on her knee, resting her chin on her fist.

"I think I might be."

"Jimmy says she's senior to you at your company."

Ryan glanced over his shoulder at Jimmy. "Did he now?"

"I plead the fifth." Jimmy scrubbed the pot in front of him.

"I think she's amazing, Mom." Blowing out a breath, Ryan ran his fingers through his hair. "She's got so many different layers, and I want to know all of them." He shoved his hands in his pockets. "The tattoos? Do they bother you?"

His mother laughed and motioned to Jimmy. "Uh…"

Ryan rolled his eyes. "True."

"Stuff like that doesn't matter to your father or me. You know that. I will say, I was a bit surprised when I first saw them, but only because she looks more like Jimmy's type, not yours."

"Weird, huh?"

"Just unexpected, yet I see how you two have been looking at each other all evening. There's definitely something there. I'm happy for you, just…" She tilted her head to the side, a thoughtful smile gracing her lips. "Take it slow. Let it grow, son."

"Feelings have grown pretty quick with her. Like an instant connection. I don't know if slow is in the cards, but I hear you."

Jimmy strolled over, a dishtowel thrown over one shoulder. "Mom, he's been denying his feelings since I've been home. If you ask me, he needs to make her his girl already."

"No one asked you, boy wonder." Ryan chuckled and caught the towel mid-air when his brother tossed it at him. "Well, at least not today."

"You'll figure it out." His mother stood. "Take it outside before I beat both your butts. Don't think I won't just because you're grown. Vamoose. Out of my kitchen, now." She laughed and walked back outside.

CHAPTER THIRTY-SIX

Maiya stayed quiet in the front seat, listening to the music play from the radio on the ride back to Ryan's home. The whole evening had been overwhelming in a wonderful sort of way. Jacob was out like a light, snoozing in the backseat. Poor kid had tired himself out playing with his cousins.

It was interesting seeing Ryan's family interact with one another. She'd had friends growing up who had siblings, but most of those kids were from the same trailer park and didn't have the best families. Not all, but most.

Aside from the few times she'd gone to her college roommate's home for visits, she hadn't been around a family like Ryan's. Of course, they had to have their faults; no family was without them, but they were the closest thing to the Brady Bunch she'd ever encountered.

They'd charmed her for sure. She shouldn't have been surprised since it was exactly how Ryan made her feel most of the time, too. She fit but didn't *exactly* fit, which she realized made no sense at all.

Ryan rubbed her thigh. "Whatcha thinking about?"

"I should call my mother and check in on her."

"Probably a good idea."

"I usually hear from her when I'm gone, but she's been oddly quiet this week. I have to admit I'm a little worried."

"You want to call now or wait until we get to the house?"

"I'll wait." She placed her hand over his and twined their fingers. "Thank you for taking me to meet your family. Or at least some of them. My God, you have a huge family."

"You're welcome." He raised their clasped hands and kissed her fingers. "You fit right in. Just like I said, you would."

"I don't know about that." She brushed a stray hair away from her eyes. "Everyone was really nice, though. I had fun."

"You'll see them more."

"I can't even imagine what the holidays must be like there."

"Stick around, Maiya Rossini." He glanced at her. "You'll get to see firsthand."

"Oh, boy." What in God's name did he mean by that? He couldn't have meant that he thought they'd still be involved by the time the holidays rolled around, could he? She wasn't sure she should ask.

When they got inside the house, Ryan carried Jacob upstairs and got him settled in bed, and Maiya found her spot on the back porch and called her mother. It rang until the voicemail picked up.

"Hmm, that's odd." It was only nine p.m. She dialed again and got the voicemail once more. Her mother wasn't out because she didn't go anywhere. She preferred the ass print worn into her despicable recliner to visiting someone. Maybe she was asleep. Maiya smoked a much-needed cigarette and then made her way upstairs when she was done.

Ryan was coming out of Jacob's room, and he pulled her into his arms. "How's your mom?"

"I didn't reach her. She must be sleeping or something. Odd for her not to answer, though." She nipped at his chin. "I'll try her in the morning."

He ran his hands down her back to her ass. "There's something I need to show you in here." He motioned with his head toward his bedroom.

"Oh really?" She smirked, and he walked her backward into the room and then shut the door behind them with his foot. "Slick."

Catching Maiya off guard, he scooped her up under her arms and tossed her onto the bed like he'd done the other night. She yelped when she landed and burst into giggles.

He tackled her with a growl. "I'll show you slick." He helped her out of her shirt and then ran his lips and tongue over the expanse of skin he exposed.

When she was naked, he stood and removed his clothes and then stretched out beside her. Without preamble, she straddled his hips and slid his hard length into her channel. Riding him at an easy pace, Maiya made love to him. Rolling her body in time with the rise and fall of his pelvis. Ryan sat up and wrapped his arms tight around her waist, holding her in place against his body, and they both tumbled over the edge into climax.

Paradise—sweet, unadulterated paradise. And while she struggled to catch her breath, Maiya became aware of only one thought: she wasn't sure if she could ever again deny the need to experience the paradise that was Ryan Donnelly.

———

RYAN ROLLED OVER AND LAY BESIDE MAIYA, HOLDING HER tight to his chest.

Curling against him, she shivered a little. "Let's get under the covers."

"I'm all for that." He tugged the blankets from beneath them and then covered them. Maiya rolled to her side and backed herself against his chest. Pulling her close, Ryan nuzzled her soft hair and traced the lines of her arm to her waist and then down to her thigh. "Tell me about your brother?"

"It's a sad story. Why do you want to hear that?"

"Because it's part of your past. Part of who you are." He kissed her shoulder. "I want to hear about it."

She took a deep breath and let it out. "All right, but don't get all weird if I start to cry. It happens sometimes."

Keeping quiet, he held her close to his chest. He wanted to know so much about her, especially the things that made her vulnerable yet strong.

"Once upon a time, my mother was a Vegas showgirl. Did I tell you that?"

He smiled against her hair. "Wow. No, you didn't. Must be where you got your talent for dancing."

"Ha, maybe. It didn't last too long, though. She lost the job. I still have no idea why, maybe too much partying, but once she lost it, she became a stripper. Nice, huh?"

"Ah, baby, it's okay. I'm not going to judge her or you." She took another deep breath as if she needed to calm herself again. Aside from the understandable sadness over the loss of her brother, he couldn't understand what made her so reluctant to tell him.

"Anyway, that's when her drinking really escalated. I mean, she always drank, but after she lost the showgirl gig, she took a swim in the deep end of the booze pool and never came out." Wrapping her arm around his, she pulled it closer to her chest. "Jeremy was four years older than me. He took care of me a lot when Mom worked, and when she went off the deep end, he had to take care of me pretty much all the time. She was never home, and when she was, she slept most of the time.

"I was young, but I was pretty rebellious. You know, not coming home right after school like I was supposed to, stuff like that. My poor brother." She shook her head. "Fourteen years old, and he's stuck home taking care of my rambunctious ass. I'm sure he hated it, but he never acted like it, at least not to me."

"I have this vision of what you must have looked like at ten. You were probably adorable." Chuckling, he kissed her shoulder.

She giggled and wiggled her hips. "Someday, I'll show you a picture. I was a skinny bean. No hips, no tits and long skinny legs, but I sure believed I was hot shit."

"Still do. Go on." He was trying to help lighten the mood a little because he had a feeling in a few minutes when she got into the meat of the story, there'd be no humor to be found.

"Whatever." She chuckled. "Anyway…it was a Wednesday, and Jeremy had football practice. I was supposed to go with him, but I blew it off. More interested in hanging out with my friends, I guess. Of course, Jeremy came to find me." She shivered and then pressed closer to him, but he knew it had nothing to do with being cold.

"When he finally tracked me down, I was on one of the main street corners near our trailer park. Man, he looked pissed. I saw him waiting to cross the intersection, and I ran with my friends, away from him, because I knew he was gonna tear into me, and I didn't want to hear it. I guess he ran after me. I heard him yell my name once, and then tires squealing, and someone screamed." She pulled her hand away from his and fisted it in front of her mouth.

Ryan cupped her hand in his for a moment and then stroked her hair while she cried without making a sound. Her body shook in his arms, and it resonated deep in his heart. He thought about telling her to stop, that she didn't need to go on, but he didn't. It was selfish, but he hoped it might bring her closer to him to open up in this way.

After a minute, she began again—her voice thick with tears. "One of my friends grabbed me, and we turned around and ran back toward the intersection. I couldn't see Jeremy, but a cab had stopped just past the crosswalk." Her voice shook as she spoke through her sobs. "There was a crowd already gathering, and when we got closer, I saw him. He was lying on the ground, a pool of blood beneath his head."

She stopped talking then and wept. Ryan urged her to turn over, and when she did, he wrapped her in his arms.

Maiya buried her face in his neck and cried for what seemed like forever before continuing. "It was my fault. He'd run after me instead of waiting for the light to change. Fucking cabbies are lunatics in Vegas, but Jeremy had stepped right into oncoming traffic. It was my fault. If I hadn't run or had gone home to begin with, Jeremy'd still be here."

Ryan stroked her hair and back, remaining silent and letting her cry it out in his arms. The depth of her pain was palpable, and his heart shattered into a million pieces for her.

"It was my fault—all my fault. I should've been home."

He placed his finger under her chin, raising her face to meet his. He let his gaze roam over her shadowed features. She was beautiful, even as she cried.

"You were a child, Maiya." He kissed the tears on her cheeks. "It wasn't your fault, baby."

"But—"

Holding his forefinger over her lips, he quieted her. "Baby, this couldn't possibly be your fault. You were a child. So was Jeremy. He shouldn't have had to take care of you, to begin with."

"But I know it was. Because of what I did, and also, she told me it was."

"Who?" She lay her head back down on his chest, and he stroked through her hair. "Who on earth would lay such a burden on a child?"

She sniffled. "My mother."

Fierce protectiveness and anger bloomed inside Ryan's chest. How in the hell did a mother tell her young daughter it was her fault such a horrible and traumatizing accident happened? His mind rejected the thought that a mother would be that cruel. He kissed her forehead. God, he hoped her mother hadn't meant it.

"Ah, baby," he crooned. "She couldn't have meant it. She must know it wasn't your fault."

CHAPTER THIRTY-SEVEN

Maiya took a deep breath and coughed. Her chest felt tight, and her head ached. Most likely a hangover from her emotional confession to Ryan last night. Maiya cringed. How embarrassing—she'd cried like a damn baby.

She couldn't believe she'd told him all about how Jeremy died. Except, the whole time, he'd held her in his gentle arms, listening and then tried his damnedest to relieve her guilt. She wasn't sure anything would ever be powerful enough to absolve her, but she cherished the fact that he tried. Maybe he cared about her more than she thought.

Ryan stirred behind her. He ran a warm hand up her thigh and nuzzled her hair. "Mmm. Morning, baby."

"Morning." She smiled at the feel of the other good morning pressing against her backside. "I see you're both up."

"Hey, not my fault. You're the one with a delectable ass pressed against my dick. A man can only take so much, you know." He nipped her shoulder.

"Likely story," she scoffed. "Blame me, huh? I'm so getting first dibs on the shower for that one, pal." Getting up, she swayed her hips from side to side on her way to the bathroom.

"And no, I'm not sharing." He growled, and she stuck her tongue out at him before shutting the door.

Starting the shower, she stepped under the spray and proceeded to wash away the tears from last night. Maiya closed her eyes tight. Her thoughts were a jumbled mess of past, present and future as the water ran down her body to the drain.

She'd never confessed the guilt she harbored over Jeremy's death to anyone, or also that her mother blamed her. Never before had she let herself be this vulnerable with anyone, and as a result, she felt raw. But his tender response touched a part of her soul where no one had dared to venture before. Where she'd let no one touch before.

When she stepped back into the bedroom, Ryan was getting dressed. "I grabbed a shower in the other bathroom. Save time, since we overslept a bit." He buttoned his shirt.

"Good thinking. I'll head down and get breakfast going." She turned to walk out.

"Hey, c'mere."

"Hmm?"

"Come here."

Pivoting, Maiya approached him.

"Morning, again." Leaning forward, he kissed her. "Think you might want to stay through the weekend?" He stepped away and grabbed his tie, looping it around his neck.

Maiya raised her brows in surprise. "Oh. Um. To be honest, I hadn't even thought about the fact that I'm supposed to fly home today. Damn." She frowned, and a knot formed in her throat. Did she want to stay? "Either way, I probably need to get home and check on my mother. Speaking of which, I need to call her."

"I understand. It was just a thought." He frowned a bit and then faced the mirror.

He looked disappointed. *Shit.* Maiya didn't want to disappoint him. Ever. All this time, she was convinced he'd be the one administering any hurt feelings between them. It wouldn't be her, yet here she was. The shoe, being on the other foot, turned the lump in her throat to acid. She chewed her thumbnail. "Let me give her a call and see how she's doing. I'm not promising anything, but we'll see. Okay?"

"It's all good, baby. Just figured I'd ask." He smiled, but it didn't quite reach his eyes. *Double shit.*

In the kitchen, she made Jacob a bowl of oatmeal, gave him a kiss on the top of his head and made her way to the back patio. Coffee, cigarette and cell phone in hand, she dialed her mother's number and got no answer. Again. Disconnecting the call, she tried again. No answer.

What the hell was going on? Feeling more than a little panicked, she dialed the next-door neighbor. Maiya asked Mrs. Janowick to go over and check on her mother. The woman had lived next door for over ten years, and she and Joanie had swapped keys long ago. Leaning back in the lounger, she lit another cigarette and held the phone in her palm, willing it to ring.

Ryan poked his head out the door. "Everything okay?"

"I can't reach my mother. I'm getting worried."

Ryan stepped outside, mug of coffee in hand.

"I called the neighbor and asked her to go over and check. I'm waiting for her to call back."

Sitting on the edge of the lounge, he rubbed her leg. "I'm sure she's fine. Try not to worry."

"I know. But she never leaves the house, so it's weird she isn't answering." Maiya sipped her coffee. "You make the best coffee."

"Thanks." He chuckled. "But I think you made this batch, so the credit goes to you."

"Oh. Yeah. Damn, I'm distracted this morning. I'm not going to be worth a shit today if I don't hear back from her."

He took her hand and kissed the palm. "It'll be fine, baby. Deep breath."

Thirty long minutes later, while Maiya was getting her things together, her phone rang. "Hello."

"Maiya, I couldn't wake her up. I tried, but she wasn't responding. I called an ambulance, sweetheart," Mrs. Janowick said.

"Oh my God!" Maiya grabbed her purse.

"I'm sorry; this was the first chance I had to call you back."

"It's okay. Where are they taking her?"

"University Medical Center. Are you home?"

Maiya shoved her sweater in her briefcase. "No, I'm in L.A. for work. I'll be on the next flight out of here."

"I'll head over to the hospital now. Oh, your poor mother."

"Thank you, Mrs. Janowick. I'll be there as soon as I land." Maiya disconnected the call.

Ryan came into the kitchen. "What happened?"

"They've taken her to the hospital. She was unconscious. Oh God, Ryan, I should've known last night. I should've done something." Her voice raised about three octaves as panic spread through her. "I have to fly home right now."

"Easy, Maiya. I'll get the flight changed for you."

She rubbed her forehead. "Fuck. Shit. Okay. Yes, thank you. Thank you."

She needed to get home. Now.

CHAPTER THIRTY-EIGHT

Maiya was staring at her mother's still form in a hospital bed, less than four hours after leaving Ryan's home.

Joanie lay beneath a buttercup-yellow blanket tucked neatly around the edge of the bed. Her eyes were closed, and there were two separate IVs providing medicine and fluids into her bloodstream. The metal railings sat in the raised position on both sides, caging her in place. The room smelled like antiseptic and sickness, and the knots in Maiya's stomach tightened further. Hospitals were so not her favorite place.

With her arms crossed, she waited for the doctor to come in and let her know what the hell was going on with her mother. Maiya stared at the unconscious woman in front of her. She no longer looked like her mother. Years of drinking, and Lord knows what else, had distorted the pretty face Maiya once knew.

Her mother had been beautiful when Maiya was a child. She'd had the creamiest pale skin and shiniest raven-colored hair. Her once beautiful locks were now a straggly mess of dark brown with gray laced through them. The once smooth skin had wrinkled and was tinted a yellow, almost orange color from her liver's inability to filter the bilirubin from her blood.

With a shaking hand, she smoothed the hair off her mother's forehead. "Mommy?"

No response.

"I'm here, Mommy." She stroked her mother's arm. "Just rest, okay? It's going to be all right now."

Again, no response. The only sound in the room was her mother's rattled breathing and the soft beeps of the heart monitor. Turning away from the bed, Maiya paced the room.

A man wearing a lab coat entered, carrying a binder. "Hi, I'm Dr. Guzman. You're Ms. Rossini's daughter?"

Jesus, this is the doctor? The guy looked like he was barely twenty years old. "Yes. I'm her daughter, Maiya Rossini. Nice to meet you." She shook his hand. "What's happening with my mother?"

"Let's step outside the room." After checking another chart hanging on the wall, he ushered her into the hall.

"She's an alcoholic." Cringing, she covered her mouth with her hands. The words were out before she had a chance to stop them.

"Yes, we gathered. We're giving her Valium as a precaution to avoid any complications. Is she a daily drinker?"

"Sorry. Yes. And smoker. She has cirrhosis and COPD and is under the care of two physicians for both."

"We'll need the names of her doctors to obtain her records. Do you have a medical Power of Attorney?"

Maiya shook her head. The various times she'd tried to broach the subject, her mother had flat-out refused. "There won't be any need for that shit," had been her exact words if Maiya remembered correctly. So much for not needing it. "We'll have someone come talk to you about obtaining one since this is an emergency situation."

"Great, thank you." Nodding, she crossed her arms. "Please tell me what's going on."

"It appears the ammonia levels in her blood rose extremely high. This would have affected her cognitive function, causing symptoms such as confusion and delirium, finally, unconsciousness, which is how she was brought in."

"Can you fix it? Is it treatable?"

"We've administered medication to reduce the levels. We'll know in about twenty-four hours if her body will respond. If the medicine does what it's designed to do, she'll begin to wake up."

"What do you mean? Is she in a coma?"

"Of a sort, yes. She's unconscious and unresponsive. We're doing everything we can to make sure she's comfortable. For now, she's as stable as can be expected."

Maiya's hands tingled, and she flexed them. "So, that's it? We just wait."

"Basically. Her body will heal itself if she's strong enough. We're also monitoring her oxygen levels. Her lungs are in poor condition. We'll be watching for signs of pneumonia."

Placing her hand on her forehead, Maiya closed her eyes. "She saw the doctor last week for a checkup. He wanted to do some procedure to drain the fluid in her stomach. She refused."

The doctor checked the chart again. "Yes, her abdomen is quite distended. Once we have a handle on the ammonia levels, we'll schedule her for the paracentesis procedure to drain the fluid."

"Is that why this happened? Because she didn't have the fluid removed last week?"

"Most likely, but from the results of her blood work, she's in end-stage liver disease. Unfortunately, this was only a matter of time." He closed the chart. "Feel free to ask the nurses to page me if you have any other questions."

"Thanks." Releasing a frustrated breath, Maiya walked back into the room. She should have made her mother do the damn procedure instead of letting her blow it off. Instead, she was too focused on Ryan and then ran off to L.A. for him.

Guilt welled up like a tidal wave, swamping her, and she

swallowed down the bitter taste. Sure, work had wanted her there, but in truth, the real motive for the trip had been to see him. Some good daughter she turned out to be.

Speaking of Ryan, she took a seat in the oversized vinyl recliner in the corner of the hospital room and sent him a text.

> Maiya: Hey, I'm at the hospital. It's not looking good. I'll text later.

> Ryan Painintheass: I'm sorry, baby. Is there anything I can do?

> Maiya: No. I'm fine.

> Ryan Painintheass: I'm worried about you.

She didn't respond. Whatever. He didn't need to worry about her. The man had enough on his plate. Although it wasn't his fault her mother was lying in a hospital bed, she couldn't help but feel a bit agitated at him. Maiya didn't want to deal with her own feelings, let alone his. He'd have to get over it.

A few minutes later, her phone rang. Seeing it was Ryan, she let it go to voicemail. Then, it rang again. *Dammit.* He wasn't going to give up. Again, she sent it to voicemail. Then she got a text.

> Ryan Painintheass: I'm coming out there.

Staring at the screen, it occurred to her how apropos the contact name she'd assigned him in her phone was. The bastard was still a pain in her ass and tenacious to an insane degree.

> Maiya: No. I told you I'm fine. Besides, I'm going to be at the hospital all weekend.

Ryan Painintheass: I'm coming out there, and
that's the end of it. I'll see you in three hours. I
suggest you let me know what hospital unless
you want me wandering around Vegas
searching every one of them.

Maiya: Fine. University Medical Center.

Fucking fabulous.

CHAPTER THIRTY-NINE

RATHER THAN LETTING JACOB GO TO AFTER-CARE, RYAN picked him up at school. He wanted to be sure his son understood why he was suddenly rushing out of town.

Jacob had gotten so sad when Ryan told him Maiya's mother was sick. Little man had such a kind heart; he'd colored a picture for Joanie. Ryan would be sure to hang it in the hospital room if Maiya let him.

Her short text messages and refusal to answer his call scraped liked a piece of sandpaper at the patience Ryan normally had with her. He had no idea what the hell was going on, but he intended to find out. The situation with her mother must be grave and would surely explain her curtness. At least, he hoped it would.

After Jimmy arrived to stay with Jacob, Ryan left for the airport to catch his plane. Thankful for the short flight, he grabbed a cab from the airport straight to the hospital. He sent her a text when he got there, asking her to come outside.

Plus, he figured she could probably use a cigarette. Knowing his Maiya, she hadn't stepped out of the room since she'd stepped into it.

Taking a seat on a bench down the sidewalk from the main entrance, Ryan waited.

And then she was there.

Coming to a stop when she cleared the threshold of the automatic doors, she turned and spotted him.

Ryan stood. With his arms loose at his sides, he waited. Maiya took two steps forward but then halted in her tracks. Her head fell forward, and her shoulders began to visibly shake.

Son of a bitch, she was crying. A fierce need to protect her coursed through his veins. The amount of energy it took to quell the urge to run to her, hold her, and ease her suffering was enough to launch a rocket.

Yet, he couldn't allow himself to move. After the story she'd told him last night about her brother, Ryan believed, deep in his soul, no one had taken care of her since Jeremy died. But she hadn't allowed anyone near her heart to try, either.

Maiya *needed* to reach out and then *let* someone take care of her for once, and he just so happened to be the lucky bastard she needed to reach for. It cut him to the bone watching her stand there and cry, though.

After what felt like an eternity, she looked up and then ran to him. Ryan opened his arms, sent up a silent prayer of thanks and enfolded her into his embrace. Cradling her against his chest, he stroked the back of her head. "All right, baby. It's all right."

With a death grip on the back of his shirt, her heart-wrenching sobs shook them both. When her tears ebbed, he kissed the top of her head and led her over to the bench. They both needed to sit.

"I'm sorry," she mumbled.

He stroked her hair. "You don't ever have to be sorry for crying, Maiya."

"Easy for you to say." Pulling a tissue from her pocket, she blew her nose. "Damn, I need a cigarette. I haven't had one since I landed."

"I figured you might. You've been in her room for the last eight hours straight, huh?" He rubbed her back.

"Yeah." She shook her head. "I keep waiting for her to wake up. The doctors said she wouldn't, though, not today, anyway." She lit a cigarette, inhaled and then blew out a stream of gray smoke.

"What are they saying's going on?"

"I told you she was sick, but I didn't tell you what she was sick with." She put the cigarette to her lips and took a long drag. "She's in end-stage liver disease, cirrhosis to be specific. She also has COPD, basically emphysema." She sniffled and looked over at him. "Don't look at me like that. I know I should quit."

"Babe." Wrapping an arm around her shoulders, he pulled her closer. "Yeah, sure, I would love it if you quit smoking, but it wasn't what I was thinking."

"Then what?"

"I happen to be thinking you're an incredible woman. And —" She scoffed and rolled her eyes. "Hey, now. Let me finish." He squeezed her shoulder. "And because she's all you have left, this has got to be hard on you. It's scary, baby."

Maiya leaned forward, staring at the ground. "I don't know what I feel. My relationship with my mother is far from pleasant. I mean, I love her—she's my mother, but I don't like her." She drew on her cigarette again. "Jesus, I sound like such a horrible person, huh?"

"No. You sound like a woman who grew up in a home where she never got taken care of." He stroked her back, and she looked over at him. "You sound like a woman who takes care of her mother, even though she never took care of you."

"I'm no saint, Ryan." She stubbed out her smoke. "I just do what I have to do."

"It's more than a lot of people would do."

She lit another cigarette. After a little while, she rested her head on his shoulder. "Thanks for coming, even though I said not to." She cleared her throat. "You're kind of a pain in the ass."

He chuckled. "Yeah, you've mentioned that a few times." He mussed the top of her hair. "So, I'm guessing you've not eaten, right?"

"Heyyyy. Watch the hair." Smiling, she poked him in the side. "Nope, I haven't eaten. Haven't had any coffee, either."

He raised his arms in the air in a mock stretch. "Guess it's a good thing I came anyway, then, huh?"

"Yeah, yeah. Pipe down."

"Ah, there's my girl."

"Don't make me slap you."

"Tell you what, give me your keys, I'll go drop my stuff at your house and come back with hot food and equally hot coffee. Good?"

"You don't have to do that—I mean, you can go to my house and hang out or something. You don't have to bring food or anything."

"Look at it this way, I have to eat, too, right? And besides —" he held up his hand to stop her from interrupting, "—I came here to not only take care of you, I came here to be with you. So, not another word. Now, keys, please."

She narrowed her eyes. "They're upstairs in my purse."

Standing, he held out his hand to her. "Lead the way."

She shook her head and let out an exasperated sigh, took his hand and did what he said.

About damn time.

Maiya couldn't believe he was determined to stay. In addition, he intended to take care of her. Fat chance. The level of anxiety and annoyance pulsing in her veins far outweighed her patience for his domineering bullshit. She'd managed to take care of herself for the last nineteen years since Jeremy died; she sure as hell didn't need someone stepping up now. What? Did he think he was some prince with two shiny luxury cars come to rescue her from a tower? Not quite.

For now, she'd humor him and let him do what he wanted, but she intended to nip it in the bud as soon as this ordeal was over. She didn't need or want the complication of a relationship in her life. Never mind all the heartbreak often accompanying it.

They were quiet when they entered her mother's hospital room. As expected, nothing much had changed since she'd gone downstairs. Ryan set his bag down and took a moment at the foot of the bed, looking at her mother and the various machines set around the room, she assumed. Before sending him off with her car keys, Maiya asked him to grab a sweat jacket from the mudroom closet for her. Might as well, right?

She eyed the oversized recliner. It folded out to a makeshift bed, and she wondered if they would fit in it, but then dismissed the thought. There was no reason to think he was going to be spending the night there with her. Maiya glanced at his bag, still sitting on the ground at the foot of her mother's bed. Maybe he intended to stay after all.

Ryan returned in less than an hour with a bag of clothes and some toiletries for her. Food and—thank you, baby Jesus —hot coffee for both of them. A downpour of guilt drenched her, washing away her earlier feelings of annoyance. He handed her one of the steaming cups and then pulled the rolling hospital bed table over to where she sat in the recliner.

Thanking him for the coffee, she took a sip of the fresh brew. Ryan lowered the table to a proper level, took a seat in a plastic chair and set out two containers of food for both of them. Every time she'd convinced herself he was going to let her down, he proved her wrong. He said he was here to take care of her, and maybe he meant it. Maybe he meant all of it.

He stopped what he was doing when he noticed her watching him. "What?"

"Nothing. Just watching how efficient you are."

His brows peaked as if he wasn't sure if she was being serious, but then he went back to his task.

"Thank you for this."

"No big deal, babe. It's just food and a coffee." He took a bite of his sandwich.

Maiya covered his hand with hers. "It's so very much more than food and a coffee, and I need you to know I appreciate it."

"I do. Now eat. You're going to need your strength."

"It looks delicious." She picked up a corner of the sandwich and bit in. Nodding, Ryan smiled and then took a bite of his own. She glanced at her mother. "I'm probably going to stay here tonight."

He wiped his mouth with his napkin. "I figured as much."

"I don't know if we'll both fit in this recliner."

"It's all right, I'll sleep in this folding chair if I have to. Either way, I'm not leaving." He sipped his coffee. "Well, at least not until Sunday at six to fly home."

"Where's Jacob?"

"He's with Jimmy at my house for the weekend. I'll get home, and they'll have built racecar tracks running down the stairs and through the formal living room." He chuckled.

"No doubt." She laughed with him and took another bite of her sandwich.

A nurse with short black hair and bright pink lipstick came in to hang another bag of something for her mother and check the monitors. Before leaving, she erased the prior nurse's name from the whiteboard on the wall and added her own. "If you have any questions, let me know." She smiled and left the room.

"Thank you," Maiya called after her. Not able to eat another bite, she pushed the container away and sat back in the recliner.

"Did you eat enough?"

She patted her tummy. "Yes, I'm stuffed. Thanks. Now I need another cigarette."

"Good. I'm just about full myself. Why don't you head down and have your smoke, and I'll clean up."

"You sure?"

"I got this. Go ahead; we'll be here when you get back." He started packing up their mess.

"All right." Releasing a breath, she got up and stepped next to the bed. Maiya stroked her mother's cheek with a tenderness she wasn't used to showing, and gave her a kiss on the forehead, then left the room.

When she got back, Ryan had extended the recliner into a bed and was lying down, looking all perfect and comfortable, reading a magazine. Glancing up at her, he scooted over and rolled to his side. He patted the cushion for her to lie next to him.

Fear and desperate need warred inside Maiya, and she hesitated. There was no energy within her to fight it, though. In truth, she really did want the warmth of his arms around her.

Maybe they'd fit, after all.

And the irony of the statement hadn't escaped her, either.

CHAPTER FORTY

Ryan wasn't sure what time they'd drifted off to sleep, not that it mattered. What mattered was he was there, and Maiya was in his arms.

The rattle of a wet cough and then a raspy voice broke the silence. "Who the hell are you?"

Maiya jerked awake at the sound of Joanie's voice and pushed herself up on one arm. "Mommy?"

"Depends on who's asking," Joanie grumbled. "Christ, I feel like shit."

Getting up, Maiya went to her side. "How are you feeling?" She took her mother's hand.

"I just said I feel like shit, didn't you hear me?"

Ryan righted the recliner and watched the exchange between the two. So, this was Maiya's mother in action. She seemed like a peach. *Not.*

"Aside from that."

"Like I want to sleep. What happened?"

"Mrs. Janowick found you unconscious. Evidently, your liver isn't doing so hot."

Joanie snorted but didn't comment. Maybe the snort *was* the comment.

Maiya reached for the call button. "I'll get the nurse."

Joanie caught Maiya's hand. "I want to go home, Emmie."

"No way in hell. You're not going anywhere, Mom." Depressing the button, Maiya signaled for the nurse.

Joanie strained to sit up but started coughing and wheezing. Maiya supported her mother's back to help her lie back down. "Easy, Mommy."

Joanie struggled and swatted at her daughter, barely missing Maiya's cheek.

She grabbed Joanie's arm and restrained her. "Knock it off, Mom! I'm not screwing around with you. This is serious. Are you listening to me?"

Ryan rushed to Maiya and put his hand on her shoulder. Joanie stilled and closed her eyes, but continued coughing. Maiya turned to look at him, anger and fear burning hot as fire in her eyes. "I can't do this. I am *not* fucking doing this!" Jerking away from him, she fisted both hands at her sides.

A nurse came in and immediately examined Joanie. "Everything okay here?" She'd obviously heard Maiya's outburst from the hall.

Tension filled the room, and Ryan took a step back. Maiya wrapped her arms around her stomach and stayed quiet.

The nurse grabbed a package from the cabinet and then fitted oxygen tubing across Joanie's face. When she was done, she raised the angle of the bed, elevating Joanie's head higher. "She needs to stay calm. I'll page the doctor and let him know she's regained consciousness."

Maiya paced, chewing on her thumbnail.

"I'll go get us some coffee." Ryan waited for a reply. When there was none, he put on his shoes and headed to the hospital cafeteria.

When he approached the room with two coffees and a bag of pastries, he spotted Maiya in the hall talking to who he assumed was the doctor. Giving her some privacy, he stepped into the room. And discovered a very awake Joanie.

"You're the one, aren't you?" Joanie let out a gravely wheeze.

Ryan set the items on the table. "I guess it depends on what you mean by 'the one'."

Joanie coughed a couple times. "Another smart ass. You two must get along real nice then."

"That's one way of looking at it." Chuckling, he stepped over to her bedside. "Nice to meet you, Ms. Rossini. My name's Ryan Donnelly." He took her limp hand in his and gave it a gentle squeeze.

"Polite, too." Her lips curved into a weak smile. "You're the one that's *not* the flavor of the month." Closing her eyes, Joanie drew in a shallow breath.

"I beg your pardon?"

"Don't play dumb, I can already see you're a smart dude. C'mere." Joanie waved him closer, and he bent forward.

Placing a shaking hand on his cheek, she gazed into his eyes. Hers might've been a bright blue at one time. Now, they appeared dull, tired. Sadness colored Ryan's thoughts. He felt bad her life had turned out the way it did, and he could only imagine what dreams she must've had once upon a time. Life knocked people down sometimes, and it could be so hard to get back up and move forward. It made him think of Tammy. Some people never got back up.

"Don't let her push you away, okay?" Her voice was weak, and then she turned her head away and cleared her throat. Facing him again, she continued. "My Emmie? She's stubborn. She pushes everyone away. You're different, though." She patted his cheek. "She deserves you, Mr. Donnelly, so don't let her think any different. Don't let her run you off with her hard exterior, understand?"

"Yes, ma'am." Ryan took the hand she held to his face and then kissed the back of it. "Rest for a bit, okay?"

"Sure, sure." She looked up at the ceiling. "Christ, I want

a cigarette." She snorted and coughed but then closed her eyes and appeared to fall asleep.

Maiya walked back into the room and found Ryan bent over her mother. She was talking, but Maiya couldn't hear what she was saying. Then Ryan took her mother's hand in his and kissed it. What in the world could her mother have said to make him do that? Noticing the coffees he'd bought, Maiya grabbed one off the table.

Ryan approached and took the other cup. "What did the doctor say?"

She took a sip before answering, letting the hot brew warm her too-cold insides. "They're concerned about her lungs. It's the reason for the oxygen tubing. Good chance she's got pneumonia now."

Opening the bag, he took out a cheese Danish for her. "That doesn't sound good."

Maiya took the offered pastry and nibbled the edge. Frustration pricked at her nerves. It bugged the ever-loving crap out of her that he'd talked to her mom, and she hadn't been there. Not like he wasn't allowed or anything, she just...she wanted to know what the woman, who never said anything nice to anyone, said to him. With her mother, one never knew what might come out of her mouth. Screw it. "What did she say to you?"

He paused, mid-sip, and stared at her over the rim of the foam cup. "She said I wasn't good enough for you."

"Shut up! She did not, did she? Oh my God, I am so sorry." She put her hand on her forehead and shook her head.

How mortifying. But it was *her* mother, after all. The woman said what she wanted to whoever she wanted. Didn't matter if they were the damn President of the United States, if Joanie Rossini didn't like a person, she had no problem telling them.

"Shh, baby, relax." He chuckled. "I'm kidding. That's not what she said."

Maiya frowned. "Not funny. That's absolutely something she *would* say, you know." She huffed and took another bite of the Danish. "Thank you for breakfast," she said around a mouthful.

He leaned forward and kissed her, her mouth still full of food. "Mmm."

She swallowed. "That's kinda gross."

"Nope, just makes you sweeter." He smiled.

"Will you two shut up? Trying to sleep over here." Joanie groaned.

"Nice to see your disposition is still normal, Mom."

"Find a way to get me a drink and a cigarette, and my disposition'll be just fine."

"Sorry, no can do." Maiya went to her. "Get some rest. We'll go downstairs for a bit. Okay?" She smoothed her mother's hair back from her forehead.

"Quit fussing over me, Emmie. Go with your man there. I'm not going nowhere."

Leaning in, Maiya kissed the top of her head. "Yes, Mother. I love you, too." Maiya picked up her coffee and what was left of her pastry and headed for the door. She didn't look back, assuming Ryan was following.

When they got outside, and she'd lit her first cigarette of the day, he spoke up. "She told me to take care of you."

Maiya glared at him and exhaled a plume of smoke. "My mother would never say something like that."

Ryan sat on the bench. "Well, she did. She said a few other things, but I think I'll keep those to myself. For now."

"That's fucked up." She took another draw on the filtered tip.

"Yeah, well. You'll get over it." He nudged her shoulder.

"Contrary to what you believe, babe, your mother might love you."

"What? Five minutes with her, and suddenly you're a Joanie expert?" She shook her head. "I'm sure she loves me, she just has a really fucked up way of showing it."

"Maiya, come on. I'm saying she cares about you. She wants you happy."

"She said this to you?"

He rubbed her back. "More or less."

"Well," she took another drag and exhaled, "I'm glad you see it 'cause I don't. But, whatever." She stood and walked to the edge of the sidewalk—the urge to keep walking and not turn back thrummed in time with her heart. Everything about the conversation had Maiya gritting her teeth with annoyance. Words were cheap, after all.

Fuck it. Fuck everything.

"I'll be back." She walked off, determined to clear her head and expel some of her agitation. She'd gone from zero to pissed off in one hot nanosecond, and she didn't want or need him near her right now. Chewing on the inside of her cheek, Maiya shook her hands at her sides, trying to release some of the energy building inside her body.

She just needed to breathe.

RYAN WATCHED WHILE MAIYA WALKED AWAY FROM HIM. IT WAS obvious she was annoyed—the stress of the situation getting to her. He wasn't going to take any of her behavior to heart. She'd be bound to lash out, and if she lashed out at him, then so be it. He'd handle it.

After waiting on the metal bench for an hour—ass gone numb—Maiya returned. Reclaiming her seat beside him, she lit a cigarette. "I'm sorry."

"It's okay." He stroked his fingers through her soft hair. "Feeling any better?"

"Yeah, I just needed to clear my head." She leaned forward and tapped her cigarette, dropping ashes onto the pavement in front of them. "I need a shower."

He rubbed her back. "I think that can be arranged."

Nervous tension roiled off her in waves he could practically see and feel. How things would turn out with her mother and the reality of powerlessness was enough to build his own barrel of nervous energy.

His sole focus was Maiya and being there to support her, and like her mother said, not allowing her to push him away. Though he knew he had no way of stopping her if that's what she chose. Once Maiya set her mind on something, there was no arguing with her, no changing her mind. But Ryan was all in now. No going back. He'd just have to show her and find a way to make her believe.

"Let's go back upstairs."

The sound of her soft, raspy voice pulled Ryan from his thoughts. "Sure, babe."

Taking her hand in his, they made their way back to her mother's room. Joanie appeared to be in a deep sleep, and while Maiya showered in the small stall in the attached bathroom, he spoke with the nurse. They'd given her a sedative to force her body to rest. Her lungs had gotten worse; apparently, pneumonia was a common complication in situations like this.

Maiya emerged from the shower, looking a whole hell of a lot better than when she went in. His heart ached as he relayed the information the nurse had given about Joanie's decreasing condition. Her face fell, and she turned on her heel and left the room.

Ryan gathered a fresh change of clothes and took his own shower. It was almost lunchtime, and although Maiya probably didn't have much of an appetite, he intended on making sure she ate anyway. As he got under the warm spray, the only thing occupying his mind was Maiya. Visions of the last few weeks, and even prior to the start of their affair, played before his eyes, soothing the ache in his heart.

Fighting with her, debating with her, and now loving her was by far the best damn thing on the planet.

Ryan was in love with her, and he wouldn't trade it for anything.

When he finished making himself presentable, he grabbed his cell and made a quick call home to check on Jacob. Of course, his son was doing fine with his Uncle Jimmy, and he didn't even want to get on the phone with Ryan. Instead, his son yelled in the background, "I love you, Daddy. Kiss Maiya for me."

Jimmy laughed and started to relay the message. Ryan chuckled and let him know he'd heard Jacob loud and clear, and then thanked his brother for giving him the help he needed in order to be there for Maiya.

During the call, he remembered the picture Jacob had colored for Joanie. When Maiya came back in the room, looking on the verge of tears, he showed it to her. "Jacob colored it when I was packing for my flight. He wanted me to hang it where your mother could see it and feel better."

She took the crayon-colored picture from his hands and stared at it. Then the tears came.

"Aw, my girl. It's okay."

She shook her head, tears streaming down her cheeks. "None of this is okay."

WHEN MAIYA GOT THE WATERWORKS UNDER CONTROL, SHE sent Ryan to get some tape from the nurse's station. The child had to be the sweetest boy on the planet. She missed him and his bright, inquisitive eyes and gentle smile. A lot. And his hugs...she missed his endearing little hugs, too.

Damn, she'd grown attached to Jacob fast. Maiya swiped away the wetness on her cheeks. Jesus, would she ever stop crying? She was already in too deep with Ryan, and now she'd fallen head over heels in love with his son.

Ryan returned with strips of tape stuck to two of his fingers, on each hand. "Those nurses are *really* protective over their tape. Seriously, they wouldn't let me take the roll. This was their solution. Help, please?" He whimpered. "I think they did it just to see if I'd let them."

"I think you're right. Come here, sticky digits." She waved him closer. "Don't get any ideas there, dude. You just keep those fingers away from my pockets." With a grin, she pulled the first strip of tape free and taped one corner of the picture to the wall, and then followed with the other three.

Together, they took a step back and admired Jacob's artwork. Ryan snaked his arm around her waist, and she let herself lean into him. "It's adorable. He's such a sweet boy."

He rubbed her side. "You think she'll like it?"

"With my mother? You never know, but she might. I'm wondering if she'll get to see it." Maiya glanced over her shoulder at her mother.

"She will, babe." He pulled her into an embrace.

Wrapping her arms around him, she buried her face in his neck and took a deep breath. His scent flowed into her lungs, the special scent that was all Ryan. "I'm scared," she mumbled against his skin.

"I know, baby. I know." He stroked the back of her head. After a moment, he pulled away and kissed her cheek. "That's from Jacob. He told me a bit ago on the phone to make sure I gave you a kiss from him. I almost forgot."

Cupping her face in his hands, Ryan tilted her head up and kissed her slow and tender on her lips. "That one's from me."

She sighed and rubbed her nose over his. The comfort of his kisses and words, and the strength of his arms, grounded her. Made her believe she was being cared for. And though unfamiliar, the feelings settled within her heart and mind like they belonged there.

As she drifted off to sleep in the extended recliner, nestled in Ryan's arms, she let herself imagine a perfect fantasy, one where Ryan had become a home for her and this soft haven, within his embrace, was her safe place.

The next morning, things weren't looking much better for her mother. Her lungs were getting worse, and her liver function had decreased too. There were times throughout the day where she'd become conscious and engaged in brief conversation with Maiya and Ryan, but she wasn't all there—more groggy and disoriented than anything else.

As the time for Ryan to leave grew nearer, panic rose at a steady pace in Maiya's chest. Although she'd fought it at first, having him there had made the whole situation easier to take somehow. She would've been fine without him, but falling asleep in his arms the past two nights had been a balm to her soul.

And she didn't want him to go.

CHAPTER FORTY-ONE

Ryan found an outdoor patio attached to the cafeteria for them to eat lunch. He sipped his soda. "Has she always called you Emmie?"

"It's what Jeremy called me when I was a baby. Easier to say than Maiya, I guess." She shrugged. "After that, it stuck."

"I like it, it's cute."

"Don't even think about it." She rolled her eyes. "My mother insists on calling me that. And really, I wish she didn't. It's a constant reminder of Jeremy."

"It's not wrong for you to remember him, Maiya." Taking her hand, he nudged her shoulder with his. "I didn't know him, obviously, but I can't imagine he'd want you blaming yourself for an accident."

"I loved my brother." She traced the edge of her cup with her fingertip. The expression on her face was dark, and a small crease formed between her brows from her frown. "When I was young, I used to go to sleep at night and wish it'd been me. Sometimes, I still feel that way."

"Maiya, look at me."

She didn't look up. Her shame more obvious to him than

if she had a thick, black blanket wrapped around her. One she could suffocate in. In his opinion, right now, she *was* suffocating. He could only assume her mother's abrupt decline in health must feel like another thousand pounds added to the already heavy weight she carried daily. He reached around her waist. She startled, and he tugged her onto his lap.

"Ryan! Good God, there are other people out here." She glanced around, a frantic look in her eyes.

"I don't give a rat's ass who's around." He gripped her chin and turned her face toward his. "Listen to me. Everything happens for a reason, babe." She tried to avert her eyes, and he was having none of it. "Maiya, look at me." He kept his tone stern. He needed to get her attention.

She complied and raised her gaze to his.

"Everything happens for a reason, and that means *you* were meant to be here. Would it be better to have not lost Jeremy? Yes. Absolutely. But he's gone, baby. Look at all you've done with your life." He shook her when she avoided his gaze again, but then she snapped her eyes right back to his. "I'm serious, dammit! If Jeremy had lived, who knows if you would have fought so hard to make a life for yourself? Who's to say you would've been the success you are? You're here for a reason, baby."

"Why are you pushing me on this?"

"Because it matters to me. You fucking matter to me, Maiya. Don't you get that?"

"We're friends, so yeah, I get it. You care. Just let it go, please?"

He recoiled in shock. "Is that what you think this is? That I merely just *care*, and it's tied to some sort of *friendship*?"

She frowned again and looked away. "I don't know, Ryan. What I do know is—" she glanced back at him, "—I don't want to spend the last few minutes I have with you arguing."

"You have got to be one of the most frustrating women I've ever met."

She snorted. "Well, I guess it keeps things interesting, right?"

Ryan took a deep breath and reached for some calm. "Don't lock me out, Maiya."

"What are you talking about?"

"You know exactly what I'm talking about, and yes, I agree, let's not go there right now. I don't want to argue with you, either."

She put her arms around his neck. "Then how 'bout you shut up and kiss me." She smiled. "Then let me off your lap because we're scaring the children and old people."

Ryan guffawed. Christ, it was just like her to make him laugh when he wanted to strangle her. One more time, she boiled his blood, and then, in a matter of seconds, she calmed him. Complete craziness. So, he did what she asked and kissed her, caressing her mouth with his until her heart pounded against his chest, and she gripped his hair in her fingers. Breaking the contact, he whispered against her lips, "If we don't stop, I'll really be scaring the children and old people. I'm harder than a steel rod right now."

"I know. I am sitting on your lap. I can feel it against my ass, and damn if it doesn't make me want to wiggle a little." She giggled and nipped his bottom lip.

Letting out a groan, Ryan cupped her ass in his palm. "Don't push it. I will find a broom closet somewhere in this damn facility and fuck you senseless."

She pulled back and looked at him, one eyebrow raised. "That's not exactly a threat, Ryan."

"I know." He patted her thigh. "Believe me, I know."

She slid off his lap slow as molasses, dragging her hips over his strangled dick in his jeans. He cleared his throat, and she giggled again. Ryan checked his watch. "Time to go, baby."

"I figured. Time does fly when you're having fun."

"This is true." Standing, he held out his hand, and she took it.

Joanie glanced at them when they entered her room. An oxygen mask covered her mouth and nose, steam billowing from the vents.

Maiya walked over to Joanie's side. "Ah, a breathing treatment. It should help open her lungs a bit. I hope."

Ryan nodded and set to gathering his things. When he finished, he stepped over to Joanie and took her hand in his. Turning her face toward him, she managed a weak smile.

"I won't forget." He raised her hand to his lips and kissed it. "You focus on getting better, and I'll see you soon."

"Thank you." She exhaled a rattled breath behind the mask.

When he turned, Maiya was waiting for him at the door. "Stay here with her, babe. She's awake, and that's a good thing." Pulling her close, he kissed her forehead. "I'll call you when I land, okay?"

"Sure." She glanced at her mother and then back to him and smiled. But it lacked its normal brightness. "Thanks again."

Leaning forward, he pressed a soft kiss to her lips. "Talk soon." He turned and left the room.

Ryan needed to get home to his son, but at the same time, he wanted to be there with Maiya. Nothing like having your heart torn right down the middle. He couldn't be in two places at once, and Jacob had school. This was the only option, and taking it one day at a time would be the only way to get through it.

As he boarded his flight, his chest ached with a physical pain, and he rubbed it, praying he'd be able to be there for her again soon.

MAIYA PULLED THE SMALL CHAIR OVER TO HER MOTHER'S BED and waited while Joanie finished the breathing medicine. The nurse came in and replaced the treatment mask with the oxygen tubing and then added a syringe of additional medicine into her IV tube.

When the nurse left the room, Joanie reached through the metal side bar and grabbed Maiya's hand.

She stood and leaned over her mother. "How're you doing, Mommy?"

"Not so good, Emmie. It hurts when I cough, and I can't get a deep breath." Joanie closed her eyes.

"Just rest. We're going to get through this." Maiya smoothed her palm over the crown of her mother's head. "How about I braid your hair for you?"

Joanie nodded and then coughed. "That'd be nice."

Maiya cringed at the crackle in her mother's cough, almost louder than the cough itself. Getting up, she grabbed a brush and moved to the head of her mother's bed. "Turn your head to the side, okay?"

Joanie did, and then Maiya ran the brush through the long lengths of hair with a gentle stroke. Her mother relaxed further each time Maiya pulled through the length from crown to ends. After Maiya finished brushing the tangles out, she retrieved an elastic hair tie from her bag and returned.

"Cute picture on the wall."

"You noticed." Maiya turned her mother's head to the side again and began folding the length into a braid. "Ryan's son, Jacob, colored that for you."

"He has a son, huh? How old?"

"He's five. Sweet little boy. I'll get Ryan to send me a pic so you can see him."

Joanie coughed. "Where's the mom?"

"She passed a while ago."

"Huh."

Her mother didn't say anything else, and by the time Maiya finished the braid, she'd drifted to sleep. She'd most likely be out for the night, at least Maiya hoped she would.

Fatigue hit hard, blanketing Maiya's body like a second skin. She settled on the makeshift bed and pulled the pillow she and Ryan had shared to her chest. Pressing it to her face, she breathed in deep, taking in his scent. She dozed off with the rough cotton against her cheek.

A while later, a text came in from Ryan, letting her know he'd landed and was on his way home. He asked if she wanted him to call once Jacob was settled, and she let him know she was half asleep. He asked her to call him in the morning and let him know how things were going. In his last message, he said he already missed her and was sorry he had to leave.

She stared at the message for a long while before exhaustion won out and sleep pulled her under.

When she opened her eyes again, her mother was yelling at a nurse. *Awesome.* Rubbing her eyes, she sat up and watched the exchange in silence. Her mother must be feeling more like herself if she was hollering at the people trying to help her.

The flustered nurse left. Maiya stood, ran her fingers through her tangled hair and headed toward the bathroom. "They're just doing their job, Mom."

"How the hell am I supposed to get any sleep when they won't leave me alone?" She coughed. "Do you see the crap they brought me to eat?" Joanie pushed at the contents on the plate with her fork. "Damn eggs are a runny mess. And what's this?" She picked up the small container with a straw sticking out. "Apple juice?"

Maiya smiled, listening to her mother's complaints. For the first time ever, they were a welcome sound. After a quick shower, she dressed in the last fresh set of clothes in her bag. She'd have to run home today and get more. Grab her laptop, too. May as well get some work done while her mom got better.

"Well, don't you look spiffy. How come your man went home?"

She arranged her items in her bag. "He's not my man, Mom. And there's nothing wrong with looking nice on a daily basis."

"Who's the one in denial now, hmm?"

"I'm going to run home and get a few new changes of clothes and my computer. Do you want me to bring you anything special?" Maiya held up a hand, cutting off any wrong requests. "And no, don't say gin or cigarettes. That's not happening."

"Farthest thing from my mind. So there!" Joanie stuck out her tongue. "You ignored what I said, though." Her mother lowered the angle of the bed a bit. "You love the guy, and you're gonna fuck it up if you don't start acting like it and treat him better."

Maiya looked at her mother and let out an exasperated sigh.

"I know what you're thinking. Who'm I to tell you, right? All my attempts at love failed. But Ryan's different. Don't be stupid, Emmie."

"God forbid I choose not to fall all over him and profess my love just so he can reject me and break my heart. If that makes me stupid, then so be it." Shouldering her overnight bag, Maiya started for the door.

"He loves you, Emmie. And you're too stubborn to see it!" Joanie's voice echoed in the room, and then she broke into a coughing frenzy.

The cough got Maiya's attention. She dropped the bag. "Easy now, Mommy." Running into the bathroom, she grabbed a towel, dampened it and went to her mother's side. "I can hear you, no need to yell." She wiped her mother's brow and face with the cool rag and then raised the bed higher.

Joanie closed her eyes and nodded. Although the coughing slowed, it still persisted. With each breath, the wheeze and rattle of her mother's fluid-filled lungs made themselves known. She sounded horrible.

"Try to rest, okay? I won't be long." She kissed her mother's brow and left the room.

CHAPTER FORTY-TWO

MAIYA MADE THE DRIVE TO HER HOUSE, CONSUMED BY THE words her mother had thrown at her. Ryan most certainly did *not* love her, and even if she loved him—not saying she did, of course—Maiya wasn't going to tell him.

She couldn't ever tell him. It was ridiculous to think it'd do her any good. And so what if he wanted to date her? Fine. They could date and have fun, and fuck, and whatever else, but as far as her feelings went, they were staying locked inside her mind and heart. Where they were safe.

Stopping by her mother's trailer first, she grabbed Joanie's favorite Afghan and house robe. Both stunk like cigarette smoke, so when Maiya got to her house, she threw them into be washed and dried. She took another shower, changed her clothes and packed a bag for the week. Grabbing some snacks her mother liked, she loaded everything, including her laptop, into the car.

Maiya walked through the house again, looking around, convinced she was maybe forgetting something. *Quit stalling.* The knowledge of what awaited her at the hospital had a knot forming in her stomach, and she clutched her arms around herself. Giving herself a kick in the ass, she left and headed back to the hospital.

When Maiya entered the hospital room, her mother was asleep, an oxygen mask in place of the tubing. They must have given her another treatment. She settled in the chair and opened her laptop.

"Good afternoon, Miss Rossini. Do you have a moment?" Dr. Guzman said.

The hair on the back of her neck stood on end, and a chill spread down her spine. "Of course." Standing, Maiya followed the doctor into the hall.

"I'm sorry to report your mother's liver is barely functioning." He glanced at the chart in his hands. "The pneumonia has worsened, too. We're using a full oxygen mask rather than the nasal cannula." He closed the chart and looked back at her. "In addition to the medication to control the toxins building in her blood, we've sedated her to help keep her comfortable. I'm sorry, but there's nothing more we can do for her."

"What about putting her on a ventilator?"

"That's an option, however, because her liver is so bad it may only prolong the inevitable."

Maiya crossed her arms. "So, you're saying just let her die?"

"Miss Rossini, her body isn't recovering as we'd hoped, and the pneumonia has only complicated things further."

"That wasn't an answer." She glared.

"Her vital signs are decreasing. She may not make it through the night, even with breathing support. I'm sorry."

Avoiding the doctor's eyes, Maiya leaned against the wall. His words burst the hope her mind had been holding on to. Maybe it was denial. Regardless, she'd shoved the fear of losing her mother far from her mind. And now, she wasn't ready to face it.

"I'll check back in a few hours. Would you like the hospital chaplain to visit?"

His question halted her attempts to ignore what was happening. *My mother is dying, and she needs her last rites given.* Tears filled her eyes, and she nodded.

"I'll have the nurses put in a call. Again, I'm sorry."

"Thank you." Wiping the wetness from her cheeks, she walked back into the room. She gathered the Afghan she'd brought and draped it over her mother's still form and then sat in the plastic chair next to the bed.

Taking her mother's limp hand in her own, she studied the too-thin skin and short nails. Riddled with dark patches, her skin looked bruised. Once upon a time, she'd had beautiful hands. Long, straight fingers and nails. As a child, Maiya had perched by her mother's side while she painted them to perfection.

"Tomorrow, I'll bring some pretty pink polish and paint your nails for you. You'd like that, right?" she asked without expecting a response. "If things get really dull, I'll do your toes too, though those puppies might need a professional." Maiya chuckled and smoothed her hand up her mother's arm, noticing how frail she felt beneath her touch.

"I brought some of your favorite cookies. And those crackers you love so much. When you wake up, you can have some." Standing, she kissed her mother's forehead and then paced the room.

Fear burned the back of her throat, and sweat gathered on her palms. Maiya would be alone. After everything she and her mother had been through, this couldn't be how it all ended. Nothing had gotten better, the way Maiya always hoped it would, between them.

A while later, a tall, white-haired man entered the room, wearing the standard Catholic priest uniform: Black pants, black shirt, little white collar and a Bible in hand. "Miss Rossini?" He motioned toward her mother. "May I?"

Maiya nodded, and he approached the bed, love and compassion evident in his gray eyes. "She's dying." Cringing, she bit her tongue to stop herself from saying more.

"I understand. I'll send her home to our Father with a cleansed soul."

Maiya walked to the farthest corner in the room. Her mother was sedated, so she couldn't make confession, and he couldn't give her Communion, but she wouldn't listen. She didn't want to hear the words he'd say.

She tried to think back to the last time they'd gone to church. Was it when Jeremy died? Her mother was Catholic and had baptized them both and made sure they made their First Communion, but aside from that, they didn't go to church. Religion wasn't something they practiced in their home. How ironic the woman who'd cursed God several times during drunken fits was now being absolved of her sins and given the sacrament to pass on to eternal life within God's kingdom.

My mother is dying. My mother is dying. Reality hit Maiya in the face like a freight train. *Oh, God.* Wrapping her arms around her stomach, she moved to the foot of the bed.

These were the final things a person clung to after everything was said and done, the little quiet moments. Moments to be cherished once the pain faded.

"May the Lord Jesus Christ protect you and lead you to eternal life." The priest made the sign of the cross over her mother, and Maiya blessed herself. When he finished, he faced her. "Would you like Communion?"

She rubbed her arms. "No, thank you, Father."

"Very well. God bless you." He gave her a warm, calming smile and left the room.

In the end, everyone was granted a second chance, even people like her mother.

Maiya stayed at the foot of the bed for what felt like an eternity. Memories, good and bad, of her childhood ran around her mind. She tried to focus on the good ones. The happy times when she and Jeremy were little, and her mother was home more.

"Where've you been?"

"Here with you." Maiya touched her mother's foot through the blankets. "How're you feeling, Mommy?"

"I couldn't find you, and Jeremy said you'd run off again." Her voice was muffled beneath the plastic oxygen mask.

"I—what did you say?" Maiya moved to the side of the bed.

Her mother sucked in a rattled breath and moaned. "I'm sorry, Emmie."

Maiya stroked her cheek. "What for?"

"It wasn't your fault." Joanie coughed. "I blamed you, and it wasn't your fault."

"Mommy, don't." Maiya wiped the tears trickling from the corners of her mother's eyes, and her own began to fall.

"Jeremy told me I needed to let you know." Her mother sucked in another strangled breath. "I'm sorry, baby girl. I should've been there to take care of you."

With her own tears dripping down her face, Maiya stroked her mother's forehead and listened to an apology for the blame Joanie had laid on her for Jeremy's death. Maiya never expected or felt, she deserved one. "You're going to make it harder to breathe if you don't stop crying."

Her mother nodded. Another rattled wheeze and then another cough. The sound made Maiya's stomach fold over on itself, and bile rose in her throat. Her mother sounded like she was drowning in her own phlegm. After wiping under her eyes, she pushed the nurse call button. They needed to suction her mother and give her another breathing treatment.

Her mother grabbed her by the arm, a panicked look on her face. "Listen to me, Emmie. Don't push Ryan away. You understand? Don't give up something good because of all the bad in your past."

"Shh, it's okay. All right, Mommy." Maiya stroked her cheek, trying to calm her down.

"Promise me." Rattled breaths sawed in and out of her mouth behind the mask. "Promise me, Maiya Anne Rossini."

"I… Mommy, please. It's okay. It's going to be okay."

Holy shit, Maiya needed to calm her down.

Her mother dug her fingers in and squeezed Maiya's arm with a strength she shouldn't have been able to possess and then raised her head off the pillow, pinning Maiya with a glare so fierce it raised goose bumps on her skin. "Promise me!"

Why is she doing this? Damn her for doing this! "Fine, Mommy. I promise."

"Good. I love you, Emmie. Jeremy says he loves you, too." Joanie released a long, rattling sigh.

"I love y—"

One of the machines in the room started a high-pitched beeping. Maiya looked over at it and then back to her mother. Her head had fallen back on the pillow, and her eyes were closed. Her face looked peaceful, almost younger than she had in years.

"Mom?" Maiya shook her mother's shoulder. "Mommy, can you hear me?"

All hell broke loose. Two nurses came running in, followed by Dr. Guzman, and one other doctor Maiya didn't recognize.

"What's happening?" Maiya's voice barely split the noise level in the room.

Someone pulled her away from the bed and walked her to the far wall. Everything went from bad to worse, and only bits and pieces of what they were saying registered in her ears.

"She's in cardiac arrest," Dr. Guzman said. "Bag her now!"

Dr. Guzman lowered the bed. "Begin chest compressions."

"Get ready to intubate," the other doctor said.

Maiya stood with her back glued to the wall, watching the

horrific scene play out in front of her. This looked nothing like it did on TV.

"Get the crash cart in here and clear the room."

One of the nurses approached her. Her lips were moving, but Maiya wasn't registering anything coming out of her mouth. Maiya looked over the woman's shoulder at her mom.

Taking Maiya's arm, the nurse tried to lead her to the door. "Miss Rossini, please step out of the room."

She'd heard her that time, but couldn't take her eyes off her mother. And her legs wouldn't cooperate. Then, everything went from high-speed chaos to slow motion.

The bed was reclined all the way; her mother's head tilted back at a severe angle while they shoved a tube down her throat. Her chest was bare, and a man was pushing on it, and it caved in and out with each thrust of his hands.

Maiya cringed, closing her eyes.

None of their efforts mattered, though. She knew it. It was just a matter of time before the doctors and nurses knew it, too. Pulling her arm free from the nurse's grip, Maiya grabbed her purse and left the room.

Her mother was already gone.

CHAPTER FORTY-THREE

Maiya sat downstairs on the same bench she'd occupied many times in the last four days. Her mother was dead. She didn't need the doctors or nurses to confirm it—she knew it at a bone-deep level.

And she felt…nothing.

Lighting a cigarette, she played the last several minutes over in her mind. Her mother had mentioned Jeremy, not once, but twice. She couldn't have seen or spoken to her dead brother, but who was Maiya to question such a thing?

What she said, though, had been hard to hear and even harder to accept.

"I blamed you, and it wasn't your fault. Jeremy told me I needed to let you know. I'm sorry, baby girl. I should've been there to take care of you."

Blowing out a breath, Maiya tried to wrap her mind around each word. For the first time since she could ever remember, her mother, Joanie Lynn Rossini, had admitted her wrongs and apologized.

Maiya checked her cell and found two missed calls and several text messages from Ryan. Shutting it off, she put it in her purse and went back upstairs. She couldn't talk to him right now.

Dr. Guzman stopped her in the hall. "I'm sorry, Miss Rossini. We did all we could."

"Thank you."

"Assuming you would prefer some time alone with her, we haven't moved her yet."

"Oh…um. I hadn't—" Maiya shook her head, trying to gather her thoughts.

"Take all the time you need. When you're ready, let the nurse know."

"I hadn't expected…"

The doctor squeezed her shoulder. "I understand. If you'd rather we—"

"No. No, it's fine. Thank you. I won't be long."

"Take care of yourself, Miss Rossini." He held out his hand, and she shook it.

Maiya entered the room with measured steps and approached the bed. The machines were off, and the IV lines and the tube they'd used to intubate her were gone. There was no sound save for the pounding of Maiya's heart in her ears.

Her mother lay there, eyes closed and at peace. With a trembling hand, she stroked the loose strands of hair—still in the braid she'd put it in the night before—back from her mother's face. Her skin looked waxy, a mottled yellow and grayish-blue color. The woman had led such a hard life and abused her body with reckless abandon. Too far in the abyss to ever come back out.

Maiya traced the line of her mother's nose down to her dry, chapped lips with a shaky fingertip and then traced her jawline. Deep sorrow and regret settled in her heart, forcing a lump into her throat.

She perched on the edge of the bed, took her mother's lifeless hand in her own and stroked the top of it. "I love you, too." She sniffled. "You left before I had a chance to finish telling you, Mommy." Maiya bent and kissed her hand. "And I'm sorry too." Tears welled and dripped down her cheeks. "I'm sorry I wasn't a better daughter. I'm sorry for so many things, Mommy." Maiya raised her mother's cool hand and pressed it against her damp cheek. "I wanted things to be different, and I tried, but it was so hard. Always so hard between us, but I loved you. Even though I didn't always act it, I did, Mommy. I'm sorry I didn't act it."

Maiya lay her head on her mother's lifeless chest and placed her limp hand on the back of her head, wishing she could hear her heartbeat and feel her fingers through her hair.

And she cried. She cried for herself, for Jeremy *and* for her mother. She cried for all of them and the life they'd all lost.

She didn't know how long she stayed there, but when her river of tears finally stopped flowing, she sat up and kissed her mother's forehead one last time.

Gathering her things, Maiya left the room.

CHAPTER FORTY-FOUR

Ryan couldn't get a hold of Maiya, and it was driving him out of his mind. All day, a bad feeling had been settled like a brick in his stomach, and he couldn't shake it. He'd texted several times and called twice. Knowing he had to get up early in the morning, he finally gave up and went to sleep sometime after one in the morning.

Somehow, he managed to get up on time and get his son off to school, checking his phone six million times during the process. Finally, on the drive to the office, his phone rang. He pulled the car over. "Hi."

"She's gone."

"Shit. I'm sorry, baby. When?"

"Last night. I'm sorry I didn't call. I just needed…" She blew out a breath. "I needed some time."

"It's okay. How are you doing?"

"I don't know, really. I said my goodbyes, but now I feel numb."

"That's understandable. God, I'm so sorry. I'll be there tonight, provided I can make arrangements for Jacob."

"No. It's fine. You don't have to come."

"I want to."

"Ryan, you don't need to come. I'm fine."

"Are we back to this again? Jesus, Maiya." He tapped his thumb on the gearshift, frustration burning in his gut, and not quite able to believe she was shutting him out yet again. Especially now.

"Look, I need some space. Is that too much to ask?"

Her clipped words got his attention and also pissed him off. "I really wanted to be there, but if space is what you want, then that I can give you." Ryan tried to keep his tone neutral but failed. He rubbed his forehead, knowing he sounded like an asshole. It was too hard to deal with the push and pull with her. At the hospital, she'd dropped her walls and let him in, and because she had, he thought they'd moved past this. He was wrong.

"I knew you'd be like this. This is why I didn't call you last night. I don't fucking need rescuing, Ryan."

Great. Not only was she shutting him out, she'd rebuilt her damn brick wall too. He envisioned the impassive mask she'd used so often sliding into place. "Christ, Maiya. I'm not trying to rescue you; I'm trying to support you." He pinched the bridge of his nose, and his head began to throb. "Can I come to the funeral at least, or will you be shutting me out of that as well?"

"I'm not having a funeral. Not a traditional one anyway." The sound of her lighting a cigarette resonated in his ear. "She'll be cremated on Saturday, and then I'm having a Catholic mass. I don't think it's necessary for you to come."

"Great. Thanks for letting me know exactly where I fit in your life." He gripped the steering wheel and clenched his teeth.

"This isn't about you and me, Ryan. And I don't really need this shit right now. You want to support me? Then fucking respect what I need and give me some goddamn space!"

"Respect your needs? Tell you what, Maiya, when you

figure out where I fit in your goddamn space, you let me know." Fury lanced through his veins and boiled in his stomach. He disconnected the call without giving her a chance to reply—and before he said anything else in anger.

Maiya had lost her mother, and all he wanted to do was be there for her, take care of her, and what did she do? She slammed the proverbial door right in his face. *She wants space? Fine, she'll get her fucking space.* Peeling out into traffic, Ryan resumed his commute to work.

He stewed for the next few days until his anger settled into a plain old-fashioned river of hurt. She'd hurt him. As a result, he'd lashed out at her in anger. Jodi had barely spoken to Maiya, either, and although knowing that made him feel a little better, it also made him worry. She'd walled herself off from everyone who cared about her. Hopefully, Heather was there with her.

To top off the perfect shitty week, he'd gotten a call from his attorney. There would be no mediation around the new visitation request. He wasn't interested in mediating anyway. He'd rather hit them head-on in court and send them back to Washington with their tails between their legs. A court date was set for three months from now. Fucking fabulous, as Maiya would say.

Saturday came, and he paced the house like a caged animal. Was she okay? Knowing he was in no condition to focus on his child's needs, Ryan sent Jacob to his parent's house for the weekend.

Unable to stand it any longer, Ryan packed a bag and got in the Porsche. Enough was enough.

AFTER THE FUNERAL, MAIYA SAT ALONE ON HER BACK PATIO, sipping her coffee and chain-smoking cigarette after cigarette. She'd spent the majority of the week planning her mother's small service alone, too. No reason for now to be any different.

A few of her mother's friends attended the mass, as well as some of Maiya's. Heather was there, of course, and cried the whole time. But Maiya had kept one eye on the door of the church almost the entire mass, half expecting Ryan to show up.

He hadn't. And why would he? She'd basically kicked him to the curb on Tuesday when they'd last spoken or...argued rather. The sound of the doorbell jerked Maiya from her thoughts. She bolted up from the lounge chair on the patio and ran into the house. Swinging the door open, she froze— speak of the devil and...

"Are you going to let me in or just stand there staring?" Ryan shifted his weight from one foot to the other. "It was a long drive."

She peeked out to her driveway. His Porsche sat ticking and pinging as the engine cooled from what was no doubt a speeding trip from Los Angeles to Vegas.

"Maiya?"

She jerked her focus back to him. "I can't believe you're here."

"Can I come in?"

"Shit. Yes, of course. Sorry." Swallowing past the lump in her throat, she stepped aside.

He walked in, dropped his bag on the floor and turned to face her. Closing the door, she met his gaze. Her tongue had molded itself to the roof of her mouth. Nervous energy vibrated in her palms. He looked pissed. She bit her bottom lip and smoothed both hands down her T-shirt.

Ryan stepped forward, his mouth set in a firm line, and she backed up until she met the hard wood of the door. He positioned one hand above her head and placed the other on her waist, fencing her in. But his warmth wrapped around her, and her heart began to race.

"I'm pissed at you." He stared into her eyes, and his voice was deeper than it'd ever been before. She avoided his intense stare and zeroed in on the ticking muscle in his jaw instead. "Nothing to say, hmm?" Leaning forward, he ran his nose up the side of her neck. "I'm so fucking pissed at you, I drove damn near five hours to see you. Without stopping." He squeezed her side.

"Oh. God." Her body trembled from his light touch. "I'm sorry."

"I know." Ryan kissed her neck. "Let's go." He grabbed her hand, tugged her up the stairs and into her bedroom.

Powerless to stop him, she let him lead her. He'd come for her. The man had gotten in his car and drove across the desert.

For her.

Ryan sat her on her bed. "Stay," he commanded and walked into her bathroom. She heard the shower start, and a few moments later, he emerged stark naked. "Stand up and undress, now."

She hesitated a moment but then did what he said. When she was naked, he took her by the hand, walked her into the bathroom and then stepped into the shower, taking her with him.

Ryan pushed her under the spray. The water ran over her head, dampened her hair and trickled down her face. Maiya leaned her head back under the full spray. He placed a gentle kiss on her neck and ran his fingers through her hair. Pulling her away from the spray a bit, he reached for her shampoo.

"I can do—"

"Shh." Pouring some of the pale lavender liquid into his hand, Ryan lathered the shampoo into her hair. He turned her and spread the bubbles through the long lengths, and then massaged her scalp.

She sighed, enjoying the feel of his hands. "That feels so good."

When he was done, he turned her again and edged her under the spray to rinse the suds out. She reached for the conditioner, and he took the bottle from her. "Let me do this for you." He kissed the tip of her nose. "Let me take care of you. I need to do this."

Maiya pressed her palms to his chest and stared up at him while he smoothed the creamy product through her hair. Ryan dipped his head and kissed her. Soft and slow…sweet. The gentleness in his touch had tears welling, and she swallowed them down with his kiss.

Pulling away, he grabbed the body wash and poured a generous amount into his palm. After building the liquid into a lather, he smoothed his soapy hands over her skin, massaging her shoulders and down her arms. She held on to his shoulders, entranced, gazing deep into his eyes. The tender expression in them swamped her senses and made her feel off-center, yet grounded…as long as she held on to him.

Ryan moved his hands over her collarbones to her breasts, palming and kneading each mound of flesh. Going to his knees before her, he smoothed the soap over her stomach and onto her hips. "Spread your legs for me."

She did as he asked and shuddered when he spread her labia and washed her most intimate parts.

"You have such a beautiful pussy." Ryan's voice had gone deep and gravely.

Maiya's stomach jumped, and she gripped the skin of his shoulders, digging her nails in. Ryan continued down her thighs, washing each leg, from hip to ankle. He lifted each foot and washed over the sole with his palm. His brow was furrowed, his lips in a tight line, like he was concentrating on every part of her skin, making sure he didn't miss a spot. It was the most sensual thing she'd ever experienced, and as her heart raced, all she could do was watch him with wonder.

Ryan rose to his feet, his gaze steady on hers. The care he showed her would be her undoing. She knew as he washed her with precise motions, he broke down her walls, brick by solid brick. Maiya didn't have a chance of resisting him.

Again, he pushed her beneath the spray to rinse her. Pressing his warm, wet body against hers, he ran his hands up and down her sides and then over her back and bottom, washing the soap away. "Let me take care of you, baby."

Cupping her face in his hands, he kissed her—an endless, open-mouthed kiss.

Maiya let herself sink into him. His lips were soft, his tongue firm and hot against hers. She undulated against him and explored his back and firm buttocks with her hands. His body was perfect. His erection, thick and hard, pressed to her belly between them.

No man had fit this perfect against her body before.

Moving a hand down her back, Ryan held her tight against him. Maiya moaned into his mouth, threading her fingers through his wet hair. He gripped her jaw with his other hand, controlling the kiss—controlling everything.

Ryan pulled away and pressed his forehead to hers. "I love you." He licked his lips. "I'm in love with you, Maiya."

Her vision blurred, and the small space of her shower spun around her. She wasn't sure if it was from the kissing or from the declaration of his love. She closed her eyes and swallowed, then drew in a deep breath. "I need you inside me."

Holding her tight, he turned them and pressed her to the shower wall. He gripped both of her thighs and raised her off of her feet. Maiya wrapped her legs around his waist and sank down onto his erection. His length filled her completely, and she sucked in a breath and bit his shoulder. She couldn't say *I love you* back; couldn't allow those three little words to escape her lips.

Emotions raced through her veins, and her pulse beat in her ears. It was overwhelming and wonderful and so very terrifying. He'd taken care of her physical needs and then possessed her heart and soul. Maiya could only give him this part of her, as she'd done many times before tonight.

But this time, for the first time, she let herself make love to him, against the wall in her shower and then after, again in her bed.

She fell asleep in his arms, with his words echoing in her mind.

RYAN LAY THERE, LISTENING TO HER BREATHE, RELISHING THE softness of her skin and the warmth of her body. The tension that'd been building all week had peaked when he'd arrived. After seeing her face and then ordering her into the shower, he'd lost it, no longer able to hold back his feelings. He loved her, and there was no going back for him.

She'd been so vulnerable once they'd gotten into the shower as if he'd finally pushed past her walls. Then, after, while making love, she'd been more tender with him than ever before. Even though she hadn't said *I love you* back, he *felt* her love to the bottom of his soul. Ryan held her closer to his body. She couldn't push him away while she slept, that he was quite sure of.

The next morning, he woke when Maiya shifted, snuggling against him. "I have to leave soon," he whispered.

She didn't respond, only nodded, and he stroked his fingers through her hair. After a bit longer, she got up, pulled on her robe and walked to the door. "I'll go make a pot of coffee."

Awkwardness settled between them in the kitchen, neither of them having much to say. He'd said the words, and it was as if they'd fallen between them on the floor, creating another hurdle for them to climb over. *Dammit, this is hard.*

He wasn't willing to take them back, though.

She walked him to the door and kissed him, then wrapped her arms around his neck, holding him tight to her chest.

"I meant what I said last night." Burying his face in her hair, he breathed her in. "They weren't just words in the heat of the moment."

She took a step back. "I know."

"I'll talk to you soon." Ryan placed a small kiss on her cheek and then turned and left.

The ball was in her court.

CHAPTER FORTY-FIVE

Maiya took the next two weeks off from work, taking the time she needed in order to settle her mother's affairs. There wasn't much to be done, and no close family members to distribute anything to. Her mother had a sister somewhere in the Midwest, but Maiya hadn't seen her or heard anything about her since she was a child.

Most of her time was spent cleaning out the trailer. And crying. Lots of crying while she sorted through piles of paper, old photographs and clothing. The photographs had been easier than she expected. Mom, when she was young and vibrant, Maiya and Jeremy, as kids—both with cheesy big grins, playing in one of the casino hotel pools. Days long gone. Who were those people she stared at in the photographs? It felt like a lifetime ago in a whole different world.

The bedroom closet was last; most of the clothes were too old to even bother donating. Maiya pulled out item after item, tossing each into a pile on the floor until she unveiled a hidden treasure. She sucked in a breath at what she'd found: three showgirl costumes remained in sealed zippered vinyl bags in immaculate condition. Had her mother even known they were still in there?

Maiya pulled them out, laid them on the bed and unzipped each bag. Each costume was a different color, sequins twinkling in the light above. She ran her hand down the bodice of the red one with reverent care.

So beautiful…her mother had been beautiful too when she'd last worn these. Maiya sat on the bed, closed her eyes and pictured her, clear as day, in the corner of this very room, spinning in front of the full-length mirror.

Joanie swung the skirt side to side. "Look, Emmie, look! Isn't it beautiful?"

"Yes, Mommy. Yes!" Little Maiya giggled and danced around her mother.

"You make them look beautiful, Mom." Jeremy's pride was evident in his tone.

Maiya shook herself out of the memory, grabbed yet another tissue, wiped her tear-streaked cheeks and blew her nose. She sealed the dresses back in their bags; those would be coming home with her.

She stepped onto the front stoop, lit a cigarette and thought about Ryan. He'd have been knee-deep in all of this mess helping her if she'd let him. As expected, he called, letting her know he'd arrived home safe after leaving Vegas the morning after the funeral. Their conversation had been brief, detached—almost cold.

He hadn't said he loved her again, and although it'd over-whelmed her the night he confessed it, she'd hoped to hear it again. But they hadn't spoken since. Things could be different for them with her mother gone. She could move to L.A. There was no reason not to now. They could see each other as much as they wanted. They could be a couple.

Except Ryan had nothing to say to her anymore. Maiya sat on the step and drew in a long drag. *I really fucked this one up.*

Thinking back on their time together, she'd been the one

to keep him at arm's length. *He* had been the consistent one, the one to pursue her with fervor. *He* had fallen in love with her and *wasn't* afraid to tell her. Ryan had been the one to keep it going for them, and the only consistent thing *she'd* done was pull him close and then push him away.

And she did love him. That much she at last admitted to herself. But in spite of the undeniable love she felt for him, she continued to push him away. Why? *Easy way out and stupid.* Because she was afraid he'd leave her—that he'd eventually change his mind and leave her.

Had she pushed him so far he wasn't coming back? All in the name of fear? There was only one way to find out, and it sure as hell wasn't going to happen here in Vegas. She needed to get her shit in order and get her ass out to L.A. Now.

CHAPTER FORTY-SIX

Ryan spent his days immersed in work and his nights immersed in Jacob. He hadn't talked to Maiya in two weeks, and it was driving him bat-shit crazy.

He missed her. Jacob missed her, too, but Ryan needed to stand his ground. He was tired of chasing her, tired of being the one to always pursue. Hell, he'd even told her he loved her, and what he'd gotten in return was a whole lot of nothing.

She needed space; he understood. He hadn't been prepared to lose touch with her like this, though. Granted, she'd just lost her mother and had a lot on her plate, but he hated not being by her side to help her take care of everything. Ryan prayed that when she got through the mess, she'd be willing to talk.

Jimmy had gone home to Manhattan the prior week, and thank God because his brother would be telling him daily to suck it up and wait it out. "She'll come back if you're meant to be together," had been his words before he left town. What-the-fuck-ever. He did not want to hear that crap again.

Ryan stepped off the elevator and into the main reception area of the office. He headed straight for the break room to grab some coffee and then *casually* stopped by Jodi's office again to *casually* ask her if she'd heard from Maiya.

"Morning, Jo—" He stopped short, coffee sloshing out of the cup and down his hand.

"Oh, shit, Jodi, give me a napkin!"

"Classic." Jodi stood, bypassing Maiya, and handed Ryan the napkin. "You didn't tell him you were coming, did you?" She shook her head. "You need relationship training, girl. I swear."

Ryan wiped up the spilled coffee, thanking God it hadn't been very hot.

Maiya was here.

Maiya. Here.

He stared at her. "When the hell did you get into town?"

She crossed her arms. "Late Friday night."

"And you didn't call me? What. The. Fuck, Maiya!"

"I'm going to take a walk." Jodi excused herself from her own office.

"Thanks, Jodi." He moved aside, and Jodi closed the door behind her.

"I'm sorry." Maiya let out a breath and rubbed her forehead. "Look, I really want to talk to you, I just... Can you come meet me later at the hotel?"

He stepped back and looked at her. Really looked at her. What was it with this woman? Why her? She was broken, wild, smart and beautiful, and so many goddamn things he couldn't even begin to list them all. But right then, he was so frustrated and confused, he thought he might strangle her.

It didn't help how gorgeous she was in her long, fitted pencil skirt and tight sweater, making her body look like one long, curvaceous roller coaster of deliciousness. *Stay focused, Ry. You're pissed, remember?* She made it hard to stay mad when she looked this good, and that pissed him off even more. She knew *exactly* what she was doing, dressing that way—evil minx.

"Ryan, you're staring at me like you don't know whether you want to fuck me or strangle me."

"Bingo. Fine, I'll meet you at the hotel. Four thirty. Don't be late." He turned and walked out of Jodi's office before he did exactly what she suggested he was thinking.

Damn her.

Maiya paced the foyer of her hotel, waiting for Ryan. It was past four-thirty. "Don't be late," he'd said, and now *he* was late. *Fucking fabulous.*

She shook out her hands and decided to head back up to her room. She texted him her room number and got on the elevator. He could come upstairs when he got there, and she could pace in private without her heels on.

An hour…or maybe just five minutes later, there was a knock at the door. *Finally.* Opening it, she was treated to a frustrated-looking Ryan. He blew past her into the room without saying anything.

"Come in," she mumbled under her breath and shut the door. "Are you okay?"

"Fine. Had to make arrangements for my son." He sat in the desk chair. "I'm here. You wanted to talk. So, talk."

"Okay, well." She swallowed, her mouth gone dry. Jeez, he sounded furious. She grabbed her water, took a sip and then began again. "I owe you a huge apology." She looked at him.

He leaned forward, resting his elbows on his knees.

"I was wrong for treating you the way I did, Ryan. And I'm not sure if it even matters now, but I figured I would explain why, you know?" She paced. "I'm a little fucked up, I guess." She let out a nervous laugh, but he remained silent. God, he was *not* going to let her off the hook *at all*. "I was scared. Plain and simple. And, you know, convinced I didn't deserve you, and you would leave me, but there's this problem now." She made another round of the room and then faced him again. "The problem is I love you, and I'm moving here, but now I think I've lost you." *Don't cry. Don't cry.* Dammit all to hell! She was getting damn tired of crying. "I lov—"

One second, she was standing; the next, she was flat on her back on the bed, Ryan hovering above her. "I want you, Maiya." He pressed his lips in a firm line, and his jaw ticked.

"I can feel that, but—"

"No!" Ryan shook his head. "Well, yes, but that's not what I mean. I want you, baby. Always. Forever. Twenty-four seven."

Shock bolted through her. "What are you saying?"

"I'm saying I want you to move in with me." He kissed her. "I'm saying I'm in love with you, and I don't want to waste any more fucking time. These last two weeks have been hell, and I don't care to relive them."

"Are you serious?" Her anxiety level went from a ten to a fifty in a matter of two words. Move in? Fucking, move in? Here she was, thinking she'd get an apartment and see if he wanted to see her. Her brain couldn't process what her ears were hearing. What if— Her mother's voice came rushing back and, along with it, her tears. *Don't give up something good because of all the bad in your past. Promise me, Maiya Anne Rossini.* "You'd want that with me?"

Ryan rolled them to the side and cradled her head against his chest while she wept.

"You're my girl. Please come home with me, baby? We can take care of each other. Always."

"I love you, Ryan. I'm so scared." She clung to him. Could she do this? Really do this? She wanted him for sure.

"I've got you. I'm not letting you go, Maiya. Come home with me."

All she managed was a nod while Ryan kissed her tears from her eyes, her cheeks and then found her lips. A familiar jolt of electricity shot through her body and straight to her core when their tongues touched. The kiss grew frantic, and she clawed at his shirt.

Ryan rolled onto his back, tugging up her skirt. He stopped when he reached her upper thigh. "My little slut. You're wearing thigh-highs and a garter."

"I had to pull out all the stops. What if you didn't take me back?"

"I knew it!" He ran his finger between the backs of her thighs, seeking her core. He groaned.

She was wet for him, and his fingers felt like heaven. Maiya bit his bottom lip. "No panties, either."

"That's it." Ryan reached between them and freed himself from his pants.

Maiya rose up on her knees, straddling him, and he pressed the head to her entrance. She slid down slow, inch by torturous inch, gazing into his eyes.

He went rigid beneath her. "Tell me you love me again." He gripped her ass. "I need to hear it while I'm inside what's now officially mine."

With him seated deep inside her core, she shifted her hips once and then said the words he wanted to hear. "I love you, Ryan." Her skin tingled in anticipation of his response.

He thrust his pelvis off the bed and squeezed her ass, holding her tight to him. "Oh, God. Again."

She ground against him. "I love you, Ryan Donnelly."

"I love you, too, baby. I love you, too." Ryan cupped the back of her neck and pulled her down for a kiss.

Maiya's heart burst with feeling, and she knew without a doubt she wanted this man, always. Ryan wrapped both arms around her waist, and she continued the motion of her hips in time with the stroke of her tongue in his mouth.

With her clit grinding against his pelvis, she pulled her mouth from his, tangled his hair in her hands and bit his shoulder. Her orgasm exploded, and her walls milked his shaft with tight little spasms.

"Yes! Mine!" He bucked against her, crying out a curse while his own release took him over.

Maiya continued to rock slowly, and with each slide in and out of her wetness, her pussy clenched and spasmed again. She laid her head down on his chest. "Mmm."

"Woman, you are going to be the death of me."

"Not yet, I hope. I mean, I just got here." Maiya gazed up at him. "Hey, can we go home? I really miss Jacob." She kissed his chest.

"I thought you'd never ask." He stroked her hair. "Jacob misses you, too."

After another moment in his arms, she climbed off him and the bed. "Chop chop!" She snapped her fingers. "Let's go!"

"Oh my God, I love you." He got up, laughing, and pulled her close.

"I hope you realize what you're getting yourself into."

"I have a pretty good idea."

"That makes one of us." She laughed. "This could get dangerous." Wrapping her arms around his neck, she kissed him and figured it was okay to let him navigate.

For once in her life, Maiya Rossini believed she deserved a little happy-ever-after.

ABOUT THE AUTHOR

Dorothy F. Shaw lives in Arizona, where the weather is hot, and the sunsets are always beautiful. She's a self-proclaimed sex scene snob and is proud of it. When she's not writing, she's thinking about writing.

With her ever-open heart, bright red hair, and many colorful tattoos, she truly lives and loves in Technicolor!

Get in bed (and read) with your favorite redhead!

Newsletter sign-up: Yes, please!
Join *Dorothy's Ruby Readers* on FB:
http://bit.ly/DFSRubyReaders
www.dorothyfshaw.com
DorothyFShaw@Gmail.com

f facebook.com/AuthorDorothyFShaw

O instagram.com/authordorothyfshaw

✖ bsky.app/profile/dorothyfshaw.bsky.social

♩ tiktok.com/@authordorothyfshaw

@ threads.net/@authordorothyfshaw

g goodreads.com/dorothyfshaw

a amazon.com/stores/author/B00DPRI5HK

BB bookbub.com/profile/dorothy-f-shaw

ALSO BY DOROTHY F. SHAW

Head to my site to find all links to my available backlist:

www.DorothyFShaw.com

Next in the Donnellys series:
Defensive Heart

The Donnellys Book 2
© 2019 Dorothy F. Shaw

Uptown girl, tattooed bad boy. Think you know which one is wild? You'd be wrong.

Greenwich Village is home to successful artist Jimmy Donnelly, and the world is his playground. A broken heart in college left him with zero interest in being tied down. But when he meets a sexy, quick-witted Manhattan attorney, he reconsiders his bad boy ways.

Sonja Martin's life is filled with work, an ex-husband who refuses to stay gone, and a teenage daughter who won't follow the rules. Jimmy, with his myriad of tattoos and piercings, looks more like one of her clients than a potential lover. But when every argument between them feels more like foreplay, she can't seem to stay out of his bed.

The heat burns through whatever defenses Sonja thought she had. And Jimmy finds his every fantasy fulfilled—and exceeded—by a woman whose fire burns as bright as her fiercely guarded vulnerability.

But his case for breaking her out of her self-imposed mold might just be dismissed. And he'll lose the best thing he's ever found.

Turn the page for a sneak peek...

Defensive Heart

Chapter One

Jimmy Donnelly's shoulder jerked forward. *What the—*

"Pardon me. Crap! Ugh."

He glanced to see who'd bumped him, and his mouth dropped open. *Whoa!* "No problem," he managed to mumble after he'd gotten his jaw working. The woman was gorgeous— and tall. Holy crap, she was tall.

"Thanks." She looked down. "Oh my God! No!" She swiped her hands down her white suit jacket.

"Shit. Let me get you a towel." Jimmy signaled the barback and then handed her the clean rag. "Was that your drink or his?"

"*His.* I was just coming to get my own. Ugh! That guy didn't even apologize." Her tone was filled with annoyance as she swiped at the front of the jacket, then down one thigh.

Jimmy let his gaze roam down her body. She was tall but also petite—a complete oxymoron, but the perfect description nonetheless. He took in the white formal pantsuit she wore and continued down to her beige, very expensive-looking— *holy shit*—stiletto pumps. Jimmy whistled low. Classy for sure, but completely out of place in a dance club like Tangled. He rested his elbow on the bar. "Could be worse. Could be red wine."

She pinned him with a glare cold enough to freeze hell. "Let me know if you have anything useful to say. That's really not helping." She went back to swiping at her clothes.

"Uh…" He cleared his throat. "Yeah, sorry." Talk about feeling like his mother just scolded him. Jimmy smiled, trying to hide the sudden nervous energy filling his belly and rocketing up his throat. It made his tongue feel like someone had spread a layer of rubber cement on it. He turned away and resumed his wait for the bartender.

A few minutes later, she slid into the small space between him and another patron. Like a magnet drawn to the pull of another, Jimmy couldn't help himself and looked over, taking in her profile. Man, she really was beautiful.

She glanced at him, nodded, then turned away. After a few beats, she looked back. "You're staring."

Jimmy cringed. "Sorry." He focused back on the bartender, but after another few moments, curiosity took over, and he risked another peek. Her blonde hair was pulled up in a twist on the back of her head, appearing to defy the laws of gravity, and she had the brightest sky-blue eyes he'd ever seen. She wore little makeup and had one of those faces with skin so milky white and perfect it looked like it'd been scooped out of whipped cream.

She hit him with another glare and shifted to face him. "Is there a problem?"

He bristled at her annoyed tone, layered with a hint of a New York accent. Yup, he'd been staring, but Jesus, she didn't need to be so nasty. Jimmy looked her up and down, damn ready to give it right back to her. Being of Irish descent, he normally let things slide, but she'd definitely riled his temper. The crowd pressed in closer, and someone muscled in behind her, forcing their bodies to almost touch. "You're a little overdressed for a place like this, don't you think?"

She raised a single brow. "Aren't you a master of observation."

"Usually." Jimmy smirked. Jesus, she smelled good. "If you don't mind me saying, you're...stunning."

She cocked her head to the side with a smirk rivaling his own. "Great, thanks."

Stunning *with* an attitude. A little like fire and ice. How intriguing. Unable to resist a good game of tit-for-tat, he leaned toward her. "Nice shoes. You mug someone in a back alley to score them?"

She took a small step back and bumped the guy behind her. "Hardly."

"I'm striking out here, aren't I?"

"That's assuming you ever actually made it up to bat."

"Ouch." Jimmy rubbed the center of his chest. "Look, let me start over." She mumbled something sounding a lot like, "Do I have a choice?" but he ignored it. Jimmy held out his hand. "Hi, I'm James Donnelly. Let me buy you a drink. To— you know—make up for my sarcasm."

"I think I can manage the purchase of my own drink. Thank you anyway." She didn't take his offered hand, just turned back toward the bar.

Jimmy laid his neglected palm on the bar top and leaned close enough to almost touch her ear with his lips. "That was rude."

She jerked away as if he'd slapped her. "What was rude?"

"I got you a towel so you could wipe up a drink *I* didn't spill on you. Then I tried to apologize for staring at you, which, again, wasn't trying to be rude…then I tried to start over with you and shake your hand, and you snubbed me."

Screw this lady. He drummed his fingertips on the counter.

"I beg your pardon?" She faced him, one hand on her hip and annoyance clear in her expression. "I thanked you for the towel. Ugh, forget it. Why are you talking to me?"

"Exactly." He shrugged and turned away. Why waste time and energy on someone with an entire stick up her ass? He wanted to ask her where her broom was, but figured she'd turn him into a toad—or worse. He loved a little fire and ice in a woman, but she wasn't full of fire *or* ice. The woman appeared to be merely a regular bitch.

"Now who's rude?" She tugged on his arm, and he glanced over his shoulder at her. "Fine. Buy me a drink." She sighed. "Vodka tonic, with a lime."

Interesting. Maybe the stick wasn't embedded as deep as he thought. He faced her again. With a broad smile, he smoothed his hands down the front of his white button-up shirt. "Tell me your name first."

Who in the *hell* did this lunatic think he was? Sonja Martin stood, hand planted on one hip, studying the boy standing before her. Yes, *boy.* She took a moment to appraise his features: A head full of dark, almost black, spiky and tangled hair fell over his forehead and covered the tops of his ears, both of which were pierced. Equally dark brows framed a set of pale hazel eyes. His nose, with one nostril pierced, was thin and straight but curved slightly down at the tip. A thin goatee framed his full mouth and merged into a thin strip down his squared, narrow chin.

Plenty good-looking, no denying it, but his features weren't perfect either. He was younger than her, but then again, who wasn't in a place like this? Giving in, she held out her hand. "Sonja Martin."

He wrapped his fingers around her hand in a firm but not excessive grip. "Nice to meet you. Can't say it's been a plea-sure so far, but maybe there's hope." He winked and smiled, revealing a set of straight, white teeth and a pair of dimples some would kill for.

The smile was potent, and her breath caught in her throat. "You really know how to turn on the charm, don't you?"

"Oh, come on. Lighten up, will ya? We need a shot."

"I'm not doing a shot with you, Mr. Donnelly."

"Sure you are. Good memory with the name, by the way." He rubbed his hands together. "I'm going to order two shots along with your drink, then we'll drink them. Simple."

Sonja couldn't quite believe this guy. He was either already drunk or just plain stupid. Never mind rude, annoying and downright egotistical. She could go on and on, and should've already walked away from him. Yet she stood there, like some sort of subservient sheep—*how typical of me*—and let him order them shots and drinks.

Sonja shook her head, clenching her teeth in complete annoyance. Thing was, she wasn't sure who she was more agitated with, herself or him. Just what she needed, another pompous ass ordering her around. *Spare me. I'm full up.* The bartender returned with her vodka tonic (minus the lime), two shot glasses filled with dark fluid, and a glass of what appeared to be Guinness. When her unwelcome and distracting company slid the shot in front of her, Sonja eyed the nearly black liquid and frowned. "What is it?"

"Jägermeister." He raised his shot glass. "Come on, lift it. What shall we drink to?"

She waved her hand, signaling the bartender. She needed the lime for her drink. "I'm not drinking that."

He picked up the other shot and held it in front of her. "Sure you are."

"Mr. Donnel—"

"James. Take the shot."

"James. Whatever. You can have both." The bartender appeared. Finally. "You forgot my lime."

"It's been a while, hasn't it?" James chuckled.

"Excuse me?"

He set the shot intended for her on the bar top. "Safe to assume you're single. It's been a while since you've gotten laid, huh? Must be it."

"It has no—" Heat flooded her cheeks, and agitation pulsed through her. She was single, but her relationship status or sex life was none of his damn business. And besides, it hadn't been *that* long. Had it?

Cupping her elbow in his hand, he bent close to her ear. "You are, and it has. Drink the shot, Sonja. Trust me, you need it." His hot breath feathered over her neck, and she shivered.

Sonja cursed her body for responding in any way, shape or

form to him. She should slap him, not get aroused by him. Breathing deep, Sonja sought for some measure of calm and came up short when his masculine scent flowed through her senses like a cool stream, making her shiver again. *Crap.* Always such a sucker for the aroma of clean soap and cologne. The bartender placed a lime on the edge of her drink, and she shifted, pulling away from James. "Thanks."

James held her shot glass up in front of her again. "Drink up."

"You don't give up, do you?"

"Once I sink my teeth in, I don't let go."

Knowing it was a bad idea, Sonja took the glass from him. "Is that it? You think you've sunk your teeth in?"

"The bite is so much more pleasurable if you relax and go with it." He smiled and raised his shot. "To being stunning, Ms. Martin." He tapped her glass with the edge of his.

She paused and took in his dimples, the curve of his lips. He was too sexy. A prize chock-full of wickedness, she wasn't quite sure she wanted to collect on. "Are you trying to seduce me, James?"

"Do you want to be seduced?"

"Not particularly." With a laugh, Sonja tilted the shot to her lips. She closed her eyes and swallowed the dark liquid; the sweet licorice flavor spread over her tongue and burned on its way down her throat. When she opened her eyes, he was watching her, his gaze fixated on her lips. She licked them... slowly. *Two can play at this game.*

James's eyes flared before narrowing. He tapped the bottom of the shot glass on the bar top and drank it down.

Was that some sort of shot ritual she wasn't aware of? Hmm. "How old are you?"

He hissed through his teeth and set his glass down. "Old enough to know and still young enough to do something about it."

"How very cliché."

"And how old are you?" A smooth grin tipped the corners of his lips.

"How very impolite." She raised a brow and squeezed the lime into her vodka tonic. "Too old for you. What are you, twenty-five? Twenty-six?" She licked the remnants of lime juice from her fingertips.

"Are you trying to seduce me, Sonja?"

"Only in your wet dreams."

He leaned close again, placed his hand on her lower back and pulled her against him. "Keep licking your lips and fingers like that, honey, and you'll be the star in my wet dream tonight."

Sonja tensed, trying and failing to ignore his words and warm breath on her ear. The heat of his hand burned through her clothes, and she trembled against his hard chest. James dragged his hand from her lower back to her waist, framed it for a moment between his thumb and fingers, squeezed, then let go of her. A beat of arousal pumped through her and settled between her thighs. Sonja swallowed past the lump in her throat. Why was she letting him get to her this much?

He waved for the bartender. "I think we need another shot."

"No. No, we don't."

He smiled and winked at her. "Shh. I got this."

"I bet that smile gets you into a lot of beds, doesn't it?" She sipped her drink.

"Will it get me into yours?"

A laugh she couldn't suppress bubbled up, and she sucked the liquid down the wrong pipe. Talk about a cold splash of water. Her libido went silent as she attempted to breathe.

"Shit. Sorry." James grabbed a napkin and handed it to her, and then rubbed her back while she tried like hell to appear dignified while coughing up a lung.

Sonja wiped her mouth with the napkin. "No. Not likely."

She coughed again and cleared her throat. "Don't you have a girlfriend around here somewhere you should be annoying?"

He grabbed the freshly delivered shots. "Nope. I'm all yours. Here."

"Oh God. Are you trying to get me drunk?"

"Will it get me into your bed?"

"Not a chance." She smirked but took the shot and tossed it back, this time with no hesitation.

He shook his head. "You didn't wait for the toast. Bad form, Sonja. Bad form."

"Aw. You'll get over it." She patted his shoulder.

"Nope. You've wounded my heart. How much of a beating do you think a guy can take?" He placed his hand over his chest. As he did, the sleeve of his shirt rose, revealing tattoo work on his wrist.

"Oh my, this wounded puppy thing is pretty pathetic. Go ahead, make a toast. I'll sip my drink while you toss back the second shot you insisted on having."

"Wounded puppy? *You are* relentless." He grinned. "I think you should make the toast this time."

Thanks to the alcohol kicking in, Sonja's tongue was getting looser and looser. Where were her friends, anyway? Weren't they supposed to be there to save her from situations like this? However, Sonja's libido didn't want her to be saved at this point.

The guy looked more like the clients she represented back home in Manhattan than any type of man she'd ever consider going to bed with. There was something about him, though. It made her go weak in the knees, which was more troubling than anything else. "Okay, fine." She raised her drink. "To your bedroom eyes, dimples, and wicked smile created to drop panties…though surely not mine." She nodded, feeling quite pleased with herself.

He dipped his chin and raised one brow. "Clever. Very clever."

"Thanks. Glad you liked it."

He repeated the actions from before: tapped the bottom of his glass on the bar, raised it to his lips and swallowed the alcohol. When he did, she caught a glimpse of a tattoo snaking up his neck, visible just above the collar of his shirt. She intended to ask about the little ritual with the shot, but was so distracted by the tantalizing peek of his ink, all rational thought left her mind.

He set the empty shot glass upside down on the bar. "I'm thirty."

Holy shit.

Want more?
Head to my site to find all links to my available backlist:
www.DorothyFShaw.com

Available from all major e-sellers in digital and print.

eBooks are not transferable.
They cannot be sold, shared or given away as it is an infringement on the copyright of this work.

This book is a work of fiction. The names, characters, places, and incidents are products of the writer's imagination or have been used fictitiously and are not to be construed as real. Any resemblance to persons, living or dead, actual events, locale or organizations is entirely coincidental.

Dorothy F. Shaw
Phoenix, Arizona
UNWORTHY HEART
Copyright © 2019 by Dorothy F. Shaw
ISBN-10: 0-9978310-1-4
ISBN-13: 978-0-9978310-1-6
Draft2Digital ISBN-13: 978-0-4634000-1-2
Edited by Tera Cuskaden
Cover by Kanaxa

All rights reserved. Except as permitted under the U.S. Copyright Act of 1976, no part of this book may be used, including but not limited to the training of or use by artificial intelligence (AI), or reproduced, distributed, or transmitted in any form or by any means, or stored in a database or retrieval system, without the prior written permission of the author.

Red Queen Publications electronic and print publication: April 2018

Publishing History
Digital/Print 1.0 edition / May 2015
Digital/Print 2.0 edition / August 2017
Digital/Print 3.0 edition/ May 2019

Red Queen
Publications

www.ingramcontent.com/pod-product-compliance
Lightning Source LLC
Chambersburg PA
CBHW051207120726
47905CB00004B/1019